DAEMONS

IN THE

MIST

THE MARKED ONES TRILOGY
· BOOK 1 ·

DAEMONS
IN THE
MIST

ALICIA KAT VANCIL

KORAT PUBLISHING

Daemons in the Mist

Published by Korat Publishing in California
Printed in the United States of America

This book is a work of fiction. Any references to historical events, real
people, or real locales are used fictitiously. Other names, characters,
places, and incidents are the products of the author's imagination, and
any resemblance to actual events or locales or persons, living or dead,
is entirely coincidental.

ISBN: 978-1-937288-03-7 (paperback)
ASIN: B00DRBR7T6

Book design by Alicia Kat Vancil
Cover illustration © 2013, 2014 Alicia Kat Vancil
Cover photograph © Pandorabox - Fotolia.com
Cover photograph © Oleksandr Dibrova - Fotolia.com

The text for this book is set in Liberation Serif

Third Edition

For my parents, who encouraged me to create the worlds that live within my head.

For Scott, who suffered through the kissing parts, and laughed at the clever parts.

For Sally, for always being there when I needed you the most.

And for Chris, for admitting you forgot at times that my characters weren't real people.

Pronunciation Guide

Arius *are-ee-us*
Centrina *cen-tree-nah*
Cellarius *cell-lar-ee-us*
Chancell *shan-cell*
Chancellar *shan-cell-lar*
Chancellarius *shan-cell-lar-ee-us*
Daemon *day-mon*
Daemotic *day-mah-tic*
Daenara *day-nar-ah*
Denaya *den-ay-ah*
Galathea *gala-thee-ah*
Kakodaemon *kay-koh-day-mon*
Kakodemoss *kay-koh-day-moss*
Kalo *kay-low*
Kalodaemon *kay-low-day-mon*
Lunaris *loo-nar-is*
Nikkalla *nick-a-lah*
Neodaemon *knee-oh-day-mon*
Nualla *new-all-ah*
Tammore *ta-more*

S URE, WHY NOT. WHAT HAVE *we got to lose?* is probably the understatement of the year as far as last words go. So why, in the name of all reason, did I say yes? I'm still not one-hundred percent sure, but maybe it was because Nualla was beyond tempting, and I was dying to know her secrets. Or that I was angry with my parents for never being there, and I wanted someone to be close to me. Or that I was really, really drunk. But it was probably because, when fate throws you the one thing you have always wanted, you grab hold of it and never let go.

And even though it's dangerous, and even if I have to leave everything behind, my answer is, and always will be...

Yes.

Secrets in the Mist

Monday, January 9th

NUALLA

I LOOKED OUT THE WINDOW AT the never-ending sea of fog, concealing the city as it came alive in its morning rush. In the mist, everything seemed timeless and still and wondrous. The fog drifted past buildings, their tops poking out and making it look all the world like there were castles in the sky.

San Francisco.

The exception, it seemed, to California's bright and sunny weather. It wasn't the foggiest city in the world, but it was pretty damn close. Countless people had written books based here, and songs and movies.

Even Mark Twain was quoted as saying, "The coldest winter I ever spent was a summer in San Francisco." Though if I heard one more tourist say it, I was going to hit someone.

"So, socks or leggings?"

"Huh?" I turned to see my cousin Nikki standing in the doorway holding up two types of leg coverings. One was a pair of bright purple leggings, the other was a pair of paler blue thigh-high socks with penguins dancing across them.

"Which should I wear?" she asked again as she jiggled them for effect.

Nikki and I went to Bayside Academy, a private school for the Bay Area's elite, so of course that meant uniforms. I was glad our school had gone in for the whole tieless-V-neck-knit-sweater-over-pleated-skirt look because personally, I thought ties on girls was really creepy. However since our school uniforms didn't extend to things like shoes, socks, or hair, so some students—like Nikki—went to town with their individuality.

I clicked my phone on to check the day's weather. "Nikki, it's like forty-five degrees out."

"Socks it is," she announced, sitting on the edge of my bed to slip them on.

"You're crazy!"

"Don't you know it," she replied with a wink.

I rolled my eyes at her and stood up. I had gone for the more sensible I'm-not-going-to-freeze-my-ass-off standard black leggings with tall faux fur-lined boots for good measure.

Another look at the time said we'd better head out, or we were *totally* going to be late. "Come on, Nikki. Let's not be late the first day of spring semester, okay?"

Minutes later, we coasted down the street, the buildings sliding into existence just a few seconds before we passed them, my car's engine quietly purring. Most people hated driving in the fog, but I loved it. It kept you on your toes; you had to be ready for what might appear before you at any moment.

Like this cat darting across the road in front of me.

I took my foot off the gas as she streaked past me, a flash of smoky gray, like the fog materializing into a solid form. As her paws hit the curb on the other side of the street she turned her lamp-like eyes to stare at me.

She knows me, the true me. Not this mask I have to wear each day.

There was something profoundly odd about it. That a cat could be more calm and rational than—

"*Hellooo,* earth to Nualla," Nikki said as she waved a hand in front of my face. "What are you looking at?"

The cat was gone, disappearing into the mist like a dream. "Nothing," I answered slowly. And that's when I realized the cat had used a crosswalk. Smart little thing—even *she* wasn't stupid enough to jay-walk. I mean *sure* she had just crossed against the red, but hell, at least she hadn't been mindlessly listening to an iPod as she stepped off the curb. Sometimes I thought they—cats—were smarter than people. Or maybe they just had a higher level of self-preservation.

I returned my focus to the road and hit the gas. The buildings floated past, an odd collection of shapes so far from matching it was almost funny.

The city weaved together stringent modern simplicity and Victorian mystique in a way that almost seemed intentional in its randomness. Cultures seamlessly blending into each other so slowly as to be unnoticed, while at other times changing rather abruptly—like the Chinatown Gate—announcing your passage into another world in large, imposing glory. The residences themselves were almost as odd. The houses in most cities were colors like tan, brick, and the occasional sage, but not San Francisco; it was a mélange of colors. I had even seen a house once that was lilac with chartreuse trim.

Yeah—*chartreuse.*

The light flipped to red and I drifted to a stop. I leaned back into the seat and folded my arms as I glanced over at my cousin. Nikki sipped her coffee in the seat next to me, the steam rolling off it already fogging up the windows. She wiped the window with her sleeve, so she could peer out at the buildings.

"You know it's just gonna fog up again in like two seconds," I pointed out with an amused snort.

"Then I'll just wipe it again," she answered as she slid her arm across the window like a windshield wiper.

I rolled my eyes at her and pressed my foot to the gas as the red blur in the distance shifted to green. The globes of light lining the streets floated past, the sky still too dark for them to register that it was morning.

It was like driving through a dreamland—some of the things you saw just seemed way too unreal. Like people in shiny disco ball Gaga-esque clothes dancing outside Ghirardelli Square, or joggers in tutus, or water valves painted up to look like videogame mushrooms—just a few of the crazy things I had seen on the misty streets of San Francisco.

But the mists also held a secret.

They concealed a world that existed between yours, around yours, underneath yours. Though we might have looked like you, acted like you, we were not *like* you. And so as humanity raced forward, trying to catalogue and destroy the last mysteries of this world, we eluded your grasp. Always one step ahead of you, hiding away the things you refused to believe could be possible. Allowing us to pass among you unnoticed, carrying our secrets to the grave.

And so you had carved us into your myths, into your fears, distorting us into something that no longer seemed real. And we became your stories, some of us working in your favor, while others tried to tear you down. Protectors and destroyers. A world of opposing forces battling for the upper hand. Muses, demigods, devils—the humans of antiquity gave us many names. But we claimed one for ourselves.

Daemons.

Every triumph and travesty in human history had a daemon behind the scenes. Like mist, we run through your world; seeping into your lives and disappearing when you try to look too hard. In the beginning, we tried to reveal ourselves to you. But well…let's just say concealing our true nature was just better for everyone.

Sometimes I wondered if humanity was ready to know the truth now. That we had been silent passengers all along in their struggle to thrive.

Probably not. People get crazy when you mess with their paradigms.

As we arrived at school, the fog was already giving way to lighter swells of mist. I pulled into the last above-ground spot and opened the door into the utterly cold morning.

I burrowed down deeper into my heavy black velvet pea coat with a shiver. The wind was picking up, swirling the mist past the students. I could already tell Nikki was rethinking her choice of socks over leggings by the expression on her face.

She turned to me, her teeth already starting to chatter. "Ready to go inside?"

"Naw, I think we should hang out here longer since it's a balmy forty-five degrees out."

"The weather thingy could have been wrong," Nikki said with a shivering shrug.

"By what, *thirty degrees*?" I asked dubiously.

"Sometimes you really suck," Nikki grumbled as she crossed her arms and scowled at me.

"Yeah, but you know you love me," I stated as I looped my arm through hers and started walking toward the building.

We drifted among the other students—just another set of pretty faces in a sea of prep school uniforms.

You Don't See Me

Monday, January 9th

PATRICK

E VERY MORNING THEY ARRIVED BY luxury sport
car, chauffeured town car, or taxi. I came via
MUNI. My parents were just barely well-off enough
to get me into Bayside Academy. They were apparently *not* wealthy enough to let me drive a car in the
city.

I didn't mind the bus, really—you could find the
most interesting people in San Francisco on the bus.
Foreign grandmothers chatting in a language you
couldn't understand. Convention goers with badges
that proudly touted their names for all to see. Art stu-

dents carrying more supplies than body mass. Urban yuppies playing with the newest handheld tech. A whole city's worth of culture crammed like sardines in a 320 square-foot space. If you wanted to get to know a city—I mean *really* wanted to know it—then riding its public transit was the way to go.

I never felt more at home—more like I was part of something—than when I was crammed among all the people on the bus. Just a tiny piece in the sea of life. Occasionally I would get the stares from those who recognized my school uniform and would give me that, *why's a kid like you riding the bus?* look. Mostly they just ignored me, leaving me alone to make up their life stories in my head.

I ignored one such stare and looked out the window. The fog was impressive today, drowning everything in a misty cover. The tops of tall buildings disappeared into it, leaving you to wonder just how tall they *really* were. On mornings like this you were lucky to see a block or two away.

I pulled the signal cord for my stop and fought my way to the door—always an adventure in and of itself. The stops around Market were the worst; most of the time it was like trying to swim upstream through a school of angry fish. Half the time you literally fell off the bus onto the sidewalk as people pushed past you to get on.

The bus lurched to a stop and the doors popped

open. I stepped off the bus alone. It wasn't only the students that didn't seem to ride the bus around here. Stuffy rich attitudes practically wafted through the air in this part of the city.

Sighing, I started trudging down the sidewalk toward the school. The air whipped past with a biting cold to it. January in San Francisco, cold as crap but at least it wasn't raining sideways. If you think I'm joking about the rain, I'm not. The wind in San Francisco was a tricky beast; you could walk down one street and have it gently tousling your hair, then turn the corner and get smacked in the face by a gale.

I came to the corner and took a deep breath before I crossed the street to the school. Bayside Academy was a nice enough school, but it was hard to feel at home in a place filled with the children of diplomats and CEOs.

The campus sported an impressive amount of grass and trees for being in the middle of a city. The building itself was three stories with a glassed-over atrium and underground parking—but what didn't have underground parking in the city, really?

The front of the school was nearly deserted. Like most winter mornings, everyone was in a hurry to get into the building—though most wouldn't *actually* make it to class until just before the bell rang.

As I neared the entrance of the school building, an electric blue Aston Martin Vanquish pulled into the last available spot in the above-ground parking. Everyone stared—in a parking lot of nice cars this one was in a league completely its own. The door opened, and Nualla Galathea stepped out, shuddering at the cold. I stood transfixed as she glided toward the building in front of me, arm in arm with her cousin Nikkalla "Nikki" Varris. They didn't look at me as they passed, and I fell into step behind them.

Nualla had the most beautiful hair I had ever seen. Not the short kind of long we see in magazines and movies today, but the kind straight out of a Pre-Raphaelite painting. Black loose spirals spilling down her back to just below her hips. It might have seemed old fashioned if it wasn't for the lapis-blue streaks through parts of it. Her cousin Nikki's hair was in sharp contrast—pale blond with a few light blue streaks on either side and a short a-line cut. But the two of them were extremely similar in build with the same slender waspish shapes of dancers, heart shaped faces, and large eyes.

They were some of the extremely popular kids, but theirs was an odd sort of popularity. With that much beauty and wealth, they should probably have had hordes of friends. But they didn't. Instead they seemed to spend the majority of their time with Shawn Vallen. And although the three of them were friendly to all the students, they mostly kept to themselves. But it was a self-imposed isolation; most of the students at the school looked at them with a strange sense of admiration. In a lot of towns the beautiful popular kids would have used their gifts as an excuse to abuse the other "lesser" students, but not these three.

I had never heard Nualla say anything unkind to another person. Well, aside from one really. The only person she seemed to openly despise was Michael Tammore. Which was perfectly alright with me, since he was a pretentious wank anyways. *He* was one of those people who used their power to abuse others. Michael routinely picked on the shy, the less affluent, and anyone he felt was less intelligent than himself.

My friends, on the other hand, were the kind of friends you always hung out with at school, but who never seemed to call you to do things on the weekend. Well, with the exception of my best friend Connor. There wasn't a Saturday that went by that he wasn't hanging out at my place or me at his.

My friends and I definitely weren't the most popular kids in school, but we also weren't the least popular ones either. We were somewhere in the realm of people not caring. No one aspired to be us, and no one shoved us in the janitor's closet. Our little group was made up of Connor, Sara, Beatrice, Jenny and myself. We had ended up sitting together the first week of freshman year and had just never bothered to find new seats...or friends.

After a quick trip to my locker I had walked into Trig—my least favorite class—and taken my usual seat in the back of the room next to Connor. Trig had gone by as it normally did—*painfully*. I liked Mr. Savenrue—really I did—but Trig was just about the *least* interesting thing in the world.

Connor and I left class heading for our lockers when Nualla came out of the Calculus class next to us. I opened my mouth to say something to her. "Hey."

Nualla turned back toward me, and I held my breath. She had turned, she almost *never* turned. She looked right at me. Well not at me exactly, it was more like *through* me. Her brow furrowed in confusion, and she turned back, and continued walking to her locker.

I let the breath go. I don't know why I kept trying, it was a lost cause really. I must have been less than nothing to them—to *her*.

Sigh.

Nualla and her friends mostly flat out ignored me—looked right through me—as if I wasn't even there. It was like they couldn't see me; like I was invisible. If it wasn't for the company of my friends, I might even have thought I was a ghost.

However, this did not affect my infatuation with

Nualla Galathea. I would watch her—not in a creepy stalker way, but more in observational awe—like one would admire a statue or a beautiful painting. I noticed everything about her, but she had only looked at me once, the first day I had ever seen her. She had been walking to a table in the atrium with her friends and had looked up and smiled at me through the glass.

As I watched Nualla travel down the hall to our next class, I popped my locker open. After nearly four years here, I really didn't have to look too hard to spin the dial to the correct combination. Nualla stopped at her locker and dropped her bag inside in one swift, beautiful gesture of her arm. Every movement she made was like a graceful dance. I don't know why I hadn't given up on her yet and gotten myself a real girlfriend. It was just…something in me just couldn't seem to let it go. Like some piece of me knew something I didn't. Though I did wish it would get over itself and let me in on the secret.

"Are you staring at that Galathea girl *again*?" Connor asked with a sigh as he folded his arms and leaned against the locker next to mine. His hair was a well-kept spray of dreads pulled neatly into a pony-tail. His mother had probably gotten on his case again and threatened to cut it off if he didn't keep it neat. Which—knowing Connor—would probably last for all of a few weeks before it started getting into disarray again.

Connor looked over at Nualla before looking back at me and rolling his eyes. "I'm telling you man— *never* gonna happen."

"Yeah, I know," I sighed as I turned back to my locker and tossed my bag in.

Mr. Lucas had demanded we not bring bags to Chemistry, so no one would accidentally trip over them. He had said something to the effect of, "This is chemistry, not physics. We don't need to see what happens when someone falls on their face."

"We need to get to class, you coming?"

"You go ahead, I'll catch up," I replied, though I wasn't really listening because I was still starting at Nualla without *actually* appearing to look at her—a skill in and of itself.

"Well hurry up, I heard a rumor that Mr. Lucas is switching up our seats again," Connor said and strode off toward our Chem II class.

"'Kay," I said, but he probably hadn't heard me, considering in a few seconds flat he was already halfway down the hall. But then again, he was a 6'4" black kid, and most of that was legs.

I closed my locker with a sigh. I really couldn't stand around staring anymore, and I would see her in Mr. Lucas' class anyways. So tablet in hand I started walking toward class, my eyes fixed on Nualla under the pretense that I was looking at the hallways beyond her.

After only a few steps, a sudden piercing head-ache flashed across my eyes. I stumbled and dropped my tablet on my shoe. It bounced off the white rubber tip of my black All Stars and skidded across the floor. As I bent down to get it I rubbed my temple. Things like this actually happened to me more than I wanted to admit. Though not enough that I'd ever bothered to mention it to my parents.

When I stood up, Michael was standing next to Nualla, and they were having a heated argument. They both seemed fuzzy and out of focus, like they were much farther away than they should have been. And the more I concentrated on trying to look at them the fuzzier they got and the more my head hurt.

I would have just gone to class and taken some Advil if it had not been for what I saw next.

NUALLA

I KNEW WHAT WAS GOING TO happen a split second before it did. I always knew with Michael. As good as he was with his illusionary abilities, I could always feel the impact to the air as he prepared to release it.

Michael grabbed my arm. "You're going with me

to the Winter Ball."

"No, I assure you, *I'm not*." I jerked away from him, folded my arms and glared at him with contempt.

"Then who are you going with?"

Frak! I hadn't *actually* asked anyone yet.

I looked out at the nearly vacant hall; the students that were still there were shuffling to their lockers or dashing off to class completely unaware of us. Then again, Michael *was* using his influence to make them not notice us.

"I don't have to tell you," I said, moving my hands to my hips to appear more solid. Michael was a good five inches taller than me, so I needed all the help I could get.

"I can *make* you," he said, lifting my chin with his finger so I was forced to look into his eyes.

I pushed him away with all my strength and tried to step past him. "You wouldn't *dare*." Michal's illusionary abilities weren't nearly as potent as his persuasion abilities, trust me I had learned *that* one the hard way.

In one swift motion Michael reached out and slammed me against the locker. "Enough of your games, Nualla! We both know you are not going to choose a human mate, so why do you keep picking them and not—"

"And not *you*, you mean? Because I would rather have *anyone's* company than yours."

Michael stood there silently, looking just the slightest bit stunned, but he didn't remove his hold on my shoulders. The truth was I could say all the snide things I wanted, but I couldn't get away. He was much stronger than me. He knew it. I knew it.

The bell rang and the last remaining students fled the halls. I closed my eyes and made a desperate silent plea for help even though I knew it was hopeless.

And then something weird happened.

I heard the faintest clatter—nearly inaudible to the human ear—and then an unfamiliar voice demanded, "Get your hands off of her—*now*."

My eyes shot open, and both Michael and I turned in the same moment to stare. In the hall stood a guy I had never seen before.

"Who the hell are *you*?" Michael said, in a voice that nearly betrayed just how surprised he was. Which was exactly what *I* was thinking. I had attended Bayside Academy all four years and could never remember seeing this guy before—and that's saying a lot considering the school is pretty damn small.

"It doesn't matter who I am, that's no way to treat a girl. Especially one who's *not* your girlfriend," the guy answered, glaring at Michael.

I could feel Michael's hold on my shoulders tighten. This guy had found Michael's one fatal flaw— his pride. It was common knowledge that Michael got whatever he wanted. However, only a few people knew that Michael coveted one thing more than anything else on earth. The one thing he couldn't seem to possess. Me. But somehow this guy had figured that out and had thrown it in Michael's face. The guy was either supremely lucky, or had a death wish.

"I said, let. Her. *Go*," the mysterious guy demanded, taking a step closer.

"What are you, a white knight or something?" Michael asked with disdain as his hands slipped from my shoulders.

The guy crossed his arms. "When worthless punks like *you* make me. So yeah, I guess today, I am."

Michael glared at him with a look more deadly than I had ever seen him use; his hands balling up into fists at his sides. I just gaped at the stranger, he might as well have just poked an enraged tiger with a sharp stick. This was about to get ugly.

"*Excuse me*?" Michael said in a low, deadly voice, shaking with barely contained anger. I was sure Michael had probably never been insulted like that in his entire life, and the shock had already begun to wear off.

"You heard me," the stranger said, standing up a little taller. He was about an inch shorter than Michael, but was built far more solidly—though I doubted this would help him much if they started throwing punches.

I squeezed my eyes shut; I knew what was coming,

and I really didn't want to see it.

I waited for the sound of fist meeting face, but when I didn't, I opened one eye. Michael was standing with one fist slightly out, looking at something beyond the stranger. I opened my other eye and leaned around the boys for a better look. Apparently the fates had not designed for the stranger to die today, because the one person Michael feared at the school, was coming down the hall looking at a tablet in his hands.

When he was only a few feet from us, Mr. Savenrue, Bayside Academy's only daemon teacher, finally looked up. "Mr. Tammore, Miss Galathea, what are you doing in the hall? Class started nearly five minutes ago." Mr. Savenrue looked over at the strange guy, a look of confusion briefly crossing his face. "Are you new here? I can't seem to remember your name."

"Patrick, Patrick Connolly. I'm in your first period class, sir," the stranger answered, looking equally confused.

Mr. Savenrue looked at him for a moment. "Yes— yes of course you are," he stammered uneasily before broadening his focus to the rest of us. "Like I asked before, what are the *three* of you doing in the hall?"

"I was *asking* Mr. Tammore to stop harassing Miss Galathea," the stranger—apparently named Patrick— answered as he scowled at Michael.

Mr. Savenrue fixed Michael with a fiery gaze that could have melted ice. His gaze shifted to me where it cooled considerably to a look of sympathy. "Is this true, Miss Galathea?"

Without missing a beat I answered, "Yes, Mr. Savenrue. Michael was trying to coerce me into going to the Winter Ball with him. I tried to explain I was *already* going with someone else, but he just wouldn't listen."

"No one asked you yet; you're lying!" Michael growled as he narrowed his eyes at me.

"*I* asked her," Patrick said as he fixed Michael with a deadly glare. "*And* she said yes."

Mr. Savenrue put his head in his hand and said with an exasperated huff, "Mr. Tammore, if a girl doesn't want to go with you to a dance that's her right. You can't always get what you want, you know."

"I usually do," Michael mumbled under his breath.

"What was that, Mr. Tammore?" Mr. Savenrue asked, raising an eyebrow at Michael.

"Nothing, Mr. Savenrue," Michael answered, looking sideways at nothing in particular.

Mr. Savenrue didn't look the slightest bit convinced. "*Hmm.* Well, Mr. Tammore, why don't you accompany me to the dean's office." Mr. Savenrue reached into his bag and pulled out two late passes. He handed them to me and Patrick with a strained smile. "Mr. Connolly, Miss Galathea, why don't you head to class."

As I watched the two of them recede down the hall to the stair I tried to decided what I should say next. I mean, Patrick had basically asked me to the dance without *actually* asking me. Did he really want to go with me, or was he just saying that to get Michael to back off?

I cocked my head to one side and looked up at Patrick. "*So*…I'm going with you to the Winter Ball?"

"Yeah…about that…" Patrick said as he ran his hand through his hair nervously. "You were just bluffing, right? 'Cause if you already asked someone else you don't have to go with me. I just said that to piss off Michael."

Wow, someone who liked to mess with Michael nearly as much as I did. This guy was getting better by the minute.

"No, you're right, I *was* bluffing. I hadn't actually asked anyone yet. But I'll go with you—if you ask me that is." I looked up into his eyes and was lost in the beauty of them. They were deep pools of nearly black-brown. Throughout the whole of what had just happened I hadn't really *looked* at him until now.

Patrick had a broad, square-jawed face framed by straight black hair that flared out with a slight curl at his ears. His bangs stopped just short of his eyes, which were almond shaped, hinting at a possible heritage. He was solidly built, not too skinny, but definitely not a bodybuilder either—which I liked. He was 5' 9" at best, just a few inches taller than me. The more I looked at him the more it made me giddy and restless inside. And I had to wonder how I had managed to miss him these last few years, because he was *seriously* gorgeous.

Patrick cleared his throat but kept his eyes down. I could almost feel the waves of nervous energy flowing off him. He finally swallowed hard as he looked up into my eyes. "Nualla, would you go with me to the Winter Ball?"

I was more than a little shocked that he knew my name, but I hoped it didn't show in my face. "I would love to."

Up until this point he had seemed really self-assured, cocky even, but now he just looked at me for a bit, blinking. Finally he asked in a startled voice, "You're *serious*?"

"Were you serious about asking me?"

"Well yes of course but—"

"Then yes, I'm serious, I'll go with you to the dance."

His reactions were kind of weird. He was the kind of cute that should have won him lots of female attention, but he seemed downright shocked that I had actually said yes.

"Um…okay," he said as he ran his hand nervously

through his hair again. His expression barely concealed the panic behind it.

It was almost painful watching him wrestle with himself, so I decided to throw him a safely line. "We should probably get to class."

"Oh yeah, you're probably right."

We walked the rest of the way to class in silence. His quiet, shy demeanor was in sharp contrast to the person he had been only moments before. Maybe he had a Lancelot complex or something. Or maybe he found me more intimidating than Michael—though I seriously doubted it.

As we stepped through the classroom door, Mr. Lucas turned to us with an exasperated expression, sucking in breath for a burst of lecture. But before he could get even a single word out we held up our passes.

He let the air out with a sigh and turned back to what he had been doing. "Thank you for gracing us with your presence. You two can take one of the back tables. Since you both missed out on today's earlier activity, you are now lab partners."

As we made our way back to our seats Nikki eyed me with a curious expression. Either she was wondering why I was late, or she was wondering who the hell Patrick was—or both.

Mr. Lucas didn't even wait for us to make it to our seats before he resumed his lecture about today's class work. Mr. Lucas liked to periodically switch our seats and lab partners around so no one got too comfy—or lazy. Today was apparently one of *those* days.

It wasn't until the end of his lecture that I realized I had left my tablet in my locker. *Frak me*—he was never going to let me go get it after being as late as we were. I put my head in my hands and rubbed my temples. *Blah*, this day was already starting to suck, and it wasn't even close to being lunch yet.

I heard a light clattering, and when I opened my eyes, a tablet was sitting on the table in front of me. "You can borrow mine if you like," someone offered from next to me. I looked up at Patrick and he continued. "You forgot to grab yours because of Michael."

"Yeah, I did, didn't I."

Patrick went back to quietly examining the smart board in the front of the classroom with today's assignment on it. I couldn't tell if he was shy or just nervous. The more I looked at him, the more I wondered why I hadn't noticed him before. How could I have possibly missed a cute boy like this wandering the halls for four straight years? Even if he was terribly shy I wasn't *that* blind, was I? Maybe he was a new transfer or something.

I rested my jaw in my hand and released a bit of

my own influence. "So…how long have you been a student at Bayside Academy?"

Patrick looked at me in confusion. "Four years—why?"

PARALLEL UNIVERSE

Monday, January 9th

NUALLA

"SO WHO ARE YOU GOING TO ask to the Winter Ball?" Nikki asked, staring out at the students around the atrium.

"I already have a date," I replied as I flicked through iTribe on my tablet. I was trying to see if Patrick was in any of the pictures I had taken in the last four years. Maybe he was like a vampire and wouldn't show up in photos. That would explain a lot, really.

"*Really*? Who?" Nikki asked, soda halfway to her mouth.

"Patrick Connolly," I answered still flipping through pictures.

"*Who*?"

I pointed across the atrium to Patrick. "Him."

"Never seen him before, he a new student or something?" Nikki asked as she looked curiously at Patrick.

I gave up flipping through the photos and rested my chin on my hand. "No, *apparently* he's been here all four years—which is odd because I can't remember ever seeing him before today. Hell, even Mr. Savenrue didn't remember him, and Patrick's *in* one of his classes."

Nikki stared at me in disbelief. "*What*?"

"Yeah it's weird, he's in a lot of my classes, but I can't remember seeing him before today."

"That *is* kinda weird. Hey wait, when did this happen?"

"In the hall right before Chem. Michael was trying to make me go to the dance with him and Patrick stepped in."

"So he saved you from *Michael*?"

"Yep."

"*Damn* he's good," Nikki said, with a choking laugh. "You should keep him around; Michael repellent is always a good thing to have."

"Ya *think*?" I said sarcastically.

"Though it was *your* damn fault for dating Michael

in the first—"

"*Hey*, you said you wouldn't pick on me for that anymore!" I said, pushing her.

"Sorry, it's just so hilarious how badly you frakked up there."

"I know I did, so *please* stop reminding me," I sighed in exasperation. It was nice to see that my screw-ups made for an endlessly entertaining spectacle for my family.

I poked at my lunch as I looked out at Patrick. "What nationality do you think he is?"

"A mix," Nikki replied without much thought.

"Well *yeah*, I figured that much, but a mix of *what*?" I asked as I turned my eyes away from Patrick to Nikki.

"My bet's on some European and Asian," Nikki answered after staring at him a few seconds longer.

"Yeah, I think you're right, Nikki," I agreed, turning back to look at Patrick.

"He's *really* hot."

"Most definitely," I agreed over my can of soda. Nikki nudged me, and we both burst into giggles.

"*So* ladies, what're we talking about today?" Shawn asked as he leaned between us with his tray of food.

"Nualla's date to Winter Ball."

"*Really*, who is it this time?" Shawn asked, sliding onto the bench next to us.

"Patrick Connolly," I answered, jabbing a fork at my lunch.

Shawn paused, his burrito less than an inch from his mouth "*Who*?"

"Him," Nikki said, pointing at Patrick.

Shawn looked over at Patrick, burrito still a few inches from his mouth. "Never seen him before; he new?"

"*See* what I mean? It's like he just appeared out of nowhere," I said, throwing my fork down. This was starting to get really weird, and that's saying a lot coming from people like us.

"Maybe he's here from a parallel universe and just doesn't know it yet," Nikki said, looking at Patrick curiously.

"Nikki, I think you've been watching too much of the SyFy channel," Shawn said, gesturing at her with his lunch.

"Hey, *you* watch it too!" she snapped back indignantly.

PATRICK

"THAT GALATHEA GIRL IS CHECKING you out," Connor said, in complete disbelief as he looked past me.

"Really?" I looked up, and sure enough Nualla and her cousin were looking at us—at *me* more specifically. Nualla was sitting with Nikki and Shawn, the pale January light making them look even paler. Like a handful of students at Bayside Academy, they seemed unusually pale even for foggy SF. They were all extremely pale, not in the chalky vampire sort of way, but in that I'm-Irish-and-have-always-lived-in-Seattle kind of way.

I scooted around the circular picnic table nonchalantly to be able to better look at Nualla without *actually* appearing to be going out of my way to look at her. As I did, Beatrice scooted to fill my spot without her eyes ever leaving the book in her hands.

"Wonder who she's going with to the dance this time?" Connor said, between bites of his lunch. This speculation had been torture in past years but not anymore, because I knew who she was going with this time.

"Me."

"In your *dreams*, dude," Connor said, rolling his eyes.

I pulled my eyes away from Nualla to look at Connor. "No seriously, I'm taking her to the dance."

Connor pointed at me with a french fry. "You're full of it."

"I am *not*!"

"He's telling the truth, I heard Tara Spellman

talking about it in third period," Beatrice said, without looking up as she pushed her black cat-eyed glasses back up her small nose.

"How did *she* know about it? I just asked Nualla second period!" I asked, incredulously.

"She overheard you guys on the way to the restroom." Beatrice took a sip of soda, almond eyes still firmly fixed on her book. She was always reading a book—*always*. I had never seen Beatrice outside of class without one in all the years I had known her.

"Wait, I want to know how *you* ended up asking her to the dance. I mean have you even *talked* to her once in the last four years?" Connor asked as he looked at me skeptically.

"Um, actually…no," I admitted to my lunch tray.

"*So…*" Connor said, leaning in.

"Well, that prick Michael was trying to bully her into going with him to the dance. So I stepped in and told Mr. Savenrue *I* was taking her."

"Wait, why was Mr. Savenrue there?" Connor asked in confusion.

"He came down the hall and saw me and Michael arguing. He scolded Michael and took him off to the Dean's office, and sent me and Nualla to class."

"Oh man, *seriously*? I would have *paid* to see that!" Connor said, laughing.

"Paid to see what?" Jenny, one of our other usual table mates, asked as she walked up with Sara. They placed their lunch trays on the table and sat down.

"Mr. Savenrue berate Michael and haul him off to the office," Connor answered, barely containing his laughter.

"What did Michael *do*?" Sara asked, before biting into an apple.

"He was demanding Nualla Galathea go with him to the Winter Ball, but she's already going with Patrick," Beatrice answered, over the top of her book.

"*Really*?" Sara said, nearly choking on a bite of apple, her pale green eyes wide with disbelief.

"Well actually I asked her *after* I told him she was already going with me," I admitted, running my hand through my hair.

"Well played man, well played," Connor said, clapping me on the shoulder. "That was a gamble you could have lost spectacularly."

"Yeah, tell me something I don't know," I said, with a self-deprecating smile.

"*Oh*, but I was—" Jenny sputtered, a piece of Caesar salad halfway to her mouth. Then her ice blue eyes narrowed. "Wait, I thought you had never talked to her?"

"Well no, not before today at least." *Geez*, if even my friends didn't believe me how was anyone *else* ever going to?

"And she said *yes*?" Jenny asked, in complete disbelief.

"Of *course* she did. She had the choice between Michael and Patrick. Who the hell do you *think* she would pick?" Connor said, gesturing to me.

"Thanks Connor, that's not really a winning endorsement you know," I said, flatly.

Sometimes I thought I must just be a joke to my friends. I really couldn't blame them though; I had been pining for a girl who was way out of my league for the last four years. But now that I had a shot with her—albeit a slight shot—I was at a loss as to what I should do. I had to play my cards just right, or I was going to go down in flames.

"So you were late to class because you we asking her?" Sara asked, looking at me inquiringly.

"Yeah, among other things," I answered, looking out across the atrium toward Nualla.

"That's right, she's your Chem partner now too, huh?" Connor said as he nudged me.

"Yep," I answered with a huge grin.

"Bet you're *really* glad now you didn't take Field Biology," Beatrice said, smirking over her book.

"Hey, there's nothing wrong with Biology!" Jenny said, indignantly.

"Yeah, but in Chem you get to blow things up," Connor pointed out as he demonstrated an explosion with his hands.

4

Pictures of You

Monday, January 9th

PATRICK

WHEN I GOT HOME I finally gave myself permission to freak out. I spent a good solid hour staring at my ceiling in shock. I had actually gotten up the courage to ask Nualla Galathea out, and even more shocking she had actually said *yes*. I had spent so long wishing that this would happen I hadn't given much thought to what I would do if it actually *did*. If there was a higher power out there, they were probably laughing their ass off at me.

And then the panic set in—*and* the self-doubt.

What if it wasn't real? What if I had hallucinated

the whole thing? What if some part of my brain had just snapped? I mean, I *had* been feeling really ill as I walked toward them in the hall. What if I were actually in a hospital somewhere in a coma?

And even if it *was* all real, there were so many ways this could go wrong it wasn't even funny. It wasn't as if I had dated a whole lot of girls and would know what I was supposed to do. Knowing my luck I was probably going to manage to fuck things up in the first five minutes of our date.

I tried to calm myself. *Just play it cool Patrick, it's not like you're dating her or anything. You're just going to one dance.*

But what if we *were* dating now? *Should I change my iTribe status? No...best to wait until she does. But what if she's waiting for me to change mine first?*

I jumped up and all but ran to my computer. It would probably be a good idea to at least *add* her as a friend. I looked at my page, and there was already a friend request from her. I don't think I had ever clicked a confirm button so fast in my life. But then I just sat there staring at the screen. What was I supposed to do now?

I decided to just roll with the punches; I mean what was the worst that could happen?

NUALLA

A FEW HOURS OF ONLINE INVESTIGATION had turned up quite a lot about Patrick Connolly; the boy practically lived his life online. Forum posts, videos, pictures, and social media up the wazoo. He seemed to take pictures of everything around him, and I had to admit I was a little envious of how freely he could share his life with others. I, on the other hand, had to keep most of the things about myself private, hidden, secret. Like a CIA agent or a superhero, but without the awesome costume or badge.

The pictures told me what he liked to do, who he liked to hang out with and how unbelievably geeky he truly was. But the pictures also told me more about him than he probably ever intended.

One: he was most likely an only child with parents who worked too much. Even though he had a crap ton of pictures, his family was strangely absent from all of them. Other than his friends that sat with him at lunch he didn't seem to be close to anyone else. Sure, there were other people in the pictures he took, but they all seemed to be just random strangers in even stranger costumes at some kind of event.

Two: I was pretty sure he had never left the Bay Area in his life. As far as I could tell every single picture was of somewhere in the greater Bay Area, which to me seemed a bit odd and only reinforced my previous deduction that he had busy parents who probably didn't like to go on "family trips."

Three: he was an incredibly good artist. What he couldn't take pictures of, he seemed to draw or paint instead. I found hundreds of images of everything from the mundane to the fantastic. Precisely captured or quickly expressed, but all of them beautiful.

The more I learned about him, the more I wondered how in the hell he didn't already have girls lined up around the block to date him. Their loss I guess.

It was when I was watching the same videos of him for the third time in a row that I had to admit I was entering creepy stalker territory. I finally made myself step away from the computer and go to bed. But that didn't help me stop thinking about him as I drifted off to sleep. I didn't know why he had just suddenly appeared in my life, but I was extremely glad he had.

A THOUSAND DIFFERENT WAYS

Friday, January 13th

PATRICK

THE REST OF THE WEEK was—awesome. Connor stopped getting on my case for staring at Nualla, and when I saw Michael in the hall I was pretty sure he loathed me, which just made me grin like an idiot. Best of all, Nualla talked to me in class as if we had always talked; like we had always been friends. I was so thrilled I didn't even think to ask about her complete obliviousness to my existence for the last three years.

The more I talked to her, the less nervous about the whole thing I felt. It was like just being near her was putting me at ease. And this just made me stare at her all the more, which was how I finally got a good look at the pendant she always wore. It was a weird sort of silver circular pendant a little bigger than a quarter. It looked Egyptian with a gazelle horned deity, her hands held outstretched at her sides, a small crescent moon resting between her horns. A deep lapis blue enameled background covered with tiny silver stars, filled the space behind her, and a larger crescent encircled the whole design. An inscription ran across the outer crescent, but the symbols didn't look Egyptian; they looked like something else—something I could almost remember.

"That's a cool pendant," I said as we worked on the day's assignment in Mr. Lucas' class.

"Thanks," Nualla answered with a nervous smile.

"Where'd you get it?"

"My...my dad gave it to me when I was little," she answered, a flicker of unease crossing her face.

"My mom gave me a pendant too."

"Really?" Nualla asked, looking at my bare neck.

"But I seem to have lost it this week."

"Oh."

"Yeah, and now it feels a little weird since I've been wearing it as long as I can remember. And I still haven't told—" I cut off mid sentence when Mr. Lucas' gaze drifted in our direction.

We studiously went back to work on the assignment, but I couldn't help but notice how Nualla kept unconsciously rubbing her fingers over the surface of her pendant. And I realized with a start that I had done it again. This whole week I had found myself answering all kinds of things about myself, but still learning very little about her. And even though I had spent hours looking online, I hadn't learned a whole lot from her iTribe page.

Sure, there were photos, but not a whole lot, and nothing that really revealed that much about her that I didn't already know. I couldn't believe that she didn't lead an interesting life, so why didn't she post any of it? It almost seemed like the bits that *were* online were just for show. Maybe her parents checked up on her, and she didn't want them to see what she was up to or something.

So all I had to go on was what I had learned from just observing her in class. A lot of little things that added up to a very interesting picture—well at least to *me* anyways. Her favorite color was blue, she adored cats, and she had a fondness for big black boots. She hated having to pull her hair back for Chem class, and she drank coffee to an almost obsessive level. And a thousand other little quirks that made me adore her just that much more. But mostly I had learned that there was something different about her, something hiding behind those eyes. She gave herself away in a thousand different ways each day; I just didn't know yet what all the pieces meant.

6

Let's Get Out of This Town

Friday, January 13th

NUALLA

As Nikki and I walked down the street from the coffee shop it had started to rain, making the ground on Powell Street slick. We had nearly finished walking down the steepest part when I slipped. Instinctually my lightning-fast reflexes kicked in, and I landed in a comfortable crouch not a drop of coffee spilled. I looked around without moving my head. Dozens of people were flat out gawking at me.

Great, just *great.*

A guy just behind us, pizza in hand, spoke first. "Jesus girl, are you a gymnast or something?"

Nikki grabbed my arm pulling me to my feet and flashed a radiant smile at the guy. I could feel her influence hit him like a Mack truck. "No, she's a martial arts champion."

The guy must have bought the story because he smiled and continued walking down the street.

"Martial arts champion?" I said, questioningly.

"Your boobs are *way* too big for you to be a gymnast. Martial Arts was the only thing I could think of," she answered with a shrug.

"*Right*," I said, rolling my eyes.

I looked around, everyone else on the busy street had continued on their way paying us no mind. Well *almost* everyone. Patrick—who had apparently been walking down the street behind us—just stared at me, his mouth hanging open just a bit and his eyes wide with surprise. I would have thought he was following us if it wasn't for the fact that the mall was at the end of the street.

"Oh *frak*, he totally saw that," I cursed, turning back around quickly.

"Who?" Nikki asked, looking around.

"Patrick."

Nikki looked over my shoulder completely failing at nonchalant. "Yeah, most likely."

We came out of the dress shop, our dresses for the Winter Ball in hand. With a slightly self-satisfied smile, I imagined the look on Patrick's face when he saw me in the dress. It was going to be priceless.

Nikki stopped and looked in her purse. "Frak! I left my phone in the store; I'll be right back, 'kay?"

As she dashed off back toward the dress shop, I looked around. We had stopped in front of a jewelry kiosk, so I looked through their displays to kill some time.

While I was examining one of the necklaces, the kiosk girl asked, "Can I help you with anything, miss?"

I looked up to answer her, but stopped. Michael was standing about a hundred feet behind her, looking around.

Great, just *great.*

"No I'm good," I replied as I dropped down and pretended to tie my boot. The girl looked at me suspiciously but said nothing. I looked around for a place to hide; a bookstore stood a short distance away.

Perfect!

I chanced a quick glance in Michael's direction. He was looking the other way. I took a deep breath and walked as quickly to the bookstore as I could without attracting too much unwanted attention.

I really did *not* want to have to deal with Michael, *especially* outside of school where he was less likely to get in trouble for harassing me. The boy just didn't seem to understand the word "*over.*"

I reached the bookstore and quickly stepped behind a front display shelf. I would be fine as long as he didn't come in here. I took another deep breath and peered over the top of the shelf into the mall common area.

"Is he bothering you again?" someone asked quietly from behind me.

I jerked up with a start. I whipped my head around and was met with kind brown eyes. I knew those eyes.

Patrick?

"What, are you following me or something?" It sounded just a tad bit rude, but honestly it had just popped out of my mouth.

"No, actually I come here nearly every day." He smirked at me in a friendly way. "You sure you're not following *me*?"

I opened my mouth to say something, but caught sight of Michael looking in our direction. I grabbed Patrick's hoodie and crouched down behind the short shelf of books. He looked at me, raising an eyebrow. "I'll take that as a *yes*."

"*Yes* he's bothering me," I answered, peeking around the corner of the bookcase.

After a minute or so of silence Patrick asked,

"What's in the bag?"

I turned my head quickly back toward him, meeting his eyes and almost wished I hadn't. His eyes were the type of brown that was nearly black; deep pools that looked like they would swallow me if I looked too long.

I realized I had been holding my breath and let it out in an audible puff. "Huh?"

"The bag," Patrick said as he pointed at the dress bag next to me.

I looked down at it then back up at him. "A dress."

"Is it the one you're going to wear to the dance?" he asked as he peered a little closer at the bag.

"Yeah," I answered cautiously.

"Can I see it?"

"*No*, I want it to be a surprise," I answered, scooting away from him to get a better look outside the window. Michael was still standing just outside the store and seemed to be having a heated conversation with someone on the other end of the phone.

Come on Michael go check out the food court or the theater, anything *that gets me out of here without running into* you.

"What does he want anyways?" Patrick asked, leaning over me to peer around the bookcase.

"Me," I replied without pulling my eyes from the window.

"Well I can see why," Patrick said matter-of-factly.

That got my attention; I turned quickly around to face him. *"Excuse me?"*

Patrick's expression looked queasy—pained even—like he hadn't meant for the words to *actually* be spoken out loud. "Oh *wow*, that sounded way stalkerish didn't it?"

"Yeah, just a bit. But it's okay; no one really says nice things like that to me."

"Really? I would think guys would be falling all over themselves to tell you you're pretty."

"You might think that, but you'd be wrong." I chanced a peek around the shelf again; Michael was still talking on the phone but had moved a few feet farther away. "I think I make them nervous," I said in a small voice.

"Oh I can definitely understand that," Patrick said with a slight smile in his voice.

I turned back to face him. "Do I make *you* nervous?" He stared at me open mouthed like he was unsure of what he should say. "I'll take that as a *yes.*"

"Okay, you do—a little—okay, *a lot.* It's just that—" Patrick stammered, a blush spreading across his cheeks.

"Can I help you two with something?" someone asked from behind us.

I looked up to see a very bored, college aged guy, staring down at us over a stack of books in his hands.

"Um…" I looked out the window again in time to see Michael going down the escalator. "Nope we're good." I stood up, grabbed Patrick's hand, and walked quickly to the exit.

Patrick let me drag him for several feet before he asked, "So by our quick escape I'm guessing Michael's gone somewhere else?"

"You would be correct."

I whipped out my phone and quickly texted Nikki as I walked. Looking up every few seconds to make sure I didn't run into anyone.

Please have found your phone by now Nikki.

TODAY 5:18 PM
NUALLA GALATHEA
MICHAEL'S HERE WANT TO GET OUT OF TOWN?

I wove around a pack of stroller moms but didn't lessen my pace. I hoped Patrick wouldn't think I was a complete lunatic, but after what he had seen happen between Michael and me this week, I kinda doubted he would. But still somehow what he thought of me mattered, maybe a little more than it should.

My phone buzzed and I looked down at it again.

TODAY 5:23 PM
NIKKI VARRIS
SURE I'LL CALL SHAWN & TELL HIM TO PICK

US UP OUT FRONT K.

It was then that I realized I was still dragging Patrick through the mall. I stopped and turned a little too suddenly, his hand still in mine. Unable to stop his momentum, he ran straight into me, and we crashed to the floor.

Sigh. Sometimes I forgot just how much slower human reactions were to ours.

Patrick looked at me in horror—his legs straddling my hips— before he quickly got back to his feet.

I just had to smile at him because he looked so embarrassed even though it was completely my fault. "Wanna get out of here?" I asked, broadening my smile.

After a short pause his lips slid into a grin, and he offered his hand to me. "Sure, why not."

Once back on my feet, we all but sprinted to the exit.

DREAMING OUT LOUD

Friday, January 13th

PATRICK

WHEN NUALLA HAD ASKED IF I wanted to get out of here, I hadn't considered that she had meant to another state. Which was why it had come as a total shock when I found myself standing near a ticket counter in SFO staring at Nualla as she watched the flight information flash across the screens.

After our daring escape from the mall, we had blazed a trail out of the city and down 101 to the SFO Airport. I was so caught up in the laughter of diving into a car just as Michael came out the mall doors after us that I didn't even notice we were going to the airport. I actually got all the way into the terminal before I even acknowledged anything *other* than I was with Nualla and we weren't at school. Even when I finally looked around and saw where we were I thought it was a joke, until I remembered I was with a bunch of super rich kids. Out of town to them meant something *completely* different.

But I was already in too deep by this point and I *really* didn't want to bail. I just prayed that they would at least keep it in the country because I didn't *actually* have a passport. As I fidgeted nervously I silently calculated how much money I had in my bank account. I really didn't want to have to look like a dork for being too broke to buy my ticket to the crazy place they were planning to run off to.

"So where are we going cuz?" Nikki asked Nualla, who was still staring up at the flight board.

"Wherever has a flight leaving first," Nualla answered without looking away from the board.

Nikki raised an eyebrow. "We running from something?"

Parents. Homework. Nualla's stalker punk. Life. Any one of these things seemed like perfectly logical things to run from.

Nualla eyed me covertly. "Naw, the fun is in the surprise." She whipped her head back around to look at the board causing her hair to fling out just like in a movie.

God she's beautiful.

How the hell had I gotten so lucky to end up here with them—with her? Maybe I had been hit by a bus and I was in a coma, dreaming, or dead. Naw, as unbelievable as this all was, I knew it was reality because, A: my fantasies weren't this delusional, and B: I had absolutely no idea what the inside of an airport looked like in real life—well until now.

While I was contemplating my sanity and luck, Nualla had apparently made her decision because she walked over to the ticket counter to purchase our tickets.

Shawn looked up at the flight board. "My money's on New York."

"Hawaii," Nikki chimed in cheerfully.

"LA," I guessed without even looking.

Nualla returned a few minutes later holding four tickets and thrust them toward us. "Vegas," she said with finality.

I don't know why I had been so cocky in the bookstore. I never thought I would be saying those things to her; not even in my wildest dreams. Maybe that was *why* I had said it; my brain was convinced I was dreaming. *You really can't fuck up in a dream, so what's to lose, right?* Is what was running through my head as I waited for the girls to change from their school uniforms into normal clothes.

I leaned against the wall and let my head fall back, letting out a deep breath.

"Sorry I didn't bring you anything dude, Nikki didn't mention you would be coming," Shawn said, apologetically.

I looked at him with a half-smile. He was much taller than me—like Connor, somewhere in the 6'1" to 6'4" range. Though unlike Connor, Shawn wasn't wiry like a runner; he had the broad shoulders and a solid build of a warrior with a sharply planed face like a cheetah. A tangle of wavy blond hair roughly the same shade of blond as Nikki's, spilled over his forehead nearly to his eyes and curled over the tops of his ears.

"Don't worry about it; I don't think *she* even knew I was coming."

Shawn cocked his head to one side and smiled a crooked smile at me. "You're playing it cool, but you're scared shitless aren't you?"

"Is it that obvious?" I asked, with a self-deprecating smile.

"Naw, if you weren't scared I'd know you were a conceited wank."

"*What*?" I said, nearly choking.

"The biggest pricks act all smooth in front of girls because they think they're the shit. You, on the other hand…"

"Ah. But *you* seem calm, what's that say about you?"

"*Me*? Well, I've known those two my whole life. They know about all the stupid shit I've ever done. Hard to be nervous anymore at that point," Shawn answered, looking into the distance.

"Yeah, you're probably right."

"Look, don't worry about it so much. Just relax," he advised, looking back at me with a smile.

"Easy for you to say," I said, running my hand through my hair.

"Just think about it like hanging out with friends after school, nothing serious."

"I really don't hang out with my friends that much after school. Honestly, most of the time I'm alone."

"Dude *seriously*? That's really sad."

"Yeah I know," I agreed, leaning my head back against the wall again. I don't know why I was being so honest about how truly lame I was; it wasn't going to help me.

"But I really can't say I'm much better. I mostly hang out with those two girls. Can't remember ever having many guy friends," Shawn admitted, folding his arms across his chest.

"I'd be your friend," I blurted out without giving it much thought.

Wow did I really just say that out loud? God he

probably thinks I'm even lamer now than he did before.

"*Really*? Coolness, friendship accepted," Shawn said, with a huge grin.

Wait, what?

But I really didn't have time to think about it long because something hit me in the chest. I looked down at the floor at some clothes that had apparently been thrown at me.

"Nualla, you're supposed to say 'think fast' *before* you do that, not just throw things at people," Shawn said as he pushed away from the wall.

"What are these?" I asked, bending down to pick up the clothing.

"They're *clothes* silly. You didn't think we would really make you go to Vegas in your Bayside Academy uniform did you?"

Actually that's completely what I had thought, but thanks for having a higher opinion of me than I do.

I looked at the clothes again; they were super stylish designer casual and probably cost a small fortune since we were at an airport. "Thanks. How much were they, I'll pay you back," I said, looking up.

"Don't worry about it," Nualla said with a broad smile. "Think of it as payment for letting me kidnap you this weekend."

"Okay, then how much were the tickets?"

"Don't kidnappers usually pay for the transportation of the kidnapped?" Nualla asked as she leaned in closer—*dangerously* closer.

"Um…yeah, but really I can't just—"

"Patrick, you're never going to win this so just give up," Shawn said, nudging me.

"Okay," I said uneasily.

"Now go change, our plane's gonna start boarding soon," Nualla said with a smile as she pushed me toward the restrooms.

I took a few steps then stopped. *Wait, weekend?*

Raise Your Glass

Friday, January 13th

PATRICK

VEGAS WAS...*SHINY*. THAT WAS REALLY the only word for it. I honestly didn't think I had ever seen so many lights in my life. It seemed like they basically lit up every inch of the city they possibly could. Their power bills must have been astronomical. It felt like we had entered a theme park for adults. I just couldn't help but stare out the window as we passed a pyramid, castle, and even the Statue of Liberty. I had seen this place a lot of times on TV, but it just didn't do it justice.

I didn't ask where we were going, and honestly,

I didn't even notice where we were until a bouncer asked for ID's.

Crap!

I didn't have a fake ID. I turned to Nualla to mention this, but without missing a beat she handed the bouncer four ID's and smiled. He looked at them for a second looking a little dazed. I thought we were screwed at that point; any second he was going to call the cops. I mean that's what they did when minors tried to get into nightclubs, right? But to my utter disbelief he handed the ID's back to her and stepped aside to let us pass.

Just inside the door a smiling hostess took our bags and handed all of us little keychain key cards.

"What's this?" I asked, looking at it questioningly.

"It's your Eclipse card; it tracks your drink purchases, so you don't have to carry around your belongings while you're here," the hostess answered, with a cheery smile.

"*Really*?" I said, examining the card more closely. "That's awesome."

"Just tap it here and press your thumb in the sensor," she said as she gestured to a machine beside her. "Oh, and please don't lose it, or we will be forced to charge you the maximum limit."

"Oh really, what's that?" I asked as I pressed my thumb against the reader.

"You *really* don't want to know," Nualla said,

pushing me gently away from the door.

"Enjoy your night, Miss Galathea," the hostess called behind us.

I wondered just how many times you had to come to a place like this before they remembered your name.

Being that I was in highschool and had obviously never *been* to a club before, I only had movies and episodes of *CSI* to go from. I was pretty sure most clubs didn't *actually* look like the ones on TV; however, this one totally did.

Light up dance floors, multiple levels, swirling flashing lights, music you could feel through your body. Oh, and swarms of people, pressed together; their bodies pulsing with the music. I tried not to gape at it all like an idiot as we wove through the crowds of people to an empty table.

A drink girl passed us, and Nualla said something to her I couldn't hear above the music. The girl nodded and walked off.

"Pretty awesome place," I said loudly as I looked around.

"You've never been to a club before, have you?" Shawn asked, with a smirk.

"Nope."

"Awesome! Then this should be even *more* fun," Shawn said, smiling mischievously. Something in his expression told me he was sharing a private joke with himself.

The drink girl placed some shots in front of us, and Nualla tapped her card on the drink tray sensor. It flashed green, and the girl walked away, disappearing into the throng of people.

"Bottoms up," Shawn said as he raised his shot glass.

I just stared at mine. People—mostly parents— liked to pretend that high school kids didn't drink. They were completely wrong of course, but they could keep deluding themselves if they liked. I was by no means a lush or a teenage alcoholic, but I also was not a stranger to the stuff, either. I had thought that my parents might have noticed at some point that their liquor cabinet was getting depleted, but like everything else, they didn't. But then again they would have had to have been home more to probably notice.

"You do drink, right, Patrick?" Nualla asked, in a worried voice.

I smiled up at her. "Of course, just not normally in public."

I looked back at the shot glass. Once I took one drink there would be no going back; the evening would take a completely different direction, I just knew it. But was I ready to go down that path? I looked up at Nualla, into her stunningly beautiful eyes. I didn't really have to think about it after that.

I took a deep breath, and raised my glass up to join theirs. A grin spread across all their faces, and we all downed our shots.

The shot burned its way down my throat warming my chest. "What *is* this?" I asked, looking at the glass.

"Tequila," Nikki answered grinning.

"Good tequila," Shawn amended with a huge grin as he nudged me with his elbow.

I decided it was best not to ask how much "good tequila" cost in a place like this.

A shot or two later Nualla finally grabbed my hand and dragged me into the throng of people on the dance floor. The lights washed everyone in a golden-red light like—well an eclipse actually. People moved against each other, bodies slick with sweat. I was sure there must have been air conditioning running at full-blast, but it really wasn't doing all that much to ease the heat out on the dance floor.

As Nualla began to pulse along with the music, I thanked everything holy that I actually *knew* how to dance. She moved with the music hypnotically, and I tried to burn the image in my mind. I was sure I was never going to get this lucky again, and I wanted to remember this forever.

Someone brushed up against me and I turned; Nikki and Shawn had joined us on the dance floor. Something in their movements—their eyes—told me they were more than *just* friends, but I doubted they had figured that out yet. It was interesting to see a different side of them all, the one they didn't show at school. I had been a silent observer for so long that being invited into their private world was a little overwhelming. Overwhelming but welcome; it was nice to be on the inside for once.

Nualla grabbed my hand and pulled me a little closer. I nearly froze, but then I released all my fear and just went with it. I let the music wash over me, directing my movements. My body moved closely to hers, a cushion of hot air the only thing keeping us from touching.

The music went through several changes before Nualla pushed me softly away and turned her head to Nikki. "Ready, Nikki?"

Nikki smiled broadly as if they were sharing a private joke. "Yep."

"Three…two…one," the girls said softly.

And then the music changed, and they were standing in the center of the dance floor. Their hips swiveled, arms thrust, feet stepped in perfect unison. Their precise movements would rival any professional dance squad and put any cheer team to shame. Their bodies pulsed with the music. Body rolls, hip pops, and spins that fit the music perfectly as if made for it.

Nikki was hot and a good dancer in her own right, but she had nothing on Nualla. Nualla's hips rolled and popped in time with music. No, she didn't move with the music—she *was* the music. Nualla was song in liquid form; undulating in smooth sensuous movements. She was sex appeal incarnate. It rolled off her in nearly visible waves, affecting everyone around her. All the guys stared at her and so did half the women.

A guy elbowed me gently and leaned in. "She's hella hot."

My protective defenses kicked in. "She's with me."

The guy folded his arms and looked me up and down, appraising. "You're damn lucky. That girl is *never* here with anyone. She always just seems to be dancing for herself."

"What do you mean?"

He unfolded his arms and pointed at Nualla. "Look at her eyes. She's looking straight at *you*. She never looks at anyone when she dances."

"Really?" I said, looking back at Nualla as she spun, her hair flowing out in a beautiful wave of soft black spirals.

"Yeah…look, she's a little sex rocket. You better be careful, or you might get burned."

"I'll keep that in mind," I said without looking at

him, but no answer came. I looked next to me, the guy was gone. I looked back at the girls and was hit full force by Nualla's captivating eyes. They glowed as if illuminated from within.

The girls popped their hips and dropped to the floor as the song ended. I just kinda gaped at them as everyone else cheered. I somehow got the feeling they did this a lot. Just how often did they come to places like this anyways?

Nualla stood up in one fluid movement, looking at me from beneath her lashes. And then everything fell away; there was nothing but her. I had never seen anything so sexy and enchanting in my life. *Never*. She glided over to me and reached out a hand to run her finger down my chest. I opened my mouth to say something, but nothing came out. It suddenly felt very warm; *too* warm.

Nualla pulled me dangerously close and brought her face close to mine. Her lips brushed against my ear as she let out a breath. It was hot and full of temptation. An electric shock ran through my body making my vision sway in and out. I caught a glimpse of something—something curved near her ear, but as I tried to focus on it, it shimmered farther from my vision.

I looked away then looked back at her, this time trying to avoid her eyes. My pulse seemed to be running a fifty yard dash, and it was hard to remember to breathe. "I'll…be right back."

I nearly ran to the men's room passing one of the drink girls as I went. I snatched a shot off her tray, as I tapped my card to it. I didn't look to see if it turned green, I figured if it didn't she would find me. I downed it in a few seconds flat and clunked it down on a table as I passed. I turned a corner and pushed open the door into the blessedly cool restroom.

Breathing hard I braced myself with my arms over the sink. What had I done? Nualla had always seemed so cool and reserved in school, but somehow I had unleashed a tigress. If I wasn't careful, I would give in to her *more* than tempting body language. Before Monday, Nualla had never really paid attention to me, and now she seemed to have eyes for nothing *but* me.

I threw cold water on my face, running it back through my hair. I could do this. I looked at myself in the mirror and walked back out into the sweltering club.

When I got back to Nualla they were all back at the table doing shots with a few other clubbers. I snatched up one of the glasses and did one with them.

Nualla looked at me questioningly, "You okay?"

"Never better, just a little warm." Who was I kidding? I was powerless to resist her.

"I know! I wish I could take off more clothes," she shouted over the music as she tugged on her tank top to illustrate her point.

My brain screamed *danger*, but I ignored it.

Nikki laughed. "I'm sure the *guys* wouldn't mind Nualla." She was more than wasted. Just how many drinks had they had while I was gone?

I swallowed hard and gestured to the dance floor. "What was that about?"

Nualla moved closer, pressing against me. "Oh the dance routine?"

I looked down into her eyes, which was a big mistake. "Yeah."

"Oh, me and Nikki take dance for our PE credits. Why, what do you do?"

"I just go to the boring ordinary gym. Apparently, not nearly as useful as what you do."

Nikki chimed in loudly. "She's *very* flexible."

"I am! Want to see?" Nualla asked, with a huge grin.

"I—" I was doomed; that's what I was. Either they were fucking with me, or they were smashed beyond all reason. Or *both*.

The music changed, and Nualla squealed, "Oh I love this song. Come dance with me."

I looked at her and then the dance floor and then downed another shot for good measure. This turned out to be an incredibly *bad* idea, of course. I took a step and the world began to turn out of kilter.

If you've ever been drunk, you know that there's a point when you've had too much and everything stops making any real sense. You start to feel like you're floating or walking through a dream. Yeah, I had hit *that* point.

Nualla pulled me to the dance floor and put my hands on her thrusting, popping, and swaying hips. I continued to sway with the music as I looked down at her. I was beyond resisting her and maybe she knew it.

She looked up at me questioningly. "What?"

"There's something not quite normal about you isn't there?"

"Yeah," she answered, confirming my conclusions.

"Care to enlighten me?" I asked as I raised an eyebrow.

"Sorry—can't."

"Why?"

"You'd have to marry me first," she replied in a teasing voice.

"Okay." I wasn't sure why I had said that, it had just kind of popped out of my mouth, and in the fog of this drunken dream it began to make more and more sense.

She stopped dancing and just stared at me. "*Excuse me*?"

I tried to work through the fog in my head, but gave up and said the first thing that came to mind. "Were you bluffing again?"

"No…" Nualla admitted very slowly, a smirk spreading across her face.

"Then let's go," I said as I took a step toward the door pulling her along, a big dumb grin on my face. I didn't really know why everything seemed incredibly funny when you were drunk, it just did.

"*Now*?" she asked as she looked over at Nikki and Shawn who were amidst a conversation with some fellow clubbers, all of them laughing so hard they were nearly gasping.

"Sure, why not. What have we got to lose?" I said, with a shrug.

"Okay." She smiled broadly at me, and we wove our way toward the door.

As we broke out from the club and dashed into the cool night air I had never felt more alive. We ran down the street toward the future, laughing like idiots. I couldn't remember the last time I had been this happy—this free.

Why in the name of all reason I had said yes, I will never know. Maybe it was because Nualla was beyond tempting, and I was dying to know her secrets. Or that I was angry with my parents for never being there, and I wanted someone to be close to me. Or that I was really, *really* drunk. But it was probably because, when fate throws you the one thing you have always wanted, you grab hold of it and never let go.

WAKING UP IN VEGAS

Saturday, January 14th

NUALLA

I OPENED ONE EYE. I WAS in a hotel room; it was very bright out, and I *really* needed to use the restroom. I threw the covers aside and stumbled ungracefully toward what I hoped was a bathroom. My head felt like it had made friends with a ton of bricks, and I was beyond thirsty.

I found the sink and splashed cold water onto my face. And that's when I saw it, glittering on my finger. A ring. A really *nice* ring. I took a step back and stared at myself in the mirror. Why the hell was I *naked*?

I just stared at myself in the mirror for a while.

Then something caught my attention, a mark between my hip bone and abdomen. I inspected it closer.

Is that a hickey?

"What the *hell*!" It *totally* was.

"*Ughhh...*" groaned someone's voice from the other room.

I froze. I was in a hotel room—*naked*—and I wasn't alone. This was bad. This was very, *very* bad.

I edged toward the door of the bathroom and carefully peered out. There was a guy sleeping in the bed.

Oh frak!

I stalked into the room as quietly as I could. In a swift motion I snatched a sheet from the floor that had been kicked off the bed in the night and wrapped it over me like a Grecian goddess. I crept around the bed to stand in front of the still sleeping guy. I peered closer and took a small sigh of relief. It was Patrick.

I ran my teeth nervously over my bottom lip; there was no point in putting this off any longer than I needed too. If I was awake and having to deal with this, he should be too. I reached out a tentative hand and poked him with one finger.

He groaned and opened one eye. "*Nualla?*" It came out in a groggy, slurred voice. Then his eyes went wide, and he sat bolt upright. Apparently, the fact that I was wearing a sheet had chiseled its way through his morning fog. He looked at me, looked around the room, and put his head in his hands. "Oh, *hell*."

I thrust my left hand at him. "Patrick, never mind everything else, what's *this*?"

Patrick spread his fingers to peer at the ring glittering on my finger. He dropped his hands, and his eyes went wide. He looked at me then back at the ring then back at me again. "But...I...that was just...a strange *dream*?"

"Want to try that one again, buddy?"

Patrick pulled the blanket tight to him and leapt out of the bed. He tore frantically around the seating room area of the suite in search of something. On the coffee table under a pile random junk he apparently found what he was looking for because he stopped moving. However, from this distance I couldn't see what it was.

Patrick brought his other hand up to it and the blanket dropped to the ground. "Oh, *fuck*!"

I whipped my eyes away from him lightning fast. "*What*? What is it?" I said to the wall, a blush creeping across my cheeks. He was also apparently *very* naked.

I heard him walk over, and a second later he handed me a leather folder over my shoulder. I flipped it open and stared at it blankly. It was a certificate. I said nothing for a while; just stared at it in disbelief.

Finally Patrick said, "Nualla, say something."

I whipped around to face him. "We got *married*

last night?!"

"Technically, I think it was early this morning, since it's like three in the afternoon."

"*What*?!" I yelped, looking toward the windows again.

Before Patrick could answer, I heard a buzzing. I looked over and saw the contents of my purse scattered across the floor. I dashed over and answered my phone without even checking to see who it was. "*Hello*?" I said cautiously into the phone.

"Nualla, where the *hell* are you?" Thankfully, it was Nikki and not one of my parents.

Good question. I looked around the room, but nothing screamed, *You are here, Nualla you idiot!*

"I haven't a clue. You?"

"We're at the Bellagio."

"I think we're at the Venetian," Patrick said from behind me.

"Apparently we're at the Venetian," I related back to Nikki.

"How did you get *there*? I thought you two were just going out for air?" Nikki practically yelled into the phone.

"Well we were but…um…it's a long story."

"With you, they are *always* long stories," Nikki said, and I could swear I almost heard her eyes rolling through the phone. "Can you just give me the Twitter version?"

"Look can I call you back after I find my clothes?"

"Your *what*?!" Nikki shouted on the other end of the phone, and I had to pull it away from my head.

"I'll call you back in five, 'kay?" I said quickly before I hung up the phone.

"I found your clothes," Patrick said apologetically from behind me. I looked where he was pointing; a trail of clothes lead from the door to the bed.

"Oh, *frak* me!" My hands went automatically to my face and the sheet hit the floor. Patrick put his hand over his eyes lightning fast, a deep blush spreading across his cheeks.

I rushed over and gathered up my clothes and held them in front of me as I backed toward the bathroom. I threw the clothes down and slammed the door shut. Then I wrenched the door back open and poked my head out. "Get dressed we're going downstairs in like five minutes."

"No complaints here," Patrick said, his hand still covering his eyes.

"Good, because I'm in no mood to hear any."

PATRICK

M Y HEAD FELT LIKE A two-ton truck had hit it. Nualla was still pacing back and forth waving her hands frantically and talking into her cell in a language I couldn't understand. Though she was speaking quickly, the words flowed over her lips like a beautiful waterfall. It sounded vaguely Elvish, like it was Gaelic or something. What did Gaelic sound like anyways?

She seemed upset. I mean *sure* she'd woken up to find herself married to me. But there was something else. Something she wasn't saying out loud, but I could see it in her eyes. Fear. Something was wrong—*very* wrong.

I mulled over the various possibilities in my head. Maybe she had crazy parents that would disown her or something. Or maybe she had some incurable disease. The more I thought about it the more it gnawed at my insides. I leaned my head back to stare at the fake sky while rather convincing clouds floated across it. It was like being at Disneyland; a Disneyland for adults.

I wasn't sure where exactly I had gone wrong last night. Wait, that was a lie; it was around the time I took that first drink. And even with how fucked this morning was turning out to be, I couldn't say I wouldn't have done exactly the same thing again given the option.

This morning had been so far out of my norm I had just followed Nualla down here without saying another word. I mean what was I supposed to say?

"I'm sorry I didn't mean to marry you. I was drunk and convinced I was dreaming the whole thing up." Somehow saying any of that didn't strike me as a very good idea.

I heard a sound and looked up just as Nikki and Shawn were about to reach my table. Nikki had just enough time to get out a "Hi Patrick—" before Nualla dragged her off. Shawn seemed oblivious to the whole exchange and went straight to get some coffee. Their love of coffee was starting to border on obsessive, but really, was *I* any less weird?

I went back to staring at the fake sky, letting my mind go blank. Which worked for all of five seconds before the doubts and fears started creeping in again.

I heard the scraping of metal on stone as Shawn pulled up a chair to sit with me. He leaned back in the chair so that the front feet came off the ground and stared up at the fake sky, sipping his coffee slowly. After a few more minutes of silence, Shawn finally asked, "So…how was *your* night?"

"I think we got married."

Shawn spit out the coffee and cursed something in a language I didn't know as his chair slammed back down on the ground. He looked at me, eyes wide. "*Excuse me*?"

I held last night's incriminating evidence in front of him.

Shawn ran his hand through his hair as he looked

down at the wedding band. "Well, *shit*." He sipped his coffee then stared at it before turning to the barista. "Um miss, can I get the largest espresso you have with a double shot—on second thought make that a triple."

NUALLA

I WAS RUNNING SCARED, DRAGGING NIKKI through the Venetian. I was losing it, and somehow I had convinced myself if I kept moving I wouldn't have to admit this mess was real.

When we reached the gondolas she pulled me to a stop. "Nualla, wait! What's going on?"

I reached into my purse and pulled out the marriage certificate, thrusting it into her hands. "*This*!"

Nikki looked at it in confusion, but as she began to read her eyes got wider. "Is this some kind of joke?" she asked, looking up.

"I *wish* it was," I answered before I began to pace back and forth in front of her.

"Okay, calm down. Maybe no one will find out, and you can forget the whole thing. We can just go down there and have them shred it. I mean isn't this city's slogan 'What happens here stays here' or something?"

"No, that won't work. I called the Embassy here, they *already* know."

"Well *shit*, then you have about oh I'd say a day or two until our Embassy finds out. A.k.a. your *dad*."

"I *know*, Nikki. But that's not even the worst part," I said, avoiding her eyes.

"Wait, how could this be—wait, you didn't *sleep* with him did you?" Nikki asked in a startled voice.

"Well yes, I mean no, I mean—oh hell I don't know." I sat down on the bottom railing of the bridge and put my head in my hands.

"Well its simple really, is he currently rolling on the floor in agonizing pain?"

I looked up. "Well no."

"Has he complained of his veins feeling like they're on fire?"

"Well no, I mean he didn't *mention* anything—"

"Has he complained of any pain at *all*?" Nikki asked, a little exasperated.

"Well just his head."

"I'm sure *that's* just a hangover," Nikki said as she rolled her eyes.

"Oh what does it matter anyways? I'm still screwed." I put my head back in my hands.

"Well *yeah*, but at least this way we don't have to worry about renting a private plane to transport him home."

"You always look at the bright side, don't you?" I

said sarcastically.

"There's plenty of fucked up in this situation, but look, at least you're stuck with someone who's cute, smart, funny, and well, worships the ground you walk on," Nikki pointed out as she ticked off Patrick's attributes on her fingers. "I mean hell; you could have accidentally married some jerk like Michael."

"Nikki, *anyone's* better than Michael," I said flatly.

"Well you do have a point there."

PATRICK

Nualla came and sat down at the table with impossible grace. "So the good news is, I'm almost one hundred percent sure we didn't sleep together last night. Well, I mean we slept together we just didn't *sleep* together," she said nervously.

"And that's a *good* thing?" I asked, raising an eyebrow. "I mean why the hell *else* do you drag a random stranger to Vegas?"

Nualla ran her teeth over her bottom lip and looked very unsure of herself. It was in that moment I realized that she might *actually* like me, and I had just basically called her a slut.

"Um, well I mean—that didn't come out right did

it?"

She cocked her head to one side and smirked at me. "Yeah—*not* exactly. Want to try that again?"

"Yes please," I answered, looking up at her sheepishly. She nodded as if to say, *well go ahead then*.

I looked at the wedding band on my finger. I had been infatuated with Nualla since the very moment I had first seen her. But until this week, she had never seemed to notice I even existed. Somehow she possessed an all-consuming power over me, and I braced myself as I asked the next question. "So...why *did* you drag me to Vegas?"

"Because I wanted to get out of town, and it was the first flight leaving," she answered matter-of-factly.

"No I mean why did you ask *me* to come?" I asked in an unsteady voice as I stared at my coffee.

"*Oh*—because of all the boys in school I like you the best."

I looked up; she was looking at me, chin resting on her hand. Her wedding ring glittered in the light and a broad smile crossed her face. I just looked at her. I had never thought in a thousand years that I would be here—or for that matter, *anywhere* with her—but here she was smiling at me, and I was *married* to her.

I cleared my throat and continued on with our conversation, I really couldn't just go on staring at her like an idiot. "So...us not sleeping together is a *good* thing?"

"Trust me, in *this* case it's a good thing," she said, looking away nervously.

"Explain."

"I—I can't." She rolled her eyes down to the right, running her teeth over her bottom lip. "It's—complicated."

"*How* complicated?"

"I can't tell you..."

"Or what, you'd have to kill me?" I said jokingly.

Nualla's eyes went wide before she looked down at the table again. "Um...yeah."

I choked on my coffee. I had been entirely joking, but Nualla's eyes told me she wasn't. "What, is your dad a mob boss or something?"

Nualla had a look on her face like she was trying to teach rocket science to a fish. "Yeah...something like that."

I leaned back in my chair, covering my mouth with my hand. *Shit*, just what exactly had I gotten myself into?

Nualla reached out a tentative hand to touch mine, and I looked up. "There's more..." she said uneasily.

"The bad part?" I said, bracing myself for what else life could possibly feel like throwing at me this morning.

"Yeah...turns out we actually *did* get married last night."

10

Vanishing into Dreams

Saturday, January 14th

PATRICK

AFTER A RATHER QUICK, UNCOMFORTABLY silent late lunch, we headed to the airport and hopped a plane back to San Francisco. I had always thought on my first trip out of the state I would have wanted to do more sightseeing, but I hadn't really much felt like it at the time.

None of us talked on the plane. Shawn listened to music, Nikki flipped through one of the in-flight magazines, and Nualla stared out the window nervously playing with her necklace. I flipped through all the incriminating photos we had taken the night before on my phone. If these ever made it onto iTribe, I would be a dead man for sure.

At a little after eight we finally made it out of the airport in San Francisco on our way to the parking garage. Nualla rounded the corner then leapt back pressing herself against the wall, panic stricken. Nikki, Shawn, and I stopped dead in our tracks. Nualla looked at the other two and mouthed something to them before looking up at me. I got the distinct impression that they knew *exactly* what was around that corner because they both tensed.

Nualla took a step toward me as she rummaged around in her purse. She grabbed my hand and slapped something into it. "Patrick here's some cash, get yourself a cab."

"Wait *what*? Is it Michael again or something?"

"No, worse," she answered, not meeting my eyes.

I started running through the list of people that could possibly be worse than Michael. "Is it your *dad*?"

Nualla grabbed my hands and held them in hers. "No, but Patrick, you *really* have to trust me on this. Please go. I'll see you on Monday."

"Nualla, you're not making any sense." I tried to look around her, but I couldn't lean far enough to see past the wall.

"I know; I'm sorry. I'll explain everything to you later."

I looked back at her. "Promise?"

"Promise," she answered, sounding extremely anxious.

"*Fine,*" I relented, closing my hand around the cash.

I looked away from her eyes trying to get up enough courage for what I was going to do next. I was afraid that if I let her go this would all vanish; that I would wake up tomorrow to find that it had all been a really strange dream.

I extended my hand toward her slowly, trying to keep it from shaking. Taking a deep breath, I let the fear go like I had on the dance floor. The tips of my fingers brushed her soft hair, and I pulled her face close to mine.

"One more thing before I go." It was now or never, I swallowed hard and continued. "I've wanted to do this since the first day I saw you. And I'm not a hundred percent sure I got my chance yet, so..." And then I kissed her, for what could be the last time for all I knew.

I turned and started walking away before I could lose the calm, cool person I was currently projecting. "See you Monday before school, on the steps of the parking lot entrance, okay?"

"'Kay," she said in a small voice, so low it didn't even echo off the parking garage walls.

I didn't look back, just continued walking. I didn't need to be home. I didn't need to be anywhere really. Anywhere—but with her.

NUALLA

PATRICK BRUSHED THE TIPS OF his fingers across my hair as he pulled me closer. "One more thing before I go."

My breath caught but never escaped, his eyes were vast pools, dark mysteries pulling me into their embrace. "I've wanted to do this since the first day I saw you. And I'm not a hundred percent sure I got my chance yet, so…"

I was going to ask *"what?"* but I didn't get a chance to. Patrick leaned in and kissed me, his eyes sliding closed. He kissed me deeply, passionately. His lips were so soft, softer than I imagined lips could feel. And then he pulled away and turned to leave. "See you Monday before school, on the steps of the parking lot entrance, okay?"

I was still in shock, so the only thing that popped out of my mouth was, "'Kay," and I said it to his retreating back.

I could feel a deep sadness following him, but I couldn't do anything about it but watch him go. He was not ready for what was on the other side of the wall. Hell, *I* wasn't even ready for it.

Once Patrick was nearly out of sight, I swallowed hard and rounded the corner. In the distance the curvy form of a woman leaned against Shawn's car. When we got a few feet closer my fears were confirmed. It was Tylia, one of the Kalo Protectorate's high ranking officers. Everything about her read sleek and deadly except for her hair, which was a pulled back 'fro.

"So, how was Vegas?" Tylia asked, looking down at her nails.

I just stared dumbly at her. "How did you—?"

She stopped leaning against the car and took a step forward. "Nualla it's my *job* to ensure the safety of the Chancellarius and his family. Do you really think you could leave the state without me knowing?"

I made to push past her. "Well we're back now, so you can stop keeping tabs on us."

She put an arm out in front of me. "Not so fast, *Arius*. I would ask you *why* you were in Vegas, but I already know." Tylia reached into her back pocket and whipped out an eCopy of my marriage license.

I rocked back on my heels and nearly fell over. With a steadying breath, I reached out and took the ePaper.

"I intercepted *that* before anyone else saw it. I suggest you tell your father before Monday, or I will have to," Tylia advised, gesturing to the ePaper.

"Thanks, Tylia," I said, staring down at the simple document that was causing a lot of my current problems.

"Keeping the peace is one of my job responsibilities too, you know," Tylia said over her shoulder as she stalked off in the direction we had come—toward Patrick.

A chill ran down my spine, and I called out to Tylia. "You leave him alone, Tylia. I don't want you hurting him. I...I like him."

Tylia turned back to look at me, arms crossed in front of her. "Honey, as much as I might wish different, that boy is now part of your family for better or for worse. And so protecting his ass now falls on my list of responsibilities. Hurting him is the *last* thing I'm going to do. Your father, on the other hand, is a completely different story," Tylia stated before she turned and continued in the direction she had been going.

And this time I didn't stop her.

How to Ruin Your Life
In 48-Hours or Less

Saturday, January 14th

NUALLA

I OPENED THE DOOR QUIETLY, AND Nikki and I made for the stairs. But as I hit the first step, I heard my father Alex's voice from the living room. "Hey kids, you're back early."

I turned slowly to face my parents, hiding my ring hand behind me as I did. I looked nervously at Nikki, willing myself to stay calm before answering, "Yeah, something came up."

"Oh?" Alex said, arching an eyebrow.

I opened my mouth to say something, but nothing came out. I really should have thought up a lie *before* coming home.

There was a slight creaking on the stairs, and my sister Andraya pushed past me. "Nice rock," she said with a snide smirk to her voice.

"Rock? I thought you went to Las Vegas, did you go camping instead?" My mother Loraly asked, looking a little confused.

My sister dropped down onto one of the couches and opened her book. "No, Mom, the sparkly kind you wear on your finger, not the kind you find on the ground," she clarified as she wiggled the fingers of her left hand for effect.

"A ring?" Loraly asked, looking over at me.

I looked back at them, horrified. This was bad, at this rate they were going to figure it out before I could even tell them. And that is *never* a good thing. So I went for stupid teenager Plan B. Blurt it out quickly and hope they understand none of it.

"I got married in Vegas to a human. Please don't kill me," I said in a rush, throwing my hands in front of my face. Silence hung so heavily in the air I finally had to peek through my fingers at my family.

"Wait, did I seriously just hear that right? You got *married*?" Andraya asked incredulously, finally breaking the silence.

"Yeah..." I answered reluctantly in a voice so quiet it was more breath than noise.

"Since when were you even *dating* anyone?"

Andraya asked, dropping her book and jumping to her feet.

"Um…" I answered uneasily as I ran my teeth over my bottom lip. I had absolutely no idea how to explain the next part. I was a terrible liar and everyone knew it.

"You *were* at least dating him for a while, right?" Andraya asked as she stared at me with a slightly horrified expression.

This wasn't exactly going well, but it wasn't a disaster yet either. Until that is, Nikki chimed in from next to me. "No, actually I think Nualla just met him this week."

And that's when all hell broke loose.

In the short time after Nikki had accidentally outed my complete lack of good judgment from the weekend in front of nearly our whole family, absolute chaos had ensued. Nikki had buried herself far into the pillows of the couch to avoid my fierce glare, and my parents were sitting in stunned silence, their mouths hanging open.

"Nualla, are you out of your *mind*?!" Andraya crossed the room and gestured dramatically. "Are you trying to *expose* us or something?" I really didn't know what to say, so I didn't say anything. "You never *think*, Nualla! You never think about how what you do affects all of us!" Andraya screamed at me.

Alex finally stood up and walked over to my sister. "Andraya, that's enough," he said, placing a hand on her shoulder. "You know this was, and is, Nualla's decision to make. We can have no say in the matter."

Andraya wilted under our father's hand. As much as she would hate to admit it, he was right.

"Nualla, did you marry this boy of your own free will?"

"Yes." I looked up into his face, tears pricking my eyes. The moment he had placed his hand on Andraya's shoulder in my defense I had hung my head. I hated to disappoint him, and even though he had said it was my decision to make, disappointment still shone in his eyes. "No one forced me to make this decision. It was my own fault."

Alex raised an eyebrow. "Fault?" When I didn't answer he reached out and pulled me close for a hug. Smoothing my hair, he looked down at me. "Nualla, sweetheart, choosing a life mate is not something to be ashamed of. It *is* a big decision that is only for *you* to make." He looked over and I knew he was glaring at Andraya as he continued. "And none of us, or anyone *else* for that matter, has a right to demand explanations from you."

I loved my dad; no matter how bleak things looked or how stupid I felt, he always made me feel better.

"Really?" I asked, looking up at him.

He smiled down at me. "Really." He released me and took a step back. "Now since he is a Neodaemon, he will have to register at The Embassy and will no doubt have lots of questions."

I looked down at my shoes. "Yeah, about that… he's human."

"Yes Nualla, you mentioned that, that is why he will…" Alex stopped talking when he saw me start shaking my head.

"No I mean he's *still* human."

"*What*?" Alex said, completely taken aback.

"Way to go, Nualla, you even managed to screw *that* up," Andraya said from across the room.

"Andraya dear, you really aren't helping," Loraly said with a sigh.

"But you married him?" Alex asked, looking confused and concerned at the same time.

"Most definitely. We had fake ID's, but I'm pretty sure we spoke the oath so—"

"What do you mean by 'pretty sure'?" Alex asked, his eyes narrowing.

"Well…you see we were…" I looked at the floor and braced for the reaction to what I was about to say. "Well all three, I mean all four of us were um…really drunk."

Silence hung in the air, someone coughed but I couldn't tell who since I was still staring at the floor.

The silence drifted on till it became unbearable. Finally, I just had to look up. Alex was staring at me in complete disbelief. "You got married to a boy you barely knew while you were *drunk*?!"

"Basically," I admitted reluctantly.

"Nualla, are you completely *insane*?!" Andraya shouted, but Alex put up his hand, and she didn't continue.

Alex looked at me, and I could see barely restrained anger behind his eyes. I had only seen it on occasion since he was a really kind person but still, it was frightening. He had only questioned my judgment a few times while I was growing up. However, he never had cause to question Andraya's.

"As I said, Nualla has made her decision, and we have no right to question it. Though I would have hoped she would have had enough common sense to at least make it with a clear head. What's done is done—there is no going back. What I don't understand, however, is why he's still human?"

My voice was tight and only came out barely audible. "Well we didn't..."

"You didn't *what*?" Alex looked hopelessly confused, and I was hoping to avoid having to give him play-by-play.

Fortunately for once in her life, Andraya opened her big mouth to actually come to my aid as opposed to her normal stance of kicking me while I'm down.

"Don't you see, she married him. She just didn't *sleep* with him," she said, a wide smirk spreading across her face.

Our parents' eyebrows shot up. *"Oh!"*

Alex held up a finger and opened his mouth to say something, but then clamped it shut again. He began pacing back and forth across the floor deep in concentration before stopping and bolting out of the room and up the stairs.

I slumped into the nearest chair and hung my head back. Why wouldn't this nightmare of a weekend just end? Seriously, had I really ever done anything so bad as to deserve *this*?

A few minutes later Alex came bounding down the stairs again, a large old book in his hand. I didn't really have to look at it for more than a second to know it was *The Kalo Book of Law*. "The good news is we don't have to kill him," he announced loudly after entering the room.

I shot to my feet. *"Excuse me*?!"

"If you had told him our secrets without marrying him, the Grand Council would have had no choice but to order his execution. Since you *did* marry him, he is in no danger there. But…"

"What's the bad news?" I asked with a grimace.

"You have to turn him within the year, or they *will* have to execute him."

"Great, so I have to tell him his options are death,

delayed death, or possible death," I said sarcastically.

Alex's pleasant mood hardened. "You didn't tell him the consequences of becoming a daemon yet?"

"No. Hell, I'm not even sure I told him what we are in the first place, let alone that turning him might *kill* him."

Alex placed a gentle hand on my shoulder. "Nualla, there are only a few ways this can turn out. Either you turn him and he may possibly die, or you give him to the Council to be executed, or you annul the marriage through human means and spend the rest of your life alone until he dies." He took both my shoulders and looked at me sadly. "I wish there were more options honey, but there aren't. But whatever you choose we can have no say in it."

"Well I don't want him to be executed, so option two is out. And I cannot say with complete certainty that I didn't let any of our secrets slip, so option three is out. So I guess all that's left is option one," I said, sighing. "I'm just not looking forward to explaining everything to him."

Loraly, who had been watching us all with wide shocked eyes, finally moved closer and put an arm around me. "Nualla, honey, is he at least a nice boy?"

I thought back over the week; Patrick was more than nice really. I mean he hadn't put up any resistance to the crazy things we had dragged him off to— most would have at least put up a *slight* protest. A smile crossed my lips as I looked at her. "Yes, very."

"What is his name?" she asked, with a reassuring smile.

"Patrick."

"What's his *last* name?" Andraya asked, with a smirk.

I just stood there for a second racking my brain, I knew he had told me, now what was it?

"You married a boy and you don't even know his last name?!" Alex had his head in his hand again, but more out of loving frustration than anger.

"I do know it—I *swear*—I just can't remember it at the moment," I said quickly.

"It's Connolly, Patrick Connolly," Nikki said, coming to my rescue.

"Are you sure, Nikkalla?" Alex asked, turning to her.

"Yeah. He goes to our school—actually he's even in some of our classes. He's wicked smart. Well, at least *most* of the time anyway."

"Well that's a relief," Alex said with a slight smile.

SOLID REMINDER

Saturday, January 14th

NUALLA

THE PAST TWO DAYS HAD completely drained me, so much so that lying in the middle of my floor and staring at the blank ceiling seemed like a perfectly logical way to spend the rest of Saturday night. My life wasn't dull by any means, but it also wasn't normally *this* chaotic either.

My relationship with Patrick had gone from zero to sixty in no time flat, but it wasn't exactly *his* fault. *I* was the one who had dragged him to Vegas. *I* was the one who had gotten him wasted at the club. And *I* was the one who had brought up the stupid marriage thing. To be perfectly honest, I had been basically ruining this boy's life for the last forty-eight hours.

Gods, I was a terrible person. And soon I was going to have to tell him *everything*. The truth about what I really was. The fact that he might die. The fact that very shortly he would no longer even be human… if he was lucky.

Nikki came in and sat on the edge of my bed. She fidgeted for a while before finally asking, "Nualla, what are you going to do about Patrick?"

"The only thing I *can* do Nikki, stay married to him and tell him the damn truth. Oh, and hope he doesn't run screaming when I do."

"Are you going to call him tomorrow?"

"*How*, Nikki? It's not like I've got his phone number." *Geez that sounded bad.*

"Oh…right."

"I said I was going to meet him at school Monday," I said, still staring up at the ceiling.

"*Are* you?"

"Of *course* I am, and since everyone will be staring anyways I might as well make a show of it," I answered, smiling to myself.

"What exactly are you planning on doing?" Nikki asked suspiciously.

"Oh I don't know, walking up and kissing him in front of everyone sounds like it would be a *great* idea."

"You're going to give that boy a heart attack."

"Naw he's probably over the shock by now. But his friends, on the other hand…" I said as I turned to grin mischievously at her.

"Oh, you're *evil*."

"Whatever do you mean?" I said, feigning innocence. The response I got back was a pillow in the face.

PATRICK

T HOUGH NUALLA HAD TOLD ME to go home, I didn't—well not right away at least. Why? Because I knew what I would find there. *Nothing.* No welcoming hugs or even a stern faced, "Where the hell have you been all weekend?" My parents were always away on business.

Always.

Last summer I had tried to see how many days I could go without coming home just to see how long it would take before someone noticed. After two weeks I finally gave up. So mostly it was like living alone. Most teenagers would have loved it. I, on the other hand, hated it. I had thought about getting a pet for company, but my mother was allergic. Not that she was ever home enough for it to matter, of course.

I passed on the taxi and rode BART back into the city. I really needed the time to clear my head before I returned to the real world. So I wandered the streets until I finally decided to get myself some dinner and trudged home.

I opened the door to silence. I had a few missed calls from Connor, but I didn't feel like talking to him. He could just watch Saturday night anime by himself. There were no missed calls from my parents, but there was no big surprise there.

I ate my dinner half-heartedly at the table before trudging up the stairs to my room. Kicking off my scuffed black All Stars I flopped on my bed and rolled over onto my back. With a sigh I opened my phone's picture album and looked at the pictures again. Just to torture myself, really. These pictures were the only thing that proved that this weekend had not been a figment of my imagination. Well that, and the ring on my finger.

Looking at the ring, I decided I probably couldn't wear it to school, but I also didn't want to *not* wear it. After a lot of wrestling with myself, I opted to wear it under my shirt on a chain. It was probably silly, but I liked the idea of having a solid reminder that what I had gone through in the last week had been real.

I flopped back on the bed and flipped through the weekend's pictures until I passed out. And dreamed of nothing.

REALITY CHECK

Monday, January 16th

PATRICK

B Y MONDAY MORNING I HAD convinced myself it
had all been a dream. Even the ring under my
shirt was not enough to convince me anymore. I had
spent most of Sunday sitting at the computer waiting for Nualla to do something, *anything.* Change her
profile status, add a few innocent pictures of us, hell,
even just send me a little message.

I was pacing in front of the steps of the parking lot
entrance to the school by the time Connor showed up.

"Hey man, how was your weekend?" he asked,
punching me good-naturedly in the shoulder.

What I wanted to say was, "Great! Went to Vegas, married the girl of my dreams, can't really complain." What I actually said was, "Did something really stupid that I will hopefully never live to regret."

"*Really*? What?" Connor asked, unable to conceal his interest.

The girls showed up before I could think up a reply. "Tell you later," I said out of the corner of my mouth.

"Hey Connor, *Patrick*." Jenny's tone sounded slightly irritated when she said my name. I couldn't think of why though. "How was your weekend?"

"Mine was boring as hell, but Patrick's was apparently interesting," Connor answered as he smiled conspiratorially at me. I silently vowed to beat the crap out of him later for saying anything.

"Really? What did you do, Patrick?" Sara asked as she slid her thumbs down the straps of her backpack.

I just stared at them blankly as I racked my brain for something I could say that wouldn't get me in trouble. I was so busy trying to think of what to say in fact, that I didn't notice Nualla's approach until she was only a few feet away. "Hi Nualla, how was your—" was all that I was able to say before she slid her hand around my neck and pulled my lips to hers.

Her kiss made our previous one look like a peck on the cheek and hinted at things I couldn't quite remember from Friday night. It was definitely not the type of kiss one did in front of a crap ton of people at school that's for sure.

Eventually, Nualla pulled away slightly and smiled up at me. "Did you miss me?" I just stared at her dumbly, trying to regain my composure—or *any* brain function really. She reached up and brushed a piece of hair away from my eyes. "Care to walk with me to my locker?"

"Sure…" I answered unsteadily.

With a smile, Nualla slid her arm through mine and started walking toward the building. I didn't even resist; just let her pull me gently forward. I turned back around to see my stunned friends gaping at me, along with half the school. Today was becoming a very interesting day, and I hadn't even made it into the building yet.

By the time we got to her locker, I had mostly gotten over the shock of her sudden display of affection in front of the school. Hell, who was I kidding—I was *still* completely stunned.

Nualla opened her locker, and I leaned against the one next to it. She placed her coat inside as she looked at my hand. "Where's your ring?"

"Here," I answered, placing my hand over my royal-blue tie that poked out just above my black sweater vest and hid the lump of the ring completely.

She smiled up at me conspiratorially. "Mine too."

I looked down and saw that she now had two chains around her neck; one holding the pendant she always wore and the other disappearing under the edge of her uniform.

I had no idea what to say after that. I had been going over what I would say to her in my head, but what she had done back there in front of everyone had blown it all out of the water. So I just stood there silently watching her, trying to look as if I belonged there beside her, but probably failing miserably at it.

Nualla looked up at me with a suspicious smile. "What?"

"I'm just not sure what to say or where we stand. I see that you want to keep, well what happened this past weekend secret. I'm just wondering what I should say when people ask, because they *are* going to ask," I said as I ran my hand nervously through my hair.

"You should tell them we're dating," Nualla said as if it had been the logical answer all along. I had waited years to hear those words, had imagined what they would sound like, but to actually *hear* them coming out of her mouth was another thing entirely.

I swallowed hard; best not to look too excited in front of her, she might change her mind and decide I was crazy. So instead I asked, "So who asked whom?"

"I believe it was you who asked me," she answered with a playful crooked smile.

"That's right, because you said you would only

tell me your secrets if I married you."

"You remembered that?" she asked sheepishly. "Look, Patrick, I—"

"You know, you really don't have to tell me if you don't want to," I said, avoiding her gaze.

"I'll tell you, just not *here*, okay?" she said, looking around the halls.

"Oh, right," I said, looking around the halls as well. Everyone who passed us was doing a double take or just outright staring. "Because we're in the middle of a hall."

"*Exactly*."

"But you *will* tell me, right?" I asked, meeting her eyes again.

"A promise is a promise," she answered with a slight grimace.

"What the hell was *that* about?" Connor asked as he dropped into the desk next to mine in first period Trig.

"What?" I said, playing dumb. I knew exactly what he was asking about, but it was worth a try.

"You know what I'm talking about; that stuff that went down in front of the school like fifteen minutes ago," Connor said, leaning in and looking at me expectantly. I was acutely aware that everyone *else* near us had also leaned in to hear my answer as well.

"Oh, *that*. I'm going out with Nualla now," I answered, trying to look nonchalant, as if this was common knowledge and not that big a deal, but I think I was failing at it.

"Since *when*?!" Connor practically shouted.

I looked up to see Nikki walk into the room chatting with another girl, I think named Natalie. When Nikki saw me she smiled and waved before going back to her conversation. "Since Saturday," I answered, looking back at Connor.

Connor just continued to look at me one eyebrow raised. "So what she just called you up on Saturday and asked you go out with her?"

"It was more like Friday actually, I ran into her at the mall, and she asked me to come hang out with them." I was skirting the truth as much as I could without flat-out lying.

"So she asked you out then?"

"No actually I think I asked her—" *to marry me that is. Oh, and by the way, she totally said yes.*

"Who are you, and what have you done with my best friend?" Connor asked, looking at me suspiciously. I couldn't really blame him; this was totally out of character for me.

"Connor really, it's me it's just—" *A new better me. One that good things actually happen to.* How the hell was I supposed to end that sentence?

Fortunately I didn't have to, because Mr. Savenrue

came through the classroom door. "Okay class, settle down," he said right on cue.

Everyone took their seats, and he asked us to send him our homework. Connor continued to eye me suspiciously for a few more minutes before giving up and staring blankly at the smart board.

The next two periods went by in a similar fashion, people stared and whispered, and I tried like hell to pretend I didn't notice. It was like I had grown horns or a third eye or something. I mean *sure*, Nualla was the most gorgeous girl in school, but really it wasn't as if I was a total loser.

Never mind, scratch that, they totally had a right to stare. If I couldn't even justify this to myself, how was I going to justify it to others without making both of us seem outright nuts.

When I entered the atrium I knew this was probably going to be the longest lunch hour of my life. There was the briefest of silences the second I stepped out of the hall before everyone broke into hushed chatter. Pretending I didn't notice they were talking about me was getting harder and harder to accomplish. Maybe my friends wouldn't *also* make me feel like some awful social experiment.

"Hey guys," I said with an uneasy smile.

Jenny stood abruptly, gripping her tray so hard I thought she might crack it. "So I guess you'll want to go sit with *them* from now on, huh?" she said with a huff as she stomped away.

I looked at Connor as I set down my tray. "What was *that* all about?" He just shrugged and went back to eating his lunch.

"She wanted you to ask her to the dance. *And* she's had a crush on you since freshman year," Beatrice said without looking up. How she could follow our conversation and read a book at the same time was beyond me.

Then I processed what she had said. "You've known this the whole time, and you never bothered to *tell* me!" I just couldn't believe it.

Beatrice put down her book and turned, brown eyes flashing with irritation beneath her glasses. "Patrick, it is not my job to—" She stopped talking; something over my shoulder had caught her attention. "*Hello* cute boy!"

"Down tiger," Connor said under his breath.

I turned around to find Nualla, Nikki, and Shawn standing behind me.

"Um, *thanks*," Shawn said with a quirky smile at Beatrice, which turned into a grimace a moment later. My guess, Nikki stepped on his foot.

Nualla looked at her friends then turned back to

smile broadly at us. "Do you guys mind if we sit with you?"

"Not at all," Connor volunteered enthusiastically.

Nualla slid down onto the bench beside me, and my heart started to pick up pace. She had already made a show of us being a couple, but I somehow hadn't expected her to ever sit with us at lunch. Neither apparently, had any of the *other* students, who were now openly staring at us.

Connor reached his hand across the table to Nualla. "Hi I'm Connor, Patrick's best friend, and this is Sara," he said as he smiled at her. "And Beatrice," he continued, gesturing with his head to Beatrice who had put her book down for once.

Nualla shook his hand and smiled. "This is Nikki, my cousin, and Shawn. I'm Nualla."

"So...are you *really* Patrick's girlfriend, or has he been playing fast and loose with the truth?" Connor asked Nualla while he smirked at me.

I have the best friends, don't I?

Nualla smiled and leaned even closer to me. "Yep it's completely true."

"How about *you* cutie, seeing anyone?" Beatrice asked Shawn as she leaned across the table.

"Um," Shawn answered, looking at Nikki uncertainly.

Nikki shot Beatrice a scowl and the phrase, "if looks could kill," came to mind.

Shawn was saved from answering because Jenny came stomping back to the table. Only Nualla and I had noticed her approach since Connor had his back to her, and Nikki was still staring daggers at Beatrice, who was still ogling Shawn.

"I forgot my bag, but since *you're* here I have something to say." Jenny glared at Nualla and continued. "If I find out *this* is just some sick joke and you're just going to dump him in a week after you've had your 'fun,' I'll kick your ass," Jenny threatened. "He doesn't belong with someone like *you*."

We all just sat there for a moment, mouths open. None of us could believe that those words had *actually* come out of Jenny's mouth.

"What do you mean 'someone like me'?" Nualla asked with narrowed eyes.

Jenny folded her arms across her chest; though she was tall, her red pigtails and the spray of freckles across her cheeks made her look far from intimidating. "Yeah, popular girls like *you*. You use boys and then dump them after the thrill is over."

At this Nualla stood and folded her arms as well. "I don't know what your problem is—whatever your name is."

"It's Jenny, Jennifer Bowen. *I* have been Patrick's friend for over three years, and if you knew even a lick about him you'd know that."

"So you're accusing me of this because I don't

know your name and because you think I'm *popular*?"

"No, it's because every boyfriend you've ever had you've only dated for a week!"

"Nualla's only had one boyfriend," Nikki said, looking even more confused than the rest of us.

Jenny turned on Nikki. "*Bull*! She's had a date to every school dance for the last three years."

"Yeah, but I've never *dated* any of them," Nualla spat back.

"It's not a crime to ask someone to a dance, you know," Shawn said in Nualla's defense.

"Have you even *asked* any of them if they thought we were dating in the first place?" Nualla asked angrily, gesturing toward the students in the atrium.

"I don't *need* to, you asked Patrick to the dance and now you're dating him. That's enough proof right there."

That didn't even make logical sense. Jenny normally made perfect sense. She had either completely convinced herself that what she was saying was right, or she lost control of all rational thought when she was angry. Or both.

"I didn't *ask* Patrick, he asked *me*," Nualla said, glaring at Jenny.

Jenny's argument folded in on itself, and she turned to me. "You asked *her* out?" she blurted out incredulously.

"Well yeah." As surprising as it was, it was actually the truth.

"Even though she's been *ignoring* you for the last three years?" Jenny asked as she angrily gestured toward Nualla again.

Oh balls, why did I ever tell them that?

"I never *ignored* him. I never asked him because I thought he was dating you!" Nualla yelled back at Jenny. I wasn't entirely sure if that was the truth, but it did make a lot of sense when you thought about it.

"*Ooooo,*" came a chorus of students around us. It was at that moment we all realized everyone in the atrium was avidly watching us.

Jenny turned bright red and started fiddling with her hair nervously. "We were never dating."

"Could have fooled me," Nikki snorted, rolling her eyes.

Jenny's eyes welled up with tears, and she bolted from the atrium. Then it hit me, all the signs from Jenny that I had been missing over the years. Had she really been waiting for me to ask her out the whole time? Had she just sat there biting her tongue while I was pining over Nualla?

Crap.

I stood up. "Um, guys—I'll be right back," I said quickly before I ran out of the atrium into the front hall and stopped. I looked to the left and a girl sitting among a group of freshman girls pointed to the stairs.

"She went that way," the girl announced continuing to point toward the front right stairs.

"How did you—?"

"We saw the whole thing through the glass," she answered as she pointed out the window into the atrium.

"Ah, right," I said before I charged forward, following her directions.

I found Jenny sitting on the floor second floor hallway, knees pulled to her chest, crying. "Jenny?" I said cautiously.

"Go away," she said in a strangled voice.

I sighed and slid down the wall to sit next to her. "Jenny, I'm sorry I never realized you liked me."

"Yeah well, you have the observational skills of a grapefruit, so I'm not surprised," Jenny said into the sleeves of her black V-necked sweater that made up the top of the girls' winter uniform.

I would have laughed if she hadn't been crying. "Well that aside, I'm still sorry."

"For *what*?" She lifted her head and sniffled, mascara already leaving black trails down her cheeks.

"That I couldn't return your feelings and that I probably never will. I've found the person I want to be with. Can you understand that?" I hoped that she would get the hint because I really couldn't explain that the reason I could never be with her was because

I was already married to Nualla.

She looked away down the hall. "So she really likes you?"

"I sure hope so." If she didn't, we were both screwed.

"Well if it turns out she doesn't…" Jenny said without looking back at me.

"You'll be the first to know."

We sat in silence for a while before Jenny sniffled and stood. "I probably look awful. I'll see you later, okay?" And then she walked down the hall toward the girl's restroom without waiting for my reply.

"Okay," I said quietly as I watched her go. I felt terrible about the whole thing, but what could I do? I had absolutely no feelings for Jenny other than friendship.

With a sigh, I stood up and walked back to the atrium. It wouldn't be very nice to abandon Nualla with my friends the first time she came to sit with us. I hoped that she wasn't one of the jealous types that would see my running off after Jenny as something other than just comforting a friend.

As I walked back toward our table I tried to ignore the looks I was getting. Everyone aside from my friends was watching me as I moved through the forest of students and lunch tables. I swallowed hard as I slipped back into my seat next to Nualla. Everyone at our table was eating their lunches and not talking. And I had the distinct impression that nothing had been said since I left either.

"Hey guys," I said cautiously.

"How's Jenny?" Sara asked, looking worried.

"I think she'll be fine," I answered with a heavy sigh.

"So…Nualla, Nikki said you'd only had one boyfriend, and it wasn't any of the guys you went to the dances with." I could tell by the way Connor said it he had been dying to ask her since I left. I myself had been wondering the same thing, but would never ask her.

"Yeah," Nualla replied, putting down her fork.

"So who was it?" Connor asked, leaning a little closer.

My head shot up. "*Connor*!" I snapped, glaring at him. Connor apparently had *also* known I would never ask her.

"No it's okay, you'd probably just find out eventually anyways," Nualla said with a sigh. "It was Michael," she admitted in a voice that said she was completely disgusted with herself.

That had been the *last* name I had ever thought she would say. "*What*?"

"That prick who was harassing you?" Connor asked, sharing my total disbelief.

"The very same," Nikki answered in an uninterested manner that told me it was old news.

"*When*?" After what I had seen last week, I couldn't believe this could possibly be true.

"I made the huge mistake of dating him the beginning of freshman year," Nualla admitted, her fork hovering over her lunch like she very much wanted to stab it.

"Then she found out how much of a jerk he was," Nikki added, poking her cousin.

I rolled my soda can back and forth in my hands. "Well I guess I can see why he's so angry." I looked up into Nualla's eyes. "I'd be pretty upset to lose you too."

WHAT HAVE YOU DONE?

Monday, January 16th

NUALLA

I COULD SEE PATRICK OUT BY the parking lot waiting for me as I stepped out of the school building. Even though I had tried to reassure him of my affections in every way, he was still nervously pacing back and forth. Poor thing. I could tell, even if everyone else couldn't, that he was only barely able to handle all that the last week had thrown at him. That *I* had thrown him into.

I walked down the steps and started making my way toward Patrick. I was about halfway there when I felt a concussion to the air as someone grabbed my arm and jerked me backward. I didn't even have to look to know it was Michael.

"You're *dating* him now?" he spat venomously.

I ripped my arm from his grasp as I turned around to yell at him. But my voice caught in my throat as the ring slipped out, my rash movements flinging it from its hiding place.

Michael stared at it then recoiled in horror as if the sight of it hurt him. His eyes flicked toward Patrick. "You got...but he's not." His mouth snapped shut in a scowl then opened in a sneer, his lip curling back over his teeth. "Nualla, what have you done?"

"It's none of *your* business, Michael," I answered, a threat creeping into the tone of my voice.

He took a step forward and shoved a finger hard in my chest. "It's *everyone's* business, you broke the law. He's not one of us."

"I broke nothing. The law states I'm allowed to tell him what we are after we are married. It doesn't say anything about him having to be turned first."

Michael's eyes went huge. "You *married* him?"

I swallowed hard. *Frak.* In Kalodaemon custom, the ring around my neck only meant that we were engaged, and I could have gone on for quite a while pretending we weren't already married. However, I had let Michael get to me—*again*—and had now blown that option to shiny bits.

"And so what if I am?" I snapped defiantly back

at him.

"You're playing a very dangerous game Nualla, as he is he's a threat to all of us."

"He's a *threat* to no one," I said defensively.

A smirk crossed Michael's face, "Maybe you're right." He looked off in Patrick's direction a glint of malice in his eyes.

I let the threat curl around my words to make my point perfectly—*deadly* clear. "Michael, if you hurt him, I will kill you. Make no mistake in that."

"I'm not stupid enough to touch him *now,*" Michael said, folding his arms. "Why don't you just turn him, Nualla? What's the point in not doing it if he already knows?" My face must have given me away because Michael looked at me in shocked disgust. "You haven't told him what you are yet, have you?"

"No, not yet." I looked down, so Michael wouldn't see how nervous I was about telling Patrick my secrets.

"What are you waiting for?"

"I'm going to let him choose," I answered, still talking to my boots.

"*Excuse me*?" Michael asked in a choked voice.

"You heard me," I said, looking up at him defiantly.

Michael leaned closer. "You can't *do* that, Nualla."

"Get away from my girlfriend!" Patrick shouted from behind us. Apparently, I had shocked Michael so much his influence field had dropped without either of us noticing it.

Michael grabbed the ring around my neck and nearly ripped the delicate chain clear off. "Don't you mean your—*wife*?" Michael asked through gritted teeth. He let the ring drop as if it disgusted him.

He took a step to the side and began to move away as Patrick stepped in front of me. It was like watching two circling jungle cats hiss at each other. Michael looked Patrick dead in the eye and let his illusion slip just the slightest, so the true ferocity in his eyes would show through. Most humans would have pissed their pants, but Patrick didn't even flinch.

Michael looked around Patrick into my eyes his illusion already back in place. "You're playing a dangerous game, Nualla—a *very* dangerous game."

And with that last bit of warning he whipped around and strode off to join his group of friends. One of them—Penelope—eyed us with dark, hateful eyes. She had hated me as long as I could remember and my dating then snubbing of Michael, the one thing she coveted above all else, had only made that hatred worse. And Michael ignoring her as he pursued me in vain probably hadn't helped either.

After nearly four years of trying to get me back, Michael now had no choice but to give up on me and walk away. But the question was would he now pay attention to Penelope, or would he continue to ignore her affections?

Our conversation may have ended, but I had the feeling this was far from over.

PATRICK

NUALLA TOOK A DEEP BREATH and tucked the ring back under her black V-necked sweater. I scowled at Michael's back as he stalked off with his pack of arrogant jerks. Where did he get off acting like that?

I turned back to Nualla; she was nervously playing with her pendant. "So he knows then?"

"Unfortunately," she answered with a grimace.

"Won't he say something about it to everyone?"

"Not likely, he also has a lot to lose if people found out—*and* I'd kill him."

"Seriously? Like what has he got to lose?" I asked, gesturing toward the now nearly out of sight Michael.

Nualla sighed. "Pride. Pride is Michael's fatal flaw." Then she looked at me curiously. "If you were him, would you really go around telling everyone you had lost?"

"No...you're right, I wouldn't," I admitted as I looked back out at the parking lot.

"Look, Patrick, don't worry about Michael," she said, touching my arm. "I have to go; I'll see you tomorrow before school, 'kay?" She walked off in the direction of her car where Nikki was leaning up against the driver side, staring at the clouds.

"Okay," I said to no one but myself.

I just stood there watching her go; which in the short time I had been with her seemed to happen a lot.

"What's got him so pissed off today?" Connor asked, filling the space beside me that Nualla had left.

I was in an off mood and not really paying attention. Today had been an exhausting emotional roller coaster. "Oh I don't know, gee, maybe he's pissed that I married *his* girl." My breath caught when I realized what I had just said—out loud.

Crap.

I slowly turned to face Connor who was staring at me, mouth hanging open. "Did you just say you were—?"

I threw up my hands. "Wait, don't say it!" I looked to both sides; there were *way* too many people still milling about to be having this conversation here. Plus if anyone found out, Nualla might kill me. Or her parents might. Hell, even *my* parents might.

"Walk with me," I said as I took off toward the street. I walked quickly down the sidewalk weaving past the other pedestrians; not stopping.

After we were a good city block from the school

Connor finally called out from behind me, "Is it safe to talk *now*?"

Subtle Connor, real *subtle*.

I stopped and stepped close to a building, so I wouldn't get knocked over by a distracted pedestrian on their cell. Looking around I saw none of our class-mates; it was probably safe. *Probably*. Connor looked ready to burst with pent up questions. "Yeah, we can talk now," I said reluctantly.

"You're *married*?! Since *when*?"

"Um, since last Friday. Actually, it was more like Saturday morning," I answered as shoved my hands in the pockets of my *Bleach* hoodie and avoided his eyes.

"When were you going to tell me?"

"Never," I replied looking up, slightly chagrined.

"Dude, that's cold, I'm your best friend," Connor said, folding his arms.

"Yeah well, it was on a need-to-know basis," I said, looking nervously down the street; we were inching closer and closer to the truth.

"Hey, why wasn't I invited?"

"Um, gee, well because it was kinda spur of the moment. And I was in Las Vegas, and might I add completely *drunk* at the time." Once I had said it, I instantly wished I hadn't.

The thoughts playing across Connor's face came to a screeching halt. "Wait, when were *you* in Vegas?"

"Last weekend." I had given up trying to skirt the truth; the worst damage had already been done.

"Patrick, I'm lost here, care to fill me in?"

"Okay, I told you I ran into Nualla at the mall, and she asked me to come hang out with her and her friends right? Well apparently *their* idea of hanging out is catching a plane to Vegas."

"*Seriously*?" Connor asked in disbelief.

"Seriously. So while there, we got really drunk, and I woke up Saturday morning in a hotel room— married. That about sums it up."

Connor was silent for a moment before he spoke. "Wow you must've been really, *really* drunk."

"Oh, my head would have agreed with you on that one," I said with a slight smirk.

"So what are you going to do about this?"

"Nothing," I said firmly.

"*Nothing*?"

"What is there to do? I'm married to Nualla— *Nualla*, Connor. This is in no way a problem until she tells me it is."

Connor looked at me for a second before a smirk started to spread across his face. "Your life has gotten so weird."

"Tell me about it."

15

Please Tell Me You're Joking

Wednesday, January 18th

NUALLA

I HAD BEEN AVOIDING THIS TOO long already. I should have gone in on Monday; Tuesday was pushing it, but if I didn't go today I would be screwed. Tylia had intercepted the message, but that didn't mean it was a closed matter.

I took a deep breath and walked up the steps leading to the main West Coast branch of Kalodaemon Embassy. The main entrance was swarming with people, their steps echoing on the marble floor. I passed by them quickly and rode the elevator to the third floor running through the past week in my head.

I was so lost in thought I didn't even notice he was there until he bumped gently into me. "And what brings *you* here today?"

I turned to see the smiling face of The Embassy's resident tech genius looking down at me. "Travis!"

"You seem surprised to see me," he said with a crooked smile.

"I am." I was, to be perfectly honest. He was about the *last* person I had thought I would run into today.

Travis had been one of my best friends for a long time now. He was about three years older than me, and I had always thought he was pretty damn cute. Like Shawn, he was much taller than me now, but he hadn't always been that way. When we were younger he had actually gotten picked on a lot for being shorter than the other kids his age. But when he hit puberty and shot up a good foot and a half everyone has stopped wondering which of his parents he would take after. Now it seemed the only thing he had inherited from his Japanese mother were her eyes; almond shaped and a surprisingly brilliant shade of black-blue.

"So I ask you again, what are you up to today? Your dad's office is way on the other end of the building so you can't be going there."

"You're right, I'm actually heading to the Department of Records."

"Really?" he said, his smile broadening. "Me too."

"What for?" I asked, immediately suspicious.

"To register some new tech," he answered as he held up the device he was carrying.

"Cool, what does it do?" I asked quickly. If I could get him talking about it, he might forget to ask specifics about why *I* was there. Explaining my current fuck up was really low on my list of things I *ever* wanted to have a conversation with Travis about.

"It's a device that—hey wait, you're trying to distract me, aren't you?"

Busted.

"No I'm not!" I said, feigning disgust at his accusation.

"You can't lie to me Nualla, I've known you far too long."

"How did you know?" I asked as I crossed my arms and looked down in defeat.

"You have a tell."

My head shot back up. "*Really*, what is it? Tell me."

"No way! If I told you, then you would change it. Now you're caught, so tell me why you're here. It must be juicy, or you wouldn't have lied. So spit it out," Travis said, smirking.

"I need to register something," I said as I looked away embarrassed.

"Well *duh*, but doesn't your dad's office normally do that stuff for you?"

"They can't do this; I have to do it on my own."

I could see him sorting through possible reasons in his head. I could tell, he always looked up and got this far off look in his eyes when he was thinking. But from his expression he was coming up short. The answers were obvious, but apparently too farfetched for what he thought me capable of.

"Okay, now you *really* have to tell me."

"No," I said defiantly, folding my arms.

"That's not fair, come on!"

"*Fine*, a marriage license. *That's* what I have to register, okay!"

Travis smiled; it was more than clear he didn't believe me even though I was being completely honest. "Ha ha, very funny. Now tell me why you're *really* here." As he continued to look at me, all humor left his face. "Please tell me you're joking," he said in a startled voice.

"No, I'm not," I replied, folding my arms again and leaned against the nearby wall.

Travis stood there in front of me, unmoving. I don't think I had ever seen him look that shocked. "*Seriously*?"

"Yes Travis, *seriously*," I answered, glaring at him.

"*When*? To *whom*? And why didn't you say anything about it the last time I saw you?"

I sighed and pushed away from the wall. "Travis, I was hoping to never have this conversation, but I *especially* didn't want to have it in the hall for crying out loud!"

"My lab then," he said, gesturing with his thumb.

"I'm not going to get out of having this conversation with you, am I?"

"Not a chance in hell."

"*Fine,*" I relented with a sigh. This was going to suck, I could tell already.

He turned shakily on his heel and walked back toward his lab. If I didn't know better, I might have thought he was mad.

I walked down the hall after him in silence, trying to look like nothing was out of the ordinary. Aside from people stopping to bow to me, no one seemed to notice that anything was wrong. Travis never once looked back the whole time and if he hadn't been practically my best friend, I might have turned around and bolted for the exit.

Travis pressed his hand against the panel next to his lab which flashed green before unlocking and opening the door. His lab was full of gadgets, wires, and futuristic tech that would have made any tech geek think they had died and gone to heaven.

Since the death of his parents and little brother when he was six, he had been a ward of The Embassy and thus had lived in the orphanage a few floors up. He had always shown a talent for making things, but it wasn't until his senior year of high school that my dad had realized Travis was *actually* a genius. After that, Alex had given Travis this lab which pretty much gave him the means to create all the crazy things he could possibly dream up.

Travis placed the device he had been holding, safely on the table, and then turned to face me. After a few seconds of silence, he leaned back against one of the tables. "So…"

There was no way out of this, so I went for the quick blunt answer. "I went to Vegas with Nikki, Shawn, and a guy from school, got really drunk, and I got married. That's pretty much it," I stated with a shrug.

Travis choked and looked at me. "You married *Shawn*!"

Of course he would jump to that conclusion. He wasn't going to make this easy I just knew it. "No I did not marry Shawn; Nikki would have *killed* me." I looked at my boots and mumbled the next part. "No, I married someone else."

"The *other* guy?"

"Yep," I replied, examining the lack of dust on the floor.

"What's his name?"

"Patrick Connolly."

"Doesn't ring a bell, is he a transfer student from somewhere else in the region?"

"Nope," I answered, still not meeting his eyes.

"Then…I'm confused."

"He's *human*, alright?!" I said, finally looking up at him.

A flood of different emotions cross Travis' face as he tried to wrap his head around this one. "Woah, *seriously*?" Travis said, raising his eyebrows.

"Do I *look* like I'm kidding, Travis?"

If I thought he looked shocked before I was mistaken, because nothing topped his current expression. "Wow, just wow. I know your aunt married a human—but I never pegged you for one too."

"And before you *even* ask, he's still human."

"Wait, *what*? How can he still—?"

"I am *so* not answering that, so don't even bother asking. And now if you don't mind I have to go fill out a lot of paperwork." I uncrossed my arms and pushed away from the table.

"Wait, Nualla," Travis pleaded, grabbing my arm.

I turned around to face him. "What?"

He looked at me uneasily for a second before asking, "Do you regret it?"

I was not expecting that question, so I had to think a bit before I answered. "Even if I did, there's no going back now. Rules are rules."

"You didn't answer my question," he said in a

small voice, not meeting my eyes.

"I don't know the answer; I guess I'll find out, won't I?"

"Yeah," he agreed quietly. We stood there in silence for a few minutes before he spoke again. "I've never met this guy, and I see you nearly every Friday. So tell me, just how long, exactly, have you been dating him?"

I cringed; this was the most incriminating part of my weekend's lack of judgment. "A week and a half," I admitted with a grimace. It was technically a lie, but it sounded far better than the actual truth. I mentally braced myself for what I knew was coming as I bolted for the door.

"Are you *crazy*?!" Travis shouted from behind me.

"Apparently so," I called over my shoulder as I continued my escape.

Within seconds Travis was at my side. I should have known I couldn't get away from him that easily. We walked silently down the halls for a long time.

When we had reached the Department of Records he finally asked in a quiet voice, "What did your dad say?"

"He wasn't happy, but he said it was my decision to make."

Travis reached up and brushed a strand of my hair out of my eyes. "You know you really shouldn't make huge decisions while you're drunk, you're terrible at it."

"Tell me something I don't know."

The line for the Department of Records stretched out into the hall, but luckily I didn't have to wait in it. One of the privileges of being me, you could say. On the other hand, one of the downsides of being me was that most people knew who I was so they tended to stare—a lot.

One of the Protectorate officers nearly choked when he saw me and said rather a little too loudly as his right fist came across his body to his heart, "Arius Nualla!"

Everyone who hadn't *already* noticed my entering the room sure as hell was staring at me now. Great, because what I *really* wanted more than anything at this moment was for everyone and their brother to gawk at me as I filed my fuck up.

The officer took a few steps toward me and said in a thankfully normal tone, "Arius, what can I do for you?" I was pretty sure seeing me was about the *last* thing he had thought would happen on his shift today.

"Just need to file something," I answered, holding up a folder. "Is Mrs. Murray here today?"

"Yes, she's in her office, right this way." I really

didn't need his help finding it, but he looked so startled I just let him lead me there anyway. He opened the door to Mrs. Murray's office for me and poked his head in. "Arius Nualla to see you, ma'am."

"Oh?" came Mrs. Murray's voice from inside the private office. The officer stepped aside to let me pass, then shut the door behind me. Mrs. Murray looked a little flustered to see me, but she hid it far better than the officer had. "Arius Nualla, what brings you here today?" she asked with a broad smile.

"I need to register something," I answered in as steady a voice as I could manage.

"Of course, what did you need to register?"

"This," I answered as I slid the folder containing the marriage license toward her.

She opened it and stared at it for a while before her eyes darted up to mine. "Does the Chancellarius know about this?"

"Yes," I answered truthfully.

"Well then, all we need to do is fill out these forms here." She began typing on the keyboard in front of her while looking at the marriage license.

I swallowed hard. "I also need a human pass."

"Excuse me?" she said, looking up.

"My new husband is human."

"Well then, he would need a Neodaemon Acknowledgement Certificate, not a Blue Card."

A Blue Card was normally a pass issued to children of Kalodaemons that were born Marked Ones instead of True Born daemons. It secured their safe passage in our world until their bodies signaled that it was time for the Change.

I took a deep breath and let it out slowly. "No I mean he's *still* human."

Mrs. Murray's eyebrows shot up. "*Oh.*"

"I know it's really confusing," I said, a blush starting to creep into my cheeks.

"That *is* quite a situation. I'll have to consult *The Kalo Book of Law* for this one."

She reached over to a shelf behind her and dropped the heavy tome on the desk. I sat there watching as she flipped through the pages. *The Kalo Book of Law* was one of the only things, it seemed, that hadn't made the transition into digital yet.

"Did you inform him of the existence of our world before or after you married him?" she asked, finally looking up.

"I'm pretty sure I still haven't told him," I admitted and she stopped mid page flip and raised one eyebrow at me. "It's a *really* long story, so we'll just go with *after* okay?"

"Very well." I could tell by her expression that she was dying to ask me about it, but protocol prohibited her from doing so. She flipped through pages for a few more moments in silence before looking up at me. "Did the Chancellarius make it clear that your husband must become a daemon within one year's time or face execution?"

"Painfully clear," I said with a grimace. Mrs. Murray nodded as she closed the book and went back to typing. As time passed, I sank lower and lower in my chair. I could not wait for this to be over.

Finally, Mrs. Murray stopped typing and reached over to pull a small blue electronic card from the inscriber. To a human they looked just like a piece of translucent blue plastic or glass because they couldn't see the information printed on them. "Here is the Blue Card for your husband. When he does become a daemon you must relinquish this pass."

"Understood," I said as I took the pass from her and stood.

"Wait, Arius Nualla, we are not finished."

I just looked at her. What else could I *possibly* have to do; this day had been embarrassing enough as it was.

"You must come back on Sunday and speak before the Grand Council."

Apparently, there *was* something that could make it worse. "*What*? But the laws didn't say anything about that!"

"Yes, well, those are general laws. They do not take into account that you, as a Galathea, are one of the acknowledged heirs to the *chancellariuship*. Whom you marry *is* their concern. Those who came before you had to do the very same thing regardless of whom they married." And by *whom* she meant *what* I married. They would never say it out loud, but the fact that Patrick was a human probably mattered far more to them than what type of person he was. As accepting as our world was, it was not devoid of prejudice.

The Secrets behind Your Eyes

Friday, January 20th

PATRICK

D ATING NUALLA WAS GREAT; I mean what guy *wouldn't* want a completely gorgeous girl on his arm. I just should have left well enough alone—*should* have, but didn't.

Nualla was hiding a lot of secrets behind her eyes; it was plain to me now. She had said she would tell me, but she hadn't said *when*. So like an idiot, instead of waiting for her to tell me, I had decided to seek out the truth myself. Now I wished I hadn't. The things I had found were unbelievable at best; downright insane at worst. I kept telling myself that it couldn't *possibly* be true; that there had to be a perfectly rational explanation I was overlooking. But I couldn't believe it because something in the back of my mind told me I had found the truth.

I raced through all that I had uncovered while I stood on the street waiting for Nualla to pick me up.

"Hello Patrick," Mrs. Thompson said in a friendly voice.

I looked up at her startled. I had been so lost in my thoughts that I hadn't seen her coming up the block. She was returning from her daily evening walk with her dachshund, Arthur.

"Hi Mrs. Thompson," I said as I stooped down to pet Arthur.

Mrs. Thompson was awesome, like how I imagined a grandmother would be if mine had still been alive. She always asked about my day and dropped off delicious baked treats. Truthfully, I probably had more conversations with her than my own parents.

"What are you up to this evening?" she asked kindly.

"I'm not sure yet exactly," I replied, looking up with a smile. "My girlfriend is coming to pick me up and—"

Our conversation was abruptly cut short when Nualla pulled up in her electric blue Vanquish and opened the passenger door with a smile. I stood up and looked at Mrs. Thompson who was eyeing me with raised eyebrows. "My girlfriend," I said nervously as I gestured toward Nualla's car.

I got into the car unsteadily, and Nualla gave me a questioning look but didn't say anything.

"So where are we going?" I asked as we pulled away from the curb.

"A club," she answered with a slightly mischievous smile.

"You go to those a lot don't you?" I asked as I looked over at her. The dress she was wearing was black, flowy, and *extremely* short. Her legs were bare except for the black boots that were even taller than the ones she normally wore to school. How she could even drive with boots like that in the first place was beyond me.

"Every Friday," she answered with a smile as she turned her music up.

I had no idea how to bring up what I was dying to ask her, so I just sat there in silence as we drove through the city.

NUALLA

I T WAS JUST BARELY EIGHT when we arrived at Club Lunaris, but already there was a line around the corner and down the block. Patrick took a step in the direction of the line, but I grabbed his hand gently and led him past the line of clubbers toward the front entrance.

We had left the car in a *way*-overpriced overnight parking garage a few blocks away since we wouldn't be driving later, not if tonight went anywhere close to last Friday. Most of the time Nikki, Shawn, and I just took a taxi to the club, but I had wanted to pick up Patrick in the Vanq because he always made the funniest face when he saw it.

"Do you think they'll let me in?" Patrick asked nervously.

"Of course they'll let you in. You're with me, remember?" I said as I flashed him a smile. He looked back at me dubiously and shoved his free hand into the pocket of his hoodie. I hadn't told him what kind of club this was, so all he knew was we were two minors about to just *walk* into an exclusive nightclub.

Some of the people in line shot us dirty looks, but I paid them no mind and held my head high. Just before I reached the blue velvet rope, a very large hand shot in front of me. I looked up into the eyes of Viggo, the club's head bouncer. Viggo at one point had been a big Russian guy until he had become the mate of a daemon. And even though he was now a Neodaemon he stilled looked about as graceful as a brick wall.

"Come on Viggo, what gives?" I asked, slightly irritated; Viggo had never stopped me before.

He said nothing, but eyed Patrick, who did his best not to cower under Viggo's gaze—a lesser man probably *would* have.

I sighed and fished the Blue Card out of my coat pocket. Since I hadn't explained to Patrick what we were yet, I couldn't very well ask him to wear it. He'd think I was crazy. Well, crazier than he probably *already* did at least.

Viggo looked at the Blue Card and raised an eyebrow, but said nothing as he lifted the rope. I smiled at him silently thanking him for *not* saying anything.

As we walked past him into the club I was about to breathe a sigh of relief, but just before we had gotten out of earshot Viggo spoke, his voice rising above the music. "Your friends are already here."

I cringed slightly. How was I going to explain everything to Patrick *now*?

Ethereal vocal trance music caressed our ears as we walked further into the club; the low entrance ceiling giving way to a massive vaulted ceiling. Patrick stopped dead, and I looked over at him. His face was struck with awe, and I looked from him out at the club too. Though I had been here many times, I had to admit it was still breathtaking.

The entrance opened into a circular dance floor with tables raised on a crescent moon dais beyond that. Past the crescent dais was a massive bar lit up with blue lights. The side of the club was lined with plush velvet booths, curving in sweeping crescents from the restrooms near the bar nearly to the door. Lighting fixtures about the booths spun, lightly showering the whole club in what looked like thousands of stars. Electric blue, purple, and periwinkle lights flashed and swayed around the room.

I pulled Patrick through the throngs of people toward one of the corner booths farthest from the door. No sooner had we sat than a buxom girl appeared in front of us. Her midnight blue slinky dress left nothing to the imagination as far as her shape was concerned. The dress was splattered with luminescent paint, so she looked like the embodiment of the night sky. The girl eyed Patrick with wide eyes but turned her attention to me. I had no doubt that by now everyone that worked at the club knew *exactly* who me, Nikki, Shawn, and Travis were.

Patrick looked out at the other girls flitting about from table to booth with lit up tablets, taking drink orders. I might have been upset if I wasn't sure he was in total shock by now.

I turned my attention back to the drink girl who on closer examination turned out to be Shelby. "Hey

Shelby."

"Drinks tonight, Nualla?" she asked, tapping the screen on her tablet.

"I'll have an Eclipsed Dream," I said before turning to Patrick. "Patrick?"

He turned his attention back to me and then to Shelby. "Do you have soda?" he asked her in a dazed voice.

Before Shelby could answer, I jumped in. "He'll have a Hypnotic Blue." I turned to him again. "You'll need it—*trust* me."

He looked at me curiously for a moment before he let his eyes drift back to stare up at one of the most impressive things about Club Lunaris, the massive circular glass skylight cut into the ceiling above the dance floor. But unlike most skylights this one was filled with undulating water and swimming fish. Lights streamed through it creating interesting shapes of light and shadow on the dancers below.

As Shelby left, I watched Patrick watching the ceiling. He looked like a child watching fish at an aquarium. I wondered how our world must look to someone on the outside—to him.

A few minutes later our drinks arrived, and I downed mine quickly, slamming it back down on the table.

"What was *that*?" Patrick asked, raising an eyebrow.

"Liquid courage. Now drink yours."

"Do I have—" My look must have said everything, because he didn't finish talking and instead downed the drink.

Shelby was still standing there eyeing Patrick questioningly. "Hey Shelbs, two Blue Midnight Margaritas, okay?" I said, holding up two fingers.

"Sure thing sweetie," she said before disappearing back into the sea of dancing lights.

"Don't they care about getting in trouble for serving minors here?" Patrick asked, looking out at the bar suspiciously.

"Believe me, serving minors is the *least* of their worries here," I replied with a snort.

"Wait, *what*?" Patrick said, looking back at me.

I sat there trying to think of how to reveal to Patrick all the secrets I was currently keeping from him. Hell, I had spent most of the week trying to figure it out. I opened my mouth to speak, but when I saw Nikki bounding up to us with Shawn just a few steps behind, I clamped it shut again.

"Hey guys! Didn't think I'd see *you* here. I mean Nualla sure, but *you*, Patrick?" Nikki said before she flopped down on the booth seat. Then she said a little more quietly to me "How'd you get past Viggo with *him*?"

"It's called a Blue Card; it's like a pass to get away with anything." I answered jokingly as I twirled the

Blue Card around on my finger. And that was when fate decided to smite me for my assumptions.

Nikki's eyes got real big, and she sunk a little lower in the booth. "Nualla, heads up, my mom looks to be on a warpath, and she's coming this way."

"It there time to bolt?" I asked quickly.

"Nope," Nikki answered, grimacing. "She'll be here in three...two..."

"Nualla, can I speak with you—*now*?" Skye asked through clenched teeth as she dragged me out from the booth before I could protest.

Nikki's mom, my Aunt Skye, looked exactly like I would have, if someone had doused me in blond. Well, if I were a few years older too, of course. Skye had the same face, same eyes, same spiraling wavy curls as me and my dad. She was generally the sweetest, most fun loving person you could ever meet. That is, unless she was pissed, then she was hell incarnate. And this looked to be one of those moments. So I just let her drag me through the club, because trust me, it was safer.

When we had finally made it to her office she closed the door and turned on me, eyes full of fire. "Nualla, what on *earth* is a human boy doing with you in my club?"

I had never seen Skye this angry—*ever*. "Well..."

"Nualla, this is crazy even for you. What were

you thinking?!"

"I can explain!"

"You'd better, because those clubbers out there are about to tear him apart."

Had I not noticed the angry faces with malice in their eyes? Or was Skye just being melodramatic as usual? I couldn't dwell on this long though, because Skye looked about to throttle me.

I looked down at my boots; Skye had picked one hell of a weekend to be out of town in London launching one of her newest clubs. In our world, Skye's Kalodaemon-exclusive clubs were the places to be and be seen. And because she was always traveling between the clubs, she and Nikki had always lived with us at the family estate in San Francisco. So when I had had the conversation with my family last Saturday, she hadn't been there to hear it, and apparently no one had bothered or remembered to call her up and tell her about it this past week.

"It's a really long story," I said uneasily, running my teeth over my bottom lip.

"I've got time, now spill it," Skye said as she folded her arms under her chest and leaned back against the door. And that's when I knew there wasn't a chance in hell that I was getting out of this room without telling her.

When I was done Skye sat there in silence for several minutes before she spoke. "Nualla, can I ask a favor? Next time warn me *before* you bring a human here; there's only so much I can do, you know."

"I got him a Blue Card; I just didn't give it to him to wear yet."

"Oh, well *that* changes everything. I'll just make an announcement to my patrons, and that should calm things down," Skye said as she stopped leaning against the door that led back to the club.

"What *exactly* are you going to say?" I asked, immediately suspicious.

"Oh, what any proud aunt would do," Skye replied with a mischievous smile as she opened the door.

"You're going to punish me with embarrassment, aren't you?" I said flatly, glaring at her.

"I have no idea what you're talking about," Skye answered dismissively. "Now *out.*"

I trudged over to the table in defeat. Why was my family bound and determined to embarrass the hell out of me for this? Hadn't I already suffered enough? It was just one stupid little thing. Okay, it was a very *big* thing. Yeah, I probably deserved this.

Skye and I reached the booth, and Patrick, Nikki, and Shawn looked up at me questioningly as I dropped back down onto the seat. A least our drinks had arrived while I was gone.

Skye reached out her hand to me. I didn't even look up as I slapped the Blue Card into her palm. "I'll be back in a second, dears. I just need to take care of one small thing," Skye said with a broad smile.

Without waiting for a response, Skye walked away, and I quickly turned to Patrick. "I'm going to apologize in advance for what she's about to do."

"Why, what's she about to do?" Patrick asked, looking a little panicked. At that all the lights stopped moving and focused on the crescent dais just before the tables. The music drifted to silence, and everyone stopped and stared.

"*This,*" I answered with a groan; I could already feel the blood creep into my face.

Skye was standing on the dais, microphone in hand, lit up for everyone to see. People began to cheer and whistle. I couldn't blame them; in what she was wearing she looked like a silver screen movie star.

"I apologize for interrupting your evening, but I need a moment to clear something up before any hostility breaks out in my club. This—" she said, gesturing out toward Patrick, "is my niece's new husband. He will soon be one of us, and you need not fear him." Skye smiled a wicked smile at the crowd as she held up Patrick's Blue Card. "And if one of you lays a finger on him I will personally kill you myself before I send your dead and broken body to The Embassy for assaulting a Blue Card-carrying human."

I heard a choking sound from next to me which was probably Patrick having a heart attack.

Skye's lips slid back into a pleasant smile. "Now a round of drinks on the house in honor of the happy couple."

The tension in the room visibly lifted at that, and a cheer went up. Funny how free booze usually has that effect on people.

I put my head in my hands in embarrassment and peeked over at Patrick, who looked for the first time like he wanted to bolt from the room. "So...that would be my Aunt Skye."

"My mom," Nikki said, looking at Patrick.

"She runs a *nightclub*?" Patrick asked in a shaky voice.

"No dude, she *owns* the nightclub; a few actually," Shawn said before taking a sip of his drink. "Why else do you think we hang out in them all the time?"

"Because you're really cool?" Patrick answered, shrugging.

Unnatural Selection

Friday, January 20th

NUALLA

Aᴇᴛᴇʀ Sᴋʏᴇ ʜᴀᴅ ꜰɪɴɪsʜᴇᴅ ᴇᴍʙᴀʀʀᴀssɪɴɢ the *crap* out of me, she walked over to us looking rather pleased with herself. My family had spent the last few years teasing me for being dumb enough to date Michael; I wondered just how long they were planning on poking fun at me for Patrick. With the way my luck was going, it was probably going to be for the rest of my life.

Skye smiled down at Patrick. "Hello, I'm Skye Varris. You must be Patrick Connolly."

"Yes, I am," Patrick answered nervously.

"Sorry we had to meet like this. Sometimes Nualla doesn't think about how her actions will affect others," Skye said, her eyes drifting to me. Which was a polite way of saying I fucked up.

"I'm not too good at that myself, either," Patrick admitted as he nervously ran his hand through his hair.

"So what did *your* parents say about this?" Skye asked Patrick as she leaned over the table and pulled the ring from under his shirt.

A bright blush shot across Patrick's face. "Um, they don't exactly know," he admitted, shooting me a panicked look.

"Probably a good thing, not everyone's as under-standing as I am," Skye said with a crooked smile. I coughed, and she shot me a sidewise glance.

"Your club's really awesome; I mean, not that I've really seen a lot of them but..." Patrick said in a rushed, unsteady voice.

"Why, thank you dear," Skye said with a huge grin.

One of the drink girls appeared behind Skye. "Skye, the bartenders want to know what type of drinks they can give out for free."

"I'll be right there Kristin," Skye said to the girl before turning back to us. "Duty calls," she said with a smile as she handed Patrick's Blue Card back to me. She took a few steps away before turning around to point at us. "You four stay out of trouble for the rest of tonight, okay?"

Shawn looked up from his drink startled. "Does that mean no more drinking?"

"No *Shawn*, it means no causing trouble, disrupting my patrons, or other shenanigans that would warrant me calling your parents to haul your asses home."

"We'll be good, Mom," Nikki promised with a not too reassuring smile.

"*Sure* you will," Skye said as she rolled her eyes at us and turned to walk away.

"Did she just seriously say *shenanigans*?" Shawn asked with a snort.

I turned to Patrick. "Here, put this on before someone decides to kill you or something," I said, handing Patrick the Blue Card.

"Um, okay," Patrick said as he slipped the cord over his neck. He looked at it suspiciously for a while before looking up and asking, "Hey Nualla, can I ask you something?"

"Sure," I answered, taking a sip of my drink.

"What on earth is a *Blue Card*, and since when did people specify that they were human to others?"

I all but choked. *Geez* he didn't miss a thing, did he?

"That would be our cue to go," Shawn said, grabbing his drink and jumping up.

"Oh look, I think I see Natalie—" Nikki announced

abruptly, following his lead, and the two of them all but bolted from the booth.

Patrick looked at me questioningly. I held up a finger and took a big gulp of my drink. I knew I was going to have to tell him everything, but I just couldn't find a good starting point.

I looked at him, putting my drink down. "If I promise to answer *all* of your questions will you agree to start off with something a little easier to answer?"

"Sure…um, okay your hair then."

"My *hair*?"

"The dye job always looks so fresh. I dyed mine for an anime convention once, and it didn't look that nice for long. So do you have to dye it like every week or something?"

This question was and wasn't easy to answer at the same time. "It's natural."

"Wait, *what*? How could it possibly be—?"

"I'll get to that, so could you pick something else, please?"

"Okay." Patrick looked around the club, sipping his drink. Finally, he looked back at me. "Your aunt seems to be taking our news rather well. My parents would probably kill me if I told them—well *anything* about this, really."

"You didn't see her in the office," I said, stirring my drink, "she was *plenty* scary."

"Speaking of your family," Patrick said as he ran

his hands down the side of his glass. "When will I get to meet the rest of them?"

"Soon," I answered, still idly stirring my drink.

"*Soon*?" he asked, looking at me.

"Tomorrow."

"*Tomorrow*?" Patrick asked, looking a little confused.

"Because the dance you asked me to is tomorrow," I replied before taking a sip of my drink.

"Oh yeah..." Patrick said, a little dazed.

"You *did* remember the dance was tomorrow, right?"

"Of *course*, what do you take me for? I've wanted to go with you for nearly four years!" And then he realized what he had said, and a deep blush spread across his cheeks. He ran his fingers nervously through his hair and looked up at me. "Sorry, I say a lot of stupid things around you. I'm just kinda nervous, I guess."

"It's okay—so am I," I said with a shy smile.

We both sat there sipping on our drinks as the music rushed in to fill the would-be silence. After a while, Patrick finally asked, "Nualla, why are we here?"

"It's a safe place. Public, but the wrong ears won't hear."

"*Safe*? We're in a freakin' club," Patrick snorted, gesturing with his hand out at the dancers. Then his expression changed abruptly. "*Oh*."

"What?"

"That explains a lot…" he said, still staring out at the crowd.

"*What* does?" I asked a little exasperated. I had absolutely no idea what he was referring to.

"What your aunt said earlier," Patrick replied, looking back at me.

"You're not making any sense," I said, furrowing my brow.

"I think I know what you are now," Patrick said, looking at the table.

I swallowed hard. "You *do*?"

He looked up at me. "I *think* I know, but I'm not sure, so I'd rather you just tell me."

I couldn't keep putting this off, couldn't keep making him ask different questions because I was afraid to tell him the truth. I took a deep breath and prepared myself for his reaction. "I'm—everyone here aside from you—is a daemon."

"I thought so," Patrick said with a small smirk.

I stared at him dumbly. "*What*?" This was not the response I had been expecting; not even slightly. Running and screaming, sure—but not this.

"I suspected you were, but I didn't know for sure. That's why I needed to hear it from you," he admitted, looking up at me cautiously.

I stared at him in shock. "How did you…how did you *know*?" Patrick didn't answer; just pointed at me.

"*Me*?" I asked confused.

"Your necklace."

"My *necklace*?" I replied, looking down at it.

"That's the goddess Daenara, sometimes mistaken as the Egyptian goddess Hathor. The symbolism looks Egyptian, but the inscription around the outside is in Daemotic. It reads, 'May the stars protect us.' You rub it when you're worried or nervous because it's supposed to protect against evil and bring you good luck."

I sat there gaping at him; letting what he had just said sink in before I asked, "How could you possibly know *that*?"

"You give yourself away in a thousand different ways each day; it was just a matter of putting the pieces together. Once I knew what that necklace meant, I just let the internet lead me around until I found the truth."

"Are we—am *I* that obvious?" I asked, more than a little startled.

"No, probably not to someone who doesn't have a nearly eidetic memory."

"Which you have?"

"Which I have," he confirmed like he had just admitted some grievous sin.

I let the air out of my lungs I hadn't noticed that I had been holding.

"So what *are* you exactly?" Patrick asked carefully.

"Huh?"

"The internet can only take you so far. Most of it is speculative or referencing thousand-year-old texts. And there are different interpretations of daemons. The Greeks, the Egyptians, the Christians, they all had different versions."

I had to shake my head to clear it before answering. The conversation had taken a completely different direction than I had expected. *"Oh.* Um…the Greeks hit the mark closest. There are two types."

"The Kalodaemons and the Kakodaemons; the good and the bad," Patrick said simply as if it was just common knowledge.

"Yeah…" I looked at him questioningly.

"Wikipedia," he said with a small smile.

"You know you can't trust everything you read on the internet, right?"

"Yeah, that's why I'm checking the source," Patrick answered as he flashed me a huge grin.

"So yeah good and bad; we Kalodaemons are kind of like angels, and the Kakodaemons are what you would normally think of as demons. We're like minor deities, much more powerful than humans, but not gods either. We can influence the humans around us, what they feel, what they see."

Patrick sat back with his arms folded. "If you daemons are so much more powerful than humans, why hide? Why aren't you ruling us all?"

I knew this question would come up. Funny, I had asked the same thing as a child. And so I decided to use the explanation my dad had used. "Think about it like a hunting party."

"*Excuse me*?" Patrick asked, raising his eyebrows.

"Just go with me on this one, okay." Patrick nodded, and I continued. "Though the bear, stag, and lion may be more powerful than a human in one-on-one combat, the creature stands no real chance when vastly outnumbered. Basically, you humans vastly outnumber us even though our race most likely predates yours."

"Oh, well I guess that makes sense."

I looked at him curiously. "You know, you're taking this rather calmly."

"Well I mostly got over my hysteria at home," Patrick admitted as he ran his hand through his hair.

"Ah ha," I said, raising an eyebrow.

"But apparently not all my stupidity," Patrick groaned, covering his face with his hand. There was another long pause before he spoke again. "So are you immortal?"

Gee how to answer this one. "Kinda—well not *exactly*. We *do* die; we just live longer since we age much slower than you. Also most human means can't kill us."

"What can?"

"Drowning, dismemberment, starvation. Fire, but not so much the flames as the smoke; our bodies are considerably tougher than yours, but we need to breathe same as you. And then there's our kryptonite."

"Which is?" he asked, raising an eyebrow.

"Titanium." I shuddered just *saying* the word.

"*Really*? I thought it would be something weird like garlic or silver bullets."

"It's not funny, Patrick. We're *allergic* to it. If the skin is broken with a titanium blade or bullet, the skin will never stop bleeding, never close up, or heal. If ingested, it's instant death. If we even touch it, we get a chemical burn." And then a horrible thought crossed my mind. "Why are you so interested in what can harm us?"

"Because I want to know what I have to protect you from," Patrick answered, leaning forward.

"You're worried about protecting *me*?" I had to smile at this.

Patrick looked down at his hands. "I don't want anything bad to happen to you." He looked up into my eyes. "You're...very important to me," he stated in an odd voice.

I played nervously with the ring hanging from my necklace. What had I been to this boy? I had just met him, but he already seemed deeply attached to me. If he had been a daemon, I would have thought I was his One. But since he wasn't, it must have just been a *him* thing.

Patrick looked at me as I continued to play with the ring. "That holds a special power over you doesn't it?"

"Kalodaemons don't love like humans; we choose our mates for life."

"Don't you have divorce? What if you…what if you fall in love with someone else?"

I looked down. "Even if we *did*—we can't choose another unless our mate dies."

"Oh, so kinda like penguins."

I looked up at Patrick, raising an eyebrow. "Did you just compare me to a flightless arctic bird?"

"Yeah..sorry," Patrick answered, looking down at his drink.

"No it's okay, I like penguins; they're cute," I said, with a crooked smile.

Patrick was silent again; nervously stirring his drink. I was secretly hoping he wouldn't ask if I loved him. It wasn't that I didn't think I ever could; it was just I wasn't sure *what* I felt yet. But thankfully he asked something completely different. Either he was thinking it and was afraid to ask, or it hadn't crossed his mind. "Most of you choose other daemons, don't you?" he asked, looking back at me.

"Yes most do, but some choose humans," I answered quietly. "Skye did."

"She *did*?" Patrick sat up straighter and looked

around. "Do I get to meet him too?"

"No. He—died."

"Oh—how?" Patrick asked cautiously.

I cringed; I hadn't wanted to tell Patrick this until much later in the night. Preferably after he had had a few more drinks. "His body rejected the retrovirus. He died instead of becoming a daemon. It's not common, but it does happen."

Patrick sat bolt upright. "Wait, *what* virus?"

I looked down at the table. "Remember how I said not sleeping with me was a good thing?"

"*Yeah*?" Patrick said slowly.

"Well um—if I sleep with you, you will become one of us," I confessed, still not meeting his eyes. I could feel the blush creeping across my cheeks.

"How exactly?"

I swallowed hard. "We carry a retrovirus in our blood. It re-encrypts your DNA, so you become a daemon."

"Wait, so daemons are a *disease*?"

"In the very broadest of terms—yes."

"Are there any side effects *other* than death?"

"No, and death isn't very common. Some people's bodies just contain a self-destruct button. Instead of letting your DNA be rewritten, it just kills you."

"Sounds—fun," Patrick said with a grimace. "Is it a quick death?"

"Unfortunately no, it isn't," I answered reluctantly. "Once passed to your body, it will take three to five days for it to rewrite your DNA. I've heard it's a very painful process; like being on fire from the inside out."

"Now those descriptions for demons and fiery hell make a lot more sense," Patrick said with a wry smile.

"Yeah, funny that," I said nervously.

Patrick fell silent again and took a few large gulps of his drink, finishing it off. I finished mine as I flagged down one of the passing drink girls to get us another round.

When the next set of drinks arrived Patrick finally asked, "So why are you telling me all your secrets? How do you know I'll decide to become one of you?"

"One, I *promised* I would if you married me. You did, so I'm keeping my promise," I answered holding up one finger. "Two, I made the assumption that you would like to keep on living," I said, holding up a second finger.

"Wouldn't everyone?" Patrick asked with an ironic smile.

"Since I cannot prove without a doubt to the Grand Council that I didn't tell you our secrets last Friday, that leaves you with only two choices. Either you refuse to become a daemon and they execute you, or you become one of us and either die in the dae-monification process, or we live happily ever after." I took a long pause studying his face. "You have no idea how sorry I am about all this."

"*I'm* not. Living happily ever after with you sounds a lot better than anything I could have hoped for in life."

"So you've decided?" I asked slowly.

"Do I have a *choice*?"

"No, not really. But you still have to make it—formally."

"*What*?" Patrick asked, wide-eyed.

"We have to go before the Grand Council on Sunday, and you have to speak your intent to become a daemon."

"*Seriously*?" Patrick asked in a choked voice.

I nervously fiddled with my necklace. "Yeah, I just found out about that myself on Wednesday. I thought I could just file the license and get you a Blue Card, but no such luck."

"Blue Card, isn't that that thing your aunt was talking about?"

"Yeah, that pass you're wearing tells daemons not to kill you," I answered, pointing at the Blue Card hanging from his neck.

"Oh." He picked it up and squinted at it. "Is *that* what it says?"

"You won't be able to read it, so don't even bother. It's inscribed in a spectrum only daemons can see."

"*Oh*—cool," Patrick said, staring at it with far more interest. "So do people always have to get these?"

"No, they were originally intended for the children of Kalodaemons that were born human."

Patrick looked back up at me quickly. "That can *happen*?"

"Not often."

"But I'm not one of those, so why do I have one?" Patrick asked questioningly.

"You're a special case, but the intent is the same. You're not a daemon yet, but you will be soon."

Patrick's eyebrows shot up. "Oh, I was supposed to *already* be a daemon by now, wasn't I."

"Yeah, you were," I said with a small smile. "This is kinda unprecedented for the most part. It must have happened at some point since there are rules and procedures for it, but I've never heard of it happening."

There was a long pause, and Patrick's face reddened. Without looking up from his drink he asked, "Is *it* the same as it is for humans?"

"What? *Oh*! Um—I've heard it's much better," I answered, turning equally red.

Patrick's eyes darted up to mine. "*Really*?"

I coughed. "Yeah, we release a euphoric toxin that's supposed to help you through the next week's pain."

Patrick took a big gulp of his drink; the blush in his cheeks had not disappeared if anything it had gotten redder. "Nature thinks of everything, doesn't it?"

"Sure does." I took a few more sips of my drink and looked over at Patrick's—which was empty. I gulped the rest of mine and turned to wave down Shelby. I held up two fingers, and she nodded before heading to the bar again, which was hopping because of the free drinks.

"If I didn't know better, I'd think you were trying to get me drunk again," Patrick said with a crooked smile.

"*Again*? I didn't force them down your throat before," I said with mock outrage.

"Yeah, you're right," Patrick said, looking at his empty glass. "I'm in no way a stranger to these things."

I smirked at him. "Neither am I." But my smile fell when I saw his face. There was something there, a sadness that hadn't been there before. I was debating asking if there was something bothering him, but I decided it was probably just all the stuff I had thrown at him. None of these were inconsequential school-yard secrets. These were the life-changing kind; the dangerous kind that could get you killed if you weren't careful.

Shelby arrived with our next round of drinks, and Patrick looked at his for a while before looking up at me. "So if you're a daemon, how come you look just like a normal human girl?"

"I don't, you just can't see what I really look like," I admitted as I nervously pushed a strand of hair behind my ear.

"Why?" Patrick asked in confusion.

"We are masters of illusion. We refract the light around us, altering your perception, so we appear to be humans like you. We can also influence you, your thoughts, ideas, emotions."

"Like the muses?"

I raised an eyebrow. "Where do you think the idea of muses came from?"

"So you can't show me what you really look like?"

"No I can—it's just really hard. Our illusionary fields are second nature to us. It takes a lot of concentration to drop them."

"Oh," Patrick said dejectedly.

"I can try, it's just—I'm afraid that you won't like me anymore once you see what I really look like," I confessed avoiding his eyes.

Patrick put a hand on mine. "That's not *even* a possibility."

I looked up into his eyes; they were warm and inviting. "Okay...I'll show you what I really look like—just promise me you won't bolt for the door okay?"

Your Eyes

Friday, January 20th

PATRICK

"OKAY...I'LL SHOW YOU WHAT I really look like—
just promise me you won't bolt for the door
okay?" Nualla looked so frightened as she said it,
as if she truly feared I would. I tried to speak but
couldn't find my voice, so I just nodded. She swallowed hard and squeezed her eyes shut. I looked at
Nualla unblinking, so I wouldn't miss a thing, but
nothing happened.

I began to worry. *Did I miss something?* And then
the air around her began to shimmer and change; like
a ripple in a pond, but not like it at the same time.

Slowly the image of her rematerialized into focus. Two dark blue ribbed horns swirled back from just above her ears, delicate and beautiful like a gazelle.

They were utterly captivating—that is, until she opened her eyes again. I was lost in them, their silvery blue glow drawing all of my attention as if there was nothing to look at but her. Everything around her fell away so that there was nothing but those eyes; eyes like captured moonlight. They drew you in, enticing, seductive, and luminous like a jungle cat's. A fog crept into my brain dulling my senses to everything but them.

I must have been staring at her like an idiot, because she finally averted her eyes. "Please say something," Nualla said in a small voice that was almost swallowed up by the music around us.

The minute she averted her eyes the fog in my head started to lift, and I found my voice again. "You're beautiful…" I said, my voice trailing off as her eyes shot back up to mine.

She apparently hadn't been expecting me to say that; it was plainly obvious in the look on her face. "What did you say?"

"Yes…*wait*—what were we talking about?" I couldn't think straight when I looked into her eyes. Hell, I couldn't even remember to breathe. I managed to tear my eyes away and look down at the table. "You must know how beautiful you are?"

"Then why can't you look at me?" she asked uneasily.

"Your eyes—they're so mesmerizing, I can't think straight when I look into them."

"*Oh!*" she said, startled. "Is this better?"

I looked back up; the mesmerizing twinkling glow had dissipated to a more tolerable amount. They were still enchanting, but not to the point where I was going to keel over from forgetting to breathe. "Yes."

Nualla still looked uncomfortable, but a lot less terrified. Before tonight, I had never seen her look anything other than fearlessly beautiful. She always seemed to live life like a duck in a pond, problems rolling off her back like they were nothing more than water drops.

I reached out a tentative hand trying my hardest to keep it from shaking, fearing that if it did she would bolt like a frightened deer. Quietly I asked, "Can I touch them?"

She moved back ever so slightly. "My horns?"

I nodded.

She ran her teeth over her bottom lip and looked down to the side then back up at me again. "Sure...I guess."

I extended my hand toward her, lightly touching the curved horns. They were very solid, no illusion there. I drew my hand across the ribbed surface then down her cheek letting it rest there. "How anyone could think of your kind as monsters is beyond me. You're the most beautiful person I have ever seen."

Nualla's eyes got a funny look in them, and she leapt at me. In any other situation when someone jumps you, panicking would be the proper response. But when a completely gorgeous girl jumps you, you just kinda go with it.

She slid into my lap, her dress hiking dangerously high up her thigh. Something about this felt oddly familiar. Flashes of last Friday filled my mind rapidly, and I was nearly knocked senseless by their enticing caress. *What did I do?* was the last thing that entered my mind before her lips hit mine and erased all other thought.

Nualla gripped my shirt and pulled me even closer as her lips pressed against mine. My hand seemed to move of its own accord as it slid up her thigh to the small of her back and pushed her even closer to me. Her kisses moved across to my face; her warm breath heavy in my ear. That set something off in my brain, and my eyes shot open.

"*Geez* you two, get a room. This *is* a public place you know." I looked up to see Nikki smirking at us with her hands on her hips. I had been so caught up in *what* we were doing I had completely forgotten *where* we were doing it.

Nualla sat bolt upright a deep red flush across her normally pale skin. Without a word, she slipped off my lap onto the booth seat. She was breathing heavily as if she had been jogging up the steep incline of Powell Street.

"What exactly was *that* all about?" I asked breathlessly.

Shawn just smiled as he folded his arms and leaned against the edge of the booth. "Well most teenagers have crazy hormones running through their bodies, but they don't have nothing on daemons."

"Yeah, our hormones don't just affect us, they affect everyone around us as well," Nikki said, gesturing to the room with her head.

"And when you get the two of you together, your emotions will bounce back and forth between you," Shawn said, his smile broadening.

"Right...now Vegas makes a lot more sense," I said as I took a few steadying breaths. I couldn't remember a lot about that night in Vegas, but I could remember some of the feelings.

It suddenly felt *very* hot in here.

We continued drinking at the club until way past two in the morning. I was so drunk by the time the taxi dropped me off at home I was barely able to get my front door open. I sat there stabbing my key at the door for several minutes before I was able to get it to go in.

Finally I turned the key and pushed the door open. Letting it close behind me, I flailed against the wall for the light switch but gave up. Light would have probably done more damage than good in the state I was in, anyway.

I took a few wobbly steps forward and stupidly tried to take my shoes off while still standing. With one shoe half off, I lost my balance and reached out to catch the counter; I succeeded only in sending a bowl of fruit flying as I crashed to the floor. *"Dammit!"* I cursed loudly.

"Patrick?" I looked up slowly to see the silhouette of my mother standing in the darkness on the landing of the stairs. "Did you just get home?"

This was not good; I had forgotten they would be coming home today, and currently I was piss-ass drunk, sitting on the floor with one shoe on, surrounded by a pile of spilt fruit. *Crap*, what was I going to do now? I was usually alone when I was drunk, or Connor was here and we were binging on anime. I had never actually had to pretend to be sober before.

Since she hadn't asked about the fruit, I decided not to bother explaining it; it would mean more talking. Talking too long just got you into more trouble.

Okay Patrick, concentrate. It's dark, if you don't slur your words, she won't notice you're completely wasted.

I took a deep breath and lied through my teeth. "Yeah, me and Connor went to the midnight release of *Whisper*." I took another deep breath. "I'm sorry, I didn't mean to wake you."

"Oh, okay." She turned to go back up the stairs, and I thought I was home free, but then she turned back. "What on earth are you doing on the floor with all that fruit?"

Crap, apparently she *had* noticed the mess. "Um...I was taking off my shoes, and I slipped." I hoped it didn't come out sounding too much like a question.

"Oh, well you'll clean it up, won't you? I'm going back to sleep," she said with a yawn.

"Sure Mom, no problem," I said in the steadiest voice I could.

I waited until I heard her door close before I flopped backward onto the floor. I wished I didn't have to get up; I really didn't want to tempt my fate trying to walk up those stairs just now. If it had been just me here, I would have just stayed on the floor till morning. But I wasn't alone, and for the first time in as long as I could remember, I wished I was.

Nothing Fools a Cat

Saturday, January 21st

PATRICK

I STOOD ON THE SIDEWALK OUTSIDE our townhome complex waiting for the taxi Nualla said she was going to send for me. Lots whizzed by, but none stopped.

I leaned my head back against the wall and took a deep breath. Even with all that had happened already I was still nervous. I was going to the dance with Nualla. It was really happening. It wasn't a dream. I knew that, but it still just didn't *feel* real. Somehow, this all only ever felt real when I was with her, under the gaze of those otherworldly eyes.

I had spent most of the day processing what I had learned last night—about Nualla, and her world. A world I would soon be joining. You would think becoming something else—something not human— would bother me; but it didn't. If becoming one of them meant I could be with her, it was worth it.

I pulled the ring out from under my shirt and stared at it. This small little piece of metal was all that really proved that she was real, that we were really together. It was funny that such a small little thing could mean so much.

As I was standing there staring at the ring, a sleek black limo glided to an elegant stop. Two small deep lapis-blue flags fluttered on the hood like the kind you saw on foreign dignitaries' cars; a silver lotus dancing across each of their surfaces.

A black suited chauffeur stepped out and looked about the building and street. He peered at me closer, then at the corsage box in my hand. "Mr. Patrick Connolly?"

"Yes…" I answered, looking at him suspiciously.

"I am to transport you to the Galathea residence," he announced as he opened the back door.

I just gaped at him and then the limo. When Nualla had said she was sending a car I had thought she meant a taxi or even one those black town cars. Not a freakin' *limo*.

"You have *got* to be kidding me." I had never been

in a limo before. Hell, I had never even been in a *taxi* until I met Nualla.

The driver raised an eyebrow. "Excuse me?"

"Uh…nothing," I said and got into the back of the limo.

As we cruised down Folsom to 6th I was fine, it was an area I was familiar with. But as we passed Market on to Golden Gate Avenue, it occurred to me I had absolutely no idea where Nualla lived. Over the past few years when I had pictured her in my head, it had always been of her at school. And now when I thought of her she was in the places we had been together, the mall, the club, Vegas. I had never really given much thought to *where* she actually lived.

When we entered Pacific Heights, I began to get really nervous. The houses we passed on Pacific just got larger and grander. I sank lower in my seat. Just how rich was Nualla's family?

A few blocks down Pacific we finally stopped in front of a huge pale blue Victorian house. It towered over a stone wall covered in blue morning glories; it even had one of those circular room turrets. A gate slid open and the driver turned onto a long driveway that ran along the house.

"Nualla lives—*here*?" I asked as I gaped up at the

house.

"Yes, this is one of the Galathea residences," the driver answered as the limo came to a stop.

"Wait! *One*?" I yelped, sitting bolt upright. *Crap*, not only was she beautiful, smart, and interesting, she was also apparently *way* out of my league. Now more than ever, I was certain that her family was going to hate me. I mean, what did *I* really have to offer?

The driver got out of the car and came to open my door. I looked up at the house, it was massive, ornate; everything that my home wasn't. Hell, you could probably fit my whole place in their driveway alone.

I stood there staring at the house for a while trying to get up the courage to even knock on the door. Eventually, the driver cleared his throat, and I turned to look at him. "Not that it's my place to say anything but—" he started.

"No, go ahead, say whatever you want."

"I've known Nualla Galathea a long time. She's not one to care where you're from as long as you're nice to her."

"Oh um…it's not just that. It's well…I'm meeting her family for the first time, and I kinda married her last week." I wasn't sure if Nualla would care that I was telling him or not.

The driver all but choked. I was almost positive that what I had just said was the *last* thing he thought I was going to say. "*Oh*, but you're…"

"You're one of them too, aren't you?" I asked as casually as I could. He nodded slowly. "I just found out about it all myself yesterday."

"*Really*?" he asked in disbelief.

"Yeah," I answered, looking back at the house.

"Wow, tough break kid."

I turned to him with a slightly ironic smile. "Well for her, anything's worth it."

He was quiet for a while before he spoke again. "We can stand out here all night if you want kid, but there's a beautiful girl in there waiting for you. I wouldn't keep her waiting *too* long."

"I know." I took a deep breath and walked toward the inevitable future.

A very angry face met me at the door. It belonged to a tall willowy girl with long pale blond hair, though not quite as long as Nualla's. She looked me up and down with disapproving dark blue eyes and a scowl on her face. "Here to meet the in-laws?" she asked, folding her arms across her chest and leaning against the door frame.

"Um…" I said like an idiot. Her hostility had caught me off-guard and the clever things I had rehearsed to say flew out the window. *Great*, I was making a *wonderful* impression already. I had hoped to impress them, or at the very least make sure they didn't hate me. But that was already falling apart, and I had only said one word, if you could even call it that.

"Andraya, is that Patrick?" someone called from behind her.

I was relieved when I saw Nualla's Aunt Skye pop up behind the girl whose name was apparently Andraya. "Hello, Ms. Varris," I said with an uneasy smile.

"Oh Patrick honey, call me Skye. You make me sound ancient calling me that."

"Oh sorry—*Skye...*" I said nervously. *Great*, I hadn't even made it in the door yet, and I was already going down in flames.

Skye took my arm and led me into the house. "Don't mind Andraya, she's harmless—*mostly*." *Mostly* being the operative word.

I looked around the foyer, the fact that they even *had* one said a lot. I had thought the outside of the house was impressive, but it didn't even hold a candle to the inside. An elaborate glass-topped table with a vase and a stack of mail stood in the middle of the room on a large pale blue oriental rug. Above the table was an impressive looking chandelier like one you would find in an old opera house. Intricate Victorian woodwork lined the bottom and tops of the Impressionist sky blue colored walls. They were the ornate wood carvings one only found in high-class, turn of the century homes.

I was staring at it—a little awestruck—when I heard a soft purring. I looked down to see a blueish-purple gray cat rubbing against my leg.

"*Oh*, Denaya likes you!" Skye said in an excited voice.

"Who?" I asked, looking around.

"The cat," Skye answered pointing at the gray cat currently looking up at me with curious golden eyes. "If the cat likes you, you're golden."

"Good to know," I said mostly to myself as I reached down to pet the cat.

"So do you normally do stupid things like run off and marry random strangers, or did my little sister drag you into this mess?" Andraya asked as she glared at me with disdain.

I stood up and just looked at her. There was really no answer I could give her that wouldn't come back to fuck me over later. Sure, Nualla had dragged me off to Vegas, but I had never for one *second* blamed her for anything that had happened.

"What Patrick does or doesn't do is none of your business, Andraya," Skye said, crossing her arms under her chest.

"*Sure* it is. We already have our hands full with *her* poor judgment, we don't need another one compounding the problem."

"Would the two of you stop picking on my son-in-law? He looks about to faint," a deep male voice said from the stairs.

I looked up to see a tall gentleman walking down the stairs, book in hand. He had shoulder-length wavy pale blond hair pulled back into a ponytail. His hair was a lot like Skye's and it was very clear that they were related. He also had the same unusual eyes as Nualla and Skye, periwinkle-blue with silvery flecks in them like moonlight reflecting back at you in the night.

Well this was a turn for the better; I had been expecting him to say something like, "Here's that jerk my daughter ran off and married." I swallowed hard; now to make a good impression. "Hello, Mr. Galathea, I'm Patrick Connolly, your daughter's—" somehow I couldn't get the word out.

"*Husband*," he finished for me, raising an eyebrow. "Yes, I know, and please Patrick, call me Alex. You are part of this family now. We needn't be so formal."

My brain screeched to a halt. Had he actually just said I was part of his family?

Alex placed his book on the glass entry table and reached down to scoop up the dainty little Denaya. He looked up into my eyes, and I got the feeling he was doing more than just looking. It felt more like he was reading my soul.

"It's good that Denaya likes you. You see, animals are not fooled by our illusions, only humans are. Dogs tend to not like us. But cats, cats see past *what* you are to *who* you are. They judge you by this," Alex said, pointing to his heart. "Nothing fools a cat."

"I don't have any pets," I said like an idiot. "I mean I *like* animals—I just don't have any."

Andraya didn't even try to stifle her snort as she slunk away into the next room.

I heard the sound of a door closing and looked past Alex; a lady with long straight black hair came down the hall looking at some papers. When she got closer to us, she stopped and looked up, a little startled to see us standing there in front of her.

"Ah Loraly," Alex said to her before turning to me. "Patrick this is my wife Loraly, Nualla and Andraya's mother."

Loraly smiled the kindest smile I had ever seen, and said in a soft friendly voice, "Hello Patrick, it's very nice to finally meet you." Her eyes were the same dark blue as Andraya's, but without the cold stare behind them.

"It's very nice to meet you too," I said, smiling back at her in a way I hoped looked friendly.

"Is that for Nualla?" Loraly asked, pointing at the corsage box in my hand. "It's really lovely," she said, moving closer for a better look.

I looked down at it myself. "Yeah, I got it to match her eyes." Then I realized what I had said and nervously clarified, "Um, because I didn't know what color to get since she didn't tell me what color her dress was." I ran my free hand through my hair; I had only been here a few minutes an already I was losing it.

"This must all be very strange to you," Loraly said sympathetically.

Truthfully? Yes, but to be completely honest, it was no weirder than the plots of some of the anime I had seen. Maybe that was the only reason I was keeping it together, because I was more willing to accept weird. "Um—*yeah* a little, but I'm okay."

"*Really*?" Andraya said dubiously from the other room; apparently she had been keeping up with the conversation while only *pretending* not to be interested. "Because you look like you're about to keel over any second now."

"Andraya, don't be rude," Loraly scolded her eldest daughter before turning back to me. "Patrick, be honest, do we frighten you?"

I wanted to lie at this moment more than any other time in my life, but I just couldn't. "Yeah, actually I'm terrified," I admitted reluctantly.

Loraly's shoulders dropped, and she got a hurt expression in her eyes. She looked about to burst into tears at any moment.

Oh, this is bad. This is really, really *bad.*

There was a scuffling behind us, and I turned to see Shawn coming through the door. He shut the door behind him and looked up at me, a smile on his face. "Patrick, *buddy,* how did you beat me here?"

So we were buddies now? *Um...cool?*

The smile disappeared from Shawn's face as he looked past me. "Loraly, what's wrong?"

"Patrick thinks we're scary," she almost sobbed.

Oh *fuck,* that's why she had looked so upset. She probably thought I thought they were monsters. "Oh no, that's not what I meant at all!" I said quickly. "It's not because of *what* you are. That doesn't bother me in the least, it's kinda cool really. It's just, you're her parents and well, I was terrified to death you would hate me."

Shawn, Alex, and Skye all bust up laughing, Loraly looked momentarily confused, and Andraya mumbled something unpleasant.

"Well *that* clears things right up there, doesn't it," Skye said, poking me in the ribs. "He's only terrified of what every *other* teenage boy is; his girl's parents."

Loraly looked at me questioningly, and I nodded. The smile returned to her face, and she took a few steps toward me. In one swift movement she swept me up into a hug, the papers in her hands fluttering to the ground forgotten. "Please don't be frightened Patrick, I assure you we like you very much."

I just stood there more than a little stunned. My own parents didn't normally hug me like this, and these people had never even *met* me before.

"Loraly, I think you're just making the poor boy even more nervous," Skye said with a playful smile.

"Oh, sorry," Loraly said apologetically as she released me.

Alex looked at his watch. "Well you all really should be going soon. Saturday traffic is really awful, even this time of year." He looked back up at me. "We will have more time to talk when Nualla brings you to The Embassy tomorrow."

"Embassy?" I asked questioningly.

"You have to go before the Grand Council tomorrow, didn't she tell you?" he said, looking confused.

"Oh right, she did." *Yeah right around the time she was stunning me with her eyes and revealing her secrets.* I had a really good memory; I had just been a little—*distracted*.

"I should really get going too, if I don't the club will already be swamped. But I'm not going anywhere without seeing those girls all dressed up," Skye stated before she walked over to the stairs and pushed the intercom on the wall. "You know it's rude to leave them standing down here *too* long, girls."

"He's here *already*?" Nualla yelled back into the intercom. I wondered how many floors up she had to be to have not heard our conversation.

Skye pushed the button again. "Yes, he's been here for fifteen minutes already, and at this point you guys are making *me* late too, so get your butts down here!" Skye released the button and looked over at us with a smirk. "Three…two…"

Right on cue, Nikki ran gracefully but whimsically down the stairs and into Shawn's widespread arms. He caught her as if she weighed nothing and spun her around. When he placed her on her feet again he smiled down at her now white blond and red streaked hair.

"Like it? It matches my dress better than the blue," she said with a grin as she turned her head back and forth.

"Yes…like…a lot," Shawn said rather stupidly. I was relieved to see I wasn't the *only* one here that seemed to be at a loss for words.

"You didn't say anything about my dress, Shawn," Nikki said with a slight pout.

Shawn looked slightly like a deer in highlights, and I was pretty sure what he was thinking about Nikki was not fit for public consumption.

I was trying not to laugh at the expression on his face when I heard the faintest of steps coming down the stairs. I looked up to see Nualla and nearly fell over. She didn't look like she was going to a high school dance; in fact, she looked more like she was going to a red carpet gala in the 1930's. The light satin fabric of her dress hugged every curve of her body and was nearly the color of the blue streaks in her hair. The top of the dress plunged dangerously low, and I couldn't help but gape at her. My imagination in no way compared to the girl in front of me. Not even close. And the realization that I was actually *married* to this dark-haired beauty made it very hard to breathe.

Nualla came to a stop just in front of me. "So…" she said, looking up at me through her lashes. "Do you like the dress?"

"You—you're *gorgeous*!" I blurted out.

"Aren't you glad I didn't show it to you at the mall?" Nualla asked with a slightly teasing smile.

Honestly even if she *had* shown it to me, I would still be standing here staring at her like a complete idiot. But I had enough sense to go with the easy answer. "Yes."

"I thought so," she said with a broad smile. Then she looked over my shoulder and folded her arms under her chest. "Has my family been playing nice?"

"The cat likes me," I unthinkingly blurted out again as I jerked my thumb toward Denaya the cat. And then I wanted to kick myself because I sounded like an idiot.

Nualla smiled. "Well *that's* good to know, she's hated all the others."

WHO NEEDS SELF-CONTROL?

Saturday, January 21st

PATRICK

W E STOOD IN FRONT OF the backdrop, a picturesque painting of the Golden Gate Bridge rising out of nighttime fog. Jokingly I leaned in to whisper in Nualla's ear. "So will they show up in the picture?"

"Nope," she replied with a smirk.

"*Really*, why?" I asked, looking at her.

"Give us *some* credit Patrick, we thought of that a long time ago," she answered, rolling her eyes.

"So is it that I can't see them in the picture, or is it the camera?"

"The camera," Nualla answered, looking back at the photographer.

"Interesting."

"Okay kids, smile," the photographer said before blinding us with a flash.

When my eyes had stopped seeing bright circles, Nualla and I shuffled out of the way so the next couple could get their photo taken. I looked at Nualla and finally noticed something although I had been staring at her all night. "You're not wearing your necklace." She was wearing a necklace, but not the familiar Daenarian pendant or wedding ring. This necklace looked like a strand of captured stars, delicate and dangling just above her dress.

"Yeah it didn't really go with the dress," she stated, then stopped and turned to me. "*Oh*! I hope you don't mind that I'm not wearing my ring, it's just—"

"Don't worry about it," I said with a reassuring smile. "It's just I don't think I have ever seen you without that pendant."

"You've seen me without pretty much everything else," she said with a crooked smile.

"But if I can't remember, does it really count?" I asked jokingly.

"Next time, I'll make sure you remember," she said as she pressed up close against me.

I was knocked momentarily senseless by the images in my head.

"Did I break you?" she asked teasingly.

"Maybe just a little."

With a smile, she took my hand. "Come on, let's dance."

We swayed back and forth in the dark room, pressed up close to each other. My heart was racing; this felt *way* too close to last Friday, and I quickly looked away from Nualla's eyes and caught sight of Nikki and Shawn. They were dancing together, but not quite as close as they had been at the club. "So what's up with those two?" I asked, gesturing with my head.

Nualla followed my gaze. "Oh Nikki and Shawn?"

"Yeah."

"They're either going to stay best friends forever, or one day one of them is going to make a move. The three of us have been friends since we were in diapers. Shawn's dad is my dad's best friend."

"Ah," I said, still watching them.

"He's also on the Grand Council."

I looked back at Nualla. "The people we have to talk to tomorrow?"

"Yep."

"Fun times," I said with an uneasy smile.

I looked back out at the other dancers, still avoiding her eyes. They were hard enough to withstand in the daylight, but here in a dark warm room, they were just a little too much for me to safely resist.

"Why are you acting guarded all of a sudden?"

Though I knew it was going to be a bad idea, I looked at her anyways. "Because being with you gets me in a lot of trouble."

Her brow furrowed. "What do you mean?"

"You um…make me do and say things I normally wouldn't," I admitted nervously.

"You make it sound like I'm corrupting you or something," she said with a sly smile as she pressed closer to me.

I stared at her with unfocused eyes as I lost the fight with my self-control. "Oh please, *please* corrupt me," I practically purred.

She looked at me briefly before bursting into laughter.

I swallowed hard, a blush spreading across my cheeks. "See what I *mean*, you turn my brain to mush."

"Geez, if I knew I could get that kind of reaction I might have done it more," she said, still laughing.

"You like teasing me, don't you?"

"Do you mind?" she asked with a playful smile.

No, please keep doing whatever you like to me. I'm yours completely, totally, forever. "No I…"

"Kinda like it?"

"Yeah…" I answered breathlessly.

Nualla slid her hands from my shoulders to behind

my neck and pulled me in for a kiss. I had been carefully controlling myself all night, but somehow the minute her lips touched mine that control always went out the window. I pulled her closer, pressing her body as tightly against mine as I possibly could. Her kisses pressed against my lips, hungry, needy, like she couldn't get close enough. I kissed her back meeting her need and surpassing it with my own. Normally I would be analyzing this; worrying about it in my head. But this time I couldn't help myself; my brain felt numb with pleasure much like being drunk. I parted my lips as I felt hers do the same. She flicked her tongue just inside my mouth, and I let out a soft uncontrollable moan. *Oh god* I wanted her, wanted her more badly than I had ever wanted anything.

I finally opened my eyes when I realized the whistles I was hearing were not part of the music. I jerked away from Nualla when it occurred to me *where* we were. That we were not alone, but in fact in the center of a crowded dance floor. Flushed, breathing heavy, and highly embarrassed, I looked around at my classmates.

"Is it hot in here? It's really hot in here, let's get some air," I said unsteadily as I pulled Nualla from the dance floor.

I finally stopped running when we were in the cool, brightly lit hallway far from the loud music and tempting darkness.

"Patrick, what's wrong?" Nualla asked, looking a little startled.

I took a few deep breaths. "Self-control is apparently one of the attributes I just don't have."

"What?"

I looked at her, still breathing heavy. "Every time I kiss you I start to forget where I am and...I'm afraid any day now I'm going to go a little too far."

"*Oh.*" She looked away and then looked back at me. "Self-control has never been something I had much of either," she admitted conspiratorially as she leaned in. Every time she leaned forward the neckline of her dress dipped lower revealing more of her bare skin, if that was *even* possible. Her necklace glittered in the harsh lights just above her cleavage daring me to come closer.

Oh hell, I was *so* not under control yet. I needed to get something cold to drink and clear my head, or I was going to do something that would probably get me into a lot of trouble.

In a slight panic I turned around and walked straight into Michael. I glared at him and he glared back. "Why don't you watch where you're going?"

"Were you *following* us?" I asked angrily.

"No, I'm waiting for Penelope," he answered, pointing to the bathroom.

I didn't believe him in the slightest until Penelope

actually *did* come out of the restroom eyeing us all suspiciously.

Michael looked us up and down a broad smirk spreading across his smug face. "She's *your* problem now," he said as he turned his back to us and walked away with Penelope.

21

BARELY CONTAINED

Sunday, January 22nd

PATRICK

———————

"WE'RE HERE," ALEX SAID AS we stopped somewhere in the Financial District.

I looked out the window at a building that looked a lot like every other building in the San Francisco Financial District. Pale gray stone, columns, and large glass windows on the first floor. A collection of flags jutted out from above the doors. They looked to be the flags of various countries. I would have thought nothing of it, but the longer I looked at them the more they seemed to change to flags I didn't recognize.

"What are you squinting at?" Nualla asked, looking out the window.

"Those flags, they don't look like the flags of countries, so what are they?"

"Oh, they're for the various Kalodaemon regions," Nualla replied without really paying attention. Then she froze and whipped her head around to look at me. "Wait you can *see* them?"

"Sure I can, they're right there," I answered as I gestured at the flags.

"You're not supposed to be able to see them; I mean as something—*unusual*," Nualla said, furrowing her brow.

"Really? That's kinda weird."

"Yes, yes it is." She continued to look at me in concern as the driver came around to open our door.

"Maybe your weirdness is rubbing off on me," I offered jokingly.

"Ha ha, very funny," she said, lightly pushing me.

I held up my Blue Card and looked through it at the building, but it really didn't do anything other than tint the building slightly bluish.

Nualla stepped out of the car and turned to look at me in slight exasperation. "Patrick, what on earth are you *doing*? It's not a magic looking glass, you know."

"Hey, it was worth a try," I replied with a shrug as I stepped out onto the sidewalk.

As I squinted up at the building again the design began to squiggle and change in an iridescent array of colors, like motor oil in a rain puddle, and just for a second I could see a *very* different building. Dull pale gray stone shimmering like a mirage until it became a slate blue-gray, like a rain cloud. The plain rigidly straight metal between the large glass window panes slipping into swirling shapes with a silvery patina to the metal that almost looked bluish-green. Even the stone pillars and walls took on a new form, carved with intricate sweeping edifices; a beautiful and breathtaking blend of ancient Egyptian and Art Nouveau.

"Stop that, you're going to give yourself a brain aneurysm. It's cloaked, so you won't be able to see it for what it is until we get inside," Nualla said as she bumped me. And just like that, in a blink of the eye, it was gone becoming a plain uninspiring gray stone building again.

"Here, take my hand, and close your eyes, it will be easier that way," Nualla advised with a reassuring smile.

As Alex led the way, I took Nualla's hand and closed my eyes, but only part of the way. As we stepped closer and closer to the building, things swirled and spiraled out of kilter. We passed through the main doors into a small glass entry room. People moved out of the way like we were a ambulance flashing its lights and we quickly moved to the front of the line. Someone in a blackish uniform reached out and gently grabbed the Blue Card around my neck and examined it. I looked over at them, and then wished I hadn't. His shape blurred in and out of focus in an even more nauseating way than the room.

I swayed on my feet, and Nualla almost lost hold of me. Just before she did, someone else took my other arm, and we moved through an arch out of the glass room and into the lobby proper. The second I was on the other side of that arch everything settled, but not before I had to drop to my knees.

I stared at the ground and panted until I stopped feeling like I was about to hurl.

"I *told* you to close your eyes, silly," Nualla chided as she crouched down next to me.

Geez, how embarrassing.

"Here Patrick, let me help you up." Alex looked as if he was trying very hard not to laugh as he offered me his hand.

I took hold of his hand and got back to my feet still a little dizzy. "Sorry, next time I'll listen."

When I finally looked around, I almost fell back over again. People in various strange outfits walked past us through the building, as if it was totally commonplace. The clothing was a strange fusion of Japanese and something much harder to place, and it felt an awful lot like I was at an anime convention.

I let my eyes pan around the rest of the room. The

front part of The Embassy was hollow and rose up eight floors in height, ending with a intricate blue and white stained glass ceiling. There seemed to be a reception area off to the right of us which was bustling with activity. Two grand staircases lined either side of the front room, allowing you easy access to the second floor. Hallways lined either side of the upper seven floors with wrought iron railings that allowed you to look down to the ground floor. Three hundred or so feet away the railings turned and ended at a glass-front double elevator. It was all very impressive, but it was thing directly in front of us that made my breath catch. About a hundred feet beyond us stood a large beautiful fountain, a statue of the goddess Daenara at the center, the water spilling over her hands and raining down to the pool below.

The decor of The Embassy was an interesting mix of ancient beauty and futuristic technology. Which was also a perfect description for daemons themselves, really; ancient creatures that were just a tad bit ahead of the times.

"Toto, I don't think we're in Kansas anymore," I said under my breath.

"Excuse me?" Alex asked, raising an eyebrow.

"Oh, nothing," I mumbled nervously as I looked back at the mass of people moving purposefully through The Embassy.

A woman in what looked like a kimono approached

us gracefully. Bowing slightly she spoke to Alex. "Chancellarius Galathea, may I speak with you?"

"Yes Kikyo," Alex said to her with a smile.

She looked over at me briefly before adding, "It's regarding the Kakodemoss, Chancellarius."

"Ah," Alex said, frowning. "Nualla, honey, I have to go take care of this. Go find Natasha in my office; she will guide you through everything," he said, turning toward his daughter.

"Okay Dad, see you later," Nualla said with a tight smile.

"Patrick, try to calm down a bit if you can. I promise no harm will come to you while you are here," Alex said with a reassuring smile.

Did I really look *that* bad? Yeah...I probably did; nervousness and strange swirly motion illusions really didn't mix well. "I'll try," I said with the best attempt at a smile I could manage.

Alex and the lady named Kikyo disappeared into the crowd as they moved off across The Embassy having a hushed conversation. By the way people were treating Nualla's father I was beginning to wonder what *exactly* a *chancellarius* was.

"Ready to go, or do you want to stare a little longer?" Nualla asked as she twined her fingers through mine.

"Can you really blame me?" I replied, looking at her.

"Not really; this place is pretty strange even if you are familiar with the world," she admitted with a crooked smile.

God she was gorgeous when she smiled; breathtaking, like a shooting star flashing across the night sky.

"*So...*" Nualla said, swinging my hand slightly back and forth.

"Yeah, we can go," I said, taking a deep breath and letting it out slowly.

As we moved through The Embassy in the same direction Alex and Kikyo had taken, people stopped to bow to us. Since I assumed it must be some daemon custom, I bowed back. But when they all started to give me really weird looks I stopped.

Nualla and I moved past the bank of elevators into a portion of The Embassy that was no longer hollow. As we walked I glanced around at everything; rooms lined the hallway each with a placard in a language I couldn't read—probably the same language that was on Nualla's pendant; Daemotic.

Eventually the hallway turned, and we reached a second set of elevators. These were far less crowded than the first set, but still a crowd stood in front of them.

As we walked up to join the group waiting for the elevator, a tall male daemon in normal clothes inclined his head toward Nualla. "Arius Nualla." I had absolutely no idea what *arius* could possibly mean, but Nualla was beginning to look nervous, and I got the feeling there was something she hadn't told me yet.

When we entered the elevator with a few others Nualla began to start rubbing her necklace, which I had learned was *never* a good sign. She was keeping something from me, and I really hoped it wasn't anything too bad. I was about to ask her about it when the elevator dinged, and she pulled my hand. "Our stop."

The second we were out of the elevator she let the pendant drop. Maybe she wasn't hiding something after all; maybe she just really hated elevators.

"Hey Nualla—" She looked at me with wide eyes, and I decided to switch questions. "—what's the Kakodemoss?"

Her shoulders relaxed, and she grimaced a bit as she answered. "A sect of Kakodaemon terrorists."

I stopped walking. "Should I be worried?"

"Not really, they don't really attack anymore. They're like the Bogeyman, something your parents tell you about to get you to do your homework and eat your veggies."

We walked down another long hallway before finally stopping in front of a set of large double doors. Nualla pushed the doors open without stopping and walked in. Once in the room, I immediately came to a dead stop. A woman with a long braid was whipping around a katana. She was dressed in a black kimono top and tight pants that disappeared into long black boots. A silver and blue emblem decorated the left side of her chest and black fingerless gloves covered her arms. The emblem was a rich vibrant lapis-blue and had eight silver spokes radiating out in a circle with each ending in what looked like an Egyptian lotus.

"Are you a Jedi knight or something?" I blurted out. It was probably a dumb thing to say, but it was the first thing that came to mind and I couldn't always stop those things from popping out of my mouth.

The woman turned slowly and raised an eyebrow at us. She looked positively deadly and I immediately began to regret what I had just said. The woman sheathed her sword and smoothed her hair out of her face. "You must be Mr. Connolly," she said in an authoritative voice.

"Yeah, actually I am," I answered nervously. "Who are you?"

"Natasha Jordash, Chancellarius Galathea's personal guard and captain of the Kalo Protectorate."

"Personal guard?" I didn't take my eyes off her as I spoke to Nualla out of the side of my mouth. "Just what *exactly* does your dad do?"

Natasha eyed me suspiciously. "He is the *chancellarius* of this region of the Kalodaemon Empire."

When it was clear that I had absolutely no idea what that meant she sighed. "He is the ruler of this region."

"You have *got* to be kidding me," I said in complete disbelief.

Natasha looked slightly confused. "This is no joke."

I turned to Nualla and just gaped at her. "You could have mentioned this."

"Yeah, like *when* exactly? Should I have mentioned it before or after I told you that I wasn't human?"

I had no answer to that, so I turned back to Natasha. "So when you say *region,* you mean the Bay Area, right?"

"Well yes, that is part of Chancellarius Galathea's region."

"*Part*?" I squeaked.

Oh, this is bad; this is really, really *bad.*

"The region also includes all of California and the states of Oregon, Washington, and Hawaii."

I just stared at her, trying not to faint. Finally, I turned to look at Nualla. "Your dad's ruler of the entire West Coast!"

"Yeah...pretty much. I mean, each state has at least one embassy to take care of local affairs, but this is the central embassy for the region," Nualla babled uneasily.

"So you're a—"

"Princess? Yeah, basically. In the event of my dad's death, my sister or I would then become the next *chancellarius*," Nualla stated, avoiding my eyes. The past few minutes started to make more and more sense. The people we had passed had been bowing to her *because* of who she was, and not because it was just some daemon greeting.

"I...I think I need to sit down," I said as I all but fell into a nearby chair. I put my head in my hands, starting to hyperventilate. What exactly had I gotten myself into? This kind of stuff didn't happen in real life; *especially* not to me.

Nualla knelt down next to me. "Patrick, are you okay?"

"Just—give me—a second, okay?" I answered breathlessly. I took a few more breaths, but it didn't help; my heart was beating so fast I thought it was going to beat its way out of my chest.

"I need some air," I announced abruptly. As I stood, I knew instantly that it was the wrong thing to do. My body felt weightless and the ground started to rush up at me.

Sometime later I opened my eyes. I looked over to the side and saw Nualla sitting on the floor next to me, flipping through stuff on her phone. "Hey," I said in a weak voice.

"Patrick!" Nualla dropped her phone and leaned over me. "Are you okay?"

"Yeah, highly embarrassed, but fine," I replied with a wry smile.

"Do you think you can sit up?" she asked with worried eyes. I nodded slowly, and she helped me sit up.

I looked over at her warily, "Is there anything *else* you have neglected to tell me?"

"Um…"

There was a sound behind us, and I turned to see Natasha coming through the door. "Oh good, you're awake."

Oh, 'cause you sound super *concerned.*

Natasha stopped looking at me and turned her attention to Nualla. "Arius Nualla, the Grand Council won't be able to hear your case until after three."

"*Fabulous*," Nualla said sounding less than thrilled. She turned to me with a half-smile. "Want to grab some food?"

This time we had the elevator to ourselves, so I leaned against the elevator wall and asked, "Hey, Nualla?"

"Yeah," she answered without looking over at me; she was playing with her necklace again, looking a little flustered.

"What does *arius* mean?"

"What?" she said as she turned to look in my direction.

"The man at the elevator earlier, he called you 'Arius Nualla.' So what does it mean?"

"*Oh*! Um…basically like princess."

"Figures." I looked over at her with a self-deprecating smile. "As if you needed *another* reason to be completely out of my league."

"Patrick, seriously—lighten up on yourself. I don't know where you got the idea you weren't cute but—" She looked into my eyes and stopped talking.

"But what?"

She looked away shyly before saying the rest. "I'm not the only one with distracting eyes."

"You think I have distracting eyes?" I asked in disbelief.

She moved a little closer and looked up at me through her lashes. "I think *all* of you is distracting, actually."

My heart was racing so fast it all but jumped out of my chest. Being with Nualla was like walking through a minefield of sexual tension; one of these days I just wasn't going to make it through.

I swallowed hard and the elevator door dinged and opened. We entered a crowded upscale cafeteria and headed for the food line. Why were there so many people here on a Sunday? I mean seriously, you would think they would be off doing something like going to a movie, or the park, or hell, even a mall. But no, they were milling around The Embassy like it was a normal weekday or something. Then something occurred to me: maybe for them this *was* a normal Sunday activity.

As we moved through the line I really didn't pay too much attention to what I was grabbing; I was way too distracted to really care. So when she made it to the end of the line I just followed her to one of the empty tables.

After we had taken a few bites of lunch, Nualla looked up at me. "I'm sorry I didn't tell you about my dad on Friday. I guess I thought telling you everything at once might—"

"Fry my brain a little?"

"Yeah," Nualla admitted, slightly chagrined.

"It's okay, I understand why you did it."

"*Really*?" she asked skeptically, and I nodded. Nualla ran her teeth over her bottom lip and seemed to decide something. "Well, in the interest of not giving you an anxiety attack again, I'm giving you permission to ask me anything."

"You know that doesn't really help if I don't know what I should be asking," I said wryly. Nualla looked at me innocently, and I sighed. "Fine, what happens if a human figures out what you are? Aren't you afraid someone will expose you?"

"We're like muses, remember? We can influence people to believe what they saw wasn't real, that it was all in their head. Or that they're crazy," she replied with a slight smile.

"Oh." I guess that ability would solve a lot of problems for them.

"Also, we have people in every profession, political offices, everything."

"What if your charms of persuasion don't work on someone?"

"Um...they usually end up dead," Nualla said casually.

"Wait, *what*?" I said, dropping my fork.

"They don't tend to live very long after it is determined that they can't be reasoned with."

"Oh..." I took an uneasy breath "What about me?"

"You're safe for now. My dad vouched for your character," Nualla answered as if it really wasn't that big of a deal.

"*Really*?" I asked probably looking more than a little shocked.

"Yeah, he doesn't do that often, so don't start running amuck and expose us, okay?"

"Wouldn't dream of it," I said smiling. "I already have everything I could ever want. Why would I ruin it?"

She looked up at me with big eyes. "*Really*?"

"Why do you find it so hard to believe that you're a catch?"

"I could ask you the same thing," Nualla countered, poking me playfully.

"Touché," I replied with a crooked smile. I took a few more bites of my lunch as I looked around. "So why are people dressed so weird here?"

"*Oh*. Um…to enter certain parts of The Embassy you have to be in ceremonial dress."

"Oh really?"

"Yeah, for example, the place we're going," Nualla stated, not meeting my eyes.

"Wait, *what*?" I asked, my fork hallway to my mouth.

"The Grand Council Chamber is one of the places where you have to wear ceremonial dress."

"Oh."

"Don't worry; your outfit is upstairs. I'm sure you'll look awesome in it," Nualla said with a teasing smile.

"You're enjoying this, aren't you?" I asked warily.

"For a fish out of water, you're awfully cute," she answered, grinning at me broadly. I leaned in to kiss her and she put up her hand. "Not here."

"Why, are you embarrassed to be seen kissing a human?" I asked, hurt creeping into my voice.

"*What*? No, of course not!" she said indignantly

before she leaned closer and said in a much quieter voice, "It's just that everytime you kiss me I find myself in *really* compromising positions."

I thought back to Friday when she had all but ripped off my clothes at the club. "Yeah, I guess you're right."

A deep blush spread across her extremely pale cheeks, and she looked up at me through her lashes. "You really don't know the power you have over me, do you?"

"*Me*? *You're* the one who's driving my hormones insane!" I blurted out and then I wanted to kick myself for saying it.

"Oh, you mean when I do things like this?" Nualla let her illusion slip to reveal her true eyes.

I lost all intelligent thought and dropped my fork. It clattered loudly on the table. I could feel heat surging through my body, telling it to do things I knew would be a *very* bad idea.

"Patrick?" Nualla said, waving her hand in front of my face.

I shook my head clear and looked back in her direction. Her eyes had gone back to their human disguise. I glared at her. "Okay, that was *so* not fair."

She put a hand over her mouth to stifle a laugh. "I'm sorry, I won't do that again."

"Oh you can do it again, but just make sure you do it in a place where I can rip off your clothes." Nualla stopped laughing and her face turned as bright red as mine. "Um, that didn't come out right," I mumbled to the table.

"No, I'm pretty sure you meant that, you just didn't mean to say it out loud," she said with a snort before she leaned closer and whispered in my ear. "I know, because that's exactly what *I* was thinking."

I swallowed hard and put my forehead on the cold table. I was losing control of my barely contained urges. I took a deep breath but kept my eyes fixed on the table. "Nualla, if you don't want this lunch to end in scandal could you *please* not say things like that?"

"I'm sorry. I promise I'll be good."

I finally looked up slowly. A few people were staring, but not nearly as much as they would have been if I had given in to the urges that were currently firing through my body. "Thanks," I said in a strained voice.

Nualla looked at her phone then stood. "You done eating? 'Cause we have to go strip down now."

I clenched the table making the dishes clank loudly. If I didn't know better, I might think she was doing this just to see how much I could take. I took another deep breath as I looked up at her. "I was *not* kidding, you know."

"Sorry," Nualla said, covering her smile with her hands.

"You're not sorry in the least."

"I am—just a little."

Is This More than You Bargained for Yet?

Sunday, January 22nd

PATRICK

Normally, I would feel uncomfortable sticking out in a strange place. So I decided to pretend I was cosplaying at a convention and that helped ease my anxiety. But only by a little. As it was, the outfit was pretty damn cool and could only be best described as a men's formal kimono. The kimono top and *hakama* pants were dark blue and long; the sleeveless haori over vest was white on the outside and light blue on the inside.

"So how does it feel?" Nualla asked, looking at me as we walked down the window lined hall on our way to the Grand Council.

"If by that you mean, 'How does it feel walking down the hall in something that looks like it belongs in an anime,' then yeah, I feel fine."

"*Really*? I would have thought—"

"I go to a lot of conventions; this isn't the weirdest thing I have ever been caught wearing in public." I stopped walking and looked at her. Nualla looked far more uncomfortable than I did. "You've never been to a convention have you?"

"No."

"You're really missing out—they're awesome. I'll have to take you to Fanime in a few months."

"Okay," Nualla replied in a cautious voice.

Her outfit looked a little less Japanese than mine but not by much. It had a long deep blue floor-length kimono the color of lapis lazuli. A wide sash in periwinkle blue hung down the front from her waist and was held in place by a silver obi corset-like thing. The top half of her hair was pulled back into a loop and the rest was falling freely down her back like it normally did. Most noticeably though, was the crown; a delicate and beautiful silver lotus sitting atop her head with a pair of bars curving outward from her head on either side like silvery stag horns. And hanging from the ends of each of the bars were strands of blue and silver sparkling beads that danced like a shimmery waterfall with each step she took. Now more than ever, she looked like a princess.

I leaned a little closer to Nualla and asked quietly, "So *why* exactly do we have to go before this Council again?"

"Choosing a human isn't forbidden, just frowned upon. It casts suspicion onto the daemon in question because we don't need human mates; only Kakodaemons do. Because of *who* my dad is, that suspicion has been removed, but I still had to register you."

"Why do I suddenly feel like a stray pet?"

Nualla ignored my remark and continued. "It should be an easy process; just answer their questions truthfully."

"I have no problem answering things truthfully; that's usually what gets me into trouble in the *first* place," I admitted with a sigh. With all that had happened in the last two weeks, I wondered if my life would ever return to normal. Something told me it wouldn't.

I looked up and saw a massive set of doors; ornately carved like something you would see on a temple in a fantasy movie. Inscriptions ran across the door frame in something that I couldn't read; I really hoped they didn't say something like, "Abandon all hope ye who enter here." It was flanked by guards of some kind, dressed similarly to the way Natasha had been. Which meant they were probably also part of the same force—the Kalo something.

Nualla leaned in closer to me and whispered, "Bet you're wondering just what exactly you have gotten yourself into, aren't you?"

"Yeah, a bit," I admitted still looking at the imposing doors.

"Thinking about running?" she asked with a teasing smile.

"Not in the slightest," I answered quietly.

That was only *mostly* the truth.

The guards pushed open the massive doors, and we stepped past them. Huge ornate columns held up a domed ceiling like something you would find in the Pantheon in France. What on earth was something like *this* doing in some obscure building in the middle San Francisco?

I let my eyes trace the room until they fell on the large council table in front of us. I swallowed hard; there were nine people seated there staring down at us. At the very center sat Nualla's father, Alex, though he no longer looked like he had in the car. And I supposed he really wasn't *Alex* at the moment, but the *chancellarius*. He was dressed even more lavishly than the other councilors in a slate-gray silk kimono top with a second deep blue haori top over it and a silver lotus crown resting on his head, though it was without the stag like curving bars that Nualla's had.

The *chancellarius* stood and turned to one of the

other councilors seated next to him. "Due to the nature of these proceedings, I recuse myself as Speaker of the Council. Councilor Tammore will relieve me until these proceedings are complete."

A councilor, apparently named Councilor Tammore, stood and bowed to the *chancellarius*. "I accept," he said to the *chancellarius* before he sat down and turned his focus to us. "Be warned; if you lie before this Council, punishment will be swift and uncompromising."

Good to know.

Councilor Tammore turned his attention to Nualla. "Arius Nualla, did you choose Mr. Galathea as your mate of your own free will?"

"Yes, councilors," Nualla answered in a clear voice.

"Mr. Galathea, did you choose Arius Nualla as your mate of your own free will?"

I didn't have any clue who they were referring to until Nualla nudged me. "They're speaking to *you*, Patrick," she whispered under her breath.

"Oh! Um…yes…councilors." I hoped that was the proper way to address them, since it was what Nualla had said.

Councilor Tammore looked down at a tablet in front of him and read off another question. "Mr. Galathea, were you informed of the existence of our world before you agreed to marry Arius Nualla?"

"No, she didn't tell me till after, councilors."

"Good," he said and read off another question. "Mr. Galathea, do you understand that by marrying Arius Nualla, you have agreed to become a daemon and part of our secret world?"

"Yes I do, councilors."

He nodded and continued. "Mr. Galathea, do you understand that you must become a daemon within a year's time?"

"Um… No, actually no one mentioned that there was a time frame, but I really don't have a problem with it either, councilors."

Councilor Tammore raised an eyebrow but said nothing. He looked back down at the tablet in front of him and continued. "Mr. Galathea, do you understand that although you have married into the Galathea family you have no claim to rule, nor will you ever be allowed to hold office?"

"Yes councilors." That had never even crossed my mind. Honestly, I would have had to be crazy to ever want to be in charge of anyone. I did enough damage just managing my *own* life.

"Since Chancellarius Galathea has already vouched to the quality of your character, the Grand Council has no further questions at this time." He now turned his attention to Nualla again. "Well, Arius Nualla, since you both are legal adults, I see no reason not to approve this marriage. Mr. Galathea must come before this Council within one year's time—as a daemon. Is that understood?"

"Yes councilors," Nualla replied with a bow of her head.

"Do either of you have any questions for the Council?" Councilor Tammore asked, looking at us.

"Um…yeah, why do you keep referring to me as Mr. Galathea?" I asked, honestly confused.

They all just gaped at me, and someone even coughed. Was I missing something?

"No questions. Have a nice day councilors. Come on Patrick, we really must be going," Nualla said quickly as she all but pushed me out of the Grand Council chambers.

After the doors closed behind us, I looked at her. "What?"

She looked at me, covering her smile with her hand. "Patrick, in my world gender plays no role in whose name you take when you get married. You take the name of the person whose rank is higher."

"Wait, then why is Nikki's last name Varris? Her dad couldn't possibly have had higher rank than Skye."

"Because only the heirs have the right to the name Galathea. When Alex became the *chancellarius* Skye relinquished the name Galathea once she got married. So basically the only way Nikki would ever become a

Galathea is if every member of my family died."

"Oh," I said quietly. "So what happens if your sister becomes the next *chancellarius*?"

"You and I become Connolly's."

"That's really confusing," I pointed out as I ran my hand through my hair. "So now I'm a Galathea?"

"At least in my world you are," Nualla answered as she leaned against one of the windows lining the hall.

"But I can't hold office because I'm not an heir?"

"Actually that, *and* because you're human."

"So how high up on the scandalous scale is marrying a human if you're an heir?" I asked playfully as I leaned against the window next to her.

Nualla smiled a mischievous smile at me. "Pretty high up there."

As we walked back down the window-lined hall, I started playing the hearing back in my head and got a sick feeling in my stomach. There was something that hadn't even occurred to me till now. I wasn't a legal adult yet, and I had the distinct feeling that was going to fuck things up somehow.

"Patrick what's wrong?" Nualla asked, looking at me with concerned eyes.

"Huh? Oh um, nothing. Just a lot to take in," I lied.

"Yeah, I don't envy you in the least," she stated

with a grimace.

I turned away from her and looked out the windows that lined the walls. The sun was disappearing behind the tall buildings and the night was coming alive with light like a million fireflies set free. But the clouds and fog moving swiftly toward us were threatening to cloak it all in a veil of gray.

"Hey, do we have to wait until your dad is finished here, or can we leave soon?" I asked as I looked back at her.

"Why, what's up."

"'Cause it's after five on a Sunday, and I still haven't done the homework that's due tomorrow." It wasn't a lie since I really *did* have a pile of neglected homework collecting dust on my desk at home.

"Oh, yeah let's go, I have a ton sitting at home too," Nualla said, frowning. "But seriously, what kind of person gives out homework on a weekend?"

"People who don't have anything better to do?" I offered with a shrug.

"Or people who think *we* don't."

IN OVER MY HEAD

Sunday, January 22nd

PATRICK

THE TRUTH SAT THERE ON the screen, burning a hole into me.

I was fucked. I mean royally, totally, fucked. My marriage to Nualla wasn't and had never been legal. And worse of all, no one in Nualla's family had figured that out yet. Then something even worse occurred to me; I was a dead man. I was pretty sure that if the Grand Council found out I wasn't legally married to Nualla they would have me executed. This was bad; this was *way* beyond bad.

And so as a normal, rational teenager, I did the

first thing you do when you realize you've just royally screwed up. You curse really loudly, and then call your best friend.

Connor picked up on the second ring sounding distracted. "What's up, Patrick?"

"I'm fucked," I answered, leaning back in my chair and swinging it back and forth.

"How so?" That got his full attention. When I fucked up, I usually did it spectacularly.

"I majorly fucked up and—"

"Patrick, what on *earth* is the matter?" my mom asked from behind me.

I turned around to see her standing in the doorway of my room. I had been listening to music and had not even heard her come home. *Crap*, I needed a lie quick; I sorted through possible reasons why someone would yell expletives. "Nothing Mom, I just whacked my knee on my desk."

"Oh, okay."

I couldn't really have the conversation with Connor I had intended on having, with my mother within earshot. I needed to get out of here. So I did the next thing you normally do when you're a teenager who has just screwed up. I lied through my teeth. "Hey Mom, I'm gonna run to the convenience store, okay?"

"Alright, but don't be out too late, it's a Sunday," she said in a typical motherly fashion, which coming from her, was a tad weird.

"No problem," I said with the most reassuring voice I could muster. As she walked away, I whispered into the phone. "Meet me at the store in ten, 'kay?"

"But it's Sunday. The store is closed on Sundays," Connor pointed out in a confused voice.

"Yes I *know* Connor, but does your *mother* know that?" I asked through gritted teeth.

"Well probably not, but—"

"It's not even eight, Connor. Your mom won't care if you go one block down the damn street," I spat into the phone as quietly as I could.

"Good point. See you in ten," Connor said quickly before hanging up the phone.

I took a deep breath as I descended the stairs. My mother had gone back to watching TV and probably wouldn't notice how wound up I looked. Still, I tried to exit my house as casually as possible.

A little over ten minutes later I walked up to find Connor leaning up against the wall in front of the closed store. He pushed off from the wall as I arrived. "So what *exactly* did you fuck up this time? Last time I checked your life was looking peachy."

"You'd think that, wouldn't you," I said sourly, leaning my head against the cold wall of the building behind me. "I just realized something tonight I should have realized a fucking week ago."

"What?" Connor asked curiously.

"That my marriage to Nualla wasn't legal," I admitted with complete despair.

Connor looked confused. "Wait, how was it not—*oh*, right 'cause your birthday's not till next month."

"Exactly," I said, closing my eyes. I couldn't believe I had been this stupid.

"So just tell her. If she didn't really want to marry you, she's off the hook. And if she *did* want to marry you, then you can just marry her again in a month. Girls love weddings."

"I can't."

"Patrick—"

"No, I mean I *can't* tell her," I said, looking at Connor.

"Why?" he asked, looking confused.

"It's...complicated," I answered, avoiding his eyes.

"What is it, her family or something?"

"No, they know."

"Your family?" Connor asked, arching his eyebrows.

"No, there's no way in *hell* I would tell them about this. But no, that's not it."

"Then *what*?" Connor asked, sounding exasperated.

I opened my mouth to answer then realized I couldn't tell him the truth. If I did, they would have to kill him. As it was, they would probably have to kill *me*. I was going to have to lie. And I really sucked at lying, *especially* to people who actually knew me as well as Connor did.

I slammed my head back against the building and stared up at the cloudy sky. It would probably start raining any minute, and I had left my umbrella at home.

Great, just *great*.

I settled for a believable lie, if I strayed too far from the truth he would spot it. "She's everything I've ever wanted and now that I have her I...I don't want to lose her." I looked back over at him. "I'm afraid that if she knew the truth she wouldn't have a reason to be with me anymore." It wasn't a total lie, but I hoped it would fool Connor.

"Dude, why do you think she wouldn't want to be with you?" Connor asked, looking genuinely concerned for my mental state.

I pushed off the wall and practically yelled, "Have you *seen* her? She's gorgeous and smart and...and perfect. And there's no way a guy like me gets *this* lucky twice." I leaned back against the wall again, dejected. Even *I* was starting to believe my own lie.

But it hadn't really been a hard sell; why would she want to be with someone like me in the first place when she could have anyone?

I slid down the wall to sit on the ground. Seconds passed in silence and sure enough, big fat drops started to fall from the sky.

Finally Connor spoke. "Patrick—man you are *way* too hard on yourself."

He had believed the lie, hook, line, and sinker. But I guess it was easy to lie when it was mostly based on the truth. Aside from the supernatural stuff and my impending death what I had said had been the truth, really.

"You know you have to tell her, right?" Connor said, his hands in his pockets.

"I know. I'm just not ready yet," I answered as I looked away from him back down the street. "I just want to stay in this dream as long as I can." Even if it *was* a hopeless dream.

After a few minutes of silence, Connor looked at his phone. "Look Patrick, I have to get back and finish that paper for Miss Desborne's class. Are you going to be okay?"

"Yeah, I'll be fine," I lied. It was starting to rain in earnest now.

"You sure?" he asked mostly unconvinced.

"Yeah, I'll see you tomorrow, 'kay?"

"'Kay," he said reluctantly, and then he turned

and ran back down Mission Street.

Eventually I got up and started my walk back home, but not before I was soaked to the bone. I felt worse than I had before, if that was possible.

HIDING LIES WITH A SMILE

Wednesday, February 8th

NUALLA

O VER THE NEXT TWO WEEKS we fell into an easy routine as if it had always been that way. We spent all the time we could together at school and all eight of us had lunch together mostly without incident—*mostly*. Jenny still looked like she wished I'd just fall off the face of the Earth, and Beatrice still hadn't gotten the message that Shawn was *so* taken already.

Michael, true to his word, was now completely ignoring me as if there had never been anything between us in the first place—like someone had flipped a switch in his brain. Maybe Penelope really *had* been his One, and he had been too arrogant to see it until I was taken out of the equation. Whatever the reason, it was nice to not have to worry about him suddenly pushing me up against lockers, but it was also very weird.

And Patrick was…Patrick; warm and kind and funny and self-deprecating at times. But I could also tell that something was really bothering him. I could see it there in his eyes; he was hiding something, or more likely not telling me something. I could see it eating at him, but I didn't know how to pry the truth out of him. And I didn't know his friends well enough to get it out of them either—if he had even told them in the first place.

Originally, I had decided I needed to be patient and wait for him to just tell me. However, "patience" was not something I did well, so instead I devised a plan. I was going to take Patrick somewhere he would think was beyond awesome; somewhere humans really didn't get to go. But to pull it off I needed Travis' help, which meant a trip to The Embassy.

Sixth period had let out, and we had all converged in the main floor entry hall.

"Hey Patrick, I need to go somewhere after school so…" I said in a voice I hoped sounded nonchalant.

"No problem, it's a Wednesday anyways," he said with a huge grin, or at least as big as they got lately.

"Wednesday?" I asked a little confused, and then I remembered. "Oh right, you and Connor's thing." Some boys hung out and played video games or watched football. These two hung out at a Japanese mall and watched anime on Saturday nights. "Okay, well, see you tomorrow," I said before I gave him a kiss.

I started to walk away, but he called out, taking a few steps toward me. "Hey wait, what about the pictures? They came in today."

"Can you just pick them up and give me mine tomorrow?" I asked over my shoulder.

"Sure," he answered with a small dazed smile, the kind he usually had after I kissed him.

And then I left him there and went off to work on my devious plan. Okay, it really wasn't *that* devious. No, wait, it totally was.

PATRICK

After Nualla left, Connor and I headed over to the student office to pick up our Winter Ball photos. The crowd was huge since they had just arrived, but it didn't take us too long to get to the front.

"Name?" the student behind the counter asked

without looking up at me.

"Patrick Connolly."

The guy flipped though the photo packs until he pulled out one. He looked at it briefly before his eyebrows shot up. He looked at me. "Oh you're *that* dude."

"What dude?" I asked, getting a little concerned.

"The one who's with Nualla Galathea."

"Yeah, I'm her boyfriend," I said a little defensively.

"Lucky you," he said as he handed me the photos.

You have no idea how lucky I feel dude, trust *me.*

I moved away from the line and looked down at the photos. I stopped dead in the middle of the hall and just stared at the us in the pictures. For some reason, that fact that I was with Nualla hadn't felt as real as it did now. Like it was a dream I was going to someday wake up from, but the pictures made it fact. I looked okay in the pictures, but Nualla looked like a silver screen goddess. These were *so* going up on iTribe when I got home.

"I still can't believe you actually ended up with her," Connor said, looking over my shoulder. "I know you've been infatuated with her since Freshman year, but I never thought in a million years that you would *actually* end up with her."

I rolled my eyes at him. "Thanks Connor, your confidence in me is overwhelming," I said sarcastically.

"Hey man, you can't tell me you honestly thought it would ever happen."

I looked back at the packet of photos. "No, you're right, I didn't."

"So you want to see mine and Sara's?"

I turned to look at him. "You went with Sara?"

"Yeah, what planet were *you* on? We even saw you guys there." He looked upset for a second before his expression turned to a mischievous grin. "Oh, I know what planet you were on; Planet Nualla," he said in a teasing voice.

"I am not on Planet Nualla," I said flatly.

"No dude, you *totally* are," he said, laughing.

"Am *not*."

"So how is it on Planet Nualla?"

"Don't make me hurt you Connor," I threatened, glaring at him.

"Dude *please*, you would have to catch me first."

"You don't think I can?" I said, folding my arms.

"Are you going to even try?" Connor asked, raising an eyebrow and preparing to run.

I looked at him for a while before I gave up. "Naw, let's just go to the mall."

"Will we be going there in your spaceship, Explorer Connolly?"

"Seriously Connor, if you don't shut up, I'm going to punch you."

25

IF YOU'RE READING THIS

Thursday, February 9th

PATRICK

M Y SECOND TRIP TO THE Embassy went much better than the first; I actually listened to Nualla this time and kept my eyes firmly shut until we were all the way in. I still had absolutely no idea why we were here, but I knew it couldn't be bad. For starters, Nualla had a huge grin on her face instead of well, kicking the crap out of me for keeping things from her.

We rode the elevator up to a different floor than before and walked down another long hallway. I was seriously beginning to wonder just how many hallways they could possibly fit into this building, when we stopped in front of a door with an impressive biometric hand reader panel that looked straight out of some futuristic tech movie. Though it seemed a bit moot since the door was wide open. By the ease with which Nualla walked in, it made me think she had been here a lot; unlike the agitation she had shown on the way to the Grand Council chambers.

The room was one of those stark white spotlessly clean tech rooms except for the massive amounts of electronic parts covering nearly all the available surfaces. There was also a large array of flat screen monitors displaying wire frame models of God only knew what. It felt as if we had just walked onto the set of some Sci-fi movie.

A tall blond guy in a white lab coat stood in front of a strange but impressive set of equipment. He was built similarly to Shawn, but not quite so broad-chested and looked to be in his early twenties. The guy's hair was a tangle of wavy pale blond that swept into his eyes and curled out away from his face at his jawline making him look more like a movie star than a tech geek. I almost would have believed that he was an actor in one of those medical dramas if it wasn't for the fact that he was wearing a navy blue shirt with the statement Don't Blink, a pair of faded jeans, and bright red All Star high tops.

His head snapped up as we approached and a wide

smile spread across his broad square-jawed face. "Hey, Nualla."

"Hey, Travis," Nualla greeted him in a friendly voice.

Since everyone else here seemed to only call Nualla "Arius" or "Arius Nualla," I guessed the two of them had to have some history together.

Nualla slid onto the edge of the table next to him. "*So*...do you have it ready for me?"

The guy, Travis, smiled wider as he leaned forward, his dark black-blue eyes shining. "Did you ever have doubts it would be?"

"*Really*?" Nualla asked, clapping her hands together in excitement.

He nodded.

"You're the best, Travis," Nualla squealed as she threw her arms around him.

He let her hug him a second longer before taking a step back and saying with a bow, "Why thank you, my dear."

From their body language I was beginning to seriously wonder just what *exactly* that history was.

Travis turned around to lean against the table next to Nualla. "*So*...is this your human?" he asked, gesturing to me with his head as he nudged her with his shoulder.

Nualla leapt up from the table and ran over to grab my arm. Pulling me forward she said with pride,

"Yep! This is Patrick."

"Hi I'm Patrick, Patrick Connolly—or I guess it's Galathea now, isn't it," I said with a slight smug smile to Travis.

An emotion I couldn't quite place crossed his face before disappearing. "I'm Travis Centrina and *this* is my lab," Travis stated proudly, standing a little taller as he gestured to the array of equipment.

"Travis designed a lot of the cool things you see in The Embassy. He's a genius, really," Nualla stated as she slid back onto the edge of the table, kicking her feet back and forth through the air.

"Oh really, like what?" I asked, looking around the room; it was a little hard to tell what anything here actually *did*.

"Well like the door, the lobby illusion field, even that Blue Card you're wearing around your neck," Travis answered, ticking things off on his fingers.

"You mean that *thing* that nearly made me puke?" I asked without really thinking.

"You didn't shut your eyes, did you?" Travis said with a self-satisfied smirk as he slid back onto the edge of the table next to Nualla.

"No he didn't," Nualla said with a small playful smile.

"I did *this* time," I mumbled to myself. I didn't like them being so close; didn't like the feeling it caused to raise up inside me. It was bitter like acid

239

rolling through my veins.

After a few moments of slightly awkward silence Nualla asked Travis, "So where is it?"

"Oh, it's right over here," Travis said, leaping to his feet and trotting over to a work table on the other side of the room. He picked something up and turned around with a huge grin. "Tada," he said, holding out something that looked straight out of a steampunk movie. The glasses were sturdy brass with odd blue lenses that seemed to be glowing faintly.

"Are we going to a steampunk convention or something?" I asked. I seriously doubted it, but it was the only thing that came to mind.

"No, but it *will* help you see where we're going," Nualla answered as she slipped back off the table and moved closer to Travis to get a better look at the glasses.

"Where *are* we going?" I asked, looking back at her.

"It's a surprise," Nualla answered with an even bigger grin.

"Okay Patrick, put these on—" Travis said, handing me the glasses. "—and read that chart over there."

I looked at where he was pointing; the letters were something weird like the writing on Nualla's necklace, Daemotic, I think it was. "Sure," I said, taking the glasses and sliding them on. "No problem," I said in a slightly sarcastic voice.

When I put the glasses on, I didn't expect to see much of a difference; but I was utterly wrong. The words that had been no better than a child's made up writing before, were now in plain English. I slipped the glasses back off and the letters went back to *gobbledygook*. Slowly I slid them back on again, not taking my eyes off the chart. The minute the lenses crossed my eyes the letters began to dance into different forms. This time I actually kept them on long enough to read the message.

If you can read this, you will probably be dead in a few minutes.

"I can read it!" I said excitedly and turned quickly to face Nualla. But when I caught sight of her and Travis I fell back into the table behind me. Whatever field they naturally created to conceal their true form was gone. "I can see you!" I said in shock.

"Well *yeah*," Travis said, looking smug.

"No I mean I can *really* see you."

Nualla looked at him, folding her arms. "*Travis*."

"It was all or nothing honey. *You* asked me to make something that would allow him to see it. I can't separate out our illusions, you know. It's kind of a package deal."

"You could have *told* him first though," Nualla said, poking Travis in the chest. "I'd prefer him not to die of a heart attack, you know."

She continued glaring at him until he rolled his almond-shaped eyes and put his hands on her shoulders. "Look, I'm *sorry*, okay Nulala?" It must have been a pet name, but Nualla only looked more annoyed instead of less when he said it. Nualla glared at him even more and surprisingly instead of looking concerned a crooked smile spread across his lips.

"So how do I look?" I blurted out abruptly.

Nualla turned her attention back to me, and a wide grin spread across her face. "You look really cool, actually." She moved closer and pushed the hair away from my eyes. I just stared at her dumbly; now that I could see her for what she was I was powerless against her eyes. "Patrick?"

"Hmm…" I answered in a daze.

Nualla put her hand over her eyes and I snapped back to reality. "*Frak*, I forgot about the eyes."

She turned to look at Travis, but he just shook his head. "Sorry Nualla, I can't do anything about that."

She looked back over at me. "Sorry Patrick. I'll pick up some sunglasses or something on the way."

"You're taking me somewhere only meant for daemons, aren't you?" I asked excitedly.

"Yep," she answered with a huge grin. The second I looked at her eyes I was lost again.

"Hey Nualla, your dad said he had something he wanted to talk to you about before you left," Travis said, a hint of a smile on his lips. He probably found the eye thing to be unbelievably hilarious.

"Oh really, what about?" Nualla asked as she looked back over at him.

"I don't know, he didn't say."

"Okay then, I'll be right back," Nualla said as she walked to the door.

"Oh Nualla," Travis said raising his voice a bit. "Your dad doesn't *actually* know about the glasses. So do me a huge favor and don't mention them to him, okay?"

"Will I get in trouble for having them?" Nualla asked, crossing her arms under her chest.

"Possibly," Travis admitted sheepishly.

She sighed heavily before walking out the door. "Thanks, Travis."

"Anytime, darling," he said with a slightly mischievous smile.

Nualla reappeared a second later and pointed at Travis. "Promise you won't break him while I'm gone."

"Wouldn't dream of it," Travis promised holding up his hands palms out.

"*Sure* you wouldn't," Nualla said, rolling her eyes before disappearing out of view again.

We sat in silence for a few minutes before Travis leaned against the table next to me and said, "You know if you hurt her I'll kill you, right?"

243

"Yeah," I said without looking at him. Silence hung in the air only broken briefly by the occasional noises of others outside or the beeping of machines. "You know if you try to take her from me, I will kill you, right?" I said in a serious voice, finally looking over at him.

"Yep. Wait, *what*?!" he sputtered as he leapt away from the table to glare at me.

"I may be blind half the time, but I'm not stupid. There is, or *was* something between you two once."

Travis slumped into a chair and crossed his arms, looking away from me. "That ship has already sailed."

"You *sure* about that?" I asked, arching an eyebrow.

"Hey Patrick, I'm not sure if anyone has told you or not, but we pair off for life," he said before finally meeting my gaze. "And she already married *you*. It's a done deal. Unless you give me cause to get rid of you, there is really nothing I can do about it."

"You wanted to marry her didn't you?"

"Yep," Travis answered, leaning back to look at a poster plastered on the ceiling above him.

"So why didn't you ask her?"

He let the chair snap back up and glared at me. "Because *I*, being a sensible person, was waiting until after she at least got *out* of high school."

"Oh, right," I said sheepishly.

Silence returned, and I let my eyes wander around

the room again. When I looked back at Travis he had his head resting on the back of his chair as he swung it back and forth. I recognized the gesture instantly; it was exactly what I did when I was thinking about things. Or more often than not, beating myself up for things that I had done, or *hadn't*. Apparently, I wasn't the *only* one who had been in love with her and had done nothing about it.

I hated to admit it, but it could have just as easily have been him who had ended up with her instead of me. And if I didn't find a way to fix my current predicament, it would be him who got to be with her in the end. It was stupid really; why should a little piece of paper matter so much? As far as I could remember, the words I had spoken in the chapel had been truthful. The fact that I wasn't an adult didn't make those words—that oath—any less real or true.

Suddenly I had to know what Travis thought. I turned to him and asked rather abruptly, "Is it the paper or the oath to you?"

His head snapped up in my direction. "Huh?" He looked more than confused, and I realized I had basically started a conversation that was halfway through only in my head.

"Marriage; is it signified by an oath or by a legal document?"

Travis slumped back into the same position. "Oh um—the oath," he answered then a moment later his face turned toward me again. "Why do you ask?"

"No reason," I answered, looking away. I didn't know what else to say, and Travis sure as hell didn't look like he wanted to talk; so we sat there saying nothing.

After what seemed like hours, Nualla all but skipped back into the room. She stopped dead when the tension hit her and asked in a cautious voice, "Everything okay boys?"

"Peachy," Travis replied, looking over at her.

"*Right...* " she said in a less-than-convinced voice. "So Travis, anything I should know before Patrick and I head out?"

"You shouldn't let him wear the glasses too long; don't want him frying his brain," Travis said, though he didn't sound concerned in the least.

"Anything else I should know?"

"He'll probably be really nauseous when he takes them off; so make sure he's sitting down so he doesn't hurt himself."

"Anything *else*?" Nualla asked, starting to sound a little bit annoyed.

Travis bit his lip and stood up quickly from the chair. "Yeah, *this*," he replied and in one swift motion he had his hand behind her head, pulling her face to his lips.

Nualla let him kiss her for one dazed moment before she pushed him away. "What the *hell*—?!"

I rushed him but Nualla threw her arm out, blocking my way. I screeched to a halt just before she clotheslined me.

"Care to explain *that*?" Nualla asked, raising an eyebrow at Travis.

Travis looked her dead in the eye, opened his mouth then clamped it shut again. His hands balled into fists so tightly his nails had to be digging into his palms. "I would *love* to Nualla, but it wouldn't do either of us a damn bit of good," he stated through gritted teeth. And then he walked out the door, shoving his hands in the pockets of his lab coat. "Oh and Patrick, don't lose those or we'll have to kill you," he called over his shoulder.

"*Seriously*?" I asked, looking at Nualla.

"No Patrick, he's just messing with you. If anyone would get in trouble, it would be *him* for making the damned things in the first place," Nualla answered, putting her head in her hand. "Thanks Travis!" she yelled toward the door, though if she was thanking him for the kiss or the glasses, I didn't know. Finally, Nualla looked up at me. "Did I *miss* something?"

"Nope, I have no idea what that was about," I answered, looking at anything but her.

"You're a really bad liar, you know."

REFLECTIONS

Thursday, February 9th

PATRICK

"YOUR BIG SURPRISE WAS TAKING me to an alley?" I asked as I stared at a dingy unremarkable space between two old buildings.

"Put the glasses on, Patrick," Nualla said as she rolled her eyes.

I pulled them out of my bag, took a deep breath and slid them on. The alley was no longer an alley. The space now expanded outward to reveal a large galleria. Three floors of shops lined either side and walkways crossed the space at intervals. At the far end there was a set of escalators and a massive clock.

I looked back at her and tried not to get sucked into the unbelievable beauty of her eyes. I had a hard enough time resisting them when she had her human illusion up, but in her true form it was nearly impossible.

"What is this place?"

"The Kalo Galleria, basically a Kalodaemon mall," Nualla answered with a pleased smile.

I looked back inside. *"Really?"*

Nualla took my hand and led me forward through the Kalo Galleria. I looked up in awe at the domed glass ceiling, which revealed an amazing view of the tall surrounding buildings. This place was incredible, but the fact that it was just hiding in the middle of the city was even more amazing. It made you wonder what else was hidden here in the city in the places that humans wouldn't even think to look—or be able to see in the first place.

The daemons in the galleria didn't even look twice at me as we passed which I found a bit odd. Was it normal for humans to just go wandering through here? I seriously doubted it. Then I caught sight of my reflection in the glass of a shop window and stopped. Two glowing horns flickered just above my ears.

"What on *earth*?" I leaned in closer to the window to get a better look at the horns.

"Oh right, you wouldn't have been able to see that before," Nualla said, leaning toward me. "Your Blue

Card makes a hologram around you so no one gets ideas about killing you."

"*Really*? That's awesome!" I said, excitedly looking back at my reflection. "So this is more or less what I would look like with horns?" I had to admit, like this I looked pretty damn awesome.

"Well not at first; it takes about six months for the horns to grow in completely."

"They *grow*?" I asked in disbelief as I turned back toward her.

"*Of course*, they're not magic, you know. They're as real as anything; like hair or fingernails."

"Yeah really *awesome* fingernails," I said with a huge grin.

We continued walking through the galleria passing the strangest collection of items. Formal clothing like the ones I had seen in The Embassy. Books written in what was probably Daemotic. Electronics that did God knows what. The more I was with Nualla, the more amazing her world seemed, but I couldn't ignore the things in my normal human world like school, graduation, my future. I knew about our immediate future together, but what would our lives be like come the end of the school year; the fall; five years from now? I was almost afraid to ask, but like an idiot, I always did.

"So what school are you going to in the fall?" I

asked as casually as I could.

"I'm not."

"*What*?" There was no way she hadn't gotten into an ivy-league school; she was smart as hell and more than wealthy.

"I'm an heiress apparent. I have to attend special classes at The Embassy to prepare to take over the rule of the region in the event my dad dies."

"Oh." I guess that made perfect sense.

"Why, what are you doing?" Nualla asked with a curious smile.

"Art school."

She stopped, looking frightened for a second. "Where?"

"Here in the city, at the Academy of Art. It's one of the best art schools in the country."

"Oh, well that's good. I don't think I could do a long-distance relationship," she said with a teasing smile.

I knew what she probably meant, but I still asked, "What do you mean?"

Nualla pressed close to me, looking up at me through her lashes. "I don't think I could stand to be that far away from you."

I swallowed hard. "I don't think I could, either."

Nualla took my hand and we continued walking through the galleria. I stopped to look at something in one of the windows and saw the reflection of someone behind us. Not directly behind us, more off in the distance trying to look inconspicuous. I had seen her before somewhere, I just knew it.

I moved away from the window, and we continued walking. A few shops later I looked back at the reflection, and sure enough, the strange black female daemon was there again. "Nualla, not to sound paranoid, but I think we're being followed," I whispered quietly as I leaned closer to her.

"Oh, you're not paranoid," Nualla said in an unbelievably calm voice with just a hint of annoyance.

"I'm *not*?" I asked, a little confused.

"We *are* being followed," she stated with a huff as she turned around and made a beeline for the daemon.

The stranger was a daemon—no mistake about that—but she wasn't pale like Nualla. I had mistakenly thought they would all look similar to Nualla, Shawn and Nikki; otherworldly pale with abnormally blue eyes. This daemon however was African-American; extremely pale but still dark-skinned with a pulled back fro. Her eyes were blue, not pale blue like Nualla's, but a blue so dark it was nearly black like Travis'. The woman was wearing a black jacket with a blue and silver emblem on the left side and tight black pants tucked into long black boots. "Patrick this is Tylia, one of the Kalo Protectorate officers," Nualla said calmly as she gestured to the daemon woman with the fro.

"The *what*?" I asked, completely lost.

"It's our job to protect The Embassy and ensure the safety of the Chancellarius and his family," Tylia answered proudly but without the annoying air of superiority that had been present in Natasha's voice.

"Oh the Kalo Protectorate, that's that thing Natasha's in charge of, right? So she's like your boss?" I asked Tylia. Now that I actually looked at the emblem on her jacket, I realized it was the same as the one that had been on Natasha's kimono style top.

Tylia couldn't contain her scowl as she answered, "Unfortunately."

"Yeah, I don't really like her either; there's just something—" I shuddered, there was something off about Natasha, but I couldn't quite put my finger on it. It was almost like I knew the answer, but it was lost somewhere in my brain; which was absurd because I really had only just met her. Then something occurred to me. "You're what was on the other side of the wall in the parking garage."

Tylia eyed me with amused smile. "You're damn smart, kid." Then her look soured into something deadly. "Though, if you call me a 'what' again, I will throttle you."

"Sorry," I said, taking a step back.

"Your job's to *protect* us, not scare the crap out of him, Tylia," Nualla pointed out as she glared at her.

NUALLA

TYLIA SUSPICIOUSLY EYED THE GLASSES Patrick was wearing. "Do I even *want* to know what he's wearing?"

"No, no you don't," I answered quickly.

"Travis?" she asked, raising an eyebrow.

I nodded.

"That boy is going to get himself into a whole mess of trouble someday," Tylia said as she sighed and folded her arms.

Yeah, like tomorrow, when I go yell at him for kissing me.

"Well, you two stay out of trouble," Tylia said as she eyed Patrick meaningfully again. "And I'll try to follow you a little less obviously."

Oh, because that is so going to help me forget that you're there.

Tylia stalked away as Patrick turned to me. "Do they normally follow you, or is it just because of me?"

Truthfully they were probably following me *more* now because of him, but I wasn't about to tell him that. "No, it's not you; they always follow me."

As I looked at Patrick, I caught my reflection in the shop window behind him. The reflection moved, and I thought nothing of it until I realized *I* hadn't moved. I looked closer in shock at the me in the window, and she did the same for a brief second before she bolted, disappearing further into the crowded shop. I turned to Patrick frantically. "Did you just see that?"

"See what?"

I turned back around, but the other me was gone; only my reflection was left. "I thought I saw someone just like me."

"Well yeah, there is your reflection," Patrick said with a slight smile.

"No, not me, someone *like* me."

He looked confused and asked uneasily, "Like what, a *doppelgänger*?"

It sounded really stupid when he said it out loud. "It was probably nothing," I said as I looked back at the window.

PLAYING WITH FIRE

Monday, February 13th

PATRICK

"S O WHAT ARE WE DOING FOR your birthday? I know we normally do something *on* your birthday, but since you have a girlfriend now, we really can't do that anymore," Connor said as we walked casually through the Japantown Mall. Connor knew full well Nualla wasn't my "girlfriend," but I had told him if he ever let anyone know otherwise I would kick his ass.

"Nothing," I answered, looking away from him at a nearby window display as we passed by it. "I don't want to do anything; I can't let Nualla find out

I wasn't eighteen."

Connor stopped dead, causing a few people to nearly run into him. "Wait, you haven't *told* her yet?"

"I don't know *how* to tell her, Connor. It's not like I can just walk up to her and say, 'Hi Nualla, I know you thought we were married and all, but since I was a minor at the time I'm pretty sure we're not.'"

"Dude, you're playing against loaded dice," Connor said uneasily.

"Tell me something I *don't* know," I groaned, leaning up against a nearby wall.

"How could you not think of something to say? You're like the smartest person I know."

"Connor, smart and intelligent are two *vastly* different things."

"Apparently so," Connor said with a smirk.

We walked into the extremely crowded candy shop near the bakery and began to carefully pick our way around. I grabbed an armful of things I thought Nualla might like; a cute little stuffed gray cat, a box of chocolate with coffee centers, even some candied violets. It was the day before Valentine's Day and in typical guy fashion, I had waited till the last minute to get her something. I had been so wrapped up in the whole married-not-married thing I had lost track of the days.

"Dude, no amount of presents is gonna stop that girl from being pissed when she finds out," Connor pointed out with a snort.

"Yeah I know, but it can't hurt either, can it?" I asked with a shrug. "And besides, I haven't really ever given her anything; well, aside from the ring—I think," I admitted with a grimace.

"Wait, how can you *not* know—" Connor asked, looking at me dubiously. "Oh come on, you weren't seriously *that* drunk were you?"

"Connor, that's not the *only* thing I can't remember. Actually, the truth is I really can't remember most of it."

Connor looked at me confused. "Then how do you—"

"There were—pictures," I said with the straightest face I could.

"*Really*? Am I ever going to get to see said pictures?" Connor asked, arching his eyebrows.

"Not a chance in hell, Connor," I replied as I stepped up to the counter.

After I was done, I stepped out of the crowded candy shop to wait for Connor who was buying something. Wait, *what*? "Connor, who are you buying a present for?" I asked, looking at the box of chocolate in his hands.

"Sara," he answered with a huge grin.

I just looked at him a little shocked. "*Seriously*?" I knew he had gone with her to the dance, but they hadn't given any indication that they were an "item."

"Hey, if you weren't *always* pining after Galathea you would know that," Connor said, rolling his eyes.

"Hey it's not 'pining' if I'm married to her now," I said indignantly.

But you're not really; not legally, anyways.

Connor laughed and turned around, but when he saw my face his smile dropped. "I'm fucked, aren't I?" I said to my shoes.

"Yeah, probably," Connor sighed. "But I won't be the one who outs you."

"Thanks, Connor," I said. I finally looked up, but I didn't smile.

We went back to walking through the mall. As we walked past the kimono shop I was reminded of The Embassy—and Travis. I wondered if what I was doing counted as "hurting her" in his eyes. I sighed in anguish. "And then there's Travis."

Connor stopped walking and turned. "Who's *Travis*?"

"Someone waiting in the wings to take Nualla away when I fuck up," I answered, kicking a discarded food wrapper on the ground. "He works—with Nualla's dad and she's known him like forever. He's twenty-something, smart as hell, and cooler than I will *ever* be." I looked out at the passersby as I leaned back to sit on a nearby railing. "And he kissed her like right in front of me," I said, not meeting Connor's eyes.

Connor just stared at me for a moment before saying, "Dude, you are *so* screwed."

"Thanks Connor; you are *so* reassuring," I said, rolling my eyes.

"So, since you will most likely *not* have a girlfriend by Friday, do you want to do something for your birthday then?" he asked before bounding a safe distance away.

I looked up with a slight smile before running after him. "If you *live* that long, Connor."

I knew my plan wasn't very well thought out, but denial is a very powerful illusion.

28

Pᴌᴇᴀsᴇ Tᴇʟʟ Mᴇ Iᴛ's Nᴏᴛ Tᴏᴏ Lᴀᴛᴇ

Tuesday, February 14th

PATRICK

I HAD SPENT THE MORNING HOPING to *hell* my friends would be so distracted by the fact that it was Valentine's Day that they would forget it was also my birthday. When nothing had happened by lunch, I began to think maybe they really *had* forgotten.

Nualla and I got to the lunch table before everyone else which was highly unusual. Even Beatrice wasn't there yet—which had *never* happened ~~could think of. It was a very bad sign th~~ want to bolt from the atrium. But ~~of~~ would alert Nualla that somethin~~g~~

was the *last* thing I wanted to do.

Nualla had put the other Valentine's Day presents in her locker, but had been toting the little stuffed cat around with her all day, a giant grin on her face. The fact that no one had ever given her a Valentine's Day present was practically a crime. So currently, I was more than golden in her eyes. However, I had a sinking feeling that something was going to ruin it at any second now.

I was about to suggest we leave the table to try and avoid the inevitable, but the second I was about to stand, a small cake with a candle was shoved in front of my face. "Happy Birthday, Patrick!" came the cheery voices of my friends, who had just royally screwed me without knowing it—in three words or less.

The girls placed the cake down and sat around me. Even Shawn and Nikki were in on the fun. Connor looked like he was going to throw up; which was about how *I* felt at that moment.

"Why didn't you tell us it was your birthday, Patrick? We almost didn't have time to get you a present," Shawn said as he pushed something in front of me. Apparently Nikki and Shawn hadn't done the math, because they were completely oblivious.

Everyone was smiling good-naturedly, and then all their faces fell. I was almost afraid to look at Nualla.

"Patrick, can I speak with you—*now*?" Nualla said as she grabbed my arm painfully and pulled me to my feet.

She dragged me through the hall and out into the back parking lot before stopping. But a quick glance around revealed a bunch of students hanging out around the cars. She huffed angrily and without releasing me marched across the street to the park. When we reached the fountain she finally stopped and whipped around to face me. "Patrick, how old are you?" she asked, crossing her arms under her chest.

I swallowed hard. "Eighteen." I knew it wasn't what she meant, but it was the truth—kinda.

"How old were you when we got married in Vegas?"

I just looked at her for a while and sighed, delaying this wouldn't stop the inevitable. I braced myself and sealed my fate in one word. "Seventeen."

"When *exactly* were you planning to tell me that we were never legally married?" Nualla asked through gritted teeth; her arms had moved to form clenched fists at her sides.

"I was hoping I would never have to." It was a dumb answer, and I knew it, but it was the only one I had.

"Why the hell not?!" Nualla asked, thro~ arms out in anger.

I looked down at my black and

Converse shoes. "I thought—I thought if you knew we weren't *really* married, you would—leave."

"You thought I was only with you because we accidentally got married?"

It sounded even dumber when she said it. So dumb in fact, that I couldn't even answer her—but I did. "Yes…"

She didn't say anything; didn't even make a sound for so long I just couldn't take it anymore, and I had to look up. Tears streamed down her beautiful face. I reached out to her, I had to comfort her; her tears were breaking my heart. "Nualla I—"

"Don't touch me!" she shouted and took a step back putting herself more out of my reach. I stopped but didn't drop my hand. "It didn't cross your mind, did it, that I might actually be with you because I… because I *loved* you?"

"You *love* me?" I probably sounded more shocked than I intended, but before this moment she had never *actually* said it, and this sudden declaration had caught me off guard.

In one swift movement Nualla ripped off the necklace holding the ring from her neck and threw it at me. It bounced off my chest and into the fountain with a *plunk*.

"I did," she said with a shaking voice before she turned on her heel and ran away. And I just stood there frozen as I watched her leap aboard a passing cable car, and then she was gone.

I stood there in stunned silence for a long moment, watching the place where she had been, wondering how things had gone so very wrong. But I knew the answer; I had fucked up.

Minutes, hours, days later, the crash of thunder ripped me out of my stupor. Big fat drops started to pour down as I looked up into the sky. "You really do hate me don't you?" I asked the heavens.

It rumbled back.

"Yeah, I hate *me*, too," I said as I sat on the edge of the fountain.

Then it occurred to me that it was my self-loathing that had gotten me into this mess in the *first* place— well that *and* stupidity. If I had just believed that someone would want to be with me I wouldn't be sitting here—alone. Then it hit me, I didn't *have* to be alone; that there might actually still be a chance.

I turned around and dove into the fountain; swatting coins around until I found the ring. With it clenched in my fist, broken chain swinging, I ran back across the street to the school. I wasn't going to give up on my happiness—on her—that easily.

I ignored everyone as I ran down the hall and into the atrium. I didn't stop running until I reached our lunch table again.

Connor nearly choked on his lunch when he saw me. "Patrick, is everything—"

Royally fucked? Yeah it is.

"Why are you soaking wet," Beatrice asked, more than a little confused.

I ignored her question and turned to Nikki and Shawn. "Where would Nualla go if she was upset?"

"She just ran off, in the middle of school?!" Jenny asked shrilly, sounding horrified; I ignored her too.

"Was she on foot, or did she take her car?" Shawn asked, all earlier amusement gone.

"Foot, kinda—she hopped a cable car."

"The mall," Shawn said without a moment's thought.

"No, Union Square, on the flat square platforms; if she was headed that direction she would stop there," Nikki said, looking concerned. They still hadn't figured out what was going on, but they knew *something* was up.

"Thanks!" I said quickly and started to leave, then I remembered Nualla might want her bag and turned back.

"Patrick!" Jenny's shrill voice was getting harder to ignore.

I took a few steps back to the table and leaned down snatch up Nualla's bag, shoving the stuffed cat into it.

"She figured it out, didn't she?" Connor asked as the others looked at him in confusion.

I looked down at the necklace in my hand, then

back up at him. "Yeah, she did."

"What are you going to do?" he asked, only looking at me.

"I'm going to fix it."

"Good luck man," Connor said with a half-hearted
smile.

I turned and started to run out of the atrium. "Wait
Patrick, where are you going?" Jenny shouted after
me.

"Tell Miss Desborne I threw up, so I went home,
okay!" I called back over my shoulder as I ran through
the doors.

Nualla was right where Nikki had said she would
be. She was just sitting there in the rain looking at
nothing with her arms wrapped around her black leg-
ging covered legs, and her chin resting on her knees.
I approached slowly, trying to think of what to say.
Normally she would have turned at my approach by
now; so whether she was trying her best to ignore me,
or she was lost in thought, I didn't know.

"Nualla?" I said in a cautious voice. Her head
whipped around, and she scowled at me. She stood
and started to walk away, so I reached out to grip her
wrist gently. "Nualla, *wait!*"

She shook me off and continued walking. "Leave

me alone, Patrick."

I was going to lose her forever; she was walking away, and it was all going to end. And then it finally dawned on me what I should have said before. The answer was so simple, but I had been too blind and stupid to see it till now.

I dropped to my knees on the wet sidewalk. "Nualla, marry me!"

She stopped dead and turned around. "What did you say?"

I held out the ring as the chain slipped to the ground, splashing in a puddle. "Nualla Galathea, will you marry me?" I asked in a clear loud voice. She didn't say anything or turn away, so I took that as a sign to continue. "I know I fucked up, and I'm sorry. And even if you never give me a second chance, I promise to love you for the rest of my life!"

Her expression didn't change, but her eyes darted around. And that's when I noticed out of the corner of my eye that we were being watched by dozens of curious onlookers; being that it was lunchtime in downtown San Francisco. They said nothing, just silently waited for her answer, just like me. It was like a beautiful movie moment—that is, until a service truck cut a sharp corner and drenched me in a tidal wave of dirty gutter water. But that was SF for you—a splash of dirty gutter water in the face.

As I wiped the dirty water from my eyes with my

sleeve, I heard laughter. I looked up to see it was *her* laughter; she was laughing.

Nualla walked over slowly and crouched down in front of me. "Oh Patrick, what am I going to do with you?"

"You could marry me, but only if you really want to—*this* time."

"I wanted to marry you *last* time too, you know," she admitted as she pushed my wet hair out my face.

"So is that a yes?" I asked, looking up into her eyes.

"Yeah, that's a yes," she answered with a smile.

Most people would have slid the ring on her finger right then and there or found somewhere less public to finish their conversation. I, on the other hand, just grabbed her and kissed her for all I was worth. People cheered for a while, but eventually the crowd around us lost interest. But still, we just sat there kissing in the rain; ignoring the world.

Beautiful Disaster

Tuesday, February 14th

PATRICK

I STOOD AND OFFERED NUALLA A hand up, but as she reached out and took my hand, I nearly dropped her. The rain was falling pretty hard by now, bouncing off her hair and shoulders, but I could see it bouncing off something else—her horns.

"Patrick?" Nualla asked, sounding a little concerned.

"Huh?" I answered, refocusing my eyes on hers.

"Is everything okay?"

"Everything's fine; just a little bit light-headed I guess," I lied, dropping her hand.

She didn't look like she completely believed me, but she let it go. "We should get back," she said, looking in the direction of the school.

"Naw, we already ditched class. Besides, I want to take you somewhere," I said with a small smile.

"Then we should go back and get my car at least," Nualla said, taking a step back the way we had come.

"It's not that far," I countered, taking her hand and starting to lead her down the street. "We could just take the bus." Nualla stopped walking abruptly, and I looked back at her. "What's wrong?"

"The—*bus*?" Nualla asked with a nervous smile.

"What's wrong with the bus?" I asked, arching an eyebrow.

"I've never ridden a bus," Nualla admitted in a small voice.

"Are you *serious*?" I looked at her in disbelief. "You *are* serious!" I couldn't help but laugh.

"Don't laugh at me!" she said as she playfully whacked me with her bag.

"You've seriously never ridden a bus? How long have you lived in San Francisco?"

"My whole life."

"And you're telling me you've never ridden one, not even once?" She shook her head. "Oh come on, you *have* to at least try it once," I said as I pulled her forward again.

"But I'm not supposed—" and then she stopped

and looked at me for a minute. "You know what, I will take you up on that offer."

As we walked down the street to the 30/45 MUNI bus stop, I didn't tell her that I had started to see around her illusion; that I didn't need to squint quite as much to see what I wasn't supposed to see. It was like, because I *knew* it was there, the illusion was having less and less effect on me. I probably should have told her, but I had other things on my mind; like how hilarious her expression was when the bus rolled up with people packed in like sardines.

The bus screeched to a stop and the doors popped open. Nualla looked back at me with a slightly terrified expression as I tried not to laugh.

"You kids getting on?" the bus driver asked in a less-than-thrilled voice.

"On," I answered as I lightly pushed Nualla forward up the stairs. I tagged my Clipper Card twice and moved Nualla as far back into the bus as I could.

"Is it normally this crowded?" Nualla whispered into my ear.

"Naw, just right here. Most of the people will get off at Market Street," I replied quietly.

We hit a bump and Nualla nearly toppled over. I reached out an arm and caught her. It wouldn't do to have her get banged up her first time on public transit; she would never ride it again.

I held onto the pole and cradled her close to me; a protective hand around her waist. Nualla looked up at my scowl and burst into laughter; I couldn't help but join her. It felt good to laugh; for all this stress to finally be over. I hadn't realized how much it had been weighing on me until it was no longer there.

We passed the shop windows with their Valentine's Day displays and she looked out at them like a child on an amusement park ride. Something about it all whizzing by just made it exciting—exhilarating.

We were nearing Market, so I tightened my hold on her waist. "Now don't freak out, but when the bus makes this next S-curve it tends to lean—*a lot*. It looks like it will fall over but it never does, okay?"

"Okay," she said as she smiled up at me but then her face fell; panic seizing hold of her.

"What? It's not really that—" But I never got a chance to finish my sentence.

There was a concussion as something slammed into the side of the bus—something heavy. Glass rained over us like snow, blowing Nualla's hair back into a swirling torrent of black. And then the bus started to fall over. Things and people and broken glass flew through the air as if there was no longer gravity to hold it down. I strained to hold onto Nualla with every ounce of my strength as the world tilted crazily, but my grip on her slipped. I could only watch helplessly as she fell; fell through a sea of shattered glass. The bus slammed to the ground violently, and I finally lost purchase on the pole.

This isn't supposed to happen. Not today; not ever, was the last thing that went through my mind before I hit the side of the bus.

NUALLA

I BECAME AWARE OF SOUND FIRST; screaming, crunching, sirens. And then I opened my eyes.

Rain?

I turned my head to the side and saw objects and people and glass strewn about as if a bomb had gone off. It didn't make sense. Where was I? Where had I been before the bomb went off? And then I realized I was inside. *The bus!* We had been on a bus.

Patrick!

I sat up and looked around frantically. About five feet away Patrick lay on the ground. No *wait*, it was the side of the bus and he was slumped against one of the seats.

I inched closer to him. "Patrick!" My heart pounded in my chest violently; I couldn't tell if he was breathing.

Oh gods, please be okay.

After a few nerve-racking moments, his eyes fluttered open, and I let out the breath I didn't know I had been holding. Patrick looked around confused until his eyes fixed on me. *"Nualla?"*

I reached out a hand to touch him, and then I saw it—blood. I looked down at my hands, they were covered in blood—*my* blood.

Oh gods! Not blood, not my blood.

Patrick reached out a hand to touch me. His arms were covered in blood, and it looked like his right arm was broken.

"No! Don't touch me!" I shouted as I backed away from him in panic. "Even the smallest amount of blood could affect you."

Patrick looked confused for a moment, but then nodded.

After a few seconds, his eyes flickered shut, and I called out, "Patrick!"

His eyes shot open again, and he looked at me, but his eyes were vacant—unfocused.

I inched as close as I dared. "Patrick, don't close your eyes; you probably have a concussion." Patrick said nothing, but nodded slowly. Thankfully, his eyes stayed open, but they had a glassy faraway-look that was unsettling.

I didn't take my eyes off him as I pulled my bag around. I was really glad in that moment, that I had had my shoulder bag slung across my chest. I fished around until I found my cell; it was cracked but still turned on. I dialed the Daemon Emergency Number, and someone picked up on the second ring.

"Kalo Emergency Response, please state your emergency," a female voice said less than enthused.

"This is Nualla Galathea. There's been an accident; I'm bleeding."

I heard something on the other side of the line clatter to the floor. "We have traced your location, an EMT will be sent to your location immediately!" The voice on the other line now seemed much more alert.

I put the phone back in my bag. The Embassy was not too far away, so they would be here soon. I looked over at Patrick, and he stared back at me blankly, breathing more visibly now. I wanted desperately to hold him in my arms. But I was afraid—so very afraid. Afraid of my blood; afraid of what it could do. I wanted so badly to close my eyes, but I forced myself to keep looking at Patrick. It was utter chaos around us, but nothing mattered as long as he was still awake, still breathing.

Moments passed by slowly until I heard someone behind me. "Nualla Galathea?"

"Huh?" I looked over in the direction of the voice.

A Kalo EMT bent down next to me. "Are you Nualla Galathea?"

"Yes," I answered in a weak voice. Without another word, he lifted me up and began to carry me out of the bus. "Wait!"

"Arius Nualla, we have to get you to the emergency room immediately."

"No, not without him, not without Patrick," I said, frantically trying to look at Patrick.

The EMT stopped and looked around before he lowered his face and spoke quietly into my ear. "Arius, I don't see anyone else of *our* kind here."

"He's not—not yet, but soon." I was fighting hard to stay conscious, but it was getting harder. I looked down and saw Patrick at the EMT's feet. "*Him.*"

"Arius, we can't take him with us." His voice sounded so unbelievably sorry.

"No you don't understand, he already knows, he's already been there."

"But—"

I gripped his arm with the last of my strength. "*Please.*" He looked at my hand, my left hand and saw it there; the ring. And then he finally understood.

"Frank!" the EMT called out over his shoulder.

"What?" replied another Kalo EMT coming through the wreckage.

"We're taking this one *here* with us too," the EMT carrying me stated, gesturing to Patrick with his head.

Frank looked at Patrick in confusion. "But he's—"

"Just *take* him."

"Whatever you say, Zeke." Frank reached down to grab hold of Patrick.

"Thank you," I whispered into Zeke's shirt. I didn't know if he heard me or not because the darkness clouded out the rest of my thought and left me drifting in its dark embrace.

30

Doing Right by You

Tuesday, February 14th

PATRICK

I OPENED MY EYES AND THEN almost wished I hadn't. Everything hurt. There wasn't a part of me, it seemed, that *didn't* hurt.

I turned my head to look around. Where was I? Then I saw Nualla lying nearby. Her eyes closed, her arms covered in bandages.

"Nualla." I reached my hand out to touch her and stopped, something white was covering it. I looked down at the white form covering my right forearm.

A cast?

Then I remembered the bus crash; the screaming,

the broken glass, Nualla falling away from me. In a panic I tried to sit up, but it felt like I had been hit by a truck. Then I remembered we basically *were*.

I reached out my arm again as far as I could reach and was just able to brush her shoulder with the tips of my fingers. "Nualla! Nualla *please* wake up."

Her eyes fluttered open slowly, and she looked out at me. "*Patrick?*"

"You're not supposed to close your eyes remember? You may have a concussion."

She opened her mouth to say something, but she didn't get her chance. I heard a commotion outside, and a second later Nualla's parents burst into the room. They both had every right to be frantic, but this was the first time I had seen Alex angry.

"Nualla!" Loraly rushed to her daughter's side blocking my view of her.

"*Mom?*" Nualla said in a startled voice.

"Honey, are you okay?" Loraly asked in a barely contained voice.

"I'm fine Mom, really. I'm just a little banged up," Nualla answered, sounding a little exasperated.

Loraly finally noticed me, her expression looking even more horrified. "Oh gods, Patrick!"

Just how bad do I look?

"Nualla what were you *thinking* riding public transit!" Alex shouted. The three of us looked over at him; he didn't look concerned, he looked furious.

"Dad I—"

"Your blood could have mixed with theirs," he said angrily, gesturing to the outside. And then, with a sickening reality, I finally understood. They didn't ride in town cars and taxis because they were too proud to take the bus. They did it to protect the humans.

"It was my fault," I admitted in the clearest voice I could manage. It really *was* my fault, and I couldn't stand the thought of Nualla being blamed for this.

Alex turned. "*What?*"

"I—I made her take the bus. Nualla said she had never been—I just wanted to show her—" I took a deep breath; an extremely painful breath. "I'm sorry I—I didn't think. Was anyone—" I was about to say *infected*, but that sounded way too much like an insult—even in my current groggy state. So I said the next word that came to mind. "—changed?"

Alex's expression softened, and he put his head in his hand. "Thankfully no, but a lot of them didn't make it." He looked back up at me. "You are really lucky to be alive, Patrick."

"What about Nualla?" I asked, looking over her bandaged form.

Alex looked over at his daughter. "She'll be completely healed in a few days, but will have to continue to wear *those* for much longer to keep up appearances."

"You're *joking*, right?" I asked in disbelief. That was just too unbelievable to be true.

"Our bodies heal incredibly fast; the pain I have heard is less as well," Alex answered, looking back in my direction.

"Oh, I am *so* looking forward to that," I said, closing my eyes in pain.

"Patrick, you shouldn't close your eyes—" Nualla said anxiously.

"I know, I know; I might have a concussion," I said, forcing my eyes open again.

Loraly moved closer to me and asked in a motherly voice "Patrick, should I—should I call your parents, they might be worried?"

I shook my head. Hell, I would probably have this cast off by the time I had a decent conversation with them. "No, they're out of town on business."

She looked really concerned now. "So there will be no one at your home?"

"There never is. It's usually just me there, alone for weeks." I was in too much pain at the moment to not be self-deprecatingly honest.

"Then it's settled, you're coming home with us tonight," Loraly said in a voice that allowed no arguments. I don't know if it was sad or comforting that someone *else's* parents cared more about my well being than my own did.

The door opened again, and an older-looking

guy walked in wearing a medical coat and carrying a tablet. He was short with dark short hair. He looked up from his tablet at us. "Ah, you're both awake, excellent." Then he seemed to notice Alex and Loraly. "Chancellarius Galathea, Cellarius Loraly."

After recovering from the shock of finding the *chancellarius* and his wife in his medical room, Dr. LaCosta had given us a final medical examination. However, I got the distinct impression he was only doing it for show.

"Well, everything seems to be in order," Dr. LaCosta said, looking at the tablet in his hands. He pointed a stylus at Nualla without looking up. "Arius Nualla, stay out of public bodies of water for a few days to prevent accidental contamination." Nualla nodded and then Dr. LaCosta looked over at me. "*That*—" he said pointing at my cast, "should stay on for—" he looked at his tablet again, "—about six weeks. Then you can come back and I will remove it."

I looked at him dubiously, somehow I got the feeling he wasn't used to treating human patients.

"Thank you, doctor," Alex said as they all started moving toward the door.

I swung my legs slowly around to stand, but just

that small movement was so painful, I nearly passed out from the pain. *"Wait!"* I called out and they all turned to look at me. "Um…I know you guys are super strong and stuff, but I'm kinda still a mere mortal. So could I please, *please* get some stronger painkillers?"

Nualla and her parents turned to look at Dr. LaCosta, who looked at his tablet. "Oh yes, pain-killers, humans typically need a lot of those, don't they. I'll get right on that, you just sit tight," he stated before turning on his heel and quickly walking out the door. He wasn't exactly inspiring confidence with his lack of knowledge about humans.

"Patrick, are you really in a lot of pain?" Nualla asked, looking like she was about to burst into tears at any moment.

"Don't worry about it, I'll be fine. I just currently feel as though I lost a fight with a Buick," I answered with a smile that came out more like a grimace.

"Oh my *gods!*" We all turned to see Nikki and Shawn standing in the doorway with Skye right behind them dressed in one of her sultry clubbing dresses. Valentine's Day had to be one of her biggest nights at the club and yet, even she was here.

"Are you *okay*?" Skye asked, putting a hand on my arm.

I couldn't help wincing as I answered, "Never been better."

Shawn strolled closer, his hands in his pockets as

usual. "Dude, you have had one shitty birthday haven't you?" he said with a snort.

"Well, it wasn't *all* bad," I answered as I smiled over at Nualla. Her ring was no longer caked in blood and sparkled in the harsh lights. I looked back up and caught sight of Alex's expression. He was glaring at me; he looked pissed. And that's when I realized that he had just done the math. But being the gentleman he was he hadn't said anything about it.

Yet.

"Wait today's your *birthday*? On Valentine's Day?" Skye asked, looking at me.

"Yeah," I replied with a grimace.

"Oh that's so cute!"

"Yeah, cute like a brick to the head," I mumbled. Alex was apparently done waiting, because he opened his mouth to speak. I quickly jumped in. "Um…I have something I need to tell you all." *There is really no good way to say this and you will probably all hate me now.* "I've been deceiving you all, and I'm sorry." From the looks they were all giving me, my choice of words were apparently the worst possible thing that could have come out of my mouth. "Uh…"

Nualla sighed and looked at her family. "We're not *actually* married."

"*What*?!" came the collective response.

"Patrick was only seventeen when we got married in Vegas; so yeah, not *exactly* legal."

285

"Oooh, so *that's* why you were so mad earlier," Nikki said, turning to look at Nualla.

"Hell, I'd be mad too," Shawn said, folding his arms. He now looked about as pissed as Alex had.

I looked quickly over at Alex, he was still staring daggers at me, arms folded across his chest. He looked more than pissed now. And that's when something occurred to me. I jumped up and waved my hand frantically. "Wait, wait, I *am* going to marry her, I *promise*! See." I held up Nualla's hand showing off the ring. "So *please* don't kill me, okay?"

"Why didn't you say something *before*, I almost just decked you myself," Shawn said as he punched me good-naturedly in the arm.

I dropped to the floor like a rock. "Ow!"

"Shawn, would you please refrain from injuring my fiancé any more than he *already* is," Nualla said, crouching down next to me.

"Oh right, bus accident—sorry," Shawn said as he leaned down too. He gripped me as gently as he could and pulled me back up onto my feet.

"So you see we, could get married right now, no problem," Nualla stated, looking at her dad.

"No," I said, wincing.

"Wait, what is it *now*?" Nualla snapped, rounding on me like a viper.

She looked about to throttle me so I put up my hands. "Wait, just hear me out okay!" I took another painful breath and continued. "Since I have the option now, I want to do this right."

"Patrick..." Nualla looked as tame as a kitten again. I hoped to *hell* these were just some of those daemon hormones they had been telling me about and that I wouldn't get myself killed out of stupidity sometime soon.

I took her hand and smiled through the pain. "You deserve a big beautiful wedding in a—*wait*, what exactly do you guys do for weddings anyways?"

At that they all bust up laughing, even Alex.

"We have a ceremony similar to the ones you humans have, but in one of our temples. For example, the one here at The Embassy," Alex answered with a slight smile. Apparently, he no longer felt like killing me.

I turned back to Nualla. "And besides, you said the daemonification process takes a week or so, right?"

"Yeah..."

"So wouldn't people notice if I was gone for a while?"

"Good point," Nualla replied, running her teeth over her bottom lip. "So...Spring Break?"

"How about we wait until after graduation?" I asked, pulling her a little closer.

"*What*?" Nualla asked, glaring at me slightly.

"That's actually a really smart idea, Patrick," Alex said approvingly as he moved closer.

"Maybe that way, I could even invite my friends," I said with a hopeful smile.

"Patrick…" Nualla said in a sad voice. Something in her expression told me there was something she wasn't telling me. "That's not really a—"

"We could make that work," Alex stated.

The two of us turned to face him. "*Really*?"

"We could set up an illusion system that would only show them what we wanted them to see. You could invite whoever you wanted, really."

"That would be awesome!" I said with a smile, even though it was painful.

"I'll get Travis on it right away," Alex said as he pulled a phone from his pocket.

Okay, less awesome. "Um…about that?" I said, attempting to run my hand through my hair, but my cast made that nearly impossible now.

"Hmm?" Alex said, arching an eyebrow.

"I'm pretty sure he hates me."

"When did you meet Travis?" Alex asked, more than a little confused.

"Um—"

"It's a *really* long story, let's just go," Nualla interrupted as she nearly pushed her family out the door.

"Aww, come on, the long ones are the best!" Nikki whined in playful protest.

"I'm not telling you, so move it!" Nualla said, actually pushing Nikki this time.

"I want to hear the story," Skye said with a grin.

"No one's hearing the story!" Nualla shouted back into the room.

The rest of her family started following them out as I stood there. "If anyone cares, I'm still waiting for painkillers over here," I called out, leaning toward the door.

As we walked through the halls of The Embassy on our way out, I let the others get ahead of us. The halls were still busy even at this hour. "So your dad gets upset about you taking buses but not planes?" I asked, looking at Nualla.

She shrugged. "If the plane's going down no one's living anyways."

"Yeah, you're probably right." We walked a few more feet in silence. "You live a very protected life, don't you?"

"Yeah," she answered, still looking ahead.

"It must be very lonely."

There was a deep sadness behind her eyes when she looked over at me. She laced her fingers through mine and looked up into my eyes. "It was."

I just couldn't take it anymore; I stopped walking and pulled her close. The drugs had worked their magic, and I could no longer feel the pain. Hell, I couldn't feel *anything*. But even though I couldn't feel her against me, just knowing she was still there was enough.

Someone observing Nualla from the outside might think she was prissy or self-absorbed, but they would never know the truth. Never understand the lie she was forced to protect; never know how hard it was to get close to people when most of what they knew about you is a lie. But to still be able to smile and hold your head high; that—that takes a special kind of courage.

It's Not Wise to Tease the Animals

Tuesday, February 14th

PATRICK

WE HAD ARRIVED AT NUALLA'S house pretty late at night and had headed straight up to her room. I didn't really pay much attention to what was around me or how many flights of stairs we had climbed because by then everything had started to take on a dreamlike quality; the way things looked right before you closed your eyes.

Somewhere along the way I must have taken off my jeans, but all I was really conscious of was falling into her bed and wiggling under the covers. And I tried to fall asleep—really I did—but I just couldn't because something had been eating at me the whole ride to her house.

"Nualla?" I asked quietly, watching the way the streetlights cast the shadows of the trees across her bedroom wall.

"Hmm?" Nualla said into the pillow.

"Before, you said that one drop could affect me. What did you mean by that?"

At this Nualla sat up and looked at me. She continued to look at me for a very long time before she sighed and looked down at the bed. "The thing we carry in our blood is a retrovirus like any other. It's passed through blood, even the smallest drop."

"Well, if I'm going to become one of you anyway, why would it matter?"

"The first drop of blood starts the daemonification process, but it can only replicate so fast from such a small amount." She looked nervously up into my eyes. "Basically, you would die before the transformation was complete."

"Oh..." I sat there in silence for a while. "Well then how—?"

"With *lots* of blood. The most common way is through a replacement blood transfusion. Basically, they replace your blood with ours."

"Wait, then how could sleeping with you—?"

"We have a more concentrated amount in our—" She stopped abruptly and flushed bright red. "Well obviously the blood transfusion method is a more modern way."

"*Oh*!" I said, turning red as well.

Her voice when she spoke next was just above a whisper. "I've heard it's not *always* successful; that some people die before the transformation can complete. Basically, they die of something similar to an allergic reaction or blood poisoning."

"Sounds…real pleasant," I said with a grimace.

Nualla took my hand. "I'm really sorry, Patrick—I wish I could take this all back and you could just go on leading a normal life." Tears streamed down her face; I hadn't even heard her start to cry.

I pulled her close with my good arm and rested my chin on her head. "Nualla, whereas I didn't know *exactly* what I was getting into when I agreed to hitch a ride to Vegas with you; I haven't regretted it one bit."

She pulled away to look at me. "You really mean that?"

"Nualla, I have been in love with you since the moment I first saw you. Do you really think, after wishing to be with you for that long, I would *regret* it?"

"No, but you didn't know what I was—what I *am*."

"Well yeah sure I didn't. But I wouldn't give you up for anything; not even something as small as that."

"It's not small," she replied with a pout.

"It is to me," I countered with a reassuring smile.

I had gone back to sleep, well I had *tried* to anyways. But sleep had evaded me, so I just stared with unfocused eyes at the shadows on the wall again. I hadn't eaten anything since breakfast, but I was in no mood to eat now. I mean, it wasn't like I could feel the hunger—or *anything* for that matter.

"Patrick?" Nualla asked in a quiet voice.

"Hmm?" I said into the darkness.

"Are you...are you still in a lot of pain?" she asked in a cautious voice.

"To be perfectly honest, I haven't been able to feel a thing since we left the clinic. I'm seriously thinking of calling the health board on that guy, he knows next to nothing about humans."

Her response was a pillow to the back of my head.

"*Hey*, that doesn't mean it's okay to hit me you know," I said, turning around to face her. And that's when I realized for the first time that we were in her bed—*alone*.

"This seems strangely familiar," I said in an unsteady voice. I may have been drugged out of my mind, but I wasn't dead.

With a coy smile, Nualla pressed herself closer.

"I'm pretty sure we had a lot less clothes before."

Danger Will Robinson, Danger!

Oh, *hell*. I knew where this was about to go and there was no escaping it.

"So you can't feel *this* at all?" Nualla asked, gliding her knee across my bare thigh. I could barely feel it through all the drugs, but it was still enough to send my heart racing.

"If I answer no, does that mean you're going to stop? Because if it does; then yes, I can *totally* feel that," I said in a rush.

She smiled that unbelievably sexy smile that I knew was only for me and leaned closer, lips brushing against mine. Then she began to kiss me harder, needy and hungry, and I matched it with my own need. Her soft skin against mine sent surges through my body demanding it press closer against her. I had been numb to my senses for hours now, and this sudden flood of sensation was nearly overwhelming.

Her breath was heavy and hot on my skin, awaking every part of me that had had delusions of sleep. It was as if the fact that I couldn't feel anything made me focus more on what I *could* feel, and that was intoxicating.

I released all my anxiety and just let the heat roll over me, giving myself over to the moment. I wasn't going to make it out this time; wasn't going to be able to stop. I had been fighting an uphill battle against my urges for weeks now, and this time I knew I was probably going to lose.

And then she spoke as if she sensed I had finally lost control. "*Hmm…*we have to stop," she said, pulling away from my lips.

"No we don't," I countered, leaning back in to kiss her more.

She held her hands out in front of her, preventing me from getting closer. "Patrick, do you know *why* I didn't want to wait till after graduation to get married?" Nualla asked in a slightly breathless voice. "Because now we can't do *this* for a few more months."

I didn't even have to ask what *this* was.

Damn you, logic; you are always getting the better of me.

"Okay I changed my mind. We can get married now, I'll get my pants," I announced, moving to get up.

"Nope, you made your bed now you have to lie in it," Nualla stated, turning her head away from me.

"*Nualla.*"

"Okay, bad choice of words, but still."

I knew she was right, but it didn't stop me from wanting her. Wanting her more badly than I had ever wanted anything. "You know, you really shouldn't tease the animals, sometimes they bite back," I said with a playful glare.

"I'm counting on it," Nualla replied with a teasing smile.

I just stared at her dumbly for a few moments. Sometimes I really did think she greatly enjoyed teasing me; seeing how far she could push me before I lost control of myself. Fortunately, I kinda liked it. Unfortunately, at the moment I couldn't give in to the urges racing through my body.

"Okay, you win. I'm *so* going to bed now," I said, flopping back on my pillow and closing my eyes. "As it is I may need to go take a long cold shower."

"Oh *really*, why?" Nualla asked, feigning innocence.

"If you don't cut it out, I'm going to throw *you* in the cold shower first," I threatened, opening one eye to look at her.

"*Ugh*, no! Okay, I promise to be good—*tonight* at least," Nualla said, flopping back onto her pillow. "Night, Patrick."

"Goodnight, Nualla," I said, grinning to myself.

When all had gone quiet I pulled her close and put my arms protectively around her. It felt good, so good not to be alone.

I had never slept so soundly in my life, as I did that night.

Even the Fearless

Wednesday, February 15th

PATRICK

T HE NEXT DAY I REALLY *did* feel like I had been hit by a Buick. The painkillers had worn off, and even opening my eyes hurt.

Where am I?

I scanned the room with as little movement as I could manage until I caught sight of Nualla sitting at a computer desk across the room.

Oh right, I'm at Nualla's, in her bed. In. Her. Bed?

I sat bolt upright and then immediately wished I hadn't. I fell back in a choked back scream of pain. When I opened my eyes again, Nualla was leaning over me looking anxious.

"You know, you really shouldn't do that in the condition you're in."

"Next time remind me of that *before* I do it, okay?" I moved my right arm to push my hair out of my face and remembered a second too late that it was in a cast. "Damn it!" I cursed after I whacked myself in the forehead.

"Here, let me," Nualla said, brushing my hair out of my face with a half-hearted smile. "Do you want your painkillers now?"

"Oh *God* yes, do you even have to ask?" I moaned, squeezing my eyes shut in agony.

Nualla turned and retrieved a glass of water and some pills from her nightstand. "Here, sit up slowly."

I eyed her as I took the pills and washed them down with water. When I was finished, I leaned my head back against the wall. "How are *you* doing?"

"I'm fine."

"*Really*?" I asked dubiously, arching an eyebrow, though it proved to be painful.

"Seriously, I'm fine. My body heals a lot faster than yours, remember?"

"Must be nice." I looked around the room; the light coming through the window seemed off somehow. "What time is it?" I asked as I rubbed the sleep from my eyes with my left hand this time.

"Three in the afternoon," Nualla answered, looking over at the clock.

"Well, I guess I'm ditching school today."

"We thought it was best to just let you sleep. And besides, it's not ditching if you are *actually* ill—or hurt," Nualla said in a concerned voice before her expression turned mischievous. "*I*, on the other hand, am *totally* ditching."

I laughed slightly even though it hurt like hell.

Nualla stood. "On a side note, I think you need to have food with those pills, so we should probably fix that? Do you feel able to walk down the stairs, or should I bring you something?"

"What floor are we on, again?"

Nualla looked at me anxiously. "You don't remember?"

I shook my head.

"We're on the fourth floor."

"Do you want me still alive when we get to the bottom?" I asked with a wry smile.

"Preferably," Nualla answered with a small smile of her own.

"Then you should probably bring me something."

NUALLA

B Y THE TIME I GOT back to the room, Patrick was already unconscious again. Sighing, I put the plate on the nightstand and sat watching him sleep. He looked so fragile, so breakable, lying there bruised and pale. I was so afraid to leave him; he looked so terribly vulnerable.

I had been playing it cool, joking, teasing and what-not to cover up just how much yesterday had terrified me. Seeing him broken and bleeding in the wreckage of the bus was an image I just couldn't get out of my head. Just thinking about it hurt me deep in my chest, making it hard to breathe. And that's when I knew for sure, that I wasn't just crushing, that I wasn't just attracted to him, but that I loved him.

It was a pain I wasn't used to; that I had never really felt before. But still I knew what it meant. I didn't need someone to explain it to me, I could feel the truth of it; the ache of it.

I looked down at the ring, a physical reminder of our bond. But even if it wasn't there I knew I would still feel it as strongly as I had ever felt anything. I finally understood why we guarded our hearts so fiercely; why we didn't leap until we were dead sure. Because once felt, this pull, this all-consuming urge, this bond, could never be undone.

The fact that something—that *anything*—could

have this much power over me was terrifying. It wasn't the idea of being with Patrick that frightened me. It was knowing that if I lost him, that if he was taken from me, that it would destroy me, sure as anything.

I sat there staring at the ring, and I let myself cry until it became dark outside. Because there was only so much one person could keep locked away; only so much a dam could hold in before it broke. Only so strong one person could be before they failed, because even the fearless sometimes had to fall.

PATRICK

S OMETIME AROUND EIGHT OR SO in the evening I finally braved the stairs to walk down to the media room on the second floor. It was amazing just how very large Nualla's house was, *especially* for being in the middle of a city like San Francisco. Most of the houses in the city were tall but thin, crammed together like a folded accordion. Some of the places I had been had only a single room per floor if you can believe it. It was something TV just couldn't capture adequately; just how crowded it really was here.

Sure, most cities are crowded, but they had nothing on San Francisco.

Nualla's house was completely at odds with this, as if someone had leveled the neighboring buildings and dropped an estate out of the air. But since most of the houses on the street took up similar space I got the distinct impression they had been here a very long time and the rest of the city had just grown up around them.

When Nualla and I entered the room Shawn and Nikki were already curled up on the couch eating pizza and watching some Sci-fi show. "You watch the SyFy channel?" I asked in disbelief.

Nikki and Shawn looked up at me in confusion. "Sure, why not?"

"I'd think it would be super-fake to you guys," I said, slumping down onto the couch. Even though I had slept most of the day, I was still beyond exhausted.

"Naw, it's a lot easier to suspend your disbelief when you aren't supposed to exist," Shawn said with a smile before biting into a slice of pizza.

"Touché." I sat there for a few minutes before I realized that it was a Wednesday night and Shawn was there hanging out on the Galathea's media room couch. In fact, he was *always* there as far as I could tell. "Are you always over here?" I asked, looking at Shawn.

"Dude, you haven't noticed I live across the street have you?" Shawn asked with a crooked smile.

"Sorry, I've been out of it."

"Well you *were* in a bus accident," Nikki pointed out with a small smile.

"By the way Patrick, you look like crap," Shawn said, looking me over.

"I *feel* like crap," I said, leaning my head against the back of the sofa.

"Well, that could be because you haven't eaten in over thirty-six hours," Nualla said as she shoved a plate of pizza at me. "And I'm not giving you anymore painkillers until you eat something."

"Yes *mom*," I said, rolling my eyes playfully.

"I also won't kiss you until you do," Nualla threatened, glaring at me. I looked at her and then all but shoved the pizza into my mouth. Once I had eaten a few slices, Nualla finally held out her hand. *"Here."*

I grabbed the pills and swallowed them quickly. The pain was beginning to become unbearable, and I didn't want to show them just how much I was truly suffering. "Do I get some kisses now too?" I asked hopefully.

"Patrick, can I speak with you?" Alex asked from the doorway of the room. He looked a little serious but not angry, so I knew it couldn't be *that* bad.

"Sure," I answered, standing and following him out into the hall.

Alex leaned against the wall, folding his arms in a way that made him look friendly somehow. "Since you're not actually married to my daughter—"

"You want me to sleep on the couch?" I guessed.

Alex looked slightly taken aback. "Not where I was going, actually." I could have sworn he turned slightly red as he continued. "You are both adults, and what you want to do behind closed doors really isn't my business."

Good to know, because I really didn't want to ever tell you, either.

"No, what I was going to say was we need to get you a new Blue Card; which means you may have to go before the Council again."

"Oh, okay."

I must have looked uneasy because Alex put his hand on my shoulder. "Patrick, don't worry about it. I will speak with them, and it will all be just fine."

33

BUICKS, EXTINGUISHERS, AND DANCING PLATYPUSES

Thursday, February 16th

PATRICK

WE DECIDED TO GO TO school the next day so people wouldn't think we were dead. But as I looked in the mirror, I decided I looked somewhere between an alien plague victim and a zombie, and I felt about ten times worse. On the other hand, Nualla looked just as beautiful as ever. The skin on her arms and face had mostly healed and by the next day, it would look as if she had never even been on that bus. But she had, and it was my fault. And the guilt was eating me from the inside out, gnawing on my nerves.

I sat on the edge of the vanity counter and watched

her as she started dabbing stuff across her skin. "What are you doing?" I asked, a little perplexed.

Nualla looked over at me and gestured with the makeup sponge. "Well, whereas *you* look like you were in a horrible accident, *I* do not. So I have to play pretend."

She turned back toward the mirror and started to add fake bruises to the area around her collarbone. Watching her, I had to admit she seemed pretty good at it. Then I realized she had probably had to do things like this for the last few years.

Nualla moved her hand to her face and started to add one to her right cheek just below the eye. My heart skipped a beat, and a vision of her falling passed across my eyes; falling out of my reach.

I reached out and grabbed her wrist gently. "Please don't do that to your face."

She looked up into my eyes, startled by my reaction. "Patrick, I have—"

"Please, anywhere but your face; I just can't bear to see you that way. I—when I lost hold of you I thought I was going to lose you forever," I admitted as I looked down at my hands.

Nualla put down her sponge and wrapped her arms around me with the utmost gentleness. "Oh Patrick, what am I going to do with you?"

As Nualla and I walked up the steps to the building, people were already starting to stare at me. Because my uniform had been all but destroyed in the bus crash I had been forced to borrow one of Shawn's. And since he was a good four to eight inches taller than me I had had to roll up the bottom of the pants and was all but drowning in the dress shirt and black sweater vest.

I had pulled the white dress shirt over my cast, but it just looked way too weird, so I had settled for having it bunched up above the cast instead. Hey, if people were going to stare anyways why not give them something to stare at, right?

I didn't *really* care what they thought, since I was off in my own little dreamy world already. I had thought Dr. LaCosta was a quack before, but next time I saw him I was going to have to thank him for the wicked awesome painkillers.

Nualla let go of my hand, though a little slower than she normally did. "I'll see you later, Patrick," she said before turning to walk away.

"Wait." I reached out gently to pull her back. I slipped my arms around her waist and held her close as I looked down into her eyes. "I'm never letting you go unless I do this first; you never know when it could—"

"Be our last?" Nualla said, finishing my sentence. "Patrick, I'm almost positive that nothing bad is going to happen to you before—well, you know."

"Well, in case you're wrong, I'd like to kiss you just the same." And then I kissed her gently at first, then more hungrily. I finally let her go when I could no longer ignore the cat calls from our classmates.

Mr. Savenrue passed us on his way inside the building. "Last time I checked this was still a school, Mr. Connolly."

"But I'm not in school—*yet*," I replied in a slightly dazed voice. Kissing Nualla always did that to me and the painkillers probably weren't helping either.

Mr. Savenrue looked back at us about to say something then he actually got a look at us; at my cast. His expression turned to one of concern. "Mr. Connolly, Miss Galathea, are you alright?"

"Oh we're fine *now*, but Tuesday was another story," I answered, wincing.

"Tuesday?" Mr. Savenrue asked, raising his eyebrows.

"We were on the bus that crashed at Market Street on Tuesday," Nualla clarified with a slight shudder.

Yeah, I'm never going to get her to ride public transit again. Not a chance in hell.

"So if I seem a little loopy, it's probably just the painkillers," I said with a slight grin. Truth be told, I could have been hallucinating this whole conversation and would have been none the wiser.

"I'll take that into consideration," Mr. Savenrue said apprehensively before turning to walk into the building.

Nualla kissed me on the cheek. "Bye Patrick; try not to injure yourself in math, okay?"

"You mean like whacking myself in the head again?" I had already done that at *least* eight times this morning alone.

"Yeah, like that," she answered with a crooked smile over her shoulder as she walked into the building.

"Patrick, why did you bail on me yesterday?" Connor called out from behind me. "And since when do you not answer your—" Connor stopped dead when he got close enough to actually see me. "What the hell happened to *you*?!"

I got a feeling that most of my day was going to involve answering this question. If I was smart, I might have just passed out flyers or something.

"Did you hear about that bus collision on Tuesday?"

"Yeah…" Connor answered cautiously.

I gestured to myself with my hands.

"You were *on* it?!" Connor asked in shock.

"Yeah, Nualla too," I gestured slightly to Nualla with my head.

Connor looked past me to Nualla; she had done

a really good job on her makeup. Still, I looked far worse. "How can she still manage to look *that* good after a bus accident?"

"I really don't know," I replied, gazing at my unbelievably beautiful girlfriend; wife; *wait*, what was she now? Oh right, my *fiancée*.

Connor looked back at me. "You look like hell."

"Yeah, I know." I looked at my reflection in the front office window. "But on the bright side I can't feel a thing most of the time," I stated, turning to grin at Connor in a slightly unhinged way.

"Those must be some damn good painkillers because you look like—"

"I was hit by a Buick?" I added helpfully.

"Yeah, several times," Connor said with a smirk.

When we reached the second floor hall Connor turned around to ask, "Aren't you right-handed?"

"Yep," I answered, stopping at my locker.

"You know Miss Marshall is *so* going to kill you, right?"

"Oh *fuck*!" I cursed, looking at my busted arm. "I didn't even think about that." I looked up at him. "What am I going to do?"

"Learn to use your left hand?" Connor offered with a shrug.

"Thanks Connor, *real* helpful," I said, rolling my eyes.

"What did you do to your arm?!" I turned around to see Jenny coming toward us up the stairs. Then she stopped dead in her tracks. "What happened to the *rest* of you?!"

"Can I go home now?" I said out of the side of my mouth to Connor.

"Naw man, you're already here; you're screwed," Connor answered, unable to hide his amusement.

Jenny finally got to us with Sara and Beatrice behind her. Beatrice dropped her book in surprise when she looked up at me. "*Well*?" Jenny said, throwing out her arms dramatically.

"Riot at Starbucks," I said with a stupid grin. These painkillers were seriously doing a number on my sanity.

"*What*?!" Jenny yelped, completely flabbergasted.

"He's *kidding*, Jenny," Connor said, rolling his eyes. "He was on the bus that crashed on Tuesday."

"*Seriously*?" Beatrice asked, still ignoring the book at her feet.

"Yep, I'm living proof that bad things happen to you if you ditch class," I said stupidly.

"Is he...*okay*?" Sara asked Connor out of the corner of her mouth.

"I'm pretty sure he's high as a kite, actually; just wait, any moment he might start dancing," Connor said with a highly amused grin.

The first bell rang loudly, and my friends started moving toward our first period classes. "Um, guys?" I called out to my friends. They turned around. "Can someone open my locker? I can't seem to do it with my left hand."

They all just stared at me blankly for a minute in stunned silence.

"Patrick, that's a fire extinguisher," Jenny pointed out in a bewildered voice.

"Connor, just how many painkillers did he take?" Sara asked as she looked at me apprehensively.

"No clue, but the next hour should be fucking brilliant," Connor answered with a huge grin.

Most of the day was a wash. I'm pretty sure if I hadn't told Mr. Savenrue ahead of time about the painkillers he might have sent me to the office—*or* called the cops. As it was, I'm pretty sure I spent the hour staring at the dancing platypuses on Natalie's backpack. Grooving along with their little dance party in my head.

The other teachers looked horrified when they saw me, but didn't say a whole lot to me and Nualla about the accident. Miss Marshall, on the other hand, looked like she was going to have a heart attack when

I walked into sixth period Digital Painting.

"Patrick, what on earth happened to you?!"

I decided I really shouldn't joke with her since she already looked unstable, so I settled for the truth. "I was on the bus that crashed."

"Patrick your…your arm, aren't you right-handed?" she asked in a horrified voice as she looked at my cast. To an artist there were two things almost worse than death and an injury to your dominant hand was one of them.

"Unfortunately," I replied with a grimace; you never realize how much you use something until you can't anymore. "*So…*are you going to make me paint with my left hand, or can I just sit here?"

As it turned out, the answer to my second question was *no*. Miss Marshall still expected me to participate in class; she just wasn't going to grade any of the crap that suffered under my left hand. I really *had* tried my best, but the stylus kept getting away from me.

"Hey, Patrick?" Connor asked as he worked up a background on the digital canvas.

"Hmm?" I answered, losing my grip on the stylus again.

"Are you okay now?" he asked cautiously.

"Everything's fine, Connor, really."

"Dude, you thought the fire extinguisher was your locker just a few hours ago."

"Okay, point taken. But I assure you, I am fine now, so shoot."

"So last time I saw you your life had just exploded—*again*. But based on the way the two of you were going at it out in front of the school earlier I'm guessing everything's awesome again. So what *exactly* happened after you ran off at lunch?"

"I asked her to marry me," I said in the quietest voice I could manage; we *were* after all in the crowed computer lab, and even though music was playing in the background it wasn't *that* loud.

"I thought you already did that?"

"Yeah, but this time I actually got down on my knees and asked her."

"Didn't you do that before?" Connor asked in confusion.

"No, I'm pretty sure we just drunkenly wandered into the jewelry store at a 24-hour wedding chapel.

"*Seriously*?"

"I was piss drunk, if you will recall. The only reason I know half of what happened is because of the pictures."

"What pictures—*oh* right, the pictures you won't let me see."

"Bingo."

Miss Marshall drifted by our section of computers and we fell silent. "Thank you, Patrick, for making an effort in your condition," Miss Marshall said, looking down at me compassionately.

Geez, she makes it sound like I'm dying or something.

"If you can call it that," Connor said with a snort.

"*Hey*, I'd like to see *you* try holding this thing with your left hand," I nearly shouted as I gestured to the stylus. "It's nearly impossible!"

Miss Marshall glared at Connor slightly before looking over at me. "Don't worry; I won't be grading you on this work."

Thank God, because I think I might have had better luck trying to draw with my foot, was what I wanted to say. What I actually said was, "Thanks, Miss M."

She smiled and continued on to look over the other student's progress.

"*So…*" Connor asked expectantly.

"We're doing it for reals this time, the whole big-wedding thing after graduation."

Connor looked at me suspiciously. "*Geez*, you two don't waste any time do you?"

There were so many reasons we were rushing this wedding, I wouldn't even know where to begin. Unfortunately, I couldn't tell him any of them. "It's a really long story I can't exactly get into right now, but don't head out after graduation; I want you there."

"Oh, so you're actually going to invite me this time?"

"Yes Connor," I said, rolling my eyes. "You're

never going to let me live that down are you?"

"Nope, watching the crap you do to your life is funny as hell."

We both scribbled at the tablets for a few silent moments before he asked, "So... can I bring Sara?"

"*Of course*, she's invited too and—" I said confused, and then it dawned on me. "*Oh*, I take it things went well, then?"

"Better than well; as of Tuesday Sara and I are now officially a thing," Connor answered with a huge grin.

FACING THE MUSIC

Thursday, February 16th

PATRICK

I FINALLY WENT HOME FOR THE first time since the accident. Loraly was reluctant to let me go, and I finally got her to agree by promising to come back on Friday to stay for the weekend. In all honesty, I would have loved to stay there forever, but I really needed to get some clean clothes since everything I had worn the last few days had been Shawn's.

Nualla's family's warm, inviting nature had taken some getting used to, but now it felt entirely normal and in sharp contrast to my own parents. Her family's outward affection was like a drug and as I sat at the table eating my dinner *alone*, I missed them. Not just Nualla, but everyone, even Andraya—if only just a little.

A nauseating wave of pain surged through my body, and I was reminded that I needed to take my *actual* drugs. I pulled them out and shook one pill into my hand. The instructions on the bottle were obviously not intended for humans, because taking that amount sent me way too far into La La Land. However, I still hadn't found the magic number yet.

I stared at the TV screen but lost interest in the show that was on, and my mind began to wander. The pain hadn't subsided, so obviously *one* wasn't the magic number. I took a few more bites of my dinner, but I really didn't have an appetite, maybe it was the meds.

"Patrick, what on *earth* happened to your arm?" my father asked from behind me.

I nearly choked on my dinner as I turned around. "Dad!" I had been so lost in thought I hadn't heard him come in. He placed his stuff on the counter as he passed and walked over to look at me. I liked to pretend I didn't care that they were never there, but I *did* care, a lot.

"Patrick, your arm, what happened to it?"

I looked down at my arm trying to think of how to explain. I decided on the truth, I wasn't a really a good liar, so why risk it. "Umm...I was on that bus that crashed on Tuesday." I looked up at him in time to see my mother coming through the door. She was on the phone like she always was. *Great*, now I had to explain it to both of them at the same. It was so much harder to lie when they both were looking at me.

"I'll call you back later Paul, I'm sure you can handle *it* till then," she snapped into her phone before she dropped it into her purse.

"Jane, did you know about this?" my father asked in her direction as he crossed his arms.

"Know about *what*, Nathan?" my mother said in exasperation as she dropped her stuff on the counter as she came closer. Then she stopped dead, she had apparently just noticed my arm. "Patrick honey, what happened to your arm?"

"It got broken in a bus accident," I answered, shrugging.

"A *what*?!" my mother yelped in shock.

"I'm okay, really—" I said as quickly as I could.

"Why didn't you call us?" my father asked in a worried, disapproving voice.

Crap.

"I lost my phone in the crash, and you know how bad I am with numbers." I crossed my fingers under the table. I really *had* lost my cell in the crash, though "lost" wasn't *exactly* the right word. Destroyed beyond all repair was far more accurate.

"That aside, you should have called us when you

got home from the hospital," my father said, still looking stern.

Double crap.

"Um…I actually just got home," I admitted, trying not to meet their eyes.

"You were at the hospital this whole time?!" My mother looked like she was about to faint.

"Um, actually Nualla's parents took me back to their house. Nualla's mother didn't want me to be alone here with a busted arm, since you both were out of town."

"Well, that was nice of her," my mother said with a slight smile.

My father's jaw tightened, and an odd expression crossed his face. But before I had time to decipher what it was, it was gone. "Yes, that was very kind of Mrs. Galathea."

After a few moments of silence, my mother turned to me again. "What I don't understand is why the hospital didn't call us."

Crap. I was just digging my hole deeper and deeper. Why couldn't I just shut up? Hell, why couldn't they just ignore me like they normally did?

"Um, because Tuesday was also my eighteenth birthday, so yeah, I was an adult when I came into the hospital."

Oh and you both missed it of course, and well, probably forgot in the first place.

"Oh Patrick, I'm sorry we couldn't be here."

"It's okay Mom, I'm kinda used to it," I said with a shrug. And the sad truth of it was that I was.

"I left your present at the office; I'll be right back," my father said emotionlessly as he turned and walked to the door.

"That's not really—" I started, but he was already out the door, "—necessary." The door closed shut and he was gone again.

Wait, had he said "Mrs. Galathea"? Had *I* called her that? I stared at the door trying to trace back through the conversation in my head.

"Who's Nualla?"

"Huh?" I snapped my head back in my mother's direction.

"Who's *Nualla*?" my mother asked again. For the first time in a long time, she was staring at me while she talked instead of just looking at her phone.

Who's Nualla? Oh, she's just a daemon I happened to accidentally marry in Vegas. But it's cool Mom, it didn't count because I was a minor at the time, was the first thing that came to mind, but I settled for the less incriminating: "My girlfriend." It came out sounding more like a question than an answer, though.

"Patrick, when did you get a new girlfriend?"

"Um, about a month ago," I answered while trying to think of a way to escape the rest of this conversation. "*Wait*, what do you mean, *new*? This is the only girlfriend I've ever had."

"What about that one friend of yours, what was her name… Jenny?"

Geez, even my mother had been able to clue into Jenny, and she wasn't even *here* half the time. "No Mom, Jenny was never my girlfriend, just a friend who happens to be a girl."

"Oh well, you should invite Nualla over for dinner some time, it would be nice to meet her."

Sure mom, I'll do that when hell freezes over.

After a while, I retreated up to my room to flip through stuff on PinIt and iTribe—which is far harder than it sounds with a broken arm. One of the images sparked a flicker of an idea, and I reached for my tablet to sketch it out. But as my hand reached for it, I remembered the cast.

I hung my head back on my chair and sighed in anguish. *Ugh, how am I going to get through six weeks like this?*

I closed my eyes and the images of Nualla falling returned in horrifyingly graphic detail. They had plagued me every time I closed my eyes even for a second, like my subconscious felt the need to torture me some more.

"Patrick?" my father said from behind me, scaring

the crap out of me.

"Dad!" I turned around and he handed me a box.

"Not that you can use it at the moment with that arm the way it is, but I know you've been wanting to get a new one."

I looked down at the large box with a drawing tablet splashed across its front. Most people would have been shocked that he had known exactly what to get, but I wasn't. I had given up long ago and just made an online wish list. It's just about as idiot-proof as gift giving could ever get.

"Oh, and here," he said as he handed me a shiny new cell phone. "Since your old one is missing. Try to keep hold of it this time."

This time? Was he expecting me to get into another accident?

His eyes changed focus to the drawings covering the walls behind me. He stared for a while at them with cold eyes. "Is that her, your girlfriend?" he asked as he gestured with his head. His voice was harder than it normally was, like he was upset about something. I looked at him for a second before he clarified, "Your mother told me when I got back."

"Yeah, that's Nualla...she goes to my school," I answered cautiously; I was seriously beginning to wonder what was up.

His jaw clenched, but he said nothing. So we sat there in silence for a while; him glaring at my artwork on the wall, and me trying to figure out what on *earth* was going on.

"Well, try to be more careful in the future," my father stated firmly. And before I could say another word, he was on his way out the door, phone in hand.

Sure Dad, next time I'll make sure not to get in a bus accident. Because I totally *have control over that.*

THE DIFFERENCE OF A MONTH

Friday, February 17th

PATRICK

IT WAS FRIDAY NIGHT AND I was back at Nualla's watching TV and chowing down on Chinese food with the rest of them. Normally we went to the club on Fridays, but with my busted arm it would have sucked. So we had settled for TV and takeout.

We were laughing and having a good time when we heard the smashing of glass downstairs. *"Gods Dammit!"* Alex shouted, full of rage.

All four of us turned in unison toward the door. And a second later, the three of them sprang up and sprinted out the door, and I did my best to hobble after them.

When I arrived, they were all just staring open-mouthed at Alex and the pieces of the vase covering the foyer floor. Tylia was standing in front the open doorway behind him, and Loraly was peering anxiously from the living room.

"Dad, what's wrong?" Nualla asked in a startled voice. From her tone I was almost certain she had never seen her father like this before.

Alex looked up at us all standing there startled and confused on the stairs. He was so angry he was visibly shaking. "We need to leave—*now*."

"Why, what's wrong Alex?" Loraly asked in an anxious voice.

"Someone told the Grand Council about Patrick *before* I could. They've issued a warrant for his capture and execution."

"*What*?!" Nikki and Shawn yelped, staring at him in shock.

I clutched the railing and tried not to panic. This was bad. This was *really* bad.

"Dad, you can't let them do that!" Nualla shouted, taking a few steps down the stairs.

"I have no say in this matter, Nualla." Alex looked pained and utterly defeated.

"But you're the Chancellarius! They *have* to listen to you," Nualla said, taking another step down.

"No, they don't, Nualla. I can't break the rules

any more than anyone else can!" Alex shouted in frustration as he put his fist through the glass top of the foyer table. Powerless was probably not an emotion he felt a lot; if ever.

After the broken shards had finished scattering across the floor, Tylia took a step forward out of the shadows. "You're father's speaking the truth, Nualla. The order came down a few hours ago." Tylia wouldn't look at us. Something was wrong. And then it occurred to me *what* Tylia's job was. Her job was to protect the *chancellarius* and his family; even if that meant protecting them from themselves.

"You were sent here to capture him, weren't you?" Nualla said in a hushed startled voice, she had apparently realized the same thing I had.

"Yes," Tylia admitted in a quiet voice.

Nualla marched the rest of the way down the stairs and pushed Tylia. "You *can't* have him, Tylia. I won't let you take him away!"

Tylia's eyes darted up to Nualla. "I never *said* I was going to follow the orders."

"But, that's an act of treason," Nikki said from next to me.

"Tell me something I don't know, kitten," Tylia sighed, looking away.

Tylia was avoiding looking at me; at first I thought it was because she might be ashamed of her orders. Then I realized that if she never looked at me, she could claim under oath that she had never seen me. It was skirting the truth, and it clearly showed where her true loyalties lay.

Nualla turned around to look at Alex. "Dad, there has to be *something* we can do?"

"The best I can do is bring him before the Grand Council and hope they listen."

"You mean *surrender* him?" Nualla asked in a choking voice. He didn't answer; just watched the blood rolling off his fingers. "No," Nualla said, taking a step back. "We'll run away. They can't have him."

"*Nualla*," Alex pleaded.

Nualla took another step back. "No, they can't kill him. I *love* him, they can't kill him! We'll leave tonight. We'll go to another state and—"

"They already thought you might. It wasn't a citywide order, or even a regionwide one. It was an all-region alert bulletin," Tylia informed us, folding her arms.

"But…" Nualla breathed before she collapsed into a sobbing heap on the floor covered with broken glass and fragments of vase. "But they *can't* kill him. They just can't."

Loraly rushed from the living room and dropped to her knees beside her daughter. She cradled Nualla in her arms murmuring something I couldn't make out. It was heartbreaking to watch her; to watch the tears falling to the ground and mixing with the blood.

The room, aside from Nualla's sobbing, fell silent. No one felt like filling it. What could you say in a situation like this really?

Her world, now mine, was becoming a very dangerous place. I had known there would be risks; they had all made that abundantly clear. And I was prepared for the chance that my body could be incompatible with the retrovirus and that I would die a horrible, agonizing death. I just didn't think I would be facing death so soon.

I finally found the ability to move my legs and walked slowly down the rest of the stairs. I wanted to go to her, to comfort her, but there was a sea of glass shards between us. Images from the accident flashed before my eyes and I swayed on my feet. I tried to catch myself, but I only succeeded in banging my cast uselessly on the stair railing.

Just before I hit the ground, Tylia grabbed my arm and wrenched me back up. "*Dammit* kid, you just blew my plausible deniability."

"I won't tell if you don't," I whispered under my breath.

"Patrick we have to…" Alex said, finally looking at me.

"I know," I answered, taking a step toward the door. I was too scared even to be angry at all this.

"We're going with you," Shawn announced in a shaky voice.

Alex stopped and whipped around. "No, *you* go home. If you're involved, Roy can't be. And frankly, we *really* need him on our side."

Shawn swallowed and nodded, however, he didn't look like he liked the idea of sitting out.

Alex turned his eyes on his daughter. "Nualla, you have to stay too."

"*What*? No!" she shouted indignantly, snapping out of whatever personal hell she was seeing in her head.

"We need to go," Alex stated, ignoring Nualla's protest and turning stiffly to the door, dripping a trail of blood in his wake.

I know I should have said something—*anything*— but I couldn't find the words; couldn't get them past my throat, so I just nodded and numbly followed after him.

"No!" Nualla screamed as she rushed forward.

In a move swifter than I could track Tylia was in front of Nualla blocking her path to us.

"No, you can't take him!" Nualla screamed as she tried to claw her way past Tylia. It was a horrible sight watching her struggle against Tylia; eyes wild like a caged animal. And even as the door closed behind us the fight never left her.

I didn't know if I would ever see her again. I didn't trust enough even to hope.

NUALLA

"LET ME GO!" I SCREAMED, fighting against Tylia with all my strength. I wasn't going to break free; she was far stronger than I was, but that didn't lessen the fight in me. "*Now!*"

Tylia finally let me go and I fell to the glass covered ground. I whipped around to yell at her, but stopped when I saw the tears rolling down her cheeks. In all the years I had known Tylia I had never seen her shed even a single tear.

"I'm going after him," I stated in a cautious voice.

"I know," she replied, looking at the ground.

"You can't stop me," I said, standing up.

"I'm not going to." She finally looked up into my eyes. "This is wrong. *You* know it; *I* know it."

I couldn't find the words to say something, so I just nodded.

"You know you're risking your succession by going after him, right?" Tylia asked in an even tone.

"I don't care, Patrick's far more important than power," I answered, raising my chin.

Tylia raised an eyebrow.

"My dad holds that power now, and even *he* can't save Patrick."

Tylia moved forward and placed something in my hand, closing my fingers around it. "You know, this is something I thought a spoiled rich *arius* incapable of learning. Apparently, I was wrong."

"What?" I asked as I opened my fingers and saw a set of car keys—*my* car keys.

"That the power over life and death is a power only the gods should hold."

"Tylia, I…" I was at a loss for words.

"*Go*, you idiot!" Tylia shouted as she all but shoved me toward the door.

I didn't wait for her to change her mind, I just ran out into the pouring rain. I had to get to him, I had to save him. He whom I had never known I needed so much until now. He whom I could no longer live without. Funny that it had taken *this* to show me just how much I truly loved him.

I jammed the keys into my Vanquish and screeched out of the driveway, nearly clipping the gate in the process. I slammed my fist into the car's cloaking button and slammed my foot on the gas. I needed to get there *now*, and I didn't need to get pulled over by the cops in the process. 'Course this *also* meant I had to pay far more attention to the road, because none of the humans would be able to see my car coming. They would only feel the wind as it whipped past.

I caught air a few times as I flew through the streets of the city. The rain was coming down pretty hard, flooding the streets with water. It rushed down the streets in little torrents like a water slide, making the speed at which I was driving even more dangerous.

I made a sharp turn and knew in that instant I wasn't going to make it. My car slid across the slick road, careening out of control. I nearly obliterated a mailbox before I jerked the wheel sharply and took out a fire hydrant instead. Pedestrians looked around frantically and an alarm in my car started going off, warning me that the cloaking device was about to fail.

I made a split-second decision and backed my car into a nearby alley. Dizzily, I got out of the car and shook my head clear. I looked down the street and took stock of my situation. My car was busted and the street was shockingly devoid of taxis, which left only one option. I took a deep breath and launched myself down the sidewalk. I ran until my lungs hurt, and then I pushed myself further.

I arrived at The Embassy what seemed like hours later drenched to the bone and wheezing in pain.

"Arius Nualla?" Sam, one of the Kalo Protectorate officers, said in a startled voice.

"Move it, Sam; I don't have time for formalities now," I snapped as I brushed him aside. I liked Sam, he was a nice guy, but right now I had more important things to deal with.

The minute I crossed the threshold the alarms

sounded. Those frakkers had actually set an alarm on *me*?

"I'm sorry, Arius Nualla, it says I'm supposed to detain you," he looked terrified as he looked at the screen.

I whipped around to face him. "Have you found your One?"

"What?" Sam asked, taken aback by my blunt question.

"Have you found your *One*, Sam?" I asked a little more slowly.

"Yes..." he answered in a cautious voice.

I balled my hands into clenched fists at my side. "Then you know there isn't a damn thing in the *world* you can do to stop me from going through these doors."

"But Arius—" he sputtered, looking more and more unsure of his orders.

"They're about to execute my One because of a *stupid* technicality. Now get out of my way, or so help me, I will hurt you. And I *really* don't want to have to do that, Sam."

I'm not sure how scary I looked to him, but it must have been high up on the list of things he really didn't want to fuck with because he stepped aside without saying another word. And then I ran again, ignoring the pain—ignoring everything—just running.

PATRICK

There was a huge slam from behind me, and Nualla burst through the doors. She was completely and utterly drenched; her hair already creating puddles at her feet. Splotches of what looked like blood covered the legs of her jeans and she was missing shoes. She had never looked more frightened, or more deadly than she did in this moment. But even in the state she was in she was still breathtakingly beautiful; in the same way a lioness escaping a monsoon is beautiful.

Her eyes frantically traced the room until she met mine. "Patrick!" she called out as she launched herself forward. Her stride wasn't as graceful as it normally was; she was limping.

Oh holy hell, what did she do?

"Officers, restrain her!" Councilor Tammore ordered from the council table.

The Kalo Protectorate officers looked at each other for one shocked moment before moving. I doubted they had ever been issued such an order. With no real trouble at all they grabbed hold of Nualla; it was an unfair fight, to say the least.

It was clear she was hurt, but Nualla fought and kicked against them all the while screaming, "Get off me! I won't let you kill him!"

"Arius Nualla, if you continue this outburst we

will have to remove you from the Council chambers," Councilor Tammore sighed in aloof disinterest.

With one more look in my direction, Nualla finally stopped shouting, but her fierce expression didn't disappear. She was beyond pissed and it was only a matter of time before she would escape their grasp. I had a feeling this was probably going to end badly.

Then Nualla's anger hit me like a smack in the face. It surged through my body like an out of control fire. Everyone else must not have been affected because none of them even flinched.

Councilor Tammore turned his focus back on me. "Now, Mr. Connolly, shall we continue?"

I was shaking with anger so badly I could barely even nod.

"Mr. Connolly, you were made aware of our world before you were legally married to a daemon; as such, the punishment is death."

"But I didn't know until *after* the fact that my marriage wasn't legal." I was only barely keeping my grasp on the anger. It was writhing beneath my skin, threatening to chew its way out whether I liked it or not.

"That fact does not matter. The law is clear on this," Councilor Tammore countered without looking up at me.

There is a point when any cornered creature snaps and attacks its foe, even if it knows there's a good chance that it will get itself killed in the process. I had reached my point, and the anger writhing in my body finally boiled to the surface like acid. The councilors were hiding behind their laws. They were going to *kill* me because of a stupid technicality. It was just plain wrong, and I wasn't going to die for their ideals.

"This is complete bureaucratic crap! Your whole culture is *built* on lies! Every day you lie to millions of people. So how are *you* any different than *me*?" I nearly screamed at the Grand Council.

Silence fell in the room. I just hoped it wasn't the silence before they ordered my execution.

I took a few deep breaths to calm myself before I continued, but it didn't really help. My emotions didn't really feel like my own. They felt more like someone was pouring gasoline on the fire that was already there. I forced the anger down as best I could and continued before they silenced me for good. "I'm *sorry*; I didn't mean to cause such a mess. I know we broke your laws because I wasn't an adult, but I didn't know I was *breaking* them. And honestly, I don't think someone's life or death should depend on the difference of a month. I'm an adult now; this is my decision and my choice."

They weren't interrupting me or killing me where I stood, so I just continued rambling. I just hoped I wasn't digging my own grave in the process. "I know that none of this is textbook normal, but I swear on my *life* that I am going to marry Nualla, and I am going to become a daemon—even if it kills me."

They were silent for a long time after that before Councilor Tammore finally spoke, though he sounded rather reluctant to ask. "When were you planning to make your marriage to Arius Nualla legal?"

I was so startled by the question it took me a few seconds to process what I'd heard before I spoke. "Today if you make me, but in all honesty, we were planning on the end of June."

"The end of June?" Councilor Tammore asked looking at me curiously.

"School will be out and no one would notice my absence." And then I lied, which was probably a bad idea, but when you're up against death, you tend to make rather dumb decisions on the spot. "I would be a daemon *now*, but Nualla wanted to wait until the school year was over so no one would get suspicious."

Councilor Tammore turned his focus on Nualla who was still being restrained by the Protectorate officers though their grip on her had slackened considerably. "Arius Nualla, is this correct?" Councilor Tammore asked, raising an eyebrow.

"Absolutely," Nualla answered without missing a beat. I hadn't intended to make her an accomplice to my lies, but it was also something they could never prove was false.

I took another deep breath and spoke without

being asked to do so. "I know we're young, and I know we did a lot of dumb things, but no one has been hurt by our actions—except us," I pointed out as I held up my broken arm.

Councilor Tammore sat silent for a few moments before he looked at the other councilors. "We will discuss these new facts and make a decision on the matter." He looked back at us. "Officers, make sure they remain here."

The Protectorate officers nodded as the councilors stood and exited the room through a doorway behind the council table.

The minutes crept by, seeming like hours. But eventually the councilors came back out and sat before us, their expressions unreadable.

"Mr. Connolly, upon deliberation we have decided that your actions, while not *legal*, were in good faith. We will stay our proclamation of execution for the time being. However, you *must* be legally married here by the end of June, and you *must* become a daemon no later than July seventh. Is that clear?" Councilor Tammore asked, glaring sternly down at me.

"Perfectly," I answered in the clearest voice I could manage.

"Then our business here is complete for now."

"So you're not going to kill me?" I asked, shocked.

"Not today, Mr. Connolly, but do try not to break

any *more* laws in the future," he replied in a clear, authoritative voice before changing his focus to the room as a whole. "You are all free to go."

I turned around to face Nualla. "Did you hear that, I'm—" but I never got a chance to finish because a sobbing Nualla leapt into my arms.

I wrapped my arms around her and pulled her into a kiss. Her kisses were salty tearful kisses, but they were still welcome and nice. After a while, someone coughed behind us, and I opened an eye to look at Alex.

He leaned in and whispered, "Maybe we should leave *before* they change their minds."

I pulled my lips away from Nualla's long enough to answer, "Yeah, you're probably right."

When we got out of The Embassy something finally occurred to me. I would have thought to ask before if I hadn't been fighting for my life.

"Nualla, how did you get here?"

"I drove," she answered, not meeting my eyes.

I looked out at the empty street in front of us. "Then where's your car?"

"Oh, about seven blocks away where someone just so happened to have taken out a fire hydrant with an invisible car." Nualla answered as she started to walk down the steps.

I stopped walking and stared at her in shock. "Are you *okay*?"

"Yeah, I'm fine, but the car's frakked."

SUCCESSION OF CONSEQUENCES

Monday, February 20th

NUALLA

T HE REST OF THE WEEKEND had gone off without a hitch. None of us felt much like leaving the house—stress can do that to you. So the weekend mostly consisted of TV marathons and teasing Patrick when he was in his highly medicated state.

And so we found ourselves—Nikki, Patrick, and I, eating breakfast in the kitchen Monday morning as if the last week had never happened. Except Patrick was in my house on a school day morning—oh, *and* he had a broken arm. I was about halfway through eating my Parmesan toast when the ePrinter started printing a message.

"What on earth is that thing?" Patrick asked between bites of his breakfast.

"An electronic paper printer; pretty awesome, huh?" Nikki said with a huge grin.

"Electronic paper?" Patrick asked in confusion.

I leaned over and grabbed the ePaper from the printer and held it up for him to see.

"But there's nothing on it," he said, eyeing it dubiously.

"Sure there is, you just can't see it; just like you can't see the stuff that's on your Blue Card."

"So what does it say?" he asked, still staring at me like I was from space or something.

I looked down at it and nearly choked, it was from The Embassy, and it was addressed to *me*. Oh, this was not going to be good, I could just feel it.

I pressed my finger into the biometric seal, and it loaded instantly. "Oh, *frak* me," I said, staring at the summons in disbelief. "I've been summoned to appear before the Grand Council—today."

Nikki and Patrick looked at me open-mouthed.

"For *what*? Is it serious?" Nikki asked, trying to look over at the ePaper from across the table.

"Oh, it's nothing; I just might lose the right of succession," I said, putting my head in my hand.

"Does this have something to do with me?" Patrick asked anxiously as he put his spoon down.

"Yes and no; mostly no," I sighed as I looked into his eyes. "It's mostly because of what *I* did, not what *you* did."

"Oh," Patrick said in a quiet voice.

I pushed away from the table and stood up. "Look, I have to take care of this now. Nikki, take Patrick to school, I'll see you guys later."

"With what car? Your Vanq is in the shop," Nikki pointed out as she reenacted a car crash with her hands.

"Then have *Shawn* take you guys, or call a cab. Either way, I've got to go."

I took a few steps away before I turned back and walked back to Patrick. I had told myself that no matter what, I would never walk away without kissing him goodbye. Just in case it was a goodbye one of us wouldn't be coming back from.

He looked startled as I marched back into the room, but not half as startled as he looked when I slid into his lap. "Before I go, I need to give you something."

I didn't even give him a chance to ask *what*.

When I arrived at The Embassy it wasn't swamped yet, probably because it was a Monday morning before eight. I walked up to the counter and handed over my summons to the receptionist. She looked at it, eyebrows raised for a second before typing on the computer in front of her.

"They will be able to see you in about an hour, Arius Nualla," she said, handing the summons back to me.

"Fabulous," I groaned, rolling my eyes.

What the hell am I going to do for an hour?

Coffee. If I was going to face the Grand Council, I sure as *hell* didn't want to do it without having a proper dose of caffeine first.

I walked past The Embassy reception area to the first bank of elevators. The cafe on the third floor should be opened by now. If not, there were a dozen coffee shops on the street that certainty would be.

As I was waiting for the elevator, a familiar voice spoke from behind me. A voice I *so* did not want to have a conversation with at this time, especially in my current caffeineless state. "*So*...I heard about your outburst the other day," Travis said before sipping the coffee in his hand.

"Don't *even* start, Travis. I don't need to hear this from anyone, especially *you*." I was beginning to wish I had never gotten out of bed this morning.

The elevator door dinged, and I stepped on and pushed the close button. He was too quick and pushed back the closing doors.

"Wait, *Nualla*."

Great. We were alone in a place where I couldn't escape. "Nualla, I'm sorry, I didn't mean to—" he babbled, pulling on my arm.

I turned around to glare at him, but his eyes were kind and pleading. *Sigh.* I couldn't really stay mad at Travis for any length of time, and he knew it. Sometimes I would fight it for a while, but after the past week I was all out of fight.

"Why do I *always* run into you on days when I really don't want to talk to anyone?"

"Because those are the days when you need to talk to someone the most," Travis answered as he leaned against the wall. In one swift motion he pressed his hand against the biometric reader and pressed a button. The elevator came to a gentle stop.

"What are you *doing*?!" I asked incredulously, gripping the walls. I would never admit it to a soul, but elevators creeped me the hell out.

"It's very clear you need to talk, but the minute those doors open you're going to bolt and you know it."

I looked at him. "You know this is kidnapping, right?"

"So report me for treason," Travis answered, leaning close—*dangerously* close.

My heart started beating a frantic rhythm, and I finally had to admit it to myself. The truth. That if Patrick had never fallen into my life, I probably would have said *yes* to Travis. That I had been falling aimlessly through the last few years; waiting. Waiting for him to step a little too close. Waiting for him to give me a sign. Waiting for him to ask. And he had kept me waiting for years; until it was far past too late.

I really did *not* want to tell him about the elevator thing, but I couldn't help it, I was already starting to hyperventilate. Because I was trapped in this little cramped space or because he was so close—or *both*.

I looked up at Travis with panicked eyes and the crooked smile left his face. "Nualla are you—"

"Get me the *hell* out of this elevator, Travis!" I shouted, pressing myself against the wall.

"Elevators, *really*? How could I have not noticed that?" Travis asked with a wry smile.

Everything around me was starting to get hazy. "For the gods' sake, Travis, I'll answer all your frakkin' questions; just please, *please* get me out of here."

"Okay, look here we go," he said as he pressed his hand against the reader again, and the elevator jolted upward.

A few very tense moments later the doors opened, and I let him lead me out of the elevator. I didn't even notice where we were going until we were in his lab, amongst its familiar and comforting mixture of sterile white and tech junk.

After we had been there for gods only knew how

long, Travis finally spoke, "Well, I guess you got your answer."

"Huh?" I said, looking over at him in confusion.

"I asked you before if you regretted your decision to marry Patrick. If you did, you wouldn't have done what you did on Friday."

"*Oh*, I guess you're right," I said, a little shocked at myself. It was weird to think about how unsure I had been about the whole Patrick and me thing only a few short weeks ago. Then something occurred to me. "Wait, how did *you* find out what I did?"

"You *do* realize that there are cameras in this whole building, right? They have your whole outburst on record," Travis answered with a crooked smile.

"Oh, *frak* me," I cursed, hanging my head back in the chair.

"I'm not *even* going to respond to that; *way* too easy. And you would probably hit me."

"Travis, if it was an invitation, you would know—*believe* me."

"*Is* it?" he asked, snapping up straight.

"Not a chance in hell, Travis."

"Yeah, figured as much," he sighed, rolling his eyes. Minutes passed before he looked over at me again. "So what *are* you doing here today? It's a Monday, shouldn't you be in school?"

I held up the ePaper. "I've been summoned to appear before the Grand Council."

"For *what*?"

"A Succession hearing," I answered, gesturing dramatically with the summons.

"*What*?!" Travis sat up so quickly, he nearly fell out of his chair.

"Patrick's off the hook, but I'm not yet. I technically committed an act of treason. If they find me guilty, I will be barred from succeeding Alex as the next *chancellarius*."

"That's just crazy!"

"Yeah, but I've pushed my luck too far with them. I'm probably going to lose."

"So we would be stuck with Andraya?" Travis said, folding his arms.

"Were you honestly hoping that someday it would be me?" I asked with a derisive snort.

"Yeah actually; you'd shake things up in here," Travis replied, smirking at me mischievously.

"I'm pretty sure I do a fine job of *that* already," I said, rolling my eyes.

"Yeah, from what I hear your aunt was a wildcat too, but she seems to have nothing on you."

"Thanks, Travis." I had heard comments like that on one too many occasions; usually when I was being yelled at.

After a while, Travis came over and leaned on the table next to me. "*So*…since you're not married at the moment, can I kiss you?"

"You're actually *asking* this time?" I asked wryly.

"Yeah," Travis answered, blushing ever so slightly.

"You do and I'll punch you, Travis," I stated with a glare.

A beeping went off and the ePaper in my hands blinked.

"I guess they're ready for me, catch you later," I said, standing up and starting toward the door. "Oh and I'm stealing your coffee," I informed him, holding it up.

"*Hey*!"

"You interrupted me getting mine, so you'll just have to suffer. I have a date with some not so happy people, and I'm not doing it without coffee."

When I arrived at the Grand Council chambers it was eerily silent. Maybe it was just a morning thing. The Protectorate officers opened the doors, and I walked into the room. Only eight of the seats were filled. My dad was nowhere to be seen. It was the first time I had ever been to the Council chambers and he had not been there. It was unsettling, to say the least.

"Arius Nualla, thank you for heeding our summons. I gather you understand why Chancellarius Galathea is not with us today," Councilor Tammore said as he looked down at me.

"I do." I hadn't *really* until he mentioned it, but now I did. As far as conflicts of interest went, this would be pretty high on the list.

"Very well then, let us begin. Arius Nualla, you put your own self-interest before the law and the good of the subjects of this region. A ruler cannot do such things."

"I know, councilors." I wanted to look at my feet, away from his eyes, but I fought the urge.

"When you become ruler of a region, you must swear an oath to act in the interest of the people *first* and your family *second*."

Now I fully understood my dad's actions. He was bound. He had had no choice but to take Patrick in or face treason charges himself.

I took a deep breath. I refused to lie to them, even if that meant I would lose the right to succession. I was not ashamed of my decisions, and I would make the same ones again in a heartbeat. I held my head high and said in the strongest voice I could manage, "That is something I cannot do, councilors."

"*What*?!" Councilor Tammore asked, shocked. It was clear that he had been absolutely certain that I would bow down and accept the oath. But yielding was not something I did easily, *especially* when I didn't agree with what I was being asked to yield to in the first place.

I squared my shoulders and lifted my chin a fraction higher. "I cannot do what you are asking of me, so I guess you have your answer," I stated, purposefully leaving off the honorific.

Councilor Tammore looked at me for one dumbfounded moment before he spoke. "Then Arius Nualla, this Council has no choice than to—"

"*Wait*." They all turned to look at Councilor Reynes who had just stood. "Arius Nualla is young, in time her views may change. This decision should be put off until a time when we find ourselves without the current Chancellarius Galathea."

"I second this," Shawn's father, Councilor Roy Vallen announced standing as well.

Councilor Tammore paused for a second to look at the other nodding heads before looking back at me. "Very well; this Council will suspend this decision until such a time as the succession is necessary. You may leave, Arius Nualla."

"Thank you, councilors," I said with a slight bow before turning on my heel and getting the hell out of Dodge.

Breaking Free

Wednesday, April 4th

PATRICK

T HE NEXT SIX WEEKS PASSED by with little con-
sequence. After how chaotic my life had been
since I met Nualla, it was a welcome break. School
went on, my cast still impeded any real artistic en-
deavors, and Nualla still clung to me. The incident
with the Grand Council had had a much greater effect
on her than anyone else. I wasn't sure if something in
her had been broken or been set free. Maybe in this
case, like many others, it had been both.

Now when I was with Nualla, love practically
radiated off of her. Whatever doubts she had had

before, they were gone now. It was wonderful, like living in a little dream world. Everything was perfect in my life. Well, except for one tiny little thing.

After I ran out of Dr. LaCosta's painkillers, the headaches had started. Or maybe they had been there since the accident and the meds had just covered them up. Either way, they were growing worse and more frequent as the days passed. At first I had just ignored them, but when they started happening every day it became harder to pretend it was just normal.

I had also started to see things; things I knew I shouldn't be able to see. We would pass buildings and every so often they would flicker for a brief second, revealing what the illusion fields were hiding. But it wasn't just the buildings. My friends, my daemons friends that is, had started to do the same thing. Every few hours or so they would flicker briefly, giving me glimpses of their true forms. Not fast or frequent like a strobe light; more like a little blip and then another one a few hours later; like a TV losing signal for a second as you watched a show.

I was sitting at a table with Connor in the Japantown Mall contemplating this all when something suddenly flashed in front of my eyes.

"*Hellooo*, Earth to Patrick?" Connor said as he waved his hand in front of my face.

"What? Sorry," I said, shaking my head to clear it.

"You're going stir-crazy with that thing, aren't you?" Connor asked as he gestured to my cast.

"Is it really *that* obvious?" I asked with a wry smile.

"Patrick you're practically foaming-at-the-mouth anxious."

"Well I *am* getting it off today."

"Aww, really? But you were getting so good at using your left hand," Connor said, playfully rolling his eyes.

I punched him in the shoulder with my cast.

"Ouch! What the *hell*, man?"

"Not funny, Connor. You know I haven't been able to draw crap for almost two months now."

"And you could before?" he asked with snort.

I glowered at him until I caught sight of the time. "Oh *fuck*, I gotta go. I should have been there like, *now*."

NUALLA

A FTER DROPPING IN FOR A quick visit with Travis, I started making my way to the front entrance of The Embassy to meet up with Patrick. Turning a corner, I all but ran into Nathan Jordash, Natasha's father and our Head of Security here at The Embassy.

After staring at each other for one startled moment Nathan inclined his head with a slight bow. "Arius Nualla."

"Hello Nathan," I said with a slight smile. Nathan was pretty awesome as far as authority figures went, and he let me get away with an unbelievable amount of crap in the last few years. "I'm sorry I almost ran into you, I really should have been looking where I was going."

"No, the fault is all mine, I was a bit distracted myself," he said apologetically. "Where were you headed?"

"The front lobby," I answered.

"Care if I join you?" he asked with a friendly smile.

"Not at all," I replied, returning his smile. I normally saw Nathan a lot, but lately he had been strangely absent. On the other hand, *I* had been a lot busier, so maybe it was just that I wasn't around as much.

We started walking as he looked over at me and asked, "You are about to graduate from high school in a few short months, yes?"

"Yep."

"Then you will be coming here for classes, correct?"

"Yeah, though probably not till the end of July

because of the wedding."

Nathan stumbled a bit but regained his stride. "*Wedding*?"

I looked at him curiously. "Yes, I'm getting married to Patrick Connolly at the end of June."

Nathan was silent for a few moments before he spoke. "Yes, of course, I do believe your father mentioned that the other day." We walked a few more feet in silence. "Is it wedding preparations that brings you here today, or were you visiting with Travis?"

"Neither actually, Patrick is getting his cast off today."

Nathan stopped dead, and an odd expression crossed his face just for the briefest of seconds. "He is coming here?"

"Well yes, he should be here any minute now."

Nathan stood staring at me for a while before he pulled out his phone. He looked at it for a brief second before looking back at me. "Duty calls, my dear," he said with another bow of his head before he turned and walked purposefully back in the direction from which we had come.

I stared at him as he disappeared down the hall. *Well* that *was more than a little weird.*

PATRICK

L uckily, Nualla came down to get me at the front Embassy entrance, because walking through this place alone wasn't something I exactly felt comfortable doing. And I probably would have just gotten lost if I'd even tried. She looked like something was bothering her, but when I asked about it she said it was nothing. Which meant it was most *definitely* something.

I decided not to push it though, if she wanted to tell me she would. If she didn't, it would either end up being nothing or it would come kick my ass later. Either way, not really my problem today; today I was finally getting released from this stupid cast.

Dr. LaCosta pulled out what could only be described as a miniature electric circular hand saw. "What the hell is *that* for?" I asked apprehensively.

"To slice through the fiberglass. I assure you it won't hurt," he said as he took my arm and flicked the saw thing on.

It made a high-pitched whine as it cut into the cast. The sensation of the vibrations through my arm was a lot like the cleaning things they use at the dentist, and I couldn't help but shudder. Once he had made a cut to each side of the cast up the length of my arm, he put down the saw and pulled out some kind of bizarre pliers. I didn't even bother to ask what it was for.

He wedged it gently between the two pieces of the cast and pushed it open. The cast gave a soft *pop* in response, and he moved to the other side to repeat the same thing. Then he pulled out a large set of clippers and carefully snipped the padding of the cast. And then it was off and my arm was finally free.

I flexed my hand back and forth for the first time in six weeks, testing the movement, making sure it still moved the same way. I ran my fingers over my forearm, my skin felt weird and a little sticky. My arm felt tight, sore and a little numb. And then I had a sickening thought.

"Somebody hand me a piece of paper and a pen, quick!"

"Why?" Nualla asked as she handed me a pen from her bag and a scrap of paper.

"Because I want to make sure I can actually still draw."

DAMNED IF YOU DO,
DAMNED IF YOU DON'T

Saturday, May 5th

PATRICK

P ROM.

The peppy, cheerful energy rolling off all the girls was practically visible. For a lot of them, this had been the night they had been waiting for all year. Maybe it was a girl thing, but to me it seemed no different than Winter Ball. The same people all dressed up, different location but other than that I couldn't understand why it was such a big deal to everyone.

My slight cynicism was probably due to the fact that my head was killing me, and no amount of over-the-counter painkillers was helping. Any day now, it was going to just become too much, and I was going to have to move on to something stronger—like alcohol. Which they didn't have here because oh yeah, we were in *high school*. So I just sat there trying not to look as miserable as I felt.

I don't know if it was all my brushes with death, but the approaching end of high school just seemed kind of anticlimactic. The rest of my classmates were super-excited to be graduating and starting their new lives. I, on the other hand, was getting more and more nervous. The end of the school meant a lot of changes were coming in my life. I'd be on my way to art school, be married and, oh yeah, no longer be *human*—if I survived, that is.

My nervousness in no way meant I regretted any of my decisions, because I didn't. Being put in any amount of danger was worth it for Nualla. But that didn't mean I relished the idea of my possible demise, or the feeling of being barbecued from the inside. Even if I did have doubts about my new life, there was no turning back now; that ship had sailed a long, long time ago.

And so I found myself at prom with Nualla who was in another gorgeous, unbelievably tempting dress. But this time, unlike Winter Ball, her ring was displayed proudly, dangling right above her cleavage, daring anyone to make the connection to what it *actually* was.

I had gotten much better about being able to contain my urges when I kissed her in public, but when she dressed like this it was more than a little difficult to resist her charms. Trying to swim upstream through rapids with your arms tied behind your back would probably have been easier.

As the dance began to wind down, we all sat around one of the big tables sipping soda. It was a lot like any other day at the lunch table, except with fancier clothes and a few other additions. Beatrice's date was some guy from another school, and they were actually *talking* about books instead of ignoring each other and reading them. Jenny was ignoring her date who looked terrified to be there, which made me wonder just exactly why he *was* there.

"So what are you two planning on doing after graduation?" Jenny asked trying to sound like she really didn't care, but it was obvious she did.

"Getting married for reals," Connor said with a snort as he pushed the ice around his drink with a straw. I choked on my soda and everyone fell silent. Connor stopped moving the straw and looked up. "Oh *fuck*, did I just say that out loud?"

"Yeah Connor, you kinda did," I answered, glaring at him.

Jenny's hawk like gaze darted between Nualla and me before resting on the ring Nualla had been moving back and forth on its chain. Nualla's hand froze as she looked at Jenny and then dropped the ring as if it had burned her. The ring fell and swung back and forth just above the edge of her dress, catching the light and sparkling. It might as well have been a smoking gun.

"Married!" Jenny shouted at precisely the moment the song playing ended. Her voice rang out loud and clear in the momentarily silent ballroom. And of course, everyone turned to look at us, because hell, my luck is just *that* good. Jenny, on the other hand, was oblivious to the crowd of onlookers. A new song began to play, but Jenny was still staring open mouthed at us. "You're *married*?!"

"Getting married, we're *getting* married," I said as quickly and convincingly as I could.

"When were you planning on telling us—on telling *me*?" She was shaking with rage now.

"We didn't want it getting around school till closer to graduation," I said nervously.

"Well, that's a brilliant thought, but you could have at least told your friends," she spat, her eyes pooling with angry tears. As one tear escaped and slid down her cheek she pushed the table viciously and stood. And then she stormed out of the room like so many times before this. But this time I wasn't sure if she was going to forgive me. I wasn't as blind as I had been before. I knew she still harbored strong feelings for me; which was exactly why I *hadn't* told her. But sometimes you're just damned if you do and damned if you don't.

It was Nikki who finally broke the silence several songs later. "Is everyone else as done with this dance as I am?" she asked, flicking a bit of decoration across the table.

"After party?" Shawn suggested with a grin as he looked around the table.

"Oh *hells* yes," I said as I stood. A party would mean booze. Booze meant I could probably get rid of this damned headache and actually *enjoy* what was left of this night.

"Where to?" Connor asked as he and Sara stood as well.

"We rented a suite for the night," Nikki answered with a wicked grin.

"Can I come?" someone asked hopefully.

We all turned to look at Jenny's date who was still sitting at the table. I had completely forgotten he was even there, and apparently so had everyone else.

"Depends; do you drink?" Nikki asked, looking down at him with a mischievous smile as she twirled her purse on her finger.

39

Iᴛ Wᴀѕ Bᴏᴜɴᴅ ᴛᴏ Hᴀᴘᴘᴇɴ

Sunday, May 6th

PATRICK

Eᴘɪᴄ ᴡᴏᴜʟᴅ ʜᴀᴠᴇ ʙᴇᴇɴ ᴀ perfectly good word to describe last night's party. But loud, drunken, and funny as hell would have also fit.

I opened my eyes and rolled to my stomach. My mouth tasted terrible, and I *so* needed a shower. But at least my head hadn't started to hurt—*yet*. I got out of the bed quietly and trudged over to the bathroom. Turning the shower on as I looked in the mirror. *Geez*, I looked like crap; these headaches were definitely doing a number on my complexion.

I slipped off the little clothing I was actually still

wearing and stepped into the warm water. Tipping my head back I let the water rush over me in a soothing wave. I wasn't sure how long I was there just standing like that before I heard the shower door slide open.

"Thought you'd sneak in here without me?"

I turned around, and my jaw hit the floor. I had seen Nualla in various stages of undress in the past few months, but this was the first time I had seen her naked; well, that I could remember, at least. I just stood there for a second letting the water rush over me, unsure of what to say. I opened my mouth to speak, but my words were lost in her kiss. Soft kisses, which gave way to harshly passionate ones as she pressed closer to me.

I felt my hands sliding down her shape to rest on her hips. Felt my fingers grip the sides of them and pull her tighter against my body. She responded with a thrust of her hips, pushing me against the shower wall. Her hands moved to rest on my shoulders as her thigh slid up mine to rest below my hip. Pictures erupted into my mind; flashing lights, an impossibly soft bed, the shape of a bare hip. Vegas. It was Vegas all over again. The all-consuming fire of that night; the knowledge that no one would ever fill my head but her.

And then I slipped and whacked the water faucet with my elbow. A cold icy wave hit us and my eyes shot open. "Oh *fuck*, that's cold!" I yelped as I leapt out of the path of the water.

"You're not kidding," Nualla agreed through gritted teeth as she did the same. Then she looked up at me smiling a crooked smile. "Want to continue this in the next room?" she asked as she turned the water off.

I wanted so badly to say *yes*, to scoop her up in my arms and carry her to the bed. But now that the ice water had cleared the foggy desire that had taken over my mind, I could now think rationally. But only just barely.

I averted my eyes from her beautiful naked form so I wouldn't lose my resolve. *Dammit, why do I always have to be so rational?*

"Nualla, I want nothing more than to do that, *trust* me. But—look, you and I both know what will happen if we do."

She looked at me for a long moment before she sighed. "You know Patrick; sometimes you're too sensible for your own good."

"Don't remind me, I'm only barely strong enough to say no to you right now. It's hard enough saying no when you actually *have* clothes on, but—"

"Oh *really*?" Nualla said, sliding her arms around my shoulders and dragging her fingers down the back of my neck.

I nearly lost control then and there; I mean I *was* only human. Well at least, for a little while longer. "Oh, now you're just not playing fair."

"All's fair in love and war," she stated as she slinked out of the shower.

I whipped one of the large bath towels off the rack and captured her in it. "Well if you're going to play dirty, then so am I," I said as I scooped her into my arms.

I kicked the bathroom door open and carried her into the room. If I couldn't do *everything* I wanted to do, at least I could do this.

I dropped Nualla onto the bed and leaned over her, kissing her neck just below the ear.

"Stop, stop, *stop!*" she said, gently pushing on me.

I pulled away and looked at her. "What?"

"*Now* who's playing dirty?" Nualla asked with playful glare.

"Now we're even," I said as I moved to sit next to her.

There was a knock on the door just before it opened. Being that I was still naked, I dove for a nearby pillow. A red-faced Nikki gaped at us before slapping her hand over her eyes. "Um…we were all about to head down for breakfast and—"

"We'll be right down," Nualla stated in an unsteady voice.

Somehow Nikki managed to back out of the room without looking and slammed the door shut. I flushed bright red and looked over at Nualla who promptly burst into hysterical laughter. "You should see your face!"

"Hey, it's not funny, at least *you* had a towel!" I shouted indignantly, whacking her with the pillow.

Everyone was more staring at their breakfast than actually eating it when we arrived at the large booth table. The dark sunglasses covering everyone but Nikki and Shawn's faces made it more than a little obvious that everyone was hungover.

"Hey guys, awesome night huh?" I asked as I slid into the booth.

All my human friends groaned collectively.

"How come *you* four look so chipper?" Connor asked as he looked between me and the daemons.

"Because we normally drink a lot," Shawn answered with a small sympathetic smile before he pulled Nikki's hand to his lips and kissed it. Nualla just gaped at them, making a little choking sound.

I just smiled as I asked, "So who finally made a move?"

They both looked at each other, turning bright red.

"I believe she asked if he liked her dress, and he said it would look better on the floor, right before he stuck his tongue down her throat and left the rest of us alone with the booze," Beatrice said, rubbing her temple as she clutched a cup of coffee.

Nikki and Shawn turned even redder and Nualla actually did choke on her coffee this time.

"*Smooth*," I said with an ironic smile.

Shawn looked over at me conspiratorially. "These girls are dangerous when they get you drinking."

"Oh believe me, I learned *that* a long time ago," I said with a wry smile.

Nualla and I ordered some breakfast when the waitress came back around. I doubted either of us would eat much of it, but it made us look far less conspicuous to actually *have* food when sitting in a diner.

"So, anything else happen last night?" I asked, eyeing the rest of my friends.

Connor held up his phone. "The whole school probably knows about you getting married by now."

"*What*?!" I yelped, grabbing it from him. Sure enough it was all over iTribe; someone had even managed to get a video of Jenny's outburst. "Oh, for *fuck's* sake; how did someone even *get* that on video?"

I looked over at Nualla who looked for once like she was going to be the one to faint. "It was bound to happen sooner or later, right?" I asked nervously.

We All Fall Down

Wednesday, May 9th

NUALLA

CONNOR HADN'T BEEN JOKING WHEN he said the whole school probably knew about Patrick and me getting married. They all totally did know. I couldn't turn a corner without some random person I didn't even know commenting on it. Or speculating about it. Or trying to give me ill-conceived advice. But it was okay, I was taking it all in stride with a smile plastered on my face. I had been okay, that is until they announced it during morning announcements this morning. Now I felt like throttling the next person who was dumb enough to mention it.

Nikki, Shawn, and I walked into the atrium on our way to grab lunch. We were halfway across the room when I was struck by a feeling of dread. It felt like my heart had just frozen solid and dropped to my feet, and yet I could hear it pounding in my ears. Shawn's head jerked up a fraction of a second before mine and our eyes both darted around the atrium. But as my eyes scanned the faces nothing seemed wrong; people were chatting and enjoying their lunch hour. It was a normal day like any other, until I saw a sleek shape entering the front entry doors of the school.

A skintight suit clung to every curve of her body making it unmistakable that she was a woman. The shape of the hood covering her head also made it completely apparent that she was not human. When I looked at her my eye kept wanting to slip around her. Like she wasn't there, but she was most definitely *there*.

Her hood made it impossible to tell what kind of daemon she was, so I would just have wait and watch. She could be a Kalo Protectorate officer, or a Warrior of Kalo or she could be—

"What's wrong?" Nikki asked in confusion before she answered her own question. "Who is that?"

"I don't know yet," I answered, not taking my eyes off the mystery daemon. I couldn't do anything until she acted, but that didn't mean I couldn't prepare for the worst. "Shawn, do me a favor, go stand over by the fire alarm. If she hurts anyone you pull it, 'kay?"

"'Kay," he answered as he moved quickly but calmly to the fire alarm. Strolling toward it like he was just going to grab something from the cafeteria or his locker, but I could see the tension in his shoulders, the way he was clenching and unclenching his hands inside his pockets.

The hooded daemon just stood there, looking about, and then her hand quickly came up to fiddle with something around her neck. She shook it like one might angrily shake a piece of equipment in the hopes that it would stop spazzing out. The field around her wavered, and then she was there clear as day. Whatever the thing was it was pretty damn potent if it was effecting even us. This was not entirely suspicious, that is, until one of the security guards came around the corner, and I saw the glint of her blade as she moved her hand away from her neck.

The guard looked at the blade-carrying mystery woman in shock and said something I couldn't hear. But she paid him little heed as she sliced him with her sword. The guard crumpled to the ground like a sack of potatoes, and she stepped over him without a second glance. And that's when I knew for certain she wasn't one of the good guys. That she was Kakodemoss, and we were all royally frakked.

As I whipped my eyes away to call out to Shawn, I caught movement out of the corner of my eye; I could only look on in horror as Miss Bell came down the stairs and ran into the assassin. She looked down at the fallen guard's blood spilling out across the floor before her eyes darted quickly up to the face of the assassin. A heartbeat later she let out a blood-curdling scream that could be heard loud and clear, even in the glassed-in atrium just before Shawn pulled the alarm.

Everyone in the atrium and the halls beyond it fell abruptly silent. Slowly they all turned to stare numbly at the sleek deadly form of the Kakodemoss assassin; blood dripping off her sword. She had probably meant to enter the school unnoticed. That plan was out the window now. With a snap, all the students ran in mass panic to flee the atrium, all heading for the back doors of the school.

I grabbed Nikki's arm. "We have to find Patrick, we can't leave him here!"

The sword-toting assassin looked me dead in the eye and with no thought to the human life around her, began felling anyone in her way. Nikki was still standing stuck in place, so I shook her arm and screamed, "Nikki!" Her head snapped around to look at me. "She's coming for us. Don't think, just *run*!"

All the students were now fleeing the building by any exit possible, but mostly through the back doors. I had to find Patrick, so I threw all my weight into pushing through the crowd to the back stairs. It was like trying to swim upstream through a sea of terrified fish.

Nikki was wrenched from my hand. "Nualla!" she called out in panic.

"Go Nikki, call Alex!" I called out as she was carried away from me by the fleeing students.

I didn't wait to hear her answer, just shed my bag and kept running. Everything in my bag was replaceable; I was not.

I made it to the second floor landing before I was knocked against a wall; my head smacked against the glass case with a sickening crack. I heard the screams of fallen students drawing closer. Then I saw Patrick. I nearly clotheslined him as he came around the corner. His expression was a mix of relief and frantic terror.

"No! Not that way. We have to go down the other side!" I grabbed his hand and we ran down the hall flat-out for the other stair.

"Nualla, what on earth is going on?" Patrick asked breathlessly as we ran.

"A Kakodemoss assassin has infiltrated the school and is killing everyone in her path," I shouted over the blaring fire alarm.

"I thought you said they didn't exist?!" Patrick asked as he stopped dead.

"Apparently I was wrong, okay? Anyways, not really important Patrick; not *dying* is," I said as I jerked him forward again.

We were almost to the other set of stairs when

I remembered something very important. The stories always said that Kakodemoss assassins never fought alone, like the Warriors of Kalo they always worked in teams. Which meant that just because I had seen only one, it didn't mean there weren't others.

I put a finger to my lips and quietly wrenched open a janitor's closet next to us, dragging Patrick inside. I tried to shut the door, but the closet wouldn't shut all the way. *Crap*—of all the closets to hide in, I had picked the only one in the school that didn't shut all the way. Go figure.

Patrick bent close and whispered into my ear, "What are you doing? We could have escaped!"

"There's at least two of them," I whispered back, peering out the gap made by the open door.

"*What*?! How do you know *that*?!"

"Just *trust* me, okay?" I said, looking back at him pleadingly.

And then the floor creaked, and we fell silent. Only a second later the first assassin appeared just on the other side of our door. I held my breath and squeezed Patrick's hand tightly. Then the other one, also clearly a woman, came from the other direction, from where we would have fled to. She was much slighter and shorter than the first assassin.

"We have to go *now*. Their police have nearly arrived, and the Protectorate won't be far behind," the second assassin said anxiously. Her voice sounded suspiciously familiar, but I just couldn't place it, not with my heart beating so loudly in my ears.

"Good. Exactly as planned," the first one said in a cruel hard voice.

"*What*?" the second assassin said, startled.

"Now we move on to phase two," the first assassin stated as she turned and ran swiftly down the hall.

As the sounds of sirens wailed in the distance, the second assassin looked around once more before bolting down the hall. I let several tense moments pass before I slowly pushed the door open. The hall was empty, but I didn't trust that enough to just casually stroll down it.

I took Patrick's hand, and without a word we crept silently down the hall to the stairs. I peered around the corner, and it was also deserted. I was not completely sure that the assassins had left, but we also couldn't stay hiding here forever. When we made it to the main floor unharmed I finally breathed a sigh of relief. Then I saw the ground.

The floor was covered in blood. Students lay dead in the hall, victims of the twin blades. I was about to turn and leave the building when a hunched form caught my eye. I looked at it more closely. It was a student; a girl, a daemon girl. It was—*Penelope?* I took a step in her direction.

Patrick grabbed my hand and pulled me closer to him. He looked down at me with pleading eyes. "Let's get out of here—I don't…I don't want to lose you."

"It's okay, they're gone."

"How can you be sure? They could be hiding," Patrick countered, his eyes darting quickly around.

"'They walk unseen but they do not hide,'" I quoted.

"*What*?"

"Never mind, just trust me on this, okay?" I answered, squeezing his hand.

I took another step toward Penelope, and the floor below me creaked. Her head whipped up, dark tear tracks of mascara covered her cheeks. Penelope's eyes were wild, but they calmed as she recognized me. Now that she had moved her head, I could see a curved horn protruding from the head of a student in her lap. Penelope looked past me to Patrick and bent over the figure in her lap again, blocking them from view.

I looked into her eyes. "Penelope, it's okay. It's just Patrick; he already knows what we are."

Penelope considered this for a second before she released the body a little.

I looked down and was nearly sick. A large oozing wound covered the body from shoulder to hip. The wound was not the red it should have been had it been, but a sick acidy green. They had used titanium blades. This confirmed my fears. This was not a random attack, or even a planned attack on humans.

No, this assassination was meant for daemons. For us. For *me*.

I looked more closely at the face of the person Penelope was holding in her arms and nearly fell over backward. It was Michael.

"She came at us—at me. Michael—he jumped… he jumped in front of me. He *saved* me," Penelope said in a small trembling voice before she burst into uncontrollable tears. "They used a titanium blade. He didn't know. He died—he died to save me."

I crouched down next to her and tried to think of something—*anything* to say. I opened my mouth just as Penelope released her hold on Michael and threw her arms around me sobbing. I closed my mouth again and reached out a hand to stroke her blood-matted hair. Penelope had never been my friend. She had never even been nice to me. But this was beyond petty high school drama. This was cold-blooded murder. So I let her cry, unhindered, into my shirt.

Patrick cleared his throat and moved closer. "Um…Nualla the Police are going to come through those doors any second now and…well I can see his horns."

My heart stuttered in my chest, and I quickly looked down at Michael. Our illusion shields could withstand anything—anything but death.

This was bad, this was *beyond* bad. The human police and EMTs would be here any second, if they weren't already outside. They would see him for who he was—*what* he was. What the frak was I going to do?

I started to panic, but then an idea swirled into my head. Hell, it might even work; if it didn't kill me in the process that is.

Dropping our illusions took quite a bit of effort and concentration, but trying to extend our illusions outward was a whole different story. Making humans not notice that something was there was a skill we all possessed to a certain degree. Michael had been the best that I had ever seen until today. I myself wasn't terribly good at it; my abilities were firmly situated in the power of influence and persuasion. However, combating titanium contamination and trying to make another daemon appear human would require an unprecedented amount of effort and concentration; if it was *even* possible.

"I'm going to try something," I announced as I squeezed my eyes shut and imagined my illusion extending to Michael. I poured every bit of me, every ounce of strength I possessed into the effort. Slowly, my concentration unwavering, I opened my eyes and looked up at Patrick. "Can you still see him—I mean as something *other* than human?"

"No...but how did you—?" Patrick asked in confusion.

"No time to explain. I can't do this for long." I

turned to Penelope. "I need you to be strong for me, Penelope—for him. Can you do that?"

She sniffled and nodded. "I think so."

"Okay, the two of you need to carry Michael out of here. I have to call someone and keep this illusion up until they get here."

"*They*?" Patrick asked, a little exasperated.

"Later Patrick, I'll explain later." Now was definitely *not* the time for explanations.

Patrick and Penelope hoisted Michael up and started toward the door while I searched the floor around me until I found my bag that I had dropped earlier. It had been trampled by the stampede of fleeing students, but my phone was still safely inside the pocket. Okay maybe *safely* wasn't the right word considering the screen was shattered, but at least it still turned on.

I dialed the Daemon Emergency Number and someone picked up on the second ring.

"Kalo Emergency Response, please state your emergency," a female voice said on the other end of the line sounding anxious and distracted.

"I'm at Bayside Academy; the school that was just attacked. We have one down that needs special transport. He's dead."

The voice of the other line now sounded completely panicked. "Has anyone seen him? Have we been compromised?"

"Not that I know of, we're on our way outside now. I'm extending my illusion shield to him, but I don't know how much longer I can continue." I could already feel my strength waning.

"You're doing *what*?!"

"Please hurry," I whispered faintly into the phone.

"We're—" a loud noise sounded in the background on the other end of the line and the call cut out. Something was definitely up, but I didn't have time to think about it.

I dropped the phone and collapsed to my knees. If help didn't arrive soon, I would lose consciousness and then we'd all be royally frakked. I laid down on the ground, breathing heavy and time lost all meaning.

The next thing I was aware of was strong arms lifting me up and loading me onto a stretcher. I heard the slamming of doors and felt the bouncing of a vehicle running over the cracked and potholed streets of San Francisco.

I mumbled almost incoherently. "Weak...please help."

I felt a sharp jab in my arm, then it felt like an

electric current had run rampant through my body. I sat bolt upright nearly bumping heads with the daemon leaning over me.

I looked around wildly; a relieved Kalo EMT was looking down at me. "Thank the *gods*. That little stunt of yours nearly killed you. As it is, I'm not even sure it should have even been possible in the first place."

"Michael." I whipped my head around and saw the other stretcher next to me. Michael lay there just as dead as he had been before; there was no saving him. Beyond him sat Penelope holding his deathly pale hand, unabashedly crying.

"Never do something like that to me again," Patrick choked out under his breath.

I looked over at him a little guiltily, he looked terrible, and I could only imagine what seeing me collapse like that must have done to him. I took his hand in mine and leaned against him closing my eyes. "I'm sorry."

"I don't *need* you to be sorry. I *need* you not to scare the crap out of me like that ever again," he said as he pulled me tighter.

We arrived at the Folsom Street Kalodaemon Hospital and the EMT jumped up and opened the doors. They unloaded Michael solemnly from the back. There was no point in rushing; he wasn't coming back.

"Are you coming?" the Kalo EMT who had been

riding with us in the back asked, looking at me a little uneasily. I'm pretty sure my use of my abilities had freaked him out just a little.

"No, I'm okay." I looked over at Penelope who was staring down at Michael, still refusing to leave his side. "Could you make sure she's okay though? The person she loved just died."

"Oh," he answered sadly as he looked back over at Penelope. "Sure thing, kid."

And with one last uneasy look in my direction, they all disappeared into the building. A few minutes went by; people passed us on their way inside, but I just stood there numbly taking it all in.

"It's another one of *those* buildings isn't it?" Patrick asked, rubbing his temples.

I looked over at his pained expression. "Yeah, I'm afraid so."

"If I go in just now, I'm going to hurl," Patrick admitted as he looked at the building apprehensively.

"Want to get out of here?" I asked nervously, looking around.

"I hope to hell you don't mean to Vegas this time," he said, opening one eye.

"No, I was thinking more like to your house; it's only a few blocks from here," I answered, gesturing down the street with my head.

"Wait, there's been a daemon hospital down the street from me, and I didn't even notice?" Patrick asked taken aback.

"That's the general idea, Patrick; for you *not* to notice."

"Damn, you guys are good."

41

Nothing is Ever What It Seems

Wednesday, May 9th

NUALLA

"My room's just up the stairs. You don't mind if I change into something a little less—bloody?" Patrick asked as he looked down at himself in disgust.

I looked at him, looked at the blood; Michael's blood that had already started to eat through the fibers of the cloth. "No, not at all."

Patrick pulled his acid green stained black polo shirt off over his head as his walked up the stairs. And then I saw it, saw the mark just between his shoulder blades. I saw it clear as day; there was no mistaking it. A six horned gazelle with a crescent moon perched atop its horns; dark bluish purple like a bruise, but much darker than any bruise could ever be.

"'And they shall so be marked,'" I whispered on a startled breath, so soundlessly that I wasn't even sure I had said it aloud.

The Marked Ones. The children of Kalodaemons that were not born daemon. An anomaly in the genetic code of our species. Born with a mark identifying them for what they truly were. A mark even they couldn't see with their human-like eyes. Forced to walk the fine line between the worlds, but a child of neither world. If Patrick's parents were Kalodaemons, surely they would have told him. Or he would have at least popped up in the database when I got him his Blue Card. But he hadn't, which only left one answer.

I stepped backward knocking over some papers on a nearby mail table. This couldn't be; it wasn't true. My luck couldn't possibly be that bad. But as the papers fluttered to the ground, my fears screamed out at me plain as day. The symbol on them was unmistakable. I could deny it all I wanted, try to run away from it, but it wouldn't change a thing.

Kakodemoss.

Patrick turned to me and smiled, but his smile disappeared when he saw my face. "Nualla, what's wrong?" He took a step toward me back down the stairs, and I took two back.

I chanced a glance down at the papers. There was no mistaking it. It was there, the symbol of their order. A spike piercing through a crescent moon and ending in three downward facing Egyptian lotuses with two horns curving up, nearly encircle the design.

I looked up into his confused face and swallowed. Could I trust him, or had they gotten to him? Had this been part of their plan all along?

"Nualla, what's wrong?" Patrick asked again, looking even more concerned.

I pointed a shaking finger at the fallen mail. "Patrick, whose papers are *those*?"

He looked down at the papers then back up into my face looking even more confused. "My parent's. Why, what's going on?"

"That's the mark of the Kakodemoss Order," I said, pointing a finger at the symbol on the mail.

"That terrorist group? The people who just attacked the school?" Patrick asked, staring at me in disbelief. I couldn't bring myself to answer—answering would make it real—so I just nodded.

I took another step back and then another, inching my way back to the door.

"Nualla—I *swear* I didn't know!" he pleaded as he took a few more steps toward me.

"Have you ever gone with them?" I asked, fumbling for the doorknob.

"Gone with them *where*?"

"Patrick, *please*!"

"Nualla, I don't understand."

"Have you ever gone with them to a Kakodemoss building, a meeting, *anything*?" I demanded, still frantically trying to get the door open.

He paused for a second squeezing his eyes shut before they shot back open, and he blinked like crazy. "*What*?"

"Patrick, please just *answer* me." I was barely containing my terror at this point.

"I *am* answering you. I have no idea what that symbol means, or any of this for that matter!" Patrick looked nearly as upset as I was.

I looked up at him, tears welling up in my eyes. "How can I believe you? How can I believe a word you say when your parents are...what they are?"

"Nualla, I have never gone with them anywhere. Hell, I hardly ever see them since they are never here! The last time I remember seeing my father was when I broke my damn arm!"

"But how can I trust you?" I asked, trembling.

"I *swear*, I have nothing to do with this."

"But—"

"I swear on this bond that I would never betray you!" Patrick vowed, holding up his wedding ring. Though we were no longer legally married, the gesture was the same.

"But they're your *parents*!" I knew that he loved

me, but I just couldn't make myself believe it with all certainty anymore.

"Nualla, I gave up any ties to my old life when—"

"But they're your *family*."

"They stopped being my family a long time ago," Patrick stated, looking away.

Silence hung in the air for a long time, and then I heard the words. "'Let my arms be wings, to shield you from your fears. Let me be the sword, by which you vanquish all your foes. Let me be the cure that heals all your wounds. Let me be the light that chases away the darkness. Let me be the bond that binds you to this safe place.

"'Take my days, and fill them softly with your smiles. Take my nights, and warm them gently with your kisses. Take my love, and hold it closely to your heart and I will give you all that is mine to give.'" After a short pause he added, "Will you trust me *now*?"

"How did you—how could you remember that? I was—we were wasted."

"Actually, I didn't remember it; Alex gave me access to the Kalo online database. I looked it up there. I take the promises I make very seriously. I wanted to know what I had sworn to do."

Questions were filling up my head faster than I could track them. I knew the answers had to be there, just around a corner. All I had to do was think hard enough. I went back to the beginning of everything; the beginning of us. I raced forward to today, but nothing seemed out of place, no clues leapt out to share their secrets. And so I went back farther and tried to dredge up *any* memory of Patrick before the time he had stood up for me in front of Michael. But I couldn't, not even a fragment of him passing me in the halls.

There was something *very* wrong with that, something that screamed for my attention. No one could just appear out of nowhere, they could only be hidden. But how could you hide a person? Then the image of the assassin fiddling with something at her neck flashed before my eyes. She had had something, something that kept her hidden. Something that made me feel like my eyes didn't want to see her. Like my brain was trying to forget her. Like she was a wall, a tree, a ghost. Unremarkable, invisible, like our buildings—like my car.

If we could use this against the humans, there was no reason it couldn't be used on us. But Patrick didn't have anything like that, I had no problem seeing him, it's not like he was— And then I remembered that day back in Mr. Lucas' class, that conversation we had had that first week we had met.

"My mom gave me a pendant too."
"Really?"

"But I seem to have lost it this week."

The smoking gun.

Frak.

I now knew the answer. As impossible as it seemed, I knew deep down that it was the truth.

With a sigh, I looked up into Patrick's worried eyes.

"Your pendant, the one your mother gave you, when *exactly* did you lose it?"

Patrick froze dead still and his brow furrowed. "*What*?"

"Patrick, please just answer the question," I said in the calmest voice I could muster, but I'm pretty sure anyone would have been able to hear the strain in it.

"I lost it that first day in the hall, that first day we talked."

Frak, I hated being right. "That pendant was probably an optical shield. The wearer could appear however they liked. It's like what we use on our buildings and cars. Travis said they couldn't be made that small. Apparently, he was wrong."

"So you weren't really ignoring me—I mean on purpose?"

"No, it was just the pendant."

"But why would someone give *me* something like *that*?" Patrick asked, looking extremely uneasy.

"Because *someone* didn't want anyone to know that you were a Marked One."

"A *what*?" Patrick asked, his eyes wide.

"A Marked One, a child of daemons who's not born daemon."

"Wait, did you just say I'm not *human*?!"

"Not—*exactly…*" I said, nervously running my teeth over my bottom lip.

Patrick looked like he was going to throw up or pass out—or *both*. "And you know this how?"

"You have a mark on your back that marks you as one."

"I have a mark on my *back*?!" Patrick asked incredulously, his eyes growing even wider with shock.

"Yes, right between your shoulder blades, but I guess you wouldn't be able to see, would you."

"I don't know, I might be able to see it now," Patrick said nervously, running his hand through his hair.

It was my turn to be shocked. "*What*?"

"Well you see I—"

I held up my hand, and Patrick cut off abruptly. That feeling in my chest was back again. That feeling that had preceded the attack on the school. "Patrick, who else has keys to this place beside you?"

"Only my parents. *Why*?"

And then I heard a voice in the hall outside Patrick's home and the jingle of keys behind me. I darted past Patrick, grabbing his hand to pull him up the stairs behind me. The door to the right on the top of the landing was closed, and the one straight ahead was a bathroom, so I chanced the left door. I just hoped it was the door that lead to his room.

With barely a second thought, I hit the floor and rolled under the bed just as I heard the front door downstairs creak open. I held my breath, squeezing my eyes shut. I had made the rash decision to trust Patrick with my life; I just prayed to Daenara that it wasn't the *wrong* choice.

A woman's voice from below called out in an anxious tone, "Patrick?"

I could hear Patrick swallow hard before calling out. "Up here, Mom."

As the woman rushed up the stairs, Patrick grabbed a shirt and pulled it over his head in enough time to meet her on the landing.

"Oh, Patrick!"

"Mom, what are you doing home so early?" Patrick asked in startled voice.

"I heard what happened at your school on the news and got here as soon as I could."

That was a complete lie. There was no way it had gotten on the news that quickly and that she would have had enough time to get here. *We* had barely just made it here, and we were *at* the school. And that's when I knew for certain that they were part of the

Kakodemoss Order. I just hoped Patrick was smart enough to catch the lies too.

"Thank goodness you're alright," his mother said with relief.

"A little shaken up, but no real injuries," Patrick said uneasily.

There was a pause. Something was wrong. I wished I could peer out and find out what, but I couldn't risk it.

"Patrick dear—why is the mail all over the floor?"

Patrick let out a breath. "Oh, I knocked it over right before you came in; I was just going to pick it up."

There was another long pause. "Patrick—what's that stain on the floor?"

I looked frantically to the left, there was a smudge on the carpet from when I had dropped to the floor. I was as good as dead.

Before Patrick's mother could investigate further, her cell rang. "Hello? Yes dear, he's perfectly alright. You worry too much…" She continued her conversation as she drifted out of the room.

As quietly as he could, Patrick took a few steps toward the bed. In a barely audible voice he whispered, "You okay?"

Before I could answer, his mother reappeared in the doorway. "Honey, I need to run to the office. You'll be alright on your own, won't you?"

"I always am, Mom," Patrick replied with a shrug.

I had to take my chance now if I was ever going to know for sure. As silently as I could, I peered out from under the bed toward the doorway. Two dusky red horns rose from the shoulder-length blond hair on his mother's head. I slid silently back from the edge of the bed. My worst fears had now been confirmed. Patrick's mother was a Kakodaemon.

Five minutes after Patrick's mother left, I finally slid out from underneath the bed.

Patrick crouched down next to me. "Since I didn't give you away, do you believe me *now*?"

I swallowed hard. "Patrick, I believe you, but now I have to ask you to trust *me*."

"You know I do."

"We have to leave now. Take only what is most important to you because you can never come back."

"*Excuse me*?" Patrick asked in a strangled voice.

"Patrick, your mother is part of the Kakodemoss, and they will *kill* you if they find out about us."

He swallowed hard, fighting back tears. But who could really blame him, I had just basically told him that his mother was a monster who was out to kill us. It seemed like I was only there to continue to shatter his world.

"I know…"

"You *do*?" I asked, thrown.

"I should have told you before…I can kinda see through your illusions."

"*What*?! But that's not—" I was about to say it wasn't possible but stopped myself. "Right, not human." Thinking of Patrick as being something *other* than human would take some getting used to. I really didn't know that much about Marked Ones, so it could have been perfectly normal for Patrick to already be starting to see our world. "So what is it like?"

"You all flicker slightly between what you *actually* look like and what I'm supposed to *think* you look like."

"So you knew what she was while you were talking to her."

"Yeah…you have no idea how hard it was just now not let on that I knew."

Patrick wasted no time preparing to leave. As he shoved some clothes and other items unceremoniously into a duffle bag, I looked around the room. It looked like any other teenage boy's room, except maybe a little cleaner. Then I saw them covering the walls around his desk—drawings. I took a few steps closer and gasped. They were all of *me*.

I reached out a finger and touched them. I would have thought they were stalkerish if not for the stark vulnerability of the artist they captured. His feelings were plain in every stroke. Love. It was as if his love had flowed out of his hand onto the pages.

"They're beautiful," I said in a small voice.

Patrick took a few steps toward me and put his arms around my waist. *"You're* beautiful."

I reached out and unpinned one from the wall.

"It's okay, we don't need to take them; I already have the real thing right here," he said, holding me tighter.

A tear rolled down my cheek and bounced off the desk. "We have to take them all. We can't leave any piece of me here in this place for them to find."

Patrick sighed. "Then we'll have to take the computer too."

He reached down and unplugged the black box as I unpinned more of the drawings from the walls. There was too much to say and so naturally neither of us said a word.

We walked down the hall away from Patrick's home, me with the duffel bag slung over my shoulder and Patrick carrying the black computer box. When we reached the elevators I extended my hand to press the down button, but before I could the doors sprang open. A very pissed looking Tylia was on the other side of the doors, her arms folded across her chest.

"You should be at the hospital right now," Tylia stated in a stern motherly way as she slammed her hand against the edge of the elevator door so it couldn't close.

"I feel fine."

"You should let a doctor decide if you're *fine*," she said with a scowl. "What's all this for?" she asked, her eyes shifting to the duffel bag and then the computer box.

"Um…" I said, racking my brain for a good lie but coming up short. Tylia jerked suddenly, startling us, and the elevator door started to close. "What—?" I yelped, jumping back.

"Phone," she replied as she slammed her hand flat against the edge of the elevator door and pushed it back open again, sliding the phone out of her pocket with her other hand. "Damn vibrate; I will never get used to this thing."

Patrick leaned in toward me and whispered. "Just how old *is* she?"

I shrugged, I really didn't have any idea, and I would never ask.

Tylia's brow furrowed before her eyes went huge. "*What*?! You can't be serious?!" She tapped the screen and looked up at us. "We have to go, The Embassy was just attacked."

"*What*?!"

42

LAST KISS

Wednesday, May 9th

PATRICK

WHEN WE ARRIVED IN FRONT of The Embassy, the people on the street were paying it no mind, but I knew better.

Tylia jumped out of the car then turned around to talk to us through the window. "You two stay here. If I'm not back in ten minutes, you drive to the house in Marin and lock the doors. If anyone comes near the car, you get the hell out of here, *even* if you know them. Is that understood?"

"Yes," Nualla answered quietly as she continued to look past Tylia to The Embassy beyond.

Without another word Tylia was gone, running into the building at an alarming pace. The building flickered less than the daemons, but when it did I saw utter chaos inside. A few large shapes littered the floor; I wanted to believe they weren't bodies. But I knew better than to hope they weren't.

"Don't you find it odd that The Embassy was attacked right after the school?" I asked, looking down the streets suspiciously. "It's like they knew it would have less security and emergency personnel because they would all be on their way to the school."

Nualla looked back at me, all the color draining from her already pale face. And then she opened the door and leapt out.

"Nualla!" I rushed out of the door after her, but she was too fast. She disappeared into the field of the building without looking back, and I stumbled to a halt on the last step.

Crap.

I looked around nervously at the mostly deserted street. I really didn't want to wait out here by myself, and gods only knew what was waiting for them inside. Tylia and Nualla could be walking into a trap.

I waited for a few more moments before I just couldn't take it anymore. I gritted my teeth and ran straight on with closed eyes. I could now see better through the fields, but it still made me feel queasy and disoriented if I looked at it too long. My fingers hit the door, and I wrenched it open. I continued running blindly forward, my hands stretched out in front of me, so I didn't run into the archway.

I hit something soft but solid, and when I opened my eyes I was looking up into the confused face of my father. "*Dad*?"

"*Patrick*?" he said back, equally confused.

Then everything spun out of control, and I was lost in the blackness.

NUALLA

I SLAMMED MYSELF INTO THE DOOR, but it was locked. "Travis, it's Nualla, open the *damn* door!" I shouted as I pounded my fists against the door. They were right behind me, and if I didn't get through this door I was toast because like an idiot, I had walked into a trap.

After entering the lobby, I had tried the elevator, but it had been down. So I had been forced to settle for the stairs. I had slunk up the stairs as quietly as I could, trying to keep my rising fear under control. There were so many bodies I was afraid of what I would find when I reached my dad's office. I had stepped onto the second floor landing when I saw her in the distance, one of the assassins. In a panic I had given up all stealth and just bolted down the hallway that lead to the stairs. And now here I was in front of Travis' closed lab door hoping for a safe place to hide; hoping I wouldn't find him dead, too.

After a few long moments I heard a voice on the other side of the door, *"Nualla?"*

The door opened quickly and arms darted out. I almost screamed until I saw that they were Travis'. We were only in the room a fraction of a second before he slammed his hand against the biometric reader sealing the door shut again.

Travis took one look at me and burst into tears. "Gods, I thought you were dead," he sobbed into my hair as he hugged me fiercely. I hadn't seen Travis cry since we were children, so to see him crying now was more than a little startling.

Eventually, Travis stopped crying and sat on the floor against the wall. It was a response of his I recognized, when we were children it was something he would do if he was upset—or scared.

I sat down with him and pulled my knees to my chest, Travis' usually bright lab was dark. "Travis, why are all the lights off?"

"I don't know what they used, but it knocked out all the power. No cameras, no phones, no lights. I've been in here for hours with no way of knowing if they're still out there."

"Oh, I assure you, they are."

"*What*?!" he asked, looking at me.

"I saw one; why the hell do you think I was banging on your door?"

Travis looked like he was going to be sick. He swallowed hard. "Not that I'm not happy to see you alive, but what are you *doing* here?"

"Patrick and I escaped the attack on the school unharmed, but others—like Michael—weren't so lucky. They were using titanium blades; there was nothing the Kalo EMT's could do for him. I pulled a dangerous stunt to get him out of there unseen and paid the price for it."

"What did you *do*?" Travis asked with large eyes.

"I extended my illusion shield over him."

Travis looked at me fearfully, but he didn't speak for a long time. Finally he asked, "So Michael is…"

"*Dead*? Yeah he is. So are a lot of others at the school, and here. After we left the hospital, we went to Patrick's house and then—and then Tylia got the call and we came here."

"But the phones are all out. Even *my* cell isn't working. How were they able to call her?"

"I don't know." This whole day was getting more and more unsettling.

We sat in silence for a long time huddled on the floor like scared children in a storm. "I need to tell you something, but I need to know I can trust you first," I said, my chin resting on my knees.

"Nualla, you're my best friend, there isn't *anything* you should be afraid to tell me."

"Even if it means you would be committing treason?" I asked nervously.

"I would risk my life for you in a heartbeat, and you know that," Travis said, brushing a strand of electric blue hair away from my face.

"I can't ask for that kind of loyalty from you... I'm not—I'm not yours," I said, looking away from his eyes.

"I know that you never will be, but that still doesn't change how I feel," Travis confessed, twisting a strand of my hair around his finger. Neither of us were saying it. Neither of us had *ever* said it. We had spent over three years *not* saying it. I had thought once that I—but every time I had thought of getting close to him, of trying to be more than a friend to him, something had held me back. Something deep inside that I couldn't explain. But now it felt like those reasons—those walls—were slowly cracking, and I was afraid to be there when they came down. Because I wasn't sure I'd be able to resist everything that would come rushing through.

I looked back up at him slowly. "Even if what I tell you could be used to make me yours?"

He paused, looking at me seriously before he

swallowed hard. "It's about Patrick, isn't it?"

"Yes," I said quietly.

Travis leaned his head back against the wall. "Even if I had information that could get rid of Patrick, I wouldn't use it," he sighed as if just saying it hurt him. He squeezed his eyes shut and then they flashed open again, and he reached out, cupping my face in his hand. "Because that would mean I would also be betraying *you*," he said his face dangerously close to mine. "Okay?" he asked, raising his eyebrows.

"Okay," I said, letting all the breath out of my lungs.

"But before you say anything more let me go turn something on." He leapt up and fumbled around in the dark. A few moments later he came back and held a device out in his hand.

"What is it?" I asked, looking at the small device.

"It disrupts audio equipment; if someone was dumb enough to bug my lab they wouldn't be able to hear our conversation."

"You are even more paranoid than I thought, Travis."

He sat back down and placed the device at our feet. "It's on now, so go ahead. I promise that what-ever you say will never leave this room."

"Thanks, Travis," I said with a small smile. I took a deep breath and let it out slowly. "Patrick's a Marked One."

"*What*?!" Travis choked out in complete shock. "Did you know that all along? Did *he*?"

"No, and no."

"Well that's not really an act of treason, my brother was—" Travis stopped mid-sentence and turned to look at me with horror-filled eyes. "His parents are Kakodaemons." It wasn't a question, he didn't need to ask. He was the smartest person I knew, if anyone would have gotten it right off the bat, it was Travis.

"Yeah," I answered, avoiding his eyes.

"Are you sure?"

"I *saw* her Travis—Patrick's mother—she's most definitely a Kakodaemon."

"Okay I believe you, but you do realize she would have had to have gotten pregnant the first time, *and* carried him to term even through the daemonification process." Travis paused for a second as if he himself was processing this in his head. "The odds of that are astronomical."

"I know." It was a rarity on top of an impossibility on top of a horrible miracle.

Travis' brow furrowed. "Unless they—"

Blam, blam, blam! The sound of gunshots reverberated in the hall outside the door. We heard footsteps and something metal clinked against the door. I held my breath. They had found us; we were going to die. Travis grabbed my face and kissed me for all his worth. I couldn't really blame him; it was a nice way to die.

"Anyone alive in there?" a female voice called from the other side of the door. That voice it was— *Tylia?*

I opened my eyes and pulled my lips from Travis'. "Tylia?" I called out in an unsure voice.

"Of course, who the hell *else* would it be?" Yep, definitely Tylia, she was the only one who would answer with that much disrespect to my rank.

I stood up and moved toward the door, but then realized I couldn't open it. "Travis," I said, gesturing to the door with my head. He stared at me completely stunned. "The *door*," I said a little more slowly.

He finally snapped out of it, but only just a little. "You kissed me back," he said, staring at me in disbelief.

Oh hell.

"Well *yeah*, I thought we were about to die; it seemed like a pretty good idea at the time," I admitted with a shrug.

"But you *kissed* me," he said still dumbfounded.

"Yeah, stranger things have been known to happen, now open the *gods-damned door*!"

"Right," he said, finally moving forward and pushing his hand against the door's biometric reader.

Then something occurred to me, only Travis could open the door which meant we had been perfectly safe in here.

"You knew they couldn't get in, *didn't* you?" I asked, glaring at him.

"Um...I kinda forgot," he answered, looking at me sheepishly, and I only glared at him more. "*What*? I *swear* it didn't occur to me okay? I don't think very well when threatened," he admitted, a deep flush across his cheeks.

When the door slid open Tylia was still holding her gun, and I got the feeling it had been her who had been shooting.

"What happened?" I asked, looking apprehensively down the hall.

"Um, gee, where to begin. After I told you specifically to *stay* in the damn car, you ran in here—in an attempt to make my job just *that* much harder, might I add," Tylia replied, glaring at me. "Oh, *and* I shot one of the bad guys. Or I should say, *girls*."

"But what good would that do? They're daemons."

"A bullet's still a bullet, child. It's still gonna hurt no matter who you are," Tylia said, putting a hand on her hip. "Trust me a bullet through the heart will kill *you* just as sure as anything else would."

"I guess you're right."

Tylia's eyes suddenly narrowed, and she looked at us suspiciously. "What were *you* two doing locked in here?"

"Escaping bad guys," I answered with a shrug.

"Among other things," Travis coughed, looking up at the ceiling. I elbowed him and he gasped, "*Geez*, Nualla ow!"

"Right…" Tylia said skeptically. "Let's get the hell out of this place," she said as she turned around and walked down the hall.

"You don't have to tell me twice," Travis said, following Tylia out the door.

"Oh, and your boy's passed out on the lobby floor," Tylia called over her shoulder to me.

"*What*?!" I yelped, running after them.

PATRICK

AFTER WHAT SEEMED LIKE A very long time, I heard someone calling my name.

"Hmm?" I answered woozily.

"Oh, thank the *gods*," a female voice said, it sounded familiar, but it wasn't Nualla's.

"*Tylia*?" I guessed as I opened my eyes to see Nualla and Tylia looking down at me. The second I sat up everything pitched off-kilter. I was *so* going to hurl if I didn't close my eyes again.

"Just what exactly *were* you trying to do, kid?" Tylia asked, stifling a laugh.

"Follow Nualla."

"What made you think you could just walk in here easy as pie? Did you see a sign that said, 'Hey humans, come right in, the water's great.'" I could hear the smirk in her voice even if I couldn't see it.

"Actually technically he's not *exactly* human," Nualla confessed in an unsteady voice.

"*Excuse me*?" Tylia replied as she shifted her weight.

"I'm apparently something called a Marked One," I clarified as I rubbed my aching head, it had been hurting all day, and I'm sure smacking it on the marble floor hadn't helped.

"You're *kidding* me?" Tylia said in disbelief. When no one said anything Tylia let out a heavy breath. "And you thought this gave you a pass just to run into the building?"

"Well I mean—" *Yeah, that's* exactly *what I had thought, but thanks for making me sound like an idiot.*

"Patrick the effects of the door won't go away until *after* you're a daemon," Nualla informed me as kindly as possible.

I felt arms wrap around me and pull me to my feet. "You know, for a smart kid you're kinda dumb sometimes," Tylia said with a snort as she put my arm over her shoulder. I started to open my eyes, and Tylia stated very close to my ear, "I'd keep those closed if I were you, but then again, I like my lunch in my stomach and not on the floor."

I squeezed my eyes firmly shut and swallowed hard. Another person wrapped my other arm over their shoulder, but it wasn't Nualla. This person was far too tall.

As we began to move forward I asked, "Who else is here?"

"Travis," Nualla answered from behind us.

"Hey," Travis said from next to me.

Great, because I *really* wanted him to see me like this.

After we were down the steps Nualla asked in a worried voice, "Patrick, did you hit your head?"

"I think I saw my dad," I answered woozily.

"Yeah, he most definitely hit his head," Tylia said before I felt her lean away from me. "Here, help me get him into the car. We can check out his head when we get to the house."

"Can I open my eyes now?" I asked hopefully; being led around blindly was more than a little unnerving.

"Yeah, it's fine. We're outside," Tylia answered, letting go of me.

I opened my eyes and instantly knew it was going to be bad. We were outside, away from the illusionary field, but apparently nobody had bothered to tell my body that. I wobbled on my feet and dropped to the ground.

After I was finished losing the contents of my stomach in the gutter, I finally sat back on my heels. "So, what exactly happened in there?" I looked up into Nualla's eyes afraid of what I would find there. "Is your family okay?"

"I think so, I didn't see them among the——" She looked back at The Embassy, unable to finish her sentence.

"So those were bodies in there?" I asked as I looked past her to The Embassy.

"Yeah—a lot of them," she confirmed, looking down at her shoes.

"Just like the school."

"You know, if you hadn't had Nikki call your father, he probably would have been there when The Embassy was attacked," Tylia pointed out, all mirth gone from her face.

That sobering fact hit home, and we all sat in silence looking up at The Embassy. I suddenly felt tired, so very, very tired.

THE BONDS THAT BIND US

Wednesday, May 9th

NUALLA

T HE THREE OF US, TRAVIS, Patrick and I, stood outside the front door of my family's Marin house.
Tylia had opted to stay further out by the car and
relate the news about The Embassy to the other mem-
bers of the Kalo Protectorate. I took a deep breath and
turned the knob; I didn't know what I would find on
the other side of the door. Would my family be whole
and safe—or would someone be missing.

The door fell open, and my family rushed forward
the second they saw me. "Nualla!"

They were all there, every single one, even Shawn.

They all looked worn and stressed, but no one looked injured. I let out my breath. *Thank the gods.*

I was folded into a dozen hugs, and after today I just wanted to hold them close and never let go.

"Nualla, where have you been?" Loraly asked frantically.

I recounted the last few hours for them all. The escape from the assassins, the trip to the hospital and the graveyard that The Embassy had become. But I had left out one very important piece—the truth about Patrick.

When I was finished I looked at Alex. "I have to say something, but before I do, I have to ask, are *they* here?"

He understood my meaning and his expression turned serious. "They are not in the house, but yes, they are on the perimeter of the estate."

I pulled out the audio interrupter device Travis had given me and clicked it on. "I'm going to tell you something that can never be spoken of ever again. This counts as an act of treason, so if you're uncomfortable with that leave now." No one moved. "I'm serious."

"We're not going to betray you Nualla, we're your *family*," Skye stated sounding slightly offended.

"Shawn?" I asked, looking more directly at him.

"I'm not going anywhere," he replied, pulling

Nikki closer to him.

I opened my mouth to speak, but it turned into a surprised gasp when Shawn's father, Roy Vallen, came around the corner. "Roy!"

He surveyed us questioningly. "What's going on?"

Roy had always been like an uncle to me, but I wasn't sure I could trust him with this. I squared my shoulders. "I need to say something and I can't say it in front of you, Councilor Vallen."

Roy's eyebrows shot up in surprise. "Nualla, you have never once called me that in all the time I have known you."

"Well, it *is* what you are and because of that, I cannot have you here."

"Why?" he asked hesitantly.

"Because I'm about to commit an act of treason," I answered swallowing hard.

Roy put a hand to his face and pinched the bridge of his nose. "Didn't anyone tell her?"

"When could we have, she just got here," Andraya answered with a huff.

"Tell me what?" I asked, looking around the room at their faces.

"Nualla, the Grand Council is gone," Roy answered, looking up at me sadly.

"*What*?" I said, nearly falling over.

"The only member of the Council that survived the attack was myself. And it's actually *you* I have to thank for that."

"*Me*?"

"You had Nikki call Alex. Because of that, none of us were at The Embassy when it was attacked. So you see, sweetheart, you probably saved my life. To betray you now would say that my life was meaningless," Roy said with a weary smile.

"Thanks, Roy," I answered in an unsteady voice.

Now for the hardest part, the part I felt terrible for having to say. I swallowed hard and looked Alex dead in the eye. "You have given an oath to place the well-being of your region first and your family second. If you are unwilling to break that—leave now." I hated myself for forcing this decision on my dad, but I wouldn't betray Patrick, even for my family. Even for my dad.

Alex looked beaten down and utterly defeated. "I was forced to betray my family once. I can't—no, I *won't* do it again," he stated firmly then looked into my eyes. "I'm staying, Nualla."

With a nod, I turned to Patrick. "Patrick, take off your shirt."

Patrick looked at me scandalized. "*Excuse me*?!"

"Just do it, Patrick, *please*."

He continued to stare at me like I was insane for a moment before he finally understood. Without another word, he pulled his shirt off and turned around. They all stared in shock, and the glass Skye had been holding slipped and shattered on the floor.

"But that's a…" Nikki said barely above a whisper.

"Yes, it is," I answered quietly.

"But that means he's protected by the Marked Child Act, they can't lay a hand on him for knowing our secrets," Shawn said, grinning at his father.

"No, that law does not protect *everyone*, Shawn," Roy said, looking at his son sadly. "It only protects the children of Kalodaemons."

Shawn looked at his father in confusion for a second before realization crossed his face. "No. No *way*. He couldn't possibly be—" Shawn said as his eyes darted between his father and Patrick.

"If he wasn't, this would not be an act of treason, and Nualla would not have made us swear to silence," Alex said gravely.

"Your parents are *Kakodaemons*?" Shawn asked, staring uncomprehendingly at Patrick.

Patrick turned around and slipped his shirt back on. "Yeah…yeah, they are."

I looked at Alex; he had never looked more devastated than he did in this moment. He had realized that I had chosen Patrick over my people, over even my own family. It was a shattering and harsh reality to have to swallow in silence.

"Did *you* know this?" Andraya asked, glaring at Patrick.

Alex moved to place a hand on her shoulder. "No, I don't believe he did. Patrick is not capable of that kind of deceit. The real question is why they never told him about our world, about *what* he is." Alex stared at Patrick curiously for a long moment before a sad realization crept across his face. "You disowned your family, didn't you, Patrick?"

Patrick looked up shaking in anger. "Those *people* may have created me, but they have never been my family." And then he slumped his shoulders and hung his head. "I have no family now."

Alex was by our side in a few swift steps, pulling a shocked Patrick into a tight hug. "No, you are wrong, you *do* have a family. You are a Galathea, now and always. *We* are your family now. And I will die before I let them take you, Patrick." He pulled away to look at Roy. "I cannot let you take him, Roy."

"Who would I take him to, Alex? The Grand Council is gone, it's just you and me now."

We all stood there in silence for what seemed like forever. Eventually Loraly asked, nearly in tears, "What are we going to do? If anyone finds out they'll kill him."

"I have a plan," Travis announced as he moved away from the wall to join the rest of us.

"You *do*?" I asked, turning to face him. Travis had been standing silent this whole time, but I knew better than to think his brain had stayed quiet. Could he really have found a way out of this mess?

"A Kakodaemon Marked One is *incredibly* rare. So rare, it would be possible to say that they just kidnapped him as a child."

"*What*?!" Patrick said, nearly falling over.

Roy seemed to understand where Travis was headed and a devious smile crossed his lips. "How good are you with records?"

"I'm the one who *built* the modern records system," Travis answered, almost offended.

"Do you have any qualms about forging records?" Roy asked, crossing his arms.

"For Patrick?" Travis looked over at Patrick speculatively before adding, "None at all." Then his eyes darted quickly to me before going back to Roy. "This is a frakked up situation, and I'm all for making it less so."

"Wait, wait, *wait*," I said, putting up my hands. "What are you guys talking about?"

"They're going to make me a fake identity so no one can prove what I actually am," Patrick answered in a calm voice.

"*Excuse me*?" I said, staring blankly at them.

"I have to do this quick before the systems come back up in the main building," Travis said, typing away on a sleek tiny tablet he had pulled from his lab coat pocket only moments before. I'm sure it wasn't the *only* thing hiding in the pockets either. His pockets could seriously give Felix the Cat's bag a run for its money with the amount of random ass crap I had seen him pull out of them over the years.

"You're crazy, you can't hack The Embassy's records system from *here*!" I said incredulously as I watched code go flying across the screen.

"*Please*," Travis snorted, rolling his eyes. "I hack much worse at the Coffee Press when I'm bored."

"Remind me again why we employ him?" Roy asked, leaning toward Alex.

"Because he is a certifiable genius, and he's far more dangerous to us if we *aren't* paying him," Alex answered in an amused voice.

"Oh, right," Roy said as he stuck his hands in pockets in a gesture that was so much like his son's that there was no doubt whatsoever where Shawn had picked it up from.

"*And* Loraly would kill the both of us if we didn't do right by Josh and Misaki."

"I heard that Alex!" Loraly called from the couch.

"So who are you going to make me?" Patrick asked, leaning over Travis' shoulder.

Travis' fingers stopped typing for a brief second before he continued. "My brother."

"*What*?!" Patrick yelped, standing bolt upright in

shock.

"My family was killed in a suspicious car accident when I was little," Travis said without looking up.

My breath caught and I couldn't help but stare at him. We had been best friends nearly my whole life, and this was the closest he had gotten to telling me what had happened to his family. I knew they had died, that he had then come from Seattle to live in the orphanage in our Embassy. But he had never wanted to talk about *how* they died, and I had never been able to bring myself to ask.

"You would be willing to do that for *me*?" Patrick asked, astonished.

Travis' fingers froze for a second again. "Sure, I owe you."

"For *what*?" Patrick asked suspiciously.

Now Travis' fingers really did stop in earnest, and a slight blush spread up his cheeks. "For kissing your wife—I mean, fiancée."

"You mean when we came to get the—you mean that one time in the lab?"

"No, I mean earlier tonight, actually," Travis admitted, the blush in his cheeks spreading like mad.

Patrick, Alex, and Roy turned to look at me. "What are you all looking at *me* for? *He's* the one who kissed *me*. And we thought we were about to die, for crying out loud!" I snapped indignantly.

Patrick clenched and unclenched his fists. "Deal."

He didn't look at me, and I was glad, because I wasn't exactly sure what my expression said at the moment. "Would that even work, though?"

Travis stopped and looked up at Patrick, his expression unreadable. "Why wouldn't it? I actually *did* have a little brother, and he was a Marked One. Who's to say you're not him?"

"But he looks nothing like you, Travis," I pointed out.

Travis turned to face me with a crooked smile. "You never saw my mom."

There was a knock on the door, and Travis' eyes quickly darted toward it. In the flash of an eye his hand darted out and he slipped the audio interrupter device into his pocket.

Not even a second later the door opened, and a Kalo Protectorate Officer looked around suspiciously before looking at Alex. "Chancellarius Galathea, is everything okay in here?"

"Everything is fine," Alex answered with a tight smile.

"Better than fine," Travis added with a grin as he stood. He put an arm around Patrick's shoulders and grinned wider. "I just found my little brother, Patrick Centrina."

44

PERSONAL DEMONS

Wednesday, May 9th

PATRICK

I FELT COLD, SO VERY COLD. I turned the water on as I stripped away my clothes. I had changed clothing back at my home, but it hadn't helped, I still felt dirty, tainted, wronged. Home was the wrong word; I had no home now.

I got into the water and tipped my head back. The water rushed over me—I was still so cold. I turned the water up hotter and hotter, but it didn't help. I felt empty inside; hollow, like a tree whose insides had rotted out.

I punched the wall. Why had they kept this from

me? Why had they never said a word about what they were; what *I* was?

I heard the softest of sounds and looked up as the shower door slid open. With the way my luck was going, it would be ninja squirrels or zombies coming for me next.

"Can I...can I come in?" Nualla asked in the quietest of voices.

I couldn't speak, the lump in my throat was just too heavy, and so I just nodded.

Her hair draped over her, concealing the form of her body below, like the depictions of Eve or Aphrodite. Nualla looked up at me nervously through her lashes; I had never seen her look so vulnerable. And that's when I noticed she was crying—tears rolling down her cheeks. She always appeared so strong, so sure, that the fact that she was crying just made the day that much worse.

I reached out to her slowly and she stepped into my arms. A normal person would have been traumatized by at least half of the things that had happened to her today. But she had never let on just how much she was keeping locked up tight inside. She had spent hours standing against the tidal wave of pain, and fear and sorrow, until she could be alone. And now she was letting it all out; this torrent of tears rushing down her cheeks like rain. And it was moments like this that I realized that even though we were so very different, in this we were the same.

She cried out in such anguished pain—big choking sobs that shook her whole body—that I had to bite my lip to keep myself from joining her. And so I just stood there for a long time letting her cry, holding her gently against my body. It was an odd feeling, having her naked form pressed that tightly against me. It didn't feel exciting or sexy. Instead, it left me feeling vulnerable; defenseless; raw. I could only imagine how it made her feel; what thoughts must be passing through her mind.

When I could no longer stand the silence I reached down and gently lifted her chin. "Nualla, I'm sorry, so very sorry. I didn't know what I was, I *swear*. If I had known—"

"Would you still have loved me?"

"*Of course,*" I blurted out in a quick breath that left my lungs empty and aching.

"Then it doesn't matter," she said, holding me closer.

Even though I knew it wasn't my fault, I still felt guilty for unknowingly deceiving her. For causing her doubt. For causing her fear. For causing her even the slightest bit of pain. And knowing that I had been equally deceived did not lessen how much I hurt inside. It was that pain—that guilt—that dredged up everything I had been keeping down for the last few hours. A question that was plaguing me; gnawing its way through my mind. I was afraid to ask, to hear the truth, but still I had to know.

"Nualla, something's been bothering me. If I'm… if my parents are—what they are, does that mean I can't—" I just couldn't bring myself to ask the rest.

"Become one of us?"

"Yeah."

"I'm sorry Patrick, I…I don't know the answer to that."

I felt my legs start to give way, and I slid down the wall. I put my head in my hands. Why did things just keep getting more and more impossible? Was fate just playing a cruel sick joke by tempting me with something I would never be able to have?

I wished I had the answers. I wished I could know that everything would turn out alright in the end.

But I didn't.

45

After the Storm

Saturday, May 19th

PATRICK

L OSS IS A FUNNY THING. Sometimes you feel numb, hollow, raw; passing through your days in a fog. While other times it feels like every sound, every touch, every moment, is an electric shock to your system. This reckless abandon of emotion is the only way to really describe what Nualla went through in the next week and a half. Sometimes she smiled and laughed, but most nights she cried into her pillow when she thought I was asleep.

Me, I worked through the loss with stylus and brush. Sometimes my strokes were harsh, etching themselves into the work. While other times they were a soft, gentle nod to my fallen classmates.

When the tally finally came in, twenty students, a security guard, and one teacher had lost their lives that day and dozens more had been injured; making it one of the worst school massacres in the history of the United States. It was in every paper, on every news channel—inescapable.

They hadn't deserved to die; to have their lives cut short. To be remembered for the way in which they had died instead of the way in which they had lived. And so I drew them—every one of them. Captured them in digital form and gave them a place where they could live on in peace.

I didn't do it for the attention or the recognition the project got. I did it because it was all I had. The only way I could cope. The only way I could bring myself back from the darkness.

I had never believed in a higher power, not really, but I had to believe, had to hope that there was something after all this. That our struggle had to *mean* something in the end. That there had to be a time when we could be happy again, when we could smile again. I needed to find that place; that haven from the darkness.

The darkness that was inside me.

I didn't think it was possible to hate as much as I did; to feel that much pain. I wanted so badly to numb it, to make it go away, but I couldn't. As wrong as I might have been, it felt like it was all my fault. That *I* had somehow caused this, that they had been put in danger because of me.

I had a sick feeling that wouldn't go away; that my parents might have been a part of this unforgivable act.

The day of the memorial service was overcast as if the heavens thought that even one ray of sunlight might somehow be offensive. All it did was make the sea of black spread out before me seem more dark; more sad.

I bit back my pain as I walked silently forward with the others, Nualla's hand cold and pale in mine. Nearly the whole school, it seemed, and their families were standing there. The cold wind whipping past; making you forget the approach of summer. I wanted so badly to be anywhere but here; I just couldn't shake the guilt I felt deep in my chest.

In a break in the crowd I saw her; the one person whose sorrow encompassed us all.

Penelope.

Nualla had explained in the aftermath of the attack the full implications of Penelope's loss. That the way they loved was different than humans, that it was total, complete, ineradicable. That to lose their One was something they could never truly recover from.

Sure, Penelope might someday find a new mate, a new person to share her life with, but it wouldn't be the same. That it wouldn't be her *One*. I asked how she could tell; how she knew what Penelope was feeling. She said she could see it in her eyes. And as I looked at her now, I could finally see it too.

Penelope stood there in front of us with eyes red from so many tears shed. But it wasn't just that; there was something else in those eyes, a pain so profoundly sad and heart-wrenching, I couldn't breathe. Nualla dropped my hand and held her arms open wide for Penelope. And with a choked back sob, Penelope rushed forward into Nualla's arms and buried her head in Nualla's shoulder. The service finally started and still she clung to Nualla, refusing to look out at the proceedings. Whatever animosity had been between them had died along with Michael.

Nualla didn't shed a tear, just stood there, head bowed, a pillar of strength for Penelope. I wished someone could be my strength, because I was all out and the weight was getting to be more than I could bear. The pain in my head was becoming too much for me as well. It hadn't given me a moment's peace in so long it was hard to remember what life had been like before its constant presence. And it was getting harder and harder to hide it—the pain—from those around me.

I looked out at the service; it was surreal standing there looking at pictures of the faces of people I had seen every day, who would never walk the halls alongside me again. I had never known death before; never seen it lying there in front of me. It was something you could never erase from your mind. You could cover it up with whatever you liked, but it would always be there, waiting for you when you closed your eyes.

BROKEN HALLELUJAH

Wednesday, May 30th

PATRICK

WE NEVER RETURNED TO THE Bayside Academy campus. Two weeks after the attack most of us did return to school, but it was to a rented office building. To save us the pain of returning to the scene of the school attack, they had simply opened our lockers, boxed everything up and brought it to the new building. The students that *did* return to school were not the same people they had been. The rooms were eerily quiet, smiles were few and far between, and most of the students walked around in a daze. People jumped at the littlest of sounds, and no one sat with their back to the doors.

Classes were basically a joke; they were more like group therapy than actual learning. A place for us to work on recovering from this tragedy. But there was no place to go to escape the images that filled my head when I closed my eyes. I tried to pretend like I didn't feel hollow inside; like I couldn't feel the pain. But it was a lie that even I couldn't believe.

With a shaking hand, Nualla handed fancy packaged letters to my friends. I had no idea what they were, but apparently Jenny did. "You're still going through with it even after..." For once, Jenny couldn't finish her sentence.

Connor, Beatrice, and Sara looked utterly confused. They all looked down at the envelopes at the same time.

Nualla looked Jenny dead in the eye. "I will *not* let those people take anymore from me."

I heard the sound of ripping paper and looked over at Connor just as he pulled the contents out. "*Oh*," he said in a shocked voice. "They're wedding invites; sweet!"

I was inclined to just stay out of it; Nualla and Jenny were two people you *really* didn't want to step between, but Jenny looked at me, forcing my hand. "*Patrick*?"

I wasn't sure, but I thought I could still see a glimmer of hope in her eyes; like there still might be a chance for us. I sighed. I really hated to squash her hopes, but this had to end. I had to make her understand that the world in which she and I could have been together had died long ago, swallowed up by the choices I had made, and the choices others had made for me.

I moved closer to Nualla and took her hand as I looked up at all my friends. But mostly I looked at Jenny. "Nothing's changed; this wedding is going to happen, come hell or high water."

Jenny didn't say another word, just stood up and walked out of the cafeteria, her invitation still lying on the table. We all watched her go, but no one went after her. We had all gotten tired of chasing her when she stormed off, even Sara.

After a few minutes of silence Connor finally looked over and asked, "*So*...am I the best man?"

That thought had never actually crossed my mind since Nualla had been taking care of most of the wedding stuff. Her world required certain things of her, and so I just let her and her family plan everything. But they were now *my* family too, and I probably should have been helping.

I opened my mouth to answer, but Nualla beat me too it. "Actually, there won't be anyone in the wedding party but us."

"*Really*?" Sara asked, still holding her unopened

invitation.

Nualla, Nikki, and Shawn tried to hide their smiles.

"I'm missing something, aren't I?" Connor asked, looking at me.

I shrugged. *Don't look at me, Connor. I'm just as confused as you are.*

Nualla ran her teeth over her bottom lip before speaking, something she tended to do when trying to explain something she couldn't *actually* talk about. "Our religion dictates that only the couple and the officiator be standing during the ceremony. The bond of marriage is only between two people and no other can have a say."

"Just what kind of crazy religion are you guys, anyways?" Connor asked, looking dubiously at the daemons.

Beatrice whacked him on the head with her invitation. "*Connor*, that's a really insensitive thing to say, you know."

NUALLA

J ENNY WAS APPARENTLY *NOT* GOING to get the picture on her own. I would have to end this once and for all.

I found her alone on one of the balconies staring out at the street below. She made no movement as I opened the door, so she either didn't care or hadn't heard me.

"Jenny, can we talk?" I asked calmly.

Jenny turned to look at me before looking back out at the view. "What is there to talk about? It's clear he loves you. *Of course* he does. It would be easy to love *you*; you're beautiful—and perfect." She turned to face me, scowling as she pushed away from the balcony and made to move past me.

I stuck out my arm, blocking her way to the door. "'Love is not a victory march, it's a cold and it's a broken hallelujah,'" I quoted, not meeting her eyes. The lyrics of that song had never made sense to me before, but the truth of those words was irrefutable now.

"What?"

"Loving someone is never easy. It's a struggle against common sense and reason. It's not just fluffy clouds and hearts. It's harsh, it's painful, it's all-consuming. It leaves you vulnerable in a way that nothing else you experience *ever* will."

I looked up into Jenny's startled face. "That's why there is so little of it in this world. It's anything but *easy*, and not all of us are born good at it." I dropped my arm and looked her dead in the eye. "To love someone, to *truly* love someone, is to know with all certainty that you would lay down your *life* to protect them."

Jenny just stood looking at me in stunned silence for a long time before she spoke. "Apparently I was wrong about you," she said in a small voice. "It's clear you really do love him. But what I still don't understand is why you are both rushing into this right after high school. Are you…are you *pregnant*?" She finally met my eyes on the last word.

I nearly choked. "*What*?! No, of course not!" This line of thought hadn't even occurred to me, but was probably on the minds of most of the students by now.

"Then *why*?" Jenny asked with pleading eyes.

I took in a long breath and leaned back against the door. Somehow, I doubted Patrick had ever told his friends much about his home life aside from possibly Connor. It just wasn't in his nature to talk about his suffering. "You said you've been Patrick's friend a long time, right?"

"Yeah," Jenny answered hesitantly.

"Just how much do you know about his parents?" I asked, looking her in the eye.

Jenny looked at me in silence for a long time before she looked at her shoes. "Nothing really," she admitted reluctantly.

"Well, I can tell you that they are some of the most neglectful people I have ever known. They leave him alone for days, *weeks* on end. And when they were actually there, they're not really *there*."

"That's terrible," Jenny said, looking up at me.

"That's not even the *worst* of it. The attack happened weeks ago and most parents are still fiercely hovering over their kids. Patrick's parents haven't even called him. Not even *once*. They probably haven't even noticed that he moved out to come live with me."

"*What*?! But that's…that's just wrong," Jenny said, anger filling her eyes.

"Tell me about it. My family took him in with open arms, and have treated him like family since we started dating."

"I can understand why he ran away, but still…" It was clear she was grasping at straws, refusing to face the inevitable.

"When life hands you exactly what you want, why would you wait?" I asked, looking out at the towering buildings of the city.

"What?"

"It's something Patrick said to me, and he's right."

Jenny slumped to her knees her head hanging low; it was the posture of total defeat. I had finally won the argument, but like any victory over someone else, it was a bitter one.

I knelt down next to her and took her hands in mine; she didn't pull them away. "Jenny, I know there is someone out there just for you—it's just not Patrick."

"I know," she answered sadly. And then she surprised me for the first time since I met her; she threw her arms around my torso hugging me tightly as she cried into my black polo shirt. I put my arms around her; I would let her cry as long as she needed to. It was the least I could do after breaking her heart.

I heard the door creak open behind us and quickly looked over my shoulder. Patrick and Connor stood behind us looking bewildered. Jenny continued to sob unaware of the intruders to her breakdown. Patrick grabbed Connor's arm, and they both backed out of the door.

Smart boys.

As I sat there holding the sobbing Jenny, I thought about how weird life was. In the past month I had held two crying girls, neither of which I would have ever called a friend.

Eventually, Jenny stopped crying and wiped her eyes with the back of her hands. I stood up and offered her my hand. "Come on, let's get you cleaned up."

"Why are you being so nice to me? I all but admitted to secretly wanting your boyfriend—fiancé," Jenny said, taking my hand.

"'Because the world is too small a place for spite,'" I answered with a small smile.

"*Huh?*"

"It's something my mother used to say when I was little."

47

All the Things I Can't Say

Wednesday, May 30th

PATRICK

Nualla was off doing wedding stuff, and I really didn't want to hang out alone, so Connor and I went to the Japantown Mall after class. We had gone to the mall nearly every Wednesday for the last four years, but in the aftermath of the attack, neither of us had been out much.

We ordered our usual *taiyaki* pancake fish and snagged an empty table next to the koi fish fountain. I guess Connor knew something was up because after we had been there awhile he finally said, "Hey Patrick, can I ask you something?"

I just looked at Connor, if he wasn't flat out asking what he wanted to know, he was afraid of what the answer might be. "You can ask, but I might not be able to answer." I don't know exactly when it had started, but now there was so much of my life I couldn't share with him.

"Why do you arrive with Galathea every day? I know you're engaged and all, but don't you guys live on completely different ends of town?" I didn't say anything. I was a terrible liar and Connor knew that better than anyone. "How long have you been staying with her, Patrick?" Connor asked in a careful voice.

"Since the day of the attack," I admitted quietly to the koi fish in the nearby fountain.

Silence hung in the air broken only by the shoppers around us and the splashing of the fish. "That was like three weeks ago!" Connor finally shouted incredulously.

"Yep," I replied, flicking some crumbs on the table to the koi.

"Wait, what about your parents? Haven't they noticed you've been gone all this time?"

"Nope."

Connor fell back into his chair. "I can see why you left."

All I could offer Connor was half a smile, if you could even call it that.

"I knew they kinda left you alone a lot, but this is

just plain neglect," Connor stated with disgust.

"I'm eighteen Connor, they really can't be held accountable for that anymore."

"Yeah, but what about last summer? You stayed out for like, two weeks solid," Connor countered, folding his arms across his chest.

"You noticed?" I asked, raising an eyebrow.

"Dude, you wore like the same three shirts the whole time."

"Busted," I sighed with a self-deprecating smile.

"So did they ever find out?"

"If they did, they never said anything about it," I answered before taking another bite of my *taiyaki*.

Then something occurred to Connor and he whipped his head back up. "What did you do when you weren't at my house?"

"Wandered around," I answered matter-of-factly.

"What about at night?"

"Rode BART," I replied with a shrug.

"*What*?!"

"Joking! *Geez*, Connor. I stayed in a cheap-ass motel, okay?" I said, looking around at the other mall patrons who were now staring at us.

"And they didn't ask where your parents were?"

"It's *the city*, Connor. They have better things to worry about than kids needing a place to sleep."

"Patrick, if you had just told me what was up, I'm sure my mom would have just let you stay over the whole time."

"I'm pretty sure your mom would have called Child Protective Services, actually."

"Yeah, you might be right about that one," he agreed with a slight grimace.

We went back to munching our *taiyaki*, but then Connor stopped chewing and looked at me. "Hey Patrick, why are you marrying Galathea?"

"Because I *love* her," I replied, slightly offended.

"No, I mean why are you marrying her in a little over three weeks?"

"I really can't go into that, Connor."

"Why not? I'm your best friend!" he nearly shouted, looking hurt.

I sighed and looked away, trying to find the right words. "I've gotten into a mess there's no real way out of. But I can tell you this, the fewer questions you ask, the longer we can stay friends—okay?"

Connor was silent for a long time before he spoke. "There's something special about that Galathea girl isn't there, I mean something *more* than the obvious?"

"Yeah," I answered as I twirled my wedding ring around on its chain, a habit I had picked up from Nualla.

"Are you happy?" Connor asked in a cautious voice.

I stopped twirling the ring around. "What?"

"Are you happy with her?"

I didn't even have to think about that one. "Never been happier."

Connor leaned back in his chair again. "Then I really don't need to know your secrets, man."

I just looked at him for a while before I spoke. "Thanks, Connor. You're a better friend than I deserve."

We both fell silent. Connor leaned on one elbow and stared at the koi fish. I went back to twirling my ring as I leaned my head back.

I was so tired; the truth of what I could now see without the help of the glasses seemed to be draining my strength. My headaches were also getting worse—if that was *even* possible. And I had the sinking feeling that if I didn't become a daemon soon, the headaches would probably kill me.

PHOTOGRAPH

Friday, June 1st

PATRICK

B Y THE TIME WE REACHED Travis' lab, I felt like I was going to be sick.

The more time I spent around daemons, the worse and more frequent my headaches got. I had been self-medicating since mid-April, normal painkillers at first then small amounts of alcohol, but even that had stopped working. I didn't know how many more times I would be able to show up to school nearly drunk before someone noticed what I was doing. But keeping it from my new family was the worst. I really didn't want to tell them that it was being around them all the time that was making me sick. They would do the noble thing and take themselves out of my life; I just knew it. And even though it was probably killing me, I didn't want to be alone anymore.

"Here," Travis said as he tossed a large manila envelope at me.

"What is it?" I asked as I dumped the contents onto the table.

"Your new identity. Birth certificate, passport, Blue Card, Driver's license, and your fake ID when you hit the town," he answered with a smug smile.

"But I don't even have a driver's license *now*," I said, a little shocked.

"I even took the liberty of changing your school records, though you might have to go in and make sure they print the right name on your diploma."

"You left my birthday the same," I said, looking down at the birth certificate.

"Well yeah."

I looked up at him, pretending this all didn't feel as weird as it did. "I just thought you would change it to match your brother's."

"Actually, oddly enough his birthday is the same as yours," Travis said, leaning against the table next to me. "Weird, huh?"

"Yeah," I agreed uneasily.

"Anyways, even if it *was* different I would have

just changed the records. First thing that tips people off that it's a fake ID, is when you don't even know your own birthday."

"You watch way too many spy movies, Travis," Nualla said, rolling her eyes.

I sifted through the pile of stuff; they all looked incredibly real. I picked up the driver's license which I wouldn't be using anytime soon. To be honest, I had never even *tried* to drive a car before.

I was about to shove everything back into the envelope when I saw a photo among all the other documents. I picked it up and looked at it closer; a happy family looked back out at me. A father, a mother, and two sons; the youngest was maybe three, at best. I turned to look at Travis and Nualla. "Who are these people?"

"That would be my family; it was taken just before the accident," Travis answered with a sad tight-lipped smile.

I looked back at the picture. Travis was nearly the spitting image of the father, right down to his pale blond hair and tall movie star build. The mother was a beautiful Japanese woman with long draping black hair and eyes the same black blue as Travis'. But it was the youngest boy that caught my attention. He had the mother's dark hair, but the rest of him was a blending of the two. I had to admit I could easily pass myself off as the boy in the picture.

As I ran my finger over the photo, there was a sharp, shooting pain in my head, then a flash of blurry images, and then nothing.

NUALLA

"Is he okay?" I asked, looking anxiously at Patrick lying unconscious on the floor. He had been standing just a second before looking at the picture, and then he had just collapsed to floor like a sack of potatoes.

"No, he most certainly is *not* okay," Travis snapped angrily.

"I'm fine," Patrick said in a pained voice as he opened his eyes.

"No—you're not," Travis countered, offering Patrick his hand.

When Patrick was sitting solidly in a chair, Travis folded his arms and glared disapprovingly at Patrick. "Let me guess, you're tired all the time and your headaches are getting worse?"

"How did you know—?" Patrick asked, totally caught off guard.

"Besides the fact that you look like death warmed over; I can smell the alcohol on your breath."

I just looked at Patrick in shock, and he looked back at me guiltily. "I'm sorry I didn't say anything, Nualla, it's just with everything else that was going on, I didn't want to worry you. It's just a headache, really."

"Didn't *either* of you read the book I gave you?" Travis asked angrily.

We both just looked at him and Nualla shrugged. "I was busy."

Travis stomped over to the other end of the room grabbed something off a shelf and walked back over. He slammed a book entitled: *So You're a Marked One* onto the table in front of us.

He flipped it open to a page about two thirds of the way through and began reading. "'Once the headaches reach a constant level it is imperative that you, the Marked One, undergo the daemonification process as soon as possible.' You know *why* it says that?" Travis asked as he looked at us with anger only barely masking the fear behind it. "Because if you don't you'll *die*."

"Oh fuck, *seriously*?" Patrick said, nearly falling out of the chair.

Travis took a few deep breaths as he rubbed his temples. "Yes, '*seriously*.' The headaches are your body's way of saying it has become unstable."

I looked frantically at Patrick. "Should we change him right now?"

"No, he'll probably be fine for a little while still. We'll go take his blood and send it to Parker at the lab. If Parker thinks Patrick won't make it to the wedding, we'll start the transfusion right then and there," Travis stated in a weary voice before he looked at me. "If he does *that* again, or anything similar, you call me. I don't care where you are or what time of day it is, you *call* me."

"This is *crazy*! We should just forget everything and start the transfusion now," I said, starting to pace across the room.

Travis grabbed my wrist and pulled me back to face him. "*Nualla*—you deserve a big beautiful wedding and I, for one, am going to make sure you get it."

"Travis, it's not really *that* important."

"Don't you *even* try to pretend it isn't. You only get to do this once," Travis said before a crooked smile crossed his lips. "Okay well *you're* doing it twice, but most of us only get to do it once."

We stared each other down for a while, but like always, I folded. "*Fine*, let's go take his blood."

"We're taking my blood?" Patrick asked apprehensively.

We both turned to look at him; he looked worse than he had before if that was possible.

"Yeah, think you can walk?" Travis replied, taking a few steps closer to stand next to Patrick. It could have been my imagination, but he seemed protective of Patrick all of a sudden. Like a real older brother would be. But it was probably just wishful thinking on my part.

"Here, put these on, they'll probably help a lot," Travis said as he handed Patrick a pair of glasses similar to the ones he had made before. But these were more streamlined and normal, less steampunk, more like something he could wear in public without drawing too much attention.

Once Patrick put them on, I could see a visible difference in his face. Like he had been squinting into the light, and now someone had removed that strain.

"Does it help?" Travis asked hopefully.

"Oh *gods*, yes," Patrick answered, rubbing his temples.

"Okay, ready to go then?" Travis asked, moving toward the door.

"To get blood drawn?" Patrick asked uneasily.

"Yeah," Travis answered, raising an eyebrow suspiciously.

"If I throw up or pass out, I am really, *really* sorry," Patrick said grimly.

"Do you feel that bad?" I asked anxiously.

"No, it's just—the *needles*," Patrick shuddered.

"*Seriously*? Elevators and needles; you guys are hilarious," Travis snorted, a tiny smile threatening to creep across his lips.

"Hey, if it's so funny, what are *you* afraid of?" I

asked, crossing my arms.

"Never gonna tell you."

We stood outside the clinic waiting for them to be finished with Patrick. Travis was being unusually quiet which made me more than a little nervous.

"I know you, you're not telling me something," I said, looking at him suspiciously.

"I didn't want to say something in front of Patrick because it's a little—well, *weird* to be perfectly honest."

"Does it involve you and me?" I asked hesitantly.

"No, I've uh...I've tried to stop thinking about us like that," Travis answered with a crooked smile. After a few moments he looked away again, back at the medical clinic door. His expression was unreadable. "What I didn't want tell him was, my brother was also named Patrick."

A Truth That Changes Everything

Friday, June 8th

PATRICK

T HE CEREMONY WAS DONE. WE were now high school graduates running out to face the brave new world. The auditorium lobby was swarming with hundreds of happy people, smiling, taking pictures, congratulating each other. I searched the crowd for my new family. It felt a little strange to say that, while at the same time it just felt right. Like, now that I was part of them I was whole; as if I had been unknowingly incomplete before.

When they had called my name—my *new* name—during the ceremony, heads had turned and there had been more than a few confused whispers. I had just smiled like an idiot. Travis had said that he had changed the records, but somehow I hadn't believed him until I actually heard them reading off "Patrick Centrina."

But now all that was over. I could leave my old life behind and just be Patrick Centrina. Well, at least for another week, that is. Then I would become Patrick Galathea and leave the rest of my human life behind. I wasn't afraid anymore that I might die. Maybe it was because I had faced death so many times already in the past few months. Or that Travis had assured me that, as a Marked One, I had a ninety-nine percent chance of living through this. Or maybe it was because I believed that the universe wouldn't have put me through so much just to kill me.

With Nualla's hand firmly clasped in mine, I pushed past some people and walked straight into one of the last people I ever thought I would see again, especially *here*.

"Mom!" I yelped, releasing Nualla's hand in shock.

My mother smiled down at me like she always did, but this time something seemed—*off*. There was something unnerving about her—well *other* than the fact that she had two dusky red horns growing out of her pale blond hair. "Patrick, sweetie, why didn't you tell me your graduation was today?"

I just stared at her dumbly, unsure of what to say. What exactly *did* you say in a situation like this?

She ignored my shock and continued on as if it was any normal day, and I was sitting on the couch watching TV. "If I hadn't found the invitation in the mail, I might have missed it." Her eyes drifted to Nualla. "Aren't you going to introduce me to you friend here?"

"Patrick, we should go," Nualla said uneasily behind me.

Normally I would have listened to her—just walked away. But standing there, something inside of me finally snapped. My vision flashed white, and I could feel it bubbling up inside me; anger. I had held it in for so long that I hadn't even noticed it had been there, building through the years, threatening to boil over.

"No, I have something I need to say to her," I stated through clenched teeth as I stared down my mother. "'Why didn't I *tell* you?' Because I've been gone since the day of the attack. Four *weeks*! Have you called me even *once* in all that time? No! Did you even *notice* I was gone?" I shouted at her.

My mother looked around nervously; people were staring, but I couldn't give a crap. "Patrick honey, I know I haven't been home a lot lately, but I've been really busy at work and—"

"What kind of mother doesn't notice for four fucking weeks that her son moved out!" I screamed, my anger ripping through my throat.

"Patrick, what's this about moving out? You can't move out, you're still a child," my mother stated in a patronizing voice.

"My eighteenth birthday was months ago! But like everything *else* in my life, you missed it!"

I felt a hand on my shoulder and looked up to see Alex. He smiled reassuringly down at me before glaring at my mother. The rest of my new family moved closer around me, letting me know I wouldn't have to face this alone. I felt a slight impact to the air that signaled they were throwing up their illusions, a sensation I wouldn't have been able to feel or even *notice* a few months ago. And that's how I knew that this conversation was heading into a territory humans weren't meant to tread.

My mother briefly glared at them before looking back at me again. "Patrick, who are these people?"

"My family, who the hell did you *think* they were?" I snapped, looking at her defiantly.

"Don't be silly, I'm your—your father and I are your family," my mother sputtered, visibly shaken by my statement.

"You and Dad, *family*? Hell, I haven't seen Dad in so long I can't even remember what he looks like, and I have a nearly eidetic memory, for crying out loud!"

I screamed at her; I was beyond angry now. "No, *you* stopped being my family a long time ago. Someone— *something* like you could never be my family."

My mother just gaped at me, her eyes huge, her mouth hanging open. "How...?"

"Oh, I know what you are, I know all about it," I answered, tapping on the glasses. "It was one of the reasons I left; as if I needed more than one."

She just continued to stare at me, swallowing hard.

"Get away from my brother!" someone shouted abruptly from behind us and I whipped around to see Travis moving swiftly toward us.

"No, he's my *son*," my mother answered venomously.

Travis pushed past us to stand protectively in front of me. I was going to ask him what on earth was going on, but I thought, in his current state, it was better just to back away and ask questions later.

"He was *never* your son! You stole him from us, from *me*, you monster!"

"We only replaced what Joshua Centrina stole from us," my mother said simply, unfeelingly, her eyes cold as ice.

"Don't you *dare* say his name, you murdered him—you murdered both of them!" Travis screamed, lunging forward, fists flying.

I'm pretty sure he would have beaten her to a pulp if Alex and Shawn hadn't grabbed him. "What are you *doing*?! She has to answer for this!" Travis screamed trying to break free from their arms.

"She has a blade, Travis!" Alex shouted as he threw all his weight into pulling Travis back.

And that's when I saw it, a small silver blade with acid green stuff pulsing around it like someone had thrown dye in water. I had been so focused on her face I hadn't seen her slide out the blade. I was fairly certain that had been her plan all along; for us *not* to notice.

Glaring at us with pure hate, my mother began slowly backing toward the door until she was gone. And we could do nothing but watch her go; it was a rotten feeling.

Minutes passed and finally Alex and Shawn released their hold on Travis. He glared after my mother as if his eyes could throw knifes into her back.

"I need to get some air. I'll meet the rest of you outside," Travis announced abruptly before he took a few steps in the direction my mother had gone. Alex's hand darted out to grip his shoulder, and he whipped back around. "*What*?" he growled through gritted teeth.

"I cannot let you cause a diplomatic incident," Alex said in a firm voice.

"But she's a Kakodemoss!"

"And the Protectorate will detain her outside. She will stand trial before the Grand Council once I appoint a new one," Alex stated firmly.

"She *deserves* to die," Travis said defiantly.

"If we murder them in the streets it makes us no different than them, Travis."

They stared each other down for a very long time before Travis folded and looked away.

"I'll walk out with you to your car," Alex said, putting a gentle hand on Travis' shoulder; it wasn't an offer. "The rest of you say goodbye to your classmates and come out when you're finished."

Nualla and I came out to find Travis standing next to a glossy black Porsche, staring sourly into the distance. The others were already standing next to The Embassy car, looking uneasy. I felt a little bad making them wait for us, but I had had a lot of people to say goodbye too, most of which I would probably never see again.

Nualla wasted no time making a beeline for Travis. When she was only an arms-length from him she demanded, "Travis, what in the *hell* was all that back there?"

He pushed away from the car and opened his door. "We can't talk here, get in the car."

Travis followed after The Embassy car, his face

unreadable. Finally, after what seemed like forever, he spoke. "The results from the tests came in this morning."

Nualla looked over at him anxiously. "Is he—in danger?"

"No, he'll be fine for a little while longer," he replied, not taking his eyes off the road. His outburst back in the auditorium lobby had been too passionate to be fake. But the things he had said had left me with a lot of unanswered questions swirling around in my head. I was smart enough to know the answers, but I was afraid to let myself believe they could be true.

"This isn't about the headaches, is it?" I asked in an unsteady voice.

"No, it's not," Travis answered, looking back at me briefly before returning his eyes to the road. "When they ran your blood work, I also had them run a DNA test on us. I'm sorry, but there were just too many coincidences to ignore." He paused, swallowing hard. "The tests turned up some pretty interesting things as it turns out."

"Wait, you said *us*," I repeated cautiously.

"Yeah, turns out you really *are* Patrick Centrina," Travis said with a wry smile.

And that's when everything I thought I knew went up in flames.

JUST A FEELING

Friday, June 15th

NUALLA

"**H**EY GOOD LOOKIN', WHAT YOU up to?" Travis asked cheerily from behind me.

I turned around with a wide smile. "Hey, Travis." I gave him a hug before turning back to look at the activity in The Embassy lobby. "What's going on here?" I asked as I gestured toward all the people with equipment and what-not walking purposefully around The Embassy lobby.

"Well, after the attack on The Embassy, Nathan has really started stepping up the security around here," Travis answered before taking a sip of his coffee. "But if you ask me, I think it was an inside job."

"*What*?"

"Nualla, I know these systems, to do what they did they would had to have had extensive knowledge of how we run things around here. This wasn't just some random hit on an Embassy by Kakodemoss, this was precise."

"You sure you're not just being paranoid, Travis?" I asked, folding my arms.

Travis leaned in closer. "No, we have a mole, I bet my life on it."

"Should we call off the wedding?"

"No, with all this new stuff we should be fine," Travis answered with a reassuring smile.

"So there's no danger?"

Travis leaned in even closer and said in a voice barely above a whisper. "Not unless Nathan's the mole."

"Nathan, Head of Security Nathan? Are you *serious*?" I asked dubiously.

"Hey, it's the only way I can think of that they could have pulled off what they did," Travis answered, shrugging.

"Okay, you really *are* paranoid, Travis," I said, rolling my eyes. Then I looked at him a little concerned. I wanted to say I would believe anything he said, but this was just plain crazy. "*Please* tell me you haven't mentioned this to anyone else?"

"Nope, don't have any proof; just a feeling," Travis replied as he scanned the room with his eyes.

"Speaking of feelings, I have a *feeling* you are currently standing someone up."

"Who?" Travis asked, furrowing his brow.

"Your *brother*. You were supposed to have met up with him half an hour ago."

"Oh *fuck*!" He whipped out his phone and then grimaced at it. "Yeah, gotta go."

"Don't let him get too drunk, Travis!" I called out to him as he all but ran out of The Embassy.

PATRICK

CONNOR, SHAWN, AND I STOOD on New Montgomery street outside Connor's apartment home complex, sipping coffee and waiting for Travis to show up; he was already nearly an hour late.

"Hey guys," Travis called out as he walked quickly up the street to meet us.

"You're late," I pointed out as I sighed dramatically.

"Yeah, sorry about that I was—" he started then looked over at Connor. "—Uh, with Nualla looking over last minute stuff for tomorrow."

"Who are you?" Connor asked, as he looked Travis up and down.

"His brother, who are *you*?"

"His best friend," Connor replied, standing up a little taller until confusion spread over his face. "*Wait*, Patrick doesn't have a brother."

"Sure he does; *me*," Travis stated as he shoved his hands into the pockets of his black Air Force bomber jacket.

Connor looked over at me like he thought Travis might be crazy. "Connor, this is one of those things I *really* can't talk about," I said apologetically.

"Dude, what the *hell*?" Connor said in exasperation as he glared at me.

"Naw it's okay, we can just wipe his memory if we say too much," Travis said as he tapped my shoulder.

"*Seriously*?" Connor asked in disbelief.

"You're *already* saying too much, Travis," I said with a sigh as I rolled my eyes at him.

"Yeah, you're probably right." He pulled an object from his pocket and held it up in front of Connor's face. "Now, I want you to look right here and hold still." Connor stared transfixed at the object and then Travis whacked him on the head with it. "*Geez*, you're gullible. It's just a pen, you idiot. What the hell's wrong with you?"

Shawn and I couldn't help bursting into laughter

as Connor rubbed his head.

"I don't need a device to erase your memory. Just ask Patrick, he seems to do a pretty good job of *that* on his own," Travis said with a crooked smile.

"You're taking us drinking?" I asked, a little surprised. Since the day Travis had given me the glasses no one had let me have a drop, but I really couldn't blame them.

"Bingo," he replied with a mischievous grin.

"Sweet," Shawn said, grinning broadly.

We were going drinking, *great*. There was just one problem, Travis was twenty-one and Shawn and I had fake IDs, but Connor sure as hell didn't. But then something occurred to me. "You're going to do that same trick Nualla did, aren't you?" I asked suspiciously.

"Why Patrick, I have no idea what you're talking about," Travis said not too convincingly as he started walking back down the street.

The look on Connor's face when we all but strolled into the bar was priceless. Thankfully after the initial shock he played it cool, so no one would suspect us. We ordered a round of drinks and took a seat at one of the empty tables.

A few sips into his drink, Connor looked over at

Travis suspiciously. "*Travis*…why does that name sound so familiar?" He narrowed his eyes at Travis then a look of shocked disgust covered his face. "Wait, *Travis*, as in guy-who-kissed-Nualla Travis?"

"The very same, I'm afraid," Travis admitted, a bit chagrined.

Connor just looked at me, and I had to laugh. "It's a really, *really* long story, Connor."

"Dude, I have been okay until this point with all your secret keeping crap, but you need to explain some of this shit."

I just looked at him. I really had no idea where to start, or what would get us in trouble for telling him.

Travis put down his glass and looked at me and Shawn before he spoke. "It's okay, Patrick, you can tell him about the adoption."

I choked on my drink. So *that's* how he was going to play this.

"Adoption?" Connor asked, looking confused.

"Why don't you tell him, Travis, you know a lot more about it then I do." *Like* any *of it, for example.*

"When I was six and Patrick was nearly three our parents were killed in an accident. We had no other family, so we went to an orphanage. Patrick got adopted, but they never told him. When I found him, his adoptive parents and him had a bit of a falling out."

"Did you find out he was your brother before or

after you made a move on Nualla?" Connor asked, narrowing his eyes at Travis again.

"After," Travis answered quickly.

Connor just looked between Travis and me for a while before saying, "That's some soap opera shit right there."

You really have no idea Connor.

Sometime later at God-only-knows-thirty we all stumbled out of the bar.

"Geez, you three can drink like fish," Connor said as he tried unsuccessfully to dial his phone.

"Who you callin'?" I asked as I tried to keep my feet firmly underneath me.

"Someone to come get me," Connor answered as he kept jabbing the phone with his finger.

"Dude, don't worry about it. I wouldn't get you wasted then send you home to get yelled at," Travis said as he flagged down a taxi. It screeched to a halt at the curb and Travis steered Connor toward it with Shawn at their heels. "You guys are crashing at my place."

"Travis, if I have a hangover at my wedding tomorrow, I'm going to punch you," I slurred as I drunkenly wobbled toward the cab.

WARNINGS IN WHITE

Saturday, June 16th

PATRICK

THE NEXT MORNING FOUND THE four of us sitting in a coffee shop with dark sunglasses.

"Remind me to punch you when my head stops throbbing," I groaned at Travis as I rubbed my temples.

"Here, drink some of this. It will make you feel better," Travis said as he handed me a flask of something.

"Do I even *want* to know what this is?" I asked as I took the flask.

"Probably not."

I took a swig and nearly spit it back out. "Gods, what the hell is this crap? It tastes awful."

"Hey, I said it would get rid of your headache. I didn't say anything about it tasting good."

"Can I have some?" Connor asked, sounding equally miserable.

I passed him the flask and washed the awful taste out of my mouth with coffee. Connor took a swig, made a horrible face, and then passed it to Shawn. He took a swig as well before passing it back to Travis.

Travis put it back in his pocket and looked at me. "*So*…aside from your head, how you feeling? You nervous about today?"

"Surprisingly, no." It *was* surprising; I had always thought I would be nervous as hell, but after all the crap I had been through the last few months, I seemed to be all out of anxiety.

"Well, you're damn lucky, because if it was me, I know I'd be—" And then he stopped himself. "You know if it had to be anyone, I'm glad it was you, Patrick." Then he smiled. "I don't think I ever did tell you that."

I didn't have to ask what he meant. "Thanks, Travis."

It was nice to have a brother. To know that no matter what someone would always have my back; always be there to watch out for me. It was a good feeling to feel like I belonged somewhere. Sure, my new family had tried to make me feel welcome in their world, but I had never felt like I truly belonged there; until now. Now I had proof that I was and always should have been a part of their world—of her world.

Travis looked at his phone, and his eyes got wide. He shoved it in his pocket and stood. "Come on Patrick, we have to head out. If I make you late to your own wedding Nualla will kill me."

NUALLA

I SAT THERE STARING AT MYSELF in the mirror trying to calm my breathing. I had already done this once before, so why was I so nervous?

"Hey Nualla, I know it's your wedding and all, but we really should get out there," Nikki said as she leaned against the door frame.

"I know, Nikki. Just give me another second, okay?"

She gave me an indulgent smile and started walking out the door.

I went back to trying to calm my nerves. It was just Patrick; I was just marrying Patrick, nothing scary. Except that I would be in front of hundreds of people who were silently judging me.

I wonder if this was how Skye had felt when she got married to Nikki's dad. Knowing Skye, she probably wouldn't have given the slightest damn what people thought.

I heard the door open again and whipped around. "Nikki, I said I'll be right there!" I snapped in exasperation, but the person in the doorway wasn't Nikki, it was Natasha Jordash. "*Oh*, sorry Natasha, I thought you were Nikki."

"Your father would like to speak with you before the ceremony starts," she said with a smile.

I stood up. "Okay." He probably just wanted to say something sweet and fatherly. If there had been something wrong, he would have come to me himself.

I followed Natasha out into the hall and down one of the hallways on the way to the temple. We turned the corner and someone grabbed me, but before I could scream they placed something over my mouth. And everything went dark and silent as death.

I Should Have Known

Saturday, June 16th

NUALLA

"COME ON SLEEPY HEAD, TIME to wake up," someone said quietly as they jabbed me with a foot.

"*Nathan*?" I asked as I groggily blinked my eyes until the room came into focus.

I looked around; we were in the security office. I tried to move my hands, but they wouldn't move. No, that wasn't right. I could move my hands, they were just—*bound*? I tried to work through the fog in my head; tried to make the world around me make sense.

But I couldn't.

Why was he looking at me that way? Nathan had always been kind to me, to my family. This person, *this* Nathan in front of me was so far removed from that person I knew that I was almost positive this was a dream.

Almost.

"You, my dear, have caused me an endless series of problems," he said as he folded his arms and sneered down at me.

"Nathan, what's going on? Why are you doing this?" I asked hesitantly.

"Your Embassy is detaining my wife and I'd like her back."

"Your *wife*? Why would we have your wife?" None of this was making any sense and my "this is a dream" theory was gaining momentum. However the sick feeling in the pit of my stomach told me that this wasn't a dream.

"You mean you don't know? Tisk, tisk. I thought you were more clever than this, Nualla," Nathan said as he looked me over like I was some kind of experiment that had disappointed him by yielding an unfavorable result.

"What do you mean?" I asked cautiously.

"You didn't find it particularly odd that your school was attacked by katana-wielding assassins when your father's own personal guard is herself a world-class swordswoman? Or that she was conveniently not there when The Embassy was attacked?"

I just gaped at him in horror, my heart sputtering and skipping a beat. If Natasha was one of the assassins, that meant— I looked up at him, my eyes growing larger in shock, my breath coming up short. "You're the inside man," I stated on an exhale of breath, letting it all out until my lungs were empty. It made perfect sense now, why they hadn't found the mole. The mole was Nathan, who would have made *damn* sure he wasn't caught. It was a perfect plan, really.

Damn you Travis, for once couldn't you have just been wrong?

"Finally using that brain of yours, I see," Nathan said with a mirthless crooked smile. "Pity."

Panic started to rise in my throat as the implications of what he was saying worked its way through my mind like a poison. The person who was supposed to be protecting us, the person we had entrusted our very lives to, was out to kill us. Then I realized something even worse; people didn't tend to divulge their secrets to you if they were going to let you walk away. Which meant I was most likely about to die. But still, I just had to ask even though I knew what the answer would be. "Why are you telling me all this?"

"Oh lots of reasons, but mainly because you're not going to live very much longer."

I swallowed hard. "I'm not?" My heart was slamming so hard against my ribs I could barely hear Nathan's voice over the sound of it.

"I need to get rid of you, so she can take your place; her *rightful* place."

"*She*?"

"You're not the only one with that pretty face of yours. As it turns out there's someone that bears a striking resemblance to you, my dear." He moved to give me a clear view of the security display behind him. There stood a girl who looked exactly like me; it was like looking into a horrible mirror.

"The *doppelgänger*," I whispered as my heart shuddered to a stop.

"You two could practically be twins. The only real difference between the two of you is those blue streaks," he said, gesturing to my hair. "And that was easy enough to fake."

I swallowed hard, trying to push down my fear. "And Patrick, won't he notice it's not me?" I asked, but even as I did the horrible realization set in. Now I finally knew why the voice of the second assassin had seemed strangely familiar. Because it had been my voice.

"Oh I don't think he will," Nathan answered cryptically before he looked back at the screens. "Well, things look about to get underway, so I must bid you adieu."

He rose from the table and walked over to push

something in the corner behind me which responded with an electronic beep. As it started to hum and beep quietly, I didn't have to think hard to realize what it was; now that I was more alert I could feel the titanium resonating against my skin. A bomb. A *titanium* bomb. Could he have possibly thought of anything more deadly to us—to *me*.

"A bomb—but why, Nathan? Why would you betray us? Why would you hurt you own people?"

He leaned in conspiratorially. "Let me tell you a secret honey, I'm *nothing* like you." The air around him wavered and his horns turned a dusky red. He was a Kakodaemon. *Nathan* was a Kakodaemon. In one horrible moment the pieces all fell into place.

"Your wife's Jane Connolly isn't she? Patrick's—"

"Former mother? Why yes, yes she is," Nathan answered with a wicked smirk. "You know, it's funny really, when I found out you two got together I thought our whole plan was in the drain. But apparently, you both were too busy running around like idiots to realize the truth."

"But why, why would you want him? Why would you take him?"

"Joshua Centrina took something from me—something *very* precious; I simply returned the favor."

I couldn't find the words to speak, so I just sat there looking at him.

"But I really must be going now, I don't want to

miss that lovely wedding out there," he said as he stood back up again. He took a few steps toward the exit before he turned back around. "You know, as much as I'd like to say I'm doing all this to put you all in your place, or that the very *sight* of you disgusts me, really it comes down to this: I needed a diversion to get my wife out, and I really had no qualms about killing you or blowing up your Embassy to do so," he admitted with a shrug as if it was nothing.

I just stared at him, my heart thudding painfully fast in my chest.

"Be seeing you," Nathan said as he turned and continued toward the exit. But just as he was about the pass through the doorway he stopped and turned. "Oh wait, I guess I won't," he said with a wicked grin as the door shut and blocked him from view.

I bit back my panic as I watched the Nathan on the security screen stroll away. When I was sure he was a safe distance away I sprang into action. Despair was a luxury I *so* didn't have at this moment.

Unfortunately for Nathan, during our lovely chat, I had realized that the wooden chair I was bound to wasn't bolted to the floor. Which meant his plan was totally frakked. All I had to do was break the chair, and I would be free. And thanks to the lovely TV programming they had on lately, I knew exactly how to do that. If Nathan had been as smart as he thought he was, he should have killed me on the spot. Too bad for him I guess.

I swung the chair as violently as I could into the nearby security table, and it splintered into pieces. My arms broke free from the chair easily. Now came the second way in which Nathan had underestimated me. Those dance classes I had taken since childhood had taught me more than just fancy footwork. A deep breath and a little balancing later and I had easily slipped my bound hands to the front of my body.

I ran to the door and reached out for the latch. The second I touched it searing pain ripped through my hand as if I had been shocked. I pulled my hand back so fast I almost fell over. *That bastard!* He had changed the door latch to one coated in titanium. This was just plain evil, really. And how the hell had *he* gotten out? Well if he thought that was going to stop me, he was wrong. All I needed was some fabric to act like an oven mitt. It would still hurt like hell, but at least I would be able to escape this ticking time bomb.

I looked down at where my wedding dress should have been and for the first time I realized I was only wearing a just-barely-long-enough white slip.

Oh hells *no, that girl is not going to marry* my *Patrick wearing* my *frakking wedding dress!*

Well, screw them. I would just find some other fabric. My eyes darted around the room, there had to be something else here I could use. Sure enough, slung over one of the chairs in the corner was one of the KP Officer's jackets.

I love you SF, and your completely unpredictable weather. Even in the middle of frakkin' summer it could be fifty degrees with cold-ass wind.

I grabbed the jacket and wrapped my left hand— there was no sense in messing up the hand I *actually* used. I took a deep breath, gritted my teeth, and wrenched the door open. The second I released the door I nearly doubled over in pain. I would have dropped to my knees as well if it hadn't been for what was waiting for me on the other side of the door.

Travis stood there in his slate-gray formal kimono top and *hakama* pants, looking more shocked than I had ever seen him in my life. "*Nualla*?"

"Yes Travis, who the hell *else* would it be?"

"But—I just saw you back there, about to walk down the aisle," he said, turning back toward the temple.

"That's not me, that's a *doppelgänger*!" I shouted, wincing at the pain in my hand.

"I knew it," he announced with complete certainty as he turned back toward me.

"Wait, *what*?"

"Nualla, I've known you nearly all your life and that girl out there isn't you."

"Has anyone *else* realized that?"

"I don't think so. I only noticed because I saw the other you in the hall. That's why I was out here," he answered, gesturing to the hall before looking at me apprehensively. "So what the hell is going on?"

"Can't explain that right now, Travis, there's kind of a bomb in here," I replied, jerking my head back toward the security room.

"A *bomb*?" Travis blinked at me dumbly for a second before looking over my shoulder in disbelief.

"Yeah, one with titanium, as if a *regular* bomb wasn't enough of a bad thing."

Travis swallowed hard then grabbed me by the shoulders. "Save the others, I'll try to disarm it. If—if something goes wrong—I love you both," he stated in a shaking voice. And with one last look he pulled me into a tight hug before pushing past me into the security office.

I looked back for one terrified second at what could be the last time I would ever see him, and then I turned and ran.

No one stood in my way; the halls were empty. Everyone must already have been inside. I could hear music, soft beautiful notes drifting down the hall, an unfair reminder of what this day should have been. A reminder of how it was being cruelly wrenched from me. I was about to lose everything, my friends, my family, Patrick. Everyone I held most dear.

Everything.

No More Words

Saturday, June 16th

PATRICK

A s I watched my beautiful soon-to-be-wife walk down the aisle toward me, I almost couldn't believe that this was actually happening. Nualla had never looked more beautiful than she did in this moment. Like a goddess in white, her hair pulled back from her face to cascade down her back. The hanging beads of her crown dancing with every little step she took. Her eyes mysterious and otherworldly as ever. It stole my breath away.

She had taken me on a crazy journey these last six months into places and things that I hadn't even thought possible in my wildest dreams. We—I mostly—had made a lot of mistakes along the way, but it had all been worth it. I would go through any amount of pain again if I knew in the end I would get to be with her. I didn't need someone to tell us we belonged together; I already knew it, completely—irrevocably.

She was nearly to me now; any second she would be here, and we would speak those words that would bind us together, now and always.

I took a deep breath then I heard the sound of a door bursting open. "No! Patrick, it's a trap!" someone screamed in Nualla's voice.

Instinctually, I jerked toward the sound. From one of the side doors Nualla ran toward me barefoot, hands bound, wearing nothing but a slip. My brain couldn't make sense of what I was seeing so I turned back to the Nualla I had been watching. But the more I looked at the Nualla in the wedding dress the more I realized it wasn't her. Sure, the girl looked exactly like Nualla, but something was missing; something that told me it wasn't her.

This is like a nightmare.

I whipped my head back around to the real Nualla just as she tripped, thrown off balance by her bound hands. Everything moved so slowly, as if time was hardly passing at all. I reached out my arms to cradle her fall, and then I saw it, the shiny glint of something the *doppelgänger* was pulling from within the bouquet.

A gun!

She aimed it squarely at us; at Nualla. Without much thought, I thrust Nualla to the side putting her out of bullet's path. A normal bullet wouldn't kill her, but after the attack on the school I knew that these people—these daemons—didn't play fair.

The bullet hit its mark and we were falling. I hit the ground with a thud so hard I couldn't keep my hold on Nualla—*again*. I was in the bus again; we were crashing. A pain in my chest stole my breath; I couldn't call out to her.

An explosion of sound rocked the ground and glass rained down. "Travis!" Nualla's voice screamed from somewhere close.

Travis isn't on the bus, why is she calling for him?

"Patrick?" Nualla said in a voice that was barely audible over the chaos around us.

I tried to take a breath to answer her, but the pain was too much. Things were getting blurry—unfocused.

"Patrick!" Nualla's tear-streaked face loomed close over mine. She looked down, and her eyes went wide in fear. "Oh gods you've been shot! Please, somebody help!"

I was—*shot*? But I wasn't shot on the bus, what was she talking about? This wasn't making sense.

I forced myself to take a breath even though the pain was nearly unbearable. My head cleared marginally, and I realized I was in the temple with the shattered glass ceiling above us. We were at the wedding; the fake Nualla had tried to shoot *my* Nualla, but I had snatched her out of the way. I had protected her; even in this frail human body, I had still been able to save her. With the knowledge of that, I could rest with ease. I let out a sigh of relief, and everything got fuzzier.

"*Patrick*? Patrick, stay with me! Don't leave me Patrick, *please* don't leave me! I love you—please don't die."

I wanted to tell her not to worry, not to cry, but I couldn't find the words. And then everything faded into a peaceful black oblivion.

A Time for Miracles

Saturday, June 16th

NUALLA

W HEN PATRICK HAD SHUT HIS eyes, I had nearly lost it then and there.

"Patrick, open your eyes!" I shook him gently, but his eyes didn't open. "Patrick, *please!*" Blood was already spreading across his deep blue ceremonial *haori* kimono top staining it black.

My dad dropped down next to me and extended his hand toward Patrick. But just as quickly he pulled his hand back. "They used a—titanium bullet?" he said in disgusted horror.

Fuck that, I wasn't going to let that stop me from

saving him. I already had the burns on my hand, so I reached to pull the bullet out myself.

Before I could touch it, Alex slapped my hand away. "We can't take the bullet out here or he'll bleed to death!" He looked up at me quickly. "We have to get him to the medical clinic right away." He grabbed Patrick and prepared to lift him. "Nualla, help me!"

I held up my bound hands cursing Nathan not-so-silently in my head. "I *can't*!"

My dad looked down at my hands for a split second before his head jerked back up, "Roy!"

A second later, Roy was there, and the two of them were lifting Patrick off the floor.

It was utter chaos in the hall outside the temple; people were fleeing in all directions, unsure of where to run. I looked back at Alex and Roy and ran smack into someone. Unable to throw my hands out for balance I started to fall back, but someone caught me.

I looked up and my heart leapt in my chest at the sight of Travis in something other than a million bits. "You're not dead," I breathed, in complete shock.

"Yeah, I couldn't stop the bomb so I got the hell out of—" His expression changed from panic to horror. "Oh gods, what happened?"

I followed his gaze to Alex and Roy weaving through terrified fleeing wedding guests, carrying an unconscious and bleeding Patrick. Patrick didn't look good; his face was quickly losing color.

"She shot him—with a titanium bullet."

"These people and their *damn* titanium," Travis cursed.

"She was aiming for me, but Patrick jumped in the way," I said, my lip trembling.

"Yeah, that sounds about right." Travis looked down at me, contemplated something quickly and scooped me up. "It's faster if I just carry you."

We arrived in the medical clinic to find a cowering Dr. LaCosta. "What on earth is going on?" he asked, standing up unsteadily. "Are we being attacked again?"

"Yes, but that is not the immediate problem," Alex said as he and Roy gently placed Patrick on a table. "*He* is."

Dr. LaCosta looked at Patrick in alarm. "He's been shot."

"Yes," Travis replied, looking at his brother.

The doctor reached out a hand toward Patrick and we all yelled in unison. "No!"

"What?" the doctor yelped, startled.

"The bullet's titanium," Alex informed him.

"Then what do you want *me* to do? If I leave it in he'll die and if I take it out he'll bleed to death."

"We have to change him," Roy stated in an unbelievably calm voice.

"He'll die before the change is complete and even if he *does* make it, the titanium will poison him then," Dr. LaCosta said apprehensively.

"We have to try, start the transfusion immediately," Alex ordered, looking at Dr. LaCosta expectantly.

"If we don't time this just right, he's going to die," Dr. LaCosta said anxiously.

"And if we don't do anything, he sure as hell will!" Travis shouted.

"Will somebody please *do* something? He's dying!" I screamed, tears rolling down my face unchecked. There was only so much strength one person could possess, and when it was spent there was nothing left.

They all turned to stare at me, bloodied, bound, and wearing nothing but a slip. I dropped down to me knees, unable to keep standing on my weak and trembling legs. I was so scared, so very scared, that my luck had finally run out. That I was going to lose him.

"Nualla," Travis said in a voice so sad it nearly broke my heart, if it even was possible for it to break anymore than it already was.

He dropped gently to his knees and reached into a pocket concealed somewhere inside his slate-gray *haori*. He pulled something out and took my hands in his. In one swift movement Travis clipped the industrial zip tie that had been binding my hands together. And then he pulled me into a tight hug, cradling my head against his chest. "It's going to be okay Nualla; Patrick's going to make it."

I wanted so badly to believe him, I really did. But seeing Patrick lying there, unresponsive and barely breathing, I didn't trust my heart enough even to hope.

"We should get started," Dr. LaCosta announced in a quiet voice. "And pray to the gods for a miracle."

55

OPEN YOUR EYES

Tuesday, July 3rd

PATRICK

I OPENED MY EYES. I WOULD have thought I was dead or dreaming, but everything was too sharp—too bright. The sounds that hit my ears were loud, louder than I remembered sound being. Or maybe it was just that I could hear farther? That didn't seem right. I looked around a room that appeared to be a hotel suite of some kind and tried to remember how I had gotten there.

No luck.

I took stock of the room. A dresser stood in front of me and a small table to the right of it. I panned my eyes around the rest of the room. There was a short hallway to the left that probably lead to a bathroom and exit. At the right side of the room a balcony door stood open, and I could just see the shoulder of someone sitting there.

I got out of the bed and crept as quietly as I could toward the balcony door. I breathed a sigh of relief when I saw it was Nualla sitting in a chair, sipping what smelled like coffee. Her knees were pulled up to her chest and she was staring out at nothing. I just stared at her, her pale beautiful skin, her loose curls swaying in the breeze, her horns swirling back from that place just above her ears.

Wait, her horns?

I looked at her in shock; she no longer flickered back and forth between her illusion and what she truly was. She just sat there in all her true glory, which meant I was either dead or—

My hands shot up and hit something solid just above my ears—*horns*. They were small; no bigger than an inch, but they were definitely there. I let out a sound somewhere between a sigh of relief and a shocked gasp and Nualla's head turned slowly toward me. When she saw that it was me her eyes got wide and she leapt up, the coffee cup smashing to pieces on the ground. My hands flew to my ears and I squeezed my eyes shut.

Geez, when did everything get so loud?

"Patrick!" I opened my eyes in time to see Nualla just before she collided with me. Quicker than I would have thought possible, I moved to cradle her in my arms. "I thought you were going to die," she sobbed into my chest.

"I thought I was, too," was the only thing I could think of to say. And then Nualla convulsed in another round of sobs.

I looked over my shoulder and guided her backward to the bed without letting go of her. I was pretty sure if I did she would collapse. At this point a sensible person would have asked questions. But the first thing I did after realizing I wasn't dead was kiss her. I was so glad I wasn't dead I couldn't think of anything else but wanting to be close to her.

Eventually, I did stop kissing her and finally asked, "Nualla, what happened?"

"She shot you; we didn't think you would make it," she answered, her lip quivering slightly.

"Nualla, *who* shot me?"

"You don't remember?" she asked, looking at me with concerned eyes.

I thought back, what *was* the last thing I could remember clearly?

Waking up on Travis' couch the morning of the wedding.

I tried to remember past that but couldn't. It was all a tangle of images that didn't seem to make any real sense. "I can't remember past waking up on Travis' couch. Since I'm a daemon now did we… did we get married?" It was the first time I had ever hoped the answer was *no*. I just didn't think I could live with myself if I couldn't remember something as important as that.

"No," Nualla answered in a small voice, she had mostly stopped crying now.

One crisis averted, now to fill in the rest of the gaps in this disaster. "Nualla, can you tell me what happened—from the beginning?"

She took a deep breath. "I was just about to walk out to the temple when Natasha said Alex wanted to talk to me so I followed her. We were walking down the hall and something seemed a bit off, but just as I realized that someone grabbed me from behind and drugged me. When I woke up, Nathan had me tied up in the video surveillance room."

"Wait, the head of your security is named *Nathan*?" I suddenly had a very sick feeling in the pit of my stomach. "This Nathan, is the same person who was pretending to be my father, isn't he?"

"Yeah," Nualla answered reluctantly.

Now what I had seen the day of the attack made perfect sense. I thought I had seen my father because I actually *had*. Or should I say the person *pretending* to be my father, anyways. "Wow, he's even more of a bastard than I thought he was."

"That's not even the worst part," Nualla said timidly.

If the fact that Nathan was a double agent spy wasn't the worst part, I was afraid to know what *was*.

"Nathan had me tied up in the room with a bomb filled with titanium shrapnel. He was going to make me watch you marry *her* before I blew up."

I just looked at her in horror, my heart starting to beat uncomfortably fast. "*What*?"

"He was going to kill me, so she could take my place."

Then the sick feeling got worse. "*Please* tell me I didn't marry her."

"No, I escaped and got to you in time. That's how you got shot. She was aiming for me, but you jumped in the way. It was a titanium bullet—you saved my life."

That sounded like something I would do. I had been protecting her with complete disregard for myself practically since we met.

There was a small pricking of pain in my chest right under my left collarbone. I moved my fingers up to it; there was something there. I pulled up my shirt quickly, and I looked down at a green silvery scar just under my left collarbone in that space that stopped being my chest and sloped upward into my shoulder. I ran my fingers over it slowly, it was a pitted dent about the size of a quarter, the edges of the skin around it silvery green and pulled up around the circular dent like a moon crater. I was fairly certain it must have nicked my lung at least and that I should be dead right now. I released my hold on my shirt and looked up at Nualla in confusion.

"We couldn't take the bullet out or you would have bled to death. So we left it in while we started the transfusion and took it out at the last possible moment," she stated in an emotionless voice.

I just stared at her in disbelief. That was beyond risky; they really must have been desperate.

"We didn't know what would happen," she confirmed as she traced a circular pattern across the sheet of the bed.

"But I thought the daemonification process took a week, how did—?"

"We gave you a lot blood. My whole family— even Travis and Shawn and Roy." I just continued to look at her in shock. "We hoped that if you had blood from a lot of us at once it would change you faster." Nualla smiled up at me, but then her eyes began to glass up, and she burst into tears again. "But when you didn't wake up, I thought you never would."

She thrust herself into my arms, and I held her close. "*Shh*. It's okay, Nualla, I'm fine now." I kissed her hair and held her as close as I could. "I'm sorry I made you worry."

"You made me worry for *weeks*, you idiot," she

sniffled.

"*Weeks*, just how long have I been out?"

"About two and a half weeks."

"Two and a half *weeks*!" I said incredulously.

I wondered how many tears she had shed in those past few weeks. I think if it had been me waiting I would have cracked long before now. Knowing Nualla, she had probably held strong till it was all over. She was just that type of person. Some people broke down in the face of danger while others broke down only when they knew they had reached safety.

She wiped her eyes on the back of her hand and sighed. "Come on, we should go let people know you're okay," she stated as she stood and starting toward the door.

"Yeah, probably," I agreed as I stood. "Out of curiosity, what did you tell my friends?" I asked as I tried to run my hand through my hair. But all I did was catch my thumb on my right horn. *Sigh*, these things were going to take some getting used to.

"That—is a very long story," Nualla answered with a grimace.

Travis stopped dead and dropped what he was holding. He just stared at me, completely shocked. "I'm not a ghost, I promise," I said with an uneasy smile.

He closed the distance between us in two seconds flat and all but tackled me. He hugged me so tightly I was pretty sure that if I *had* still been human it would have broken some ribs. "You *idiot,* why did you have to go and try to get yourself killed?"

"*Me*? *You're* the one who went to defuse a bomb!" I countered indignantly.

"Yes, but *I* had enough sense to run away when I knew I couldn't win."

"Hey, I had a damn good reason for risking my life," I replied, looking over at Nualla.

Travis looked over at her as well. "Yeah, I guess she *is* a pretty good reason."

"Best reason in the world," I replied with a huge grin as I pulled her into my arms. I let my lips brush gently against hers before I closed my eyes and kissed her.

We still had a lot of problems ahead of us and even more unanswered questions. I knew the next few months would probably not be easy. In this world I had become a part of, there didn't seem to be a whole lot of *easy* to go around. But for now, I just wanted to lose myself in this perfect moment, at least for a little while.

READ ON FOR A SNEAK PEEK OF THE NEXT
BOOK IN THE MARKED ONES TRILOGY

THE STORM
BEHIND YOUR
EYES

THE MARKED ONES TRILOGY
· BOOK 2 ·

*Patrick may have survived the Change, but his
problems are just beginning...*

ENDANGERED URBAN SPECIES

Saturday, July 28th

PATRICK

"SO WHAT ARE WE DOING TODAY?" I asked Travis as we walked down the driveway of the Galathea estate. It was the first day since I had found out that he was my older brother that it would just be me and him hanging out. No Nikki, or Shawn, or Connor, or even Nualla. Not that I minded hanging out with them or anything, but it was nice to have a whole day with just us. Just the Centrina boys. No amount of hanging out now would ever make up for the fifteen years we had lost, but it was better than nothing.

"I thought we'd go driving," Travis said casually

as he handed me a coffee cup.

"Anywhere in particular?" I asked before taking a sip of the coffee.

"It's up to you," he answered as he tossed the keys at me, and I fumbled to catch them, nearly dropping my coffee in the process.

"You *can't* be serious," I said dubiously as I looked down at the keys in my hand.

"You've gotta learn sometime," he said with a shrug and walked around to the passenger side.

I just looked at his Porsche. I wasn't a car person, but even *I* had to admit it was beautiful. "You're seriously going to let me drive *this*?"

"Yep," he answered as he popped open the passenger side door and dropped into the seat.

"You know, you're not half bad," Travis said as he took a sip of his coffee.

"Really?"

"Yeah, a few more times out and you'll be better than half the people who drive here," Travis added as he put his coffee cup back in the console.

"Travis, half the people who drive here are *tourists*," I said, flatly.

He didn't answer, a crooked smile spreading across his lips. I pulled my right hand off the wheel and punched him in the arm.

"Hey, hey, hands back on the wheel!" he shouted playfully as he batted my hand away.

I returned my hand to the wheel and slid the car to a stop as the light turned red. After the first jerky stop-and-go start down Pacific, things had gotten much easier. Even with all the one-way streets, hills, and bicyclists, driving in the city wasn't proving to be that hard. I mean sure, my driving wasn't going to win any good driver awards by any stretch of the imagination, but at least I wasn't likely to get a traffic ticket today.

Hanging out with Travis was really no different than hanging out with Connor or Shawn. Laughing and poking fun at each other and all the other things guys normally did to each other. But there was a whole undercurrent to this day that neither of us was bringing up. Normally one of your parents taught you how to drive, but we didn't have any. And so in awesome older brother fashion Travis was teaching me in his sleek black Porsche. But who had taught him? I had Travis, but who had he had?

I got the feeling he hadn't had anyone, and so I didn't ask. Because I didn't want to remind him of the fifteen years. Those fifteen years when he had been alone. When he had thought I was dead.

I let my eyes drift to the pedestrians in front of us. People moved through the crosswalk, dark shapes interrupting the brightness of the day. It was too bright; I squinted against the light and the forms of the pedestrians blurred into a flickering dark mass. And then it all seemed to slow to an impossibly slow rate and everything jumped jarringly into sharp focus.

The slickness of a black leather briefcase; forty-seven silver stars dancing across a tight black tank top; the burning ember of a cigarette as the smoke swirled up through the air—all slid by so slowly as if it wasn't moving at all. And then I saw her—just on the other side of the crowd—bits and glimpses at first. Pale blond hair, bleached white by the sunlight, fluttering in the breeze. Large brilliant blue eyes in a tiny face, looking out at me. Slowly her lips parted, and her eyes filled with fear. The little girl reached out toward me, and I leaned forward even though I had no hope of hearing her.

"*Patrick*," someone called, but I ignored them, focusing on the little girl.

"PATRICK, TURN!" Travis shouted.

The scene in front of me sped up and changed in a blink of the eye. The girl was gone, the people were gone, and I realized I was about to drive into oncoming traffic. I jerked the wheel too sharply and went up onto the curb. Before I could even think to hit the breaks, I collided with a payphone.

When the universe grants you an impossible wish, you should hold on tight and hope you don't wind up dead. Because every whispered prayer to the stars comes with a heavy price.

GEEKY ARTIST PATRICK CONNOLLY IS about to get the one thing he has always wanted. But this one desperate wish is about to start a chain reaction of deadly consequences that will leave no one unscathed.

ARIUS NUALLA GALATHEA HAS SPENT her entire life pretending to be something she's not—a normal human girl. But when she accidentally agrees to marry Patrick, she may have signed up for more than she can handle. This seemingly ordinary human boy has more going on under the surface than she ever could have imagined.

RECLUSIVE TECH GENIUS TRAVIS CENTRINA has been at the fringes of Kalodaemon society since the devastating accident that claimed the lives of his family when he was six. But as his best friend Nualla's life descends into chaos, and the shadowy terrorist organization of Kakodaemons strikes blow after blow against his people, he begins to suspect that the tragedies in his past may be more at the heart of things than anyone realized.

THE SAMURAI KITTY SQUAD NEEDS YOU!

Do you have a fondness for danger, mystery, and kitty epicness? Then join the ranks of the Samurai Kitty Squad and gain advanced access to dispatches packed full of artwork, books, and other shiny extras.

Just fill out the recruitment form at Squad headquaters and start receiving dispatch transmissions from Captain Kat.

THE SAMURAI KITTY SQUAD
An epic band of kitties spreading awesome across this fair geek nation

www.KatGirlStudio.com/kitty-squad

ABOUT THE AUTHOR

Alicia Kat Vancil grew up in the heart of Silicon Valley where she amused herself by telling stories to anyone around her—her family, her friends…random strangers. Eventually she actually started writing those stories down instead of just spending hours hanging out in fake Ikea living rooms and telling her friends about them. Somewhere amongst all the character-torturing and epic explosions she managed to get a BFA in Illustration from the Academy of Art University and open a graphics studio (Multi-tasking for the win!).

Kat still lives in the San Francisco Bay Area with her husband, two very crazy studio cats, and nine overfull bookcases. And when not running amuck in the imaginary worlds within her head, Kat can usually be found performing, watching anime, or hanging out in Twitter chats.

Visit her online at:

www.katgirlstudio.com
www.twitter.com/KatGirl_Studio

ACKNOWLEDGMENTS

Daemons in the Mist was my debut novel, and actually the first novel I have ever completed. As such, there are numerous people to thank, but here are just a few:

My husband and best friend in all the world, for letting me bounce crazy ideas off of him for this book and everything else in the years to come. But mostly, for believing in me even when it was hard for me to believe in myself. My alpha readers and beta readers Scott, Jenn, Chris, Ashley, and Kate, for telling me the parts you loved, and the parts you didn't, and the parts that made you laugh out loud. For pointing out plot holes, details I only actually wrote down in my head, and generally making the story the best it could be. My editors Scott Aleric and Jennifer Vancil, for fixing all my dyslexic mistakes and making this book as shiny and awesome as humanly possible. Madeline, for hanging out in fake Ikea living rooms and letting me tell you all about my stories for hours. Sally Rose, for always volunteering to be our booth helper at events and for helping me develop the pitch for this book. My mother, and future editor (Go Mom!), Maureen, for loaning me your copy of *The Chicago*

Manual of Style. It taught me more about English than school ever did. Merrie, for always sharing awesome tech things with me like Animoto and Elegant Themes. Without you, there would be no book trailer for DITM and my site would not be as cool as it currently is. My twitter friends and the community at large for your invaluable information, support and camaraderie; without you all, I don't know how I would be able to work in the studio alone all day. All the lovely bloggers who agreed to be part of the June 2012 *Daemons in the Mist* virtual book tour. You're all awesome, wonderful, shiny people! The creators of National Novel Writing Month (NaNoWriMo) without you, this book would not have been completed as quickly as it was. The creators of Scrivener, for creating a writing program that seems especially designed for non-linear writers like me. Without you, my stories would be a horrid mess and take twice as long to write. The creators of Pinterest for creating a way to store my visual ideas and share them with the world. And as always, I am eternally grateful to my parents, Bob and Maureen Dillman for their unwavering support of all the things I do; from dance and theater lessons growing up to putting me through art school. You two are the best parents anyone could have.

—Alicia Kat Vancil

Made in the USA
San Bernardino, CA
12 November 2014